The Safety of Unknown Cities

The Safety of Unknown Cities

Lucy Taylor

Introduction by
Lucy Taylor

Overlook Connection Press
Infinity
1999

THE SAFETY OF UNKNOWN CITIES

Published by
OVERLOOK CONNECTION PRESS
PO BOX 526
WOODSTOCK, GA 30188

Phone: 770-926-1762
Fax: 770-516-1469
E-Mail: OverlookCN@aol.com
URL: http://www.OverlookConnection.com

Call, write, or e-mail for a complete catalog of OCP books.

Cover Art by Neal McPheeters © 1999
Back cover photo courtesy of Lucy Taylor. Photographer unknown.

This Infinity Edition © 1999 The Overlook Connection Press

First Trade Paperback Edition ISBN: 1-892950-12-X
First Hardcover Edition ISBN: 1-892950-14-6

The Overlook Connection Press would like to thank: Lucy Taylor, a wonderful writer and a terrific lady, Neal Mcpheeters for his terriffic cover art on this edition, Dave Barnett who's the best and does the job right – thanks Dave! And Jennifer Jackson (good luck with the new home!). And finally, to Megan, for giving me the name "Infinity" on that Fawlty Towers' ride to Orlando. Thank you, love Dave.

To Mary Ann Backman, Joan Iaconetti, and Frances McKinnon—dear friends and fellow travelers all.

Introduction
by Lucy Taylor

When Dave Hinchberger approached me about reprinting *The Safety of Unknown Cities*, I was delighted that the book would be getting a chance at a wider readership. When he added that he'd like me to write a new introduction, my reaction was slightly less enthusiastic—it's a lot easier to write objectively about other peoples' work than one's own.

In addition, I knew that writing a new introduction would require me to re-familiarize myself with the novel, which I hadn't looked at in a number of years. Now I don't how other writers feel on this subject but, in general, I seldom re-read my work once it appears in print, probably for the same reason I don't think I'd enjoy watching myself having sex on video. It all seems too ego-threatening and potentially dispiriting—what if I don't like my performance, literary or otherwise? What if I become too inhibited to carry on?

Having said that, I have to admit that, as with some trepidation I re-read *Cities*, I was, essentially, still pleased with it. Many scenes I'd forgotten having written—especially a couple that featured arch fiend and pervert-of-all-persuasions, the flamingly unrepentant bisexual, Arthur Breen. I always liked Breen—he might be a psycho sex fiend but, by God, he could pull out the correct past participle when needed and, whatever else he might let dangle, it was never a preposition.

I suppose I also have a fondness for *Cities* because it was my first published novel-writing it got me over what had, up until that time, seemed like an insurmountable hurdle—the writing and *completion* of a novel. Oh, I'd begun several novels over the years, but never had the staying power or the faith in my own work to finish one.

Cities actually was never intended as a novel. Originally, it was written as a novella for a collection of erotic fiction *called Unnatural Acts and Other Stories*, which was published by Masquerade Press in 1994. I never gave any thought to expanding it into a novel until John Pelan, my editor at Silver Salamander Press, who had already published two of my collections, suggested I consider doing so. Eventually, he published a limited edition of the novel with wonderful illustrations by artist Alan Clark. Later Titan Press reprinted *Cities* in the United Kingdom.

The year that it appeared, in 1995, *Cities* won the Bram Stoker Award for best first novel (from the Horror Writers Association), the Deathrealm Award for best novel, and the International Horror Critics Guild Award for Best First Novel. All that recognition for the book was great, although I have often wished some of it could translate into a mass market audience. I know *Cities* is somewhat extreme in the sex and violence department—it was me when I was in my early twenties. I remember arriving by train in a small Swiss town. I had walked up a steep, cobblestoned street that offered a sweeping view of the village below and a lake, which in the late afternoon light, was like a great cloudy opal. And I remember thinking, with a sense of mounting joy, that not a single soul knew where I was at that moment. No one could find me. No one could phone me. No one could see me who knew me by name. For someone whose childhood experiences had pounded home the Sartrian concept that hell, truly, is other people, that was an awesome moment. I knew, at least for that instant, that I was free.

That feeling is one I've sought to find again and again. Often I've succeeded, other times, for no reason I can figure out, the feeling of elation and freedom degenerates into a profound loneliness and sense of bitter isolation. But there's still something about arriving in a strange or unexplored city, in Hong Kong or Paris or Sydney, wandering streets one has never walked before, in a place where, only against the most astronomical odds, would one encounter a familiar face.

It's that desire for peace coupled with anonymity, for that strange serenity that sometimes comes with immersing oneself in the utterly foreign and exotic, that I suppose was at the heart of my idea for *Cities*. Adding sexual compulsion to the mix seemed a logical next step—after all, don't some people regard the body of a new sex partner as an exploring of unchartered territory, a crossing of borders, whether welcoming or guarded, a titillating voyage into the unknown? When the goal, conscious or otherwise, is a flight from intimacy, then the familiar becomes frightening, the new and unknown paradoxically reassures.

Despite the often graphic sex in *Cities*, the book is also about the desperate human need for connection. Val, of course tries to achieve it by "changing partners with the same frequency that she changed countries." In a less forthright way, Breen suffers from a similar pattern. As a young boy burglarizing houses, he realized that he could, in a sense, become intimate with those he stole from by going through their personal items, their letters, diaries, whatever. Then later, he made the jump to a darker form of intimacy—the perusal of the contents of their bodies.

I don't want to romanticize serial killing as some kind of horrifically misguided search for human connection, but at the same time, I think a case could be made that a terrible intimacy can exist between killer and victim, especially when a sexual component is added.

Although *Cities* definitely qualifies as erotic horror, I don't believe there's very much in the novel that could be considered titillating. If anything, sex is more often portrayed as a kind of Sisyphean torture—no matter how often, how unconventionally, or with how many partners the characters manage to copulate, real satisfaction consistently eludes them. In the cruel world of the City, the more they indulge in sex, the more driven they become to continue doing so, and new excesses only seem to trigger more exorbitant needs. There, perhaps, lies the cruel deception behind the compulsive search for "safety" in the untried and unfamiliar that, at heart, I wanted to convey.

And for anyone reading this now, I can only say that I hope the "City" for which Val searches more than lives up to your most outrageous expectations.

Lucy Taylor
December, 1998

The Safety of Unknown Cities

Lucy Taylor

Prologue

At dinner that night she had stolen a spoon.

She had sinned.

Had taken something that belonged to the Keepers.

The Keepers were always watching, peeking, sneaking looks at her and at the others who were confined here. Behind their sleek, syrupy smiles lay lies and cruelty.

That was the least of it. Inside their eyes, she'd realized recently, was concealed a second, vestigial pair of orbs, tiny and dark like beebee shot, like the round, rotating eyes at the end of an insect's antennae stalks. These were the eyes that really *saw*, that watched her fretting in her sleep, pursued by abominable dreams, that saw her squat on the commode to defecate, that fixed avid attention when her hand went underneath the dressing gown and probed and pinched herself to painful orgasm.

How had they missed her taking of the spoon, these omnipotent white-clad Keepers?

Unless they *wanted* her to have it.

Unless *they* knew something she did not.

What she had really wanted was a knife, but that would have been impossible. They weren't even allowed knives at the dinner table, but cut their meat—their meatloaf tasteless as ground cardboard, their hamburger patties topped with the little square slices of cheap American cheese—with the sides of their forks. Like school children or barbarians. (Which amounted to the same thing, didn't it, she thought, grateful that her years of incarceration had not robbed her entirely of wit.)

Seconds before she'd swiped it, the spoon had been inside her mouth, depositing a gelid lump of vanilla pudding on her tongue. Then it had slipped between her fingers and fallen to the floor and she, quite unaware of the miracle being offered her, had bent to retrieve it. And almost set it back upon the plate, until she realized what might be hers and what might be achieved if only she could keep these six inches of curved metal for herself.

She was wearing a long-sleeved cardigan that night and, as always, her watch, although it had stopped ticking over a year ago. No one seemed to care about time here anyway—the stark white walls were gleamingly devoid of calendars and clocks, of anything that might have pulled her from this purgatorial limbo into the stream of linear time with its schedules, its reassuring forward motion.

No, that was something else denied them here—the sensation of time's normal flow, of the passing years and seasons of their lives.

There was just one season here—and that was Hell.

She'd slid the spoon up her sleeve, securing the end beneath the wristband of her watch, and pulling the loose-fitting sweater sleeve down to cover her wrist. And finished eating the pudding with her fork, as though such a thing were normal.

As if anything were normal here.

Thank you Jesus.

The Keepers with their second sets of eyes hadn't even noticed that one minute she was spooning up the pudding, the next minute jabbing at it with a fork. How was this possible? Unless they wanted her to have the spoon? Had, in fact, arranged for her to get it? Unless they were secretly in league with her?

She didn't care.

It was the Keepers, she felt sure, who sent the dreams that had been plaguing her for months now. Dreams of such unimaginable vileness, such stomach-turning carnality in a place beyond all salvation, a place she couldn't name or identify, that if she weren't already mad from all the years spent here, she would be soon enough. The visions of perversion and debauchery haunted her sleep and intruded on her waking. She could close her eyes, but this didn't stop the images. She knew that must be because the pictures were inside her eyes, projected there by the sadistic Keepers.

Except she had them now.

She had the spoon.

Oh, thank you Jesus. Thank you.

The spoon.

That night, behind the locked door of her room, she crouched beside the bed and tried to say her prayers—impossible! Demon images capered inside her eyes, a landscape of perversion unfurled in its unholy splendor. She reached to touch herself and touched, instead, (thank God) the object of her deliverance.

Thank you, Jesus.

The Keepers must be watching, enjoying this, delighting in her torment.

She didn't care.

She'd show them.

She raised the spoon in both hands and snicked the cold tip underneath the lower lid of one eye.

And thought about another lifetime, one of privilege and comfort, when often as not, breakfast was begun with coring out the sections of a grapefruit.

Coring out the meaty pulp from its neat triangle, popping the dripping fruit into her mouth to suck the tangy juice.

(Oh God, oh God, oh God, ohGodohgodohgodohgod...)

Blood filled her head. Adrenalin lanced through her like electric shock. Something warm and oyster-like slimed wetly against her cheek.

Now the other one, the other...

Again, the sickening struggle with her stubborn flesh. Then it was done.

She collapsed in pooling blood and holy darkness.

"Thank you, Jesus! Thank you!"

She screamed it aloud, at the top of her lungs, not caring now who heard.

"Thank you, Jesus!"

Until the visions started up again in the black of her gutted eye sockets.

Then all she did was scream.

Part 1

Chapter One

In early fall in the city of Hamburg, Val Petrillo arrived late for a slave auction. It was held in the basement of Das K—, one of Europe's most notorious sex clubs and consisted of nude or semi-nude men and women, willing participants all, being auctioned off for an hour or two of use in one of the private rooms in the establishment.

Val had heard about the auction—and about a particular "slave"—only hours before and had interrupted a weekend tryst in Paris with an Iranian art student whom she'd met in a Left Bank sex club. The young man had been all testosterone and appetite and sinew. Val had told him she'd be back within a few days.

She knew it was at best a half-truth, that she would probably return to Paris, but not necessarily to him. Once gone, she seldom retraced her path.

Thus, only the possibility of something still more stimulating in the offing had enabled her to tear herself away from the brute, delicious energy of his attentions.

It was her first visit to Hamburg, and she regretted the necessity to rush directly from the Fuhlsbuttel Airport to the club. Such untoward haste was not her style. She liked to savor a city at leisure and at length, to arrive by train, preferably with the sun just coming up and to sit by herself on the platform for a few minutes. She would observe the purposeful stride of the commuters, the slink and slouch of the derelicts and whores, the foreign tourists, often timid and unsure, trying not to look so, but uncertain of the language or the proper direction in which to forge and feeling their way with caution in an alien terrain. Val never considered herself part of this joyful, seedy, bubbling throng, but rather a distant watcher, the way a pigeonkeeper might observe the milling, shitting, shuffling of the flock.

Always an invisible wall, like a second, cellophane skin, seemed to separate her from those around her, so that the flesh of others, even when penetrating her, never made more than superficial contact. She could be fucked, but never touched. The invisible wall behind which she sealed herself brought pain, but also protection.

Watching was a form of safe contact, a browsing among the multitudes of those like her, and yet not like her, those whom she could only imagine knowing through scent and taste and touch. For she was like a person blind and mute from birth. Sex was her Braille, her language and connection. Without it, Val had sometimes thought that, surely, she would cease to exist.

And yet, when she was younger, she had often wished she could do just that: cease to exist as far as any other human beings were concerned. Live in solitude and peace, an old woman in a young child's body, passing her days in some mysterious, far-off bucolic land.

In her father's study had hung an oil painting of a flat, sea-battered island, lush green and capped with toadstool-colored clouds, its flat horizon broken only by the outline of some small, medieval-looking village. Orkney Island, north of Scotland, he had told her, where he had visited briefly with his family on a tour of Europe years before, and she had conceived a fierce, romantic longing for the place.

When I grow up...had been the mantra of her childhood...I will live on the Island of Orkney and paint pictures of the sea and I will be free.

But, in that mysterious way that so many childhood dreams unravel before the adult child's eyes, none of that had ever happened.

Once, just out of her teens and a succession of foster homes, she had followed her ambition to become an artist as far as a semester at New York's Parsons School of Design, but her fascination with the subtleties of shape and texture and hue was quickly subverted to devotion of another type: for the cerulean eyes of a young ceramics teacher, the coral-tipped breasts of a roommate with whom she briefly shared a Soho flat, the magenta-headed cock of a Argentine guitarist she met in a downtown club. Each effort to satisfy one hunger ignited half a dozen more, an inundation of raw desire that made all other needs and wants fade into paltry inconsequence.

New York and the dream of becoming an artist had lasted just six months.

Then she'd moved on to Boston and after that, to Philadelphia and had kept moving, from lover to lover, and, eventually, from continent to continent, a rootless adventurer in a world in which, when she was not engaged in some erotic dalliance, she felt remote and profoundly alien.

To satisfy her continuous craving for new experiences, new ways of stimulation, she had developed the habit of changing cities and partners with the frequency that many people reserve for changing outfits. Even in the act of making love to one, she was already fantasizing about the next, feeling greater appetite for what was out of reach than for the man or woman who lay atop or underneath her.

Sometimes in a moment of private observation, on a train platform or in an airport terminal, she'd see a particularly striking face, an eye-catching design of hand or jaw, a memorable breast or ankle and, if the watched one happened to look back, a brief moment of meeting, of connection might occur, and Val would think, *You might have been my sister, brother, friend for life. You might have been my lover.*

Sometimes such people did become her lovers, but the beauty promised in that first initial gaze never quite matched Val's expectations, any more than the skylines of the cities that she visited, some gleaming, thrusting ornate minarets or towering slabs of glass proudly into the sky, others squat and shabby or drab with soot and the grit of harbored pestilence, never quite lived up to her dreams.

So she stayed on the move.

From city to city, bed to bed.

Indulging her two addictions. Wanderlust and fleshlust. The passions of her life.

Over the past few months, however, a new purposefulness had infused Val's journeying. In the sex parlors and private clubs she frequented, she'd begun to hear strange rumors. Occasionally, from a pair of lips made slack with drink or satiation, she'd heard whispered tales of a place she'd dreamed about but not yet visited, a carnal city of such perversion that it tested sanity, a place beside which the fleshpot Sodoms and modern-day Gomorrahs of the known world paled by comparison.

Always the teller of the tale was vague in his or her allusions, but more than once she'd heard tell of a man known only as the Turk. It was he, so the rumormongers claimed, who could offer entrance to the City.

It was in pursuit of the Turk then, be he real or the fabrication of minds too corrupted by venality to know truth from lies, that Val had come to Das K—. A young man from the Philippines, an unskilled laborer who loaded and unloaded cargo on the Hamburg docks by day and indulged his taste for S and M by night, was scheduled to be "auctioned off" in a few minutes.

Word had it that he had met the Turk, had even ventured to the City. Intrigued, Val was intent on meeting him.

Edgy with anticipation, she sat at a table close to the stage, sipping Courvoisier and watching a punk-haired waiter clad in fishnet tights and satin shorts as he prissed among the tables.

It was after midnight and Val had been at the club since ten. She would have liked to take a partner and retire to one of the private rooms in the back of the establishment, to and from which there'd been a constant procession of couples, trios, and groups since she'd arrived, but then she might miss out on the very reason she had come here: to purchase for herself a pretty boy and a little information. So she sat impatiently, trying to ignore the persistent throbbing of her clitoris in an atmosphere of musk and heat and pheromones, waiting for the appearance of the one she meant to buy.

In her early thirties, Val was a slender woman with black hair curtaining a tanned and oval face, grey eyes flecked with hints of emerald, and features sufficiently symmetrical and absent of expression to make her, if not quite conventionally beautiful, at least inscrutable. In a room peopled with the extraordinarily eye-catching, even freakish, her clothes and manner were almost conspicuously ordinary. She wore jeans that were snug but not tight enough to impede circulation, a loose-fitting silk blouse, and scuffed cowboy boots perhaps more suited to a Western ranch than a European sex club. Her make-up was minimal, her throat, earlobes, and fingers unadorned, except for a large sapphire ring, which she wore on her middle finger.

To anyone observing her, it would have been hard to form an opinion as to her sexual orientation, a state of affairs Val liked and cultivated.

A pair of twins, two young Nigerian women with enormous flaring nostrils and lips the size of dark red rose-petals were being auctioned off, sold at last to an older, professorial type in bifocals and tweed.

A blonde young woman, leashed and corsetted, was purchased by a leather dyke, who handcuffed her prize before leading her off the stage. Then a man, all strut and beefcake, with a complex lacery of green tattoos entwining his arms and thighs in a kind of epidermal kudzu, was sold at an outrageous price to a flamboyant creature with sequins in her false eyelashes and a bulge in the crotch of her spandex tights.

When the Filipino boy was finally brought on stage, he generated interest among several of the older men. Young and ladder-bellied, virtually hairless, his oiled skin appeared too tight for him, defining every muscle, bone, and tendon like some smooth, soft leather corset made to be ripped away in strips, the better to get at the delights below.

Val let the bidding rise, then quickly bid a sum so large no one ventured to try to top her. A few of her male competitors shot venomous looks, and she wondered briefly if the slave himself was disappointed, if performing with a woman wasn't something he could accommodate, even under duress. No matter, she had paid for him, and he was hers. At least for the next few hours.

As she was going to the cashier to pay before collecting her slave, Val felt herself observed. Turning slowly, she saw a platinum-haired young man watching her through slitted, green lynx eyes from the bar. He wore a silk shirt and loose-fitting black satin vest, a diamond stud in one ear and ghoul eyeliner that would have shamed a whore. His flesh was so pale it looked translucent, a stitching together of gossamer insect wings. When their eyes met, he raised his drink, a tiny cordial glass containing what appeared to be a gold liqueur and pantomimed a toast.

Val gave him no acknowledgement. Pretty though he was, at the moment, she had no use for any but her purchase.

Minutes later, having paid for and claimed her slave, she quickly forgot the hauntingly pale features of the apparition at the bar. She took the Filipino boy, whose name the auctioneer informed her was Santos, to an upstairs whipping room, where one whole wall was lined with a sadist's treasure trove of leather crops and cat o' nine tails and devices for restraint.

Val initiated the proceedings by removing her own clothes and Santos' and ordering the slave to fuck her. He did so with might and gusto, but after a few minutes, Val feigned displeasure and secured Santos' wrists to a pair of manacles affixed to one wall. Then, availing herself of the sturdiest of the whips, she beat the boy's naked back and buttocks until his glossy, nut-brown flesh was a tapestry of raised pink welts.

Through it all, the slave uttered not a sound, which disappointed her somewhat, as she found the chief reward of flogging to be the moans and cries of a submissive, and so she wielded the whip with greater vigor but managed to wring forth not one plea or moan.

At length, she freed Santos' hands and allowed him to fuck her to climax, her own and his, which he accomplished with much writhing and shuddering but not a single sound.

They lay still for a while then, breathing the heady, pungent odors of orgasm, hearing laughter and applause from the auction still continuing downstairs.

"I heard about you in Paris," Val began in halting German, one hand covering and idly petting Santos' cock. "I've been told you're quite the connoisseur of perversions."

Santos smiled and shrugged. It occurred to Val that perhaps he hadn't understood her or that his command of German was even more rudimentary than hers. She tried English then, but Santos only fixed on her a dullard's gaze and ran a finger lazily around one of her nipples.

Summoning up what meager Spanish she possessed, Val persevered, "Is it true you've had relations with a man known as the Turk? And that you've been to a place they call the City?"

Again, that small, half-rueful smile, rich with coquetterie, but this time Val knew he'd understood. His penis, when she uttered the words "el Turco" had twitched beneath her hand.

"You're still my slave, you know. And I asked you…"

Santos leaned forward, pressed his full mouth to hers. His lips parted, and for the first time in their encounter, he allowed her to kiss him. Val thought he was enticing her into a game of sorts: the information she was asking to be won only by more wooing. Half irritated, half intrigued, she decided to play along, entering him with her tongue and probing, thrusting, until…

She pulled back, skin goosefleshing, with a cry of surprise and disgust.

Santos gave a gleeful grin and opened his mouth so wide for her inspection that she could see his tonsils.

But then, of course, nothing was there to block the view.

His mouth was empty, a vacant cave, the stump of tongue a grey cauterized root deep in his throat. He gave a gurgling, half-formed sound, a kind of muffled oink.

Val was appalled, but didn't permit herself to flinch. Instead she snatched up her handbag and dug out a pen and paper. "Answer my questions," she commanded. "I know you understood me. Write it down."

Santos held the pen as if it were a foreign object. At the top of the page, he scrawled an "X." Val asked again and got the same response.

His cock, however, was far more communicative. Fully erect now, it pressed lewdly against Val's belly.

She slapped the offending piece of meat aside and began to dress.

She'd bought herself a mute who either was illiterate or pretended to be so. Santos would tell her nothing, and she was furious. But in another way, she realized, perhaps he'd told her more than she really cared to know.

That made her even angrier and, perversely, more anxious than ever before to see the City.

Chapter Two

Arthur Quentin Breen lifted the knife toward his pursed and finely chiseled lips and, with an expert flick of one gold-braceleted wrist, cut a notch in his victim's ear.

The damage was quite minimal. The pain, clearly, was not.

The trussed man strained against the ropes that bound him to the chair. He tried to cry out behind his gag, but managed only a muffled growl.

Breen watched the blood drip off the sliced earlobe and make a star-shaped stain on the blue and ocher pattern of the carpet. He frowned, a delicate crease that bisected his high, bronze forehead between unnaturally bright turquoise eyes.

Breen hated messes.

That was the only part of his work that he disliked, the dreadful nastiness of the human body in times of stress and the necessity for making a perfectly ungodly mess each time he opened someone up.

His craft was the bane not just of law enforcement and forensic experts throughout Europe and the United States, but of unfortunate chambermaids and next-of-kin who got stuck scrubbing out the stains and airing out the rooms where Breen had spent time torturously, methodically, helping some unfortunate expire.

But, oh, undoubtedly the rewards of his labors more than justified the unpleasant spots and smells and leakages.

Breen looked the man over and was not displeased. Although he was perfectly capable of murdering at random, he had preferences as distinct for murder victims as he did for sex partners—in Breen's experience, the two frequently amounted to the same thing. He had a penchant for men and women with dark hair and eyes and olive skin, although blue eyes matched with black hair was also a favorite combination. Light-eyed blonds like himself were not, generally speaking, to Breen's taste. He found them irritating, an affront to his vanity and a reminder that his own coloring was more artifice than nature; Breen used hair coloring and tinted contact lenses to effect a Nordic look, and he liked his partners to provide a contrast to this fairness. Thus swarthy men and olive-skinned women, those whose appearance hinted at Mediterranean or Mid-Eastern lineage, were favored playmates.

Breen had overpowered the man as his victim had been toweling dry in the bathroom of a third-floor walk-up apartment located on Paris' Rue de Moine between a bakery and, fittingly enough, a butcher shop. He was someone who'd have appealed to Breen even if his victimhood hadn't been a foregone conclusion. The name on the mailbox downstairs read Reza Farasati, a name Breen supposed was probably Iranian or Iraqui. Certainly this apartment building housed a number of Middle Eastern students. Breen had observed their comings and goings while taking his meals across the street at a cafe as he awaited the right moment.

The young man trussed to the chair in front of him was as exotic as his name: the swarthy skin, the obsidian black hair and eyes, the hooked Arab nose, even the crooked, inch-long scar that twitched at the corner of one eye each time Breen slit him. For in addition to being a murderer, an occasional cannibal, and several other things besides, Arthur Breen was also something of a romantic. The man's name and his appearance, in addition to the plethora of Oriental rugs and vases, not to mention a stunning bronze tea service on a table by the door, put Breen in mind of mosques and minarets, of splendid sultans and silk-clad harem wenches attended by mincing eunuchs.

Such images appealed to Breen's sense of the exotic.

And though his full lips didn't move, behind those shockingly azure eyes, Breen smiled.

Now Breen circled his prisoner, not malevolently but with a certain impatient eagerness. He didn't have all night.

Or rather, *he* did, but his victim, most assuredly, did not.

"Do you speak English?"

The captive nodded.

"That's good," Breen cooed, "that's lucky for you. Now listen carefully, and you may save your life."

He got down on one knee, in the position of a love-struck suitor and laid a hand on one of Reza Farasati's hirsute, muscular legs. He stroked the solid, bulging calf, caressed the bony knob of knee, then ran his hand inside the thigh where the flesh was chill and clammy from where some urine had leaked out when Breen sliced off a thumbnail.

Until now, though, there'd been only a few cuts of significance. Reza Farasati was bleeding in fewer than a dozen places. All things considered, Breen thought he'd shown exemplary restraint, leading Farasati down the path of pain as gently, as solicitously, as one would deflower a virgin.

"Look at me," said Breen, his voice all bedroom and kisses, his eyes pure ice.

The victim stared at him. His eyes were close-set, hawkish under hooded lids, so black the pupils were indiscernible from the surrounding iris. Wide nostrils flared. Beads of oily sweat slid down his temples, merged with the blood flowing down his jaw from the slashed ear.

"Do you want to live?"

Farasati nodded frantically. His Adam's apple lurched in his throat, like an elevator run amok, leaping from floor to floor.

"Or is that a foolish question?"

More head-nodding until the import of that last query sank in. Then, respectful, stillness.

"Of course you do, of course." Breen's hand moved higher up the thigh. Reza Farasati began to shiver despite the fact that Breen had turned the heat up in the apartment soon after he entered.

"You want to live. We all do. It's the nature of existence that, nomatter how painful, how agonizing even, life becomes, we still all want it to continue." His voice got softer, so soft he knew the man would have to strain to hear it.

"And you will live, too, if you'll just give me what I want."

The captive's eyes roved wildly about the room. His jaw muscles knotted beneath the gag. Breen guessed, from past such experiences, that he was trying to indicate the location of his valuables, as if Breen couldn't have easily found such booty on his own.

"Now I'm going to take the gag off," Breen said, "but one thing you must understand. I've no compunction about killing you. Try to scream and I'll slit your throat so fast you'll be gargling your own blood before anyone has heard you. And even so, I'll still have at least five minutes to work on you while you're still alive and able to feel pain." Breen stroked the side of the knife over one of the man's eyelids. "Do you have any idea how long five minutes can be? What an eternity in hell can be inflicted in that amount of time? Do you know, for instance, that when a person's terrified and their adrenalin's racing, they hardly ever pass out from pain? They feel it all—right to the end."

Breen flicked his wrist and a tiny slit opened up above the hooked nose. A bead of blood oozed out, was snared in the dark kudzu of the brows before running down the handsome nose, quivering atop one nostril like a ruby in a Bombay whore's pierced nostril.

"Contemplate your choices," Breen said, "while I go get a snack."

He set the knife down, went into the small kitchen, which occupied an alcove off the main room, and made himself at home. He was pleased to find that, unlike the stereotypical bachelor, this Farasati fellow kept a well-stocked larder. The refrigerator overflowed with various-sized dishes containing ethnic fare: tabouli and taramosalata, a dish of oily, dark green dolmades and flaky pastries made from filo dough that, when Breen bit into one, oozed honey like a lubricating vulva. And wine, enough good French and imported bottles, to suggest the man had a discriminating palate.

Breen enjoyed a glass of burgundy and spooned up samples of the food from various containers. Although he sometimes mildly rebuked himself for the childishness of the minor kitchen larcenies that so frequently accompanied his work of a more serious nature, it was an indulgence Breen allowed himself. There was a forbiddenness to other people's kitchens, an unspoken taboo on touching the contents of their pantries and refrigerators similar to the greater one against entering and perusing the contents of their skin. Whether a wedge of fine Brie and a jar of caviar or the exquisite, glistening confections found behind a pair of eyes or in an abdominal cavity, Breen considered himself a connoisseur of all.

There was fresh blood on Breen's thumb. He dunked the digit in a jar of caviar—blue-black eggs ashimmer in the ruby—and sucked it clean with a small, satisfied smack of his lips.

When he was finished eating, Breen fished a Dunhill lighter from his pocket, lit the one cigarette which he allowed himself each day, and smoked it leisurely. He found a dishrag and wiped down everything he'd touched.

Then he returned to work.

Farasati remained silent when Breen removed the gag, which was damp with blood that had flowed down from the wound between his eyes. Other cuts had bled across his chest and down his shoulders, thighs, giving him crude stripes that, to Breen, resembled the tribal markings on a celebrant at some primitive bacchanal. Only the man's abundance of chest hair interfered with the effect, the blood coagulating there in thick, unsightly clumps.

Breen knelt and laid a hand almost protectively across the man's groin.

"Where did she go?"

"She?"

"Where did she go?"

"I don't know who…"

"I think you do."

There was a brief beat, less than a second, where comprehension dawned and Reza Farasati perhaps entertained a second's thought toward chivalry and trying to protect Val. In light of his own woeful condition and the proximity of Breen's knife to his testicles, the impulse was short-lived.

"Val, you mean?"

"Unless you've had some other whore in here who used that name?"

Farasati lowered his head briefly, appeared to contemplate the blood stain glorying his left nipple.

"You are…her husband?"

Breen laughed with genuine mirth for the first time that night.

"And you think I'm here to pay you back for making me a cuckold? A fair assumption, I suppose, but hardly the case. No, I'm merely one of the many men who's fucked her, but in my case I'm going to…well, let's just say I want to reacquaint myself with Ms. Petrillo for old time's sake. But first I need to know where she is and when she's coming back. Or did you simply bore her—pun intended—to the point where she had to throw her things into a suitcase and flee into the night?"

Farasati licked blood off his lips. "If I tell you what you want to know, you'll leave? You won't hurt me anymore?"

"Of course."

"How can I believe you?"

"What choice do you have?"

"I have money. Not here but in the bank. I could..."

Breen switched the knife to his left hand, backhanded Farasati with his right.

"I don't need money." He stood up, did a princely pirouette while Farasati's head was still reeling from the blow. "I'm rich, you see. Like she is. Old money. Inherited from my wealthy... father. I can go wherever I like, do whatever I like—" he made a languid slashing gesture toward Farasati's face with the knife—"*kill* whomever I like."

A drop of blood from the wound between his eyes pooled on the tip of Farasati's nose, dripped down to stain his chest.

"I don't know if Val's coming back or not. She said she might call. She hasn't."

Breen tsk-tsked. "How very like her to be unreliable. So, tell me then, where is she?"

"She went to Hamburg."

"Just like that, she up and goes to Germany on a whim. Is that it?"

"A few days ago, she made a phone call. I don't know who she talked to or what they said, but right away she made plans to fly to Hamburg. I tried to talk her out of going. She went anyway."

"Yes," said Breen with a faint frown, "she always does."

"She was going to an auction."

"An auction? Val?" Despite himself, Breen giggled. The image of the woman he remembered poring over antique cabinets or limited edition prints or anything that wasn't capable of sweat and sighs and orgasms was simply too amusing. "To buy *what?*"

"I don't know."

"She has no taste. Whatever could she buy?"

"I don't know."

"Her hotel. What hotel was she staying at?"

"I don't know. She might have said something. We were...I wasn't really listening."

The knife flashed and the blade nicked out a chink of flesh in Farasati's abdomen. Blood unfurled from his belly like a scarlet tongue.

"I don't remember what hotel."

"But she did say she might call?"

"Yes. Yes."

Breen paced in circles around the chair.

"She'll never call. She'll never come back. I know her far better,

I'm afraid, than you do. I've spent time with her, but I'm going to spend more of it. Quality time. Exceptional, quality time."

Breen came up behind the chair and leaned against it. Inside his stylishly cut trousers, his dick was getting hard. He reached down and ran both hands down Farasati's bleeding chest, tugging gently at the thick hair, pausing at the place where he'd excised a bit of flesh to dip a finger into the blood-filled indentation.

"You wouldn't lie to me now, would you? You wouldn't harbor any ill-advised intentions of protecting the slut?"

"No, no."

"You know she's just a common whore. She's fucked hundreds of men. She told me so. We'd lie in bed and tell each other stories. Except I never told her my really best stories, of course. The ones that ended with me killing my bed partner. So she doesn't know me. Not really. Not the way you will if you don't remember the name of that hotel and remember it very quickly."

Footsteps sounded on the stairs outside. A man's voice and a woman's chattering in some tongue Breen didn't recognize. Farasati's mouth opened and he sucked in air to scream.

Breen clamped his hand across the man's mouth, held the knife up to his eyes.

"Quiet, quiet now. You mustn't try to call for help. Not now when we're just getting to the best part."

He came around the front side of the chair. With one hand, he held the knife blade up to Farasati's face. With the other, he unzipped himself, freed his erection.

"One thing I like about Val," Breen went on conversationally, "is that her tastes in men are similar to mine." He saw a different kind of terror come into Farasati's eyes and savored it, as he always did. At some point, with a certain kind of man, it was hard to tell which terrified them more—the phallic knife with its power to kill them or the blade-like phallus with its power to unman them. He opened his legs, straddling Farasati's lap so that his rigid penis was level with the man's mouth.

"Get away from me," Farasati said hoarsely.

"Oh, but I'm in need, as you can see, and Val's not here to perform her womanly duties, although if she were, I'm sure she'd be glad to service both of us. Let's see now," said Breen, reaching down to scrabble between the clenched thighs for the clutch of dark, limp genitals, "if you've found any of this arousing."

For the first time in their encounter, an emotion other than pure terror shone on Farasati's face. Through clenched teeth, the captive said, "Leave me alone. I've told you what you want to know, now leave me the fuck alone, you fucking faggot."

Breen laughed with genuine delight. He loved it when unwilling lovers attacked his sexual proclivities. As if it mattered. As if he cared. As if the whole universe wasn't one gigantic cunt open for the fucking, a humongous asshole waiting to be buggered.

"A faggot? Moi? My God, I'm wounded. What an awful thing to say?" Breen was bent over laughing now, his cock bobbing less than an inch from Farasati's face. He pressed himself against the cut between his eyes so that blood rouged the crown of his penis.

"I like to see blood on my cock," said Breen. "It makes me hard just thinking about it. Blood from a menstruating pussy, from a fresh wound."

He angled himself closer to Farasati's face. "Now you're going to open your mouth wide and suck me off. And if you try to cry out or bite me, I'll cut your lips off, and that I promise before God and Allah or anybody else you care to think of."

Still the captive's mouth stayed stubbornly shut.

Breen leaned himself away and held the knifeblade vertically against Farasati's lips.

"Cock or knife?"

He switched again, erection bobbing against Farasati's nose.

"Knife or cock?"

And switched again, the knife this time.

"Last chance."

He made a nick above the man's eyebrow.

"All right, all right. Don't cut me anymore."

Farasati bent his head, took in the bloody cockhead. His stubborn heterosexuality was underscored to Breen by the unskillful way he sucked a cock. Breen had had better from the mouths' of babes.

Still, to receive fellatio, however clumsy, from a virgin mouth was always a thrill and he jetted not long after insertion, forcing himself more deeply into the captive's mouth so that Farasati gagged and retched on the emission.

"There, now," said Breen, when it was done, "not bad. Not bad at all. Who knows, with a little practice, you might make someone a fine wife."

Farasati's eyes were full of tears, whether from rage and shame or the gag reflex, Breen didn't know.

He tucked himself back in his trousers, zipped up. Farasati spat hard and watched him with a kind of stunned despair.

"Now then, back to our discussion. Where did Val go?"

"I told you, *Hamburg*."

"But the hotel—what was the name of the hotel?"

"It was a long word in German. She only said it once."

"Last chance," Breen singsonged.

Farasati spat again. "Vier."

"What?"

"The name of the hotel…it was Fier-Jahre-something—at least that's what it sounded like."

"VierJahre," mused Breen. "The Vierjahrezeiten Hotel. On Alster Lake, reeking of snob appeal. I've stayed there myself. That's it, isn't it?"

Farasati nodded.

"Very good." Breen patted Farasati's cheek. "Very good indeed. You make a better informant than you do a fellatrice. Now then, time for your reward."

He went over to his briefcase, opened it and removed a roll of duct tape which he used to bind Farasati's mouth. Was it a look of relief that Breen imagined flickered, however briefly, in the man's eyes? Did he feel safer with one masculine orifice now tightly sealed? If so, he was misguided. Breen rarely left a murder scene with any path unviolated.

Finished with the taping, Breen flicked the knife in one expert stroke and severed the tip of Farasati's nose.

Blood spewed like red projectile vomit from a tiny mouth.

Breen bent, scooped up the morsel, and popped it in his mouth. He chewed and swallowed. Smiled.

"Turn about is fair play, isn't it? You eat me. I eat you."

Breen laughed.

"We've got a long night ahead."

And the game continued.

Chapter Three

"You didn't keep him very long. He must have disappointed you."

The voice was part cat's purr, part smoke, spiced with a faint British accent. One green lynx eye winked at her above a full mouth uptilted at one corner with amusement: the pretty young thing from the bar. He'd come up beside her when she left the Club and fallen into step.

"He was exceptional," Val said. "Quite worth what I paid."

"Except he's maimed."

"Not where it counts."

"Unless you purchased him more for what you hoped he'd say than what he'd do."

"I didn't buy the boy for conversation."

"Oh, didn't you?"

Val stopped. They were walking along a narrow street in the St. Pauli district, slightly north of the Reeperbahn's famed glitz—all neon, sizzle, and glare—and a hundred years away in atmosphere. Here winding cobbled streets converged and serpentined, dead-ended and then reemerged, a medieval maze of narrow, gabled houses illuminated by pale cones of incandescent light thrown by iron streetlamps. Alone, Val had been content to wander, even at this hour. Now she considered summoning a taxi and going back to the hotel where she'd left the overnight bag with the few belongings she'd seen fit to bring from Paris.

Tomorrow perhaps she would fly back, resume her tryst with her Iranian swain, assuming he'd not found other company in her absence.

She turned and stared into those feline eyes, darkly flecked with green and amber.

"Who are you?"

"Majeed," the boy said, extending a pale, long-fingered hand which Val ignored.

"And are you always so inquisitive about other people's sex lives?"

"If they amuse me. Your little interlude with Santos must have been quite interesting—especially after you found out he had no tongue."

"He had enough."

"Oh, did he?"

Val was tiring rapidly of this patronizing, painted-up boy. "The auction's still going on. Why don't you go back? It's late enough and people have been drinking—I'm sure someone would bid on you."

"I'm having more fun here."

Val stopped, looked Majeed up and down appraisingly. On any other night, she'd have been tempted by his flagrant vampishness, his curved, flirtatious mouth, the crotch-hugging jeans. But she was angry, thwarted. She'd come all this way, gone to much trouble and expense, all in the hope that Santos might either satisfy her obsession with the City or put an end to it.

"Please go away," she told Majeed. "Stop following me."

"I'm not following you. I only thought perhaps I might offer you what Santos, with his unfortunate speech impediment, could not."

"What do you mean?"

"I know you came here seeking information about the City. I thought it possible that I could help. But now I see I'm only bothering you. You want a hard cock like your little slave's, and here I'm offering you merely words. I'll leave. I wouldn't wish to force my company on you."

He turned to go and Val let him—for about six paces. Then curiosity overcame her pride and she called out, "Wait. You're right. I didn't come to Das K—for a hard cock. I came for information."

As it turned out, however, Majeed apparently had both. Val took note of the ostentatious bulge in the tight jeans, sculpted to the youth's body. "What can you tell me?"

"Nothing, here on the street. But my apartment's only a short way from here. I know it's late, but if you aren't too tired..."

"How do I know you know anything about the City? Have you actually been there? Or did you talk to Santos before his unfortunate amputation?"

"We'll talk about it all in due time," said Majeed. "Right now I need a pipe."

He slid an arm through Val's, leading her in and out of quiet, curving streets presided over only by stray felines and the occasional derelict, regaling her along the way with information about himself: that he was a long-time habitue of Das K—, self-educated and well-traveled, a sometimes masseur skilled in Shiatsu and Reiki and other, unspecified forms of bodywork, that he was in Germany only on a temporary visa and would be moving on to warmer climes before the winter set in.

"To the City, you mean?"

"Possibly. If I even remember how to get there. It's very far."

And he would say no more on the subject.

Majeed's apartment was a claustrophobe's nightmare. Located at the back of a dilapidated hotel, the kind where rooms are rented by the hour and the sheets are blotchy with questionable stains, it was reached only by traversing a narrow, catacomb-like hall, then crossing a refuse-littered courtyard before climbing two winding flights of stairs so low-ceilinged that they were forced to proceed crouched over, like two hunchbacks. Val felt as if she were entering the domain of a would-be troglodyte.

At the top of the stairs, Majeed unlocked the outer door to his derelict abode. There was one more bleak corridor to cross, then Majeed ushered her into a room that smelled of herbs and incense, the heady fragrance of decaying temples, untended gardens. The narrow bed was made up with a brocade spread worn thin in places, its gold fringe trailing upon a grimy floor. Scant decoration. Upon the wall a crucifix; in the window sills, a collection of incense burners and candles in every shape and size: a gold Buddha and cloissonnee-style jar, a terracotta pagoda.

Majeed lit some candles and an incense stick. The room filled with cloying fragrance, orchids past their prime or rotting camellias.

"Welcome," Majeed said, "to my little sanctuary."

He pulled Val toward him. He slid a hand behind her neck, pressed his mouth to hers, enticing her with a lithe tongue made all the more erotic by its equivalent's repulsive absence in her most recent lover's mouth. The young man smelled of musk and cloves, his lips flavored with the lingering trace of mint liqueur. He sucked and nibbled Val's lower lip as one would suck the pulp from a slice of citron.

Val reached down to massage the sweet protuberance at Majeed's groin, but he took her hand away, kissed the perfumed wrist and palm and laid it on his shoulder.

"You aren't afraid? To go late at night to the room of a man you barely know?"

Val scrutinized those subtly slanted eyes. She'd been with dangerous men before; it was, in fact, her preference. She'd taken chances all her life and was not about to change her habits now.

"There's only one thing I'm really afraid of. That's not being free to do what I please and go where I want."

Majeed laughed. "Oh, really? So what if I were to shackle you to the bed and walk away? Just leave?"

"That might be exciting."

"What if I never came back?"

"You would."

"Oh would I now? Perhaps someday we'll have to test that."

Fondly, with neither undue haste nor passion, he began disrobing her. Val allowed it, finding in the movements of the boy's long fingers a mesmerizing languor. As he undressed her, Majeed kissed her neck and eyelids, her nipples and the cleft, still moist from Santos' use, between her legs. His tongue flicked and traced the plump curves of flesh from her clit to the puckered bud between her buttocks.

"Now you," said Val. Kneeling, she unzipped Majeed, whose heavy, uncut cock lolled out into her mouth. She peeled back the foreskin, rimmed and licked the velvet head before swallowing the length of it.

Majeed had made no move still toward taking off his clothes. Perhaps, as he had undressed her, he wished to be undressed himself, Val thought. She stood up and began unfastening the buttons of his vest. Pulling this off, she commenced with the shirt itself, working open half a dozen tiny pearl buttons until she could fold back the silk—to reveal a pair of breasts bound tightly to Majeed's chest by a bra designed to flatten and minimize.

Val had seen transsexuals before, but had never partnered one. She hadn't expected this oddity of Majeed.

She tried not to show her surprise, but it must have registered on her face for Majeed was smiling, enjoying—as he must always savor it—the look on a new lover's face when he unveiled himself.

Val rolled the tight bra up and over Majeed's head. His breasts were unexpectedly full, with small nipples rouged dark as strawberries. Val sucked one into her mouth. Majeed moaned and arched his back.

"You're a man on his way to becoming a woman?"

Majeed laughed and pulled her down with him onto the bed.

"Guess again."

"A woman on her way—*well* on her way—to becoming a man?"

"Neither."

"Then..."

"Why don't you finish undressing me?"

Val stooped to remove Majeed's shoes and socks. He lifted narrow hips while she tugged down his jeans. His erection bobbed. At the base: two small but perfectly formed testicles. Behind those, where in most men the perineum would be, a moist and parted slit shaved hairless as an egg. It gaped at Val, a single eye, defined by pink and fleshy lids.

"A vagina." Val gazed in wonder at this miracle. She touched the fleshy labia, then inserted a finger inside Majeed's cunt. He contracted inner muscles, seized and squeezed. And laughed again, causing breasts and cock to wobble in jarring juxtaposition.

In all her wandering, all her years of sexing in strange places among foreign people, Val had never before encountered such a creature. Now, confronted with this marvel, she felt both aroused and awestruck. To be both male and female—that, it had always seemed to her, would be the optimal design. Anything less, she thought, resulted in a woefully incomplete condition passing for the norm, a world of people able to experience only half the spectrum of erotic experience.

"You're splendid," she told Majeed. "Beautiful. Unlike anything I've ever seen."

"Any*one* you've ever seen," Majeed corrected her. "I'm not a freak, you understand, though I've been called that and worse. It's a condition called hermaphrodism."

"When you were born, your parents...what did they...?"

"They were appalled, to put it politely. They tried to raise me, but when it became apparent there was no way to hide my condition from my siblings and schoolmates, they sent me to a home in London for the disabled and retarded. For some reason, the two groups were lumped together. The worst part was, since my so-called 'disability' wasn't something readily apparent, people tended to assume I must fit in the other category.

"When I was thirteen, I ran away and hitchhiked around Britain.

For a while, I made my living as one of the 'human oddities' in a grubby little carnival full of freaks and flimflam artists that traveled around Europe. Then for a while, I worked as a masseuse. An old Latin professor in Oxford who saw me dressed up as a woman fell in love with me. We were going to get married, but he had a stroke a month before the wedding and wound up in a nursing home with half his mouth on the side of his cheek and one eye squinting and twitching like he'd blinked in a gnat. I went to see him and pulled my skirt up and flashed him—because I was mad at him for having the stroke, I guess, for ruining my fantasy of being somebody's wife, and I wanted him to know his cocksucking little fiancee had a bigger dick than he did. I don't know if he knew what he was seeing, though. The squinting thing—that was about it for his communication skills."

"And since then?"

"I changed genders. Not physically, of course, but emotionally. I live as a man now. I could have an operation to make me more conventional—a chop job or a stitch job, as it were—but in places like Das K—, that would diminish my popularity significantly. And I know which sex I truly am, and that's male."

Val cupped and stroked the silky balls dangling behind his penis. "Do you have periods?"

From the look on Majeed's face, she might as well have accused him of public defecation.

"No. Hardly what you'd call a period anyway. Just some spotting. Sometimes not even that."

"You're awfully touchy about it. Are you ashamed of being partly female?"

"Women fall in love, get hurt. When something goes wrong, they blame themselves and do penance in a thousand masochistic ways. When men fuck up, they blame circumstances, bad luck, other people. And when they love, they hold a big part back, so they don't lose themselves."

"How little you know about love."

"And I suppose that you're the expert?"

Val gazed up into eyes as emerald as the towers of Oz. "So you'll be a man tonight?"

"As always."

"With all the limitations of that gender?"

"And all the advantages."

Majeed lay back upon the bed. Val mounted him. Grinding her

hips upon his cock, she reached back to fingerfuck his pussy. She bent forward; their breasts met and mashed together as she sucked on Majeed's lips and sent her tongue exploring the crevices and contours of his mouth.

They made love in all the ways and combinations that Majeed's wondrous anatomy allowed. For the first time in months, Val was able—for a little while—to forget about the City. For surely in Majeed she'd found a prize to please a sultan, the dream-lover of all who hungered for the novel, the bizarre, and yes, Val thought, the freakish, too. Despite his protestations to the contrary, Majeed was unquestionably a freak, though one of unsurpassing elegance and beauty and, yes, femaleness, too.

To take Majeed's erect cock in her mouth, then dip below and lap and tongue-fuck his pussy was a dizzying excursion into androgyny. To reach up to squeeze those silky breasts while the owner of those breasts drove his cock into her throat, these were pleasures beyond all Val's experience, Majeed's strange beauty an intoxicant of the most seductive sort. His body was the first she'd ever encountered that, given a way to do so, she would have exchanged willingly for her own.

They lay together afterward, hermaphrodite and woman, in a sidelong embrace, genitals still locked together in a gentle clench.

"So you know about the City?" Val began. "Is it even half-true what I've heard, that Sodom and Gomorrah would seem like places of sweet innocence and childlike games by comparison?"

"Not having visited either Sodom or Gomorrah, I wouldn't know."

"But you *have* visited the City?"

"Perhaps. Perhaps I've only listened to the rumors and drawn up my private fantasy about the place. Or maybe I'm just another drugged out sicko suffering delusions."

"Either way, you must have some tasty stories."

"I do, indeed. But if you don't mind let me indulge another of my habits now. I'm starting to lose my high." He pulled away. Their bodies separated with a gentle suction. Val rolled over onto her stomach and watched Majeed's profile—the full breasts and lolling penis—as he filled a pipe and lit it.

"Care for some?" He offered her the pipe.

"Hash? No."

"You don't do drugs?"

"Well, only…" She laughed, licked the head of his cock, "…the kind that comes in this type of container."

He lay back down beside her. The smell of the hash, sweet and cloying, competed with the other flowery aromas in the room, the air so thickly perfumed Val found it difficult to breath.

"Where did you first hear about the City?" asked Majeed.

"I've heard about it off and on for years. I never took it seriously—or didn't want to. I guess, because I knew if I ever came to believe in such a place, I'd have to find it. I'd become obsessed with going there. It would consume my life."

"And so it has, apparently. What changed your mind? What made you start to wonder if the stories were real?"

Val hesitated, watched the pale smoke eddy up from Majeed's pipe like swirling water. "You'll laugh."

"I may. But when I'm high, I laugh at everything."

"My mother."

"Your mother?" Majeed laughed, but stopped himself. "What is she, some kind of aging degenerate? A wealthy madam ready to retire and looking for someplace a little more exciting than Phoenix or Miami Beach?"

"She's in a mental institution in Virginia. She's round the bend, beyond insane. She goes through periods, though, when she's lucid, when if she wasn't sitting there in a room with a barred window and if she didn't talk about the micro-vibrater that some people called the Keepers have implanted in her clitoris to keep her constantly aroused, you'd think she was perfectly normal, almost suspiciously conventional."

"Most lunatics are," remarked Majeed.

"Not the last time I saw her, though, which was about a year ago. She'd managed to get hold of a spoon and smuggle it back with her from the dining hall."

"A spoon? You can't do much damage with a spoon."

"She took out her eyes."

"*What*?"

"She scooped them out of their sockets."

"Jesus."

"Yes, that's what she said, over and over again. Jesus. Thank you, Jesus. At least that's what the doctors told me she was saying when they found her. Then she got hysterical and went into some kind of fit."

"Was she religious?"

"Not that I know of. But then a lot of people acquire their faith behind bars. Her wounds became infected, though—apparently the spoon she'd used had penetrated other places first—and for a few days, the doctors thought she'd had it, that she was going to die for sure. So what was I supposed to do—I pay the bills on Mother's hospital, so they were finally able to reach me through my attorney."

"Full-time hospital care. You must do very well, to be able to afford that."

Val started to ignore the implicit query, then said, "I used to feel guilty over having family money that I didn't earn. Then I decided I'd earned it in the hardest way possible—by being born into a situation where I'd have to give up my childhood."

"It's over-rated anyhow, this childhood business. I don't like children anyway. Do you have any of your own?"

"I can't. I had my tubes tied years ago. It seemed the wisest course for all potentially concerned."

For some reason, her answer seemed to make Majeed uneasy. He quickly changed the subject. "Well, in any case, your mother's very lucky to have you, footing her bills at the madhouse and all."

"I'd rather you didn't call it that."

She shuddered at the memories that were crowding in like angry, pecking starlings—the call from the hospital that finally tracked her down, through her bank, in Tokyo, the rushed flight back to Virginia, the conviction (or was it hope?) that the plane was going to crash before she reached her destination—on take-off first, then into the Pacific, then surely, over the Rocky Mountains where it would go down like a silver dart slammed into a rocky bullseye, and finally—when the pilot seemed to apply the brakes far too long and hard on landing, when the entire cabin rocked and objects fell from the overhead compartments as they hit the runway going into Dulles Airport—then she knew that she was going to die, that she had sacrificed her life on this most cliched, appalling, and ludicrous of missions, to attend her blind and presumably dying mother's bedside.

"My mother didn't die, of course."

"You sound like that disappointed you."

"It would have been a relief."

Majeed gave her a sidelong looked, sucked on the pipe.

He doesn't understand, thought Val. *He thinks I'm some kind of awful, heartless daughter who wished her mother dead.*

"Anyway, she recovered, although she's blind for life, of course, and she's watched more closely. But when I visited her at the hospital, I asked her whatever'd caused her to do such a thing? What possibly could have motivated her to maim herself like that?"

She paused, saw that she had Majeed's rapt attention. "She said she'd done it so she wouldn't have to see that horrible, ungodly place again. I thought she meant the hospital, of course. I mean, what else? It's as horrible and ungodly as anything I've ever seen. Then she started to describe things. She said she saw a city of perversity, of lust, and she described things almost exactly the way I'd already been told, except I thought that the descriptions were just rumors or exaggerations, that they couldn't be real. She said there was a man pale as a lily who presided over the City and that she'd seen him, he'd talked to her in dreams she saw behind her eyes."

Majeed's shoulders stiffened and he drew deeply upon the pipe. "Sounds like either your mother thought she saw the Devil or she's been looking at too many Hieronymous Bosch paintings."

"Well, of course, the doctors thought she'd been hallucinating. But everything she said matched what I'd already heard, so you tell me, how would a crazy woman in a mental hospital in Charlottesville, Virginia be able to describe something in almost exactly the same words as people I've talked to in places like Das K—?"

"Coincidence? Horniness? I don't imagine your mother's gotten laid much in the past few years."

"I think the City exists," said Val. "And I think you know how to get there."

"Maybe I do."

"Why so coy?"

"Maybe I want to find out if you're really serious."

"I think you know the answer to that. I didn't come here to talk to Santos on a whim."

"There are people who dream of going to the City in the same way they'd like to go to Namibia or Agra or Kathmandu. They see it as just another exotic travel destination. They've no idea what they're getting into."

Val skimmed a hand across Majeed's breasts, tracing a nipple with her fingernail. "I've been to all those places you just named. I think I know the difference between another changing of geography and time zone and...something more."

"Everyone says that."

"I'm not *everyone.*" One hand stayed to fondle Majeed's breast. The other moved along the muscular striations of his abdomen, enclosed and rubbed his cock.

Majeed took a lengthy inhalation off the pipe. The ceiling above his and Val's head was restless now with swirling smoke, as though a fog were moving in above the bed.

"If you stay around a while, I may be going to the City later in the fall." His words were slow and ponderous-sounding, bloated with drug. "Perhaps I'll take you with me. We'll see."

Val's hands stopped working. "I don't think you understand. I don't want to wait around in Hamburg, and I don't want to go with you. Just tell me how I find this place, who I need to talk to, what I need to do."

"And I just told you. Be patient. Spend some time with me, and later we can talk about the possibility of becoming traveling companions."

Val removed her hands from Majeed's body. She was getting no reaction anyway. His energy was entirely devoted to the consumption of his drug—and with baiting her, she realized, with worthless promises.

"You're wasting my time."

"Oh, really?"

"I don't think you know anything about the City. I don't think you've ever been there. I don't think you plan on going there. You're playing some game at my expense."

"I wouldn't be so hasty to draw conclusions."

"Then tell me what I need to know and I'll be on my way."

"I *said* that perhaps we could go there together."

"I'm not interested in that."

"Fine." Majeed exhaled a languid ring of smoke. "Then get there on your own."

"I will."

"It's not as easy as you think."

"I'll worry about that."

Val was out of the bed, gathering up her clothes and getting dressed.

Majeed glared at her from the bed. His head was wreathed in flowing plumes of scented smoke, eyes narrowed down to panther-slits, voice gravelly and hoarse.

"You're making a mistake," he said. "You're trying to go alone to a place that many think is heaven, but more consider to be hell."

"Then I'll make up my own mind," said Val, "when I get there."

She closed the door behind her.

Chapter Four

Maybe it was the moon that made her crazy.

According to folklore, the full moon caused some people to transform into werewolves, didn't it? It drove those for whom sanity was a tightrope walk above the void to topple into madness and turned hospital emergency rooms into frantic triage units as its luminous pull spawned barroom brawls, domestic squabbles, violent assaults.

The full moon, thought Val. Maybe it was stirring up her juices, causing high tide in her bloodstream, adding a beat of syncopation to the wildness of her heart.

The moon, that must be why she was doing this.

But overhead the swell of clouds opened like an eye, revealing as its pupil only the slenderest of sickles, its magnetic pull reduced to nearly its least powerful that month.

Val almost laughed, except that to have done so—alone in the night on the notorious Reeperbahn—might have invited a kind of attention that even she wouldn't relish.

So she wasn't going to be able to get away with blaming the moon for her madness. Well, fine then, she'd have to rationalize this folly away some other way. She was walking Germany's equivalent of Times Square in a tiny leather skirt and spike heels, pretending—no, there was no pretending to it—she was, for this night anyway, a prostitute.

Two days had passed since she'd quarreled with Majeed. During that time, she'd tried to talk herself into abandoning her quest for the City and going back to Paris. Unless he'd found another in her absence, Reza should be gnashing his teeth for her right now. She'd called him several times, though, and gotten no response—either he was spending all his time at the Sorbonne or, more probably, was busy amusing himself in someone else's company.

Still, there was no reason for her to stay in Hamburg.

Or anyplace, for that matter.

She could go anywhere.

To Bangkok or to Bali, to Fiji or to Zanzibar.

That was the beauty and the terror of her life. She was free to go wherever she might want. Except, of course, to the City. Unless she could find a way to get there on her own or were willing to dawdle here and let Majeed coerce her into his manipulative games.

Earlier that evening, she'd turned a trick, her first paid sex in many months. Now the taste of that unknown man's flesh lingered at the back of her mouth like the residue of a pill that stubbornly refuses to melt upon the tongue and coats the throat with bitter residue.

The excitement of it remained as well, energizing her like the raw rush from a gulped amphetamine. She knew that turning tricks, under the best of circumstances, invited disaster. Playing the prostitute in a foreign country, where her American passport might be worth no more than a few extra weeks in jail or a one-way trip across the nearest border, was still riskier.

She didn't need the money, wasn't sure, in fact, how many Deutsche Markes exactly her blowjob-in-the-backseat man had pressed into her hand after he had dribbled so unmajestically down her throat.

The experience, overall, had been disgusting. Why had she felt compelled to do it? Why, even now, did she feel compelled to repeat it?

She hardly needed the sex. Majeed had surely fucked her well and long and, if she were still eager for some sort of erotic contact, adventures far superior in duration and kind to the average trick, could be purchased at Das K—or places like it.

But there was a hunger there, a need.

As there was power in buying sex, so there was a thrill in selling it.

Especially when she didn't need to do it.

Especially when there was no pimp lurking in the shadows,

waiting to beat her up, no kids at home, waiting for Mom to suck sufficient dicks to buy the groceries.

She chose to do this and so could tell herself it was in no way demeaning.

Something exciting. Forbidden.

Something that briefly filled her body and, for still more fleeting instants, appeared to fill the void inside her soul.

Something to take her mind off Majeed, off the City that she seemed no closer now to entering than when she'd first arrived here.

Something…dangerous.

The night was new and tarted up with neon. Lights pulsed and strobed above her, advertising everything from nude dancers to more explicit, intimate delights. Cars cruised with conveyer belt smoothness along the Reeperbahn, hustlers swaggered, hookers strolled, struck preening poses, did everything but purr.

A young man in a leather bomber jacket, a man with heavy brows like thunderclouds over darkly staring eyes cruised Val, unraveling her clothing with his gaze, zeroing in on her nipples like a sharpshooter sighting through a target. He was lanky with an S-curved spine and small, fine-boned hands that boded poorly for his other endowments and did little to put any heat into Val's blood. She decided he was not to her taste, ignored him. But he turned when she did, followed. She paused and turned to stare at him directly.

He saw her studying him and seemed to flinch, unsure apparently, of whether to admit to interest or draw back, play coy.

Val didn't move, awaited the approach. It didn't come. One minute he was staring at her with that strangely intense gaze, revulsion mixed with hunger, the next he seemed to liquify and evaporate into the passing crowd.

She continued on, disquieted. A half-block later, he came from behind her, swerving around her with right hand out-stretched, pushing some kind of form or pamphlet at her, face set with the determined mien of one issuing a summons.

"Whore." He said the word almost kindly, conversationally, as though it were her name or a term of endearment. "Pray with me. God can save you."

She was rattled by the rapid flow of German, the unexpected and bizarre approach. Before she could stop him, he grabbed her hand and forced the booklet into it. She stared at it in outrage and disbelief, as though he'd filled her hand with filth-clotted toilet tissue. Some sort of religious tract, a Save the Sinners missive. Canvassing for Christ. Ministering to the damned.

"Fuck you and fuck your God." Whether or not she was able to successfully convey this message in her limited German, Val wasn't sure, but the look on her would-be savior's face made it pretty clear he got the gist. Just to be sure, she held the pamphlet up, ripped it into quarters and flung it in his face.

Fear, astonishment, and outrage vied for dominance on the young man's pallid features. The muscles of his jaw bunched and knotted. His forehead corrugated with what Val assumed was the effort he was exerting not to physically attack her.

She slid one hand into the shoulder purse that dangled at her hip and touched the switchblade that she carried there.

Let him try to hurt her. She'd slash his face into more pieces than she'd torn the pamphlet.

The young man took a deep breath, leaned into her. He smelled of sauerkraut and nicotine. Val slid the knife out of her purse, cupped in her palm.

Come on then, do it. Do it.

"Whore," the young man whispered. "May God have mercy on your soul."

He bent to collect the pieces of his pamphlet. When he straightened, his eyes caressed Val all the way from spike-heeled feet to cleavage before turning away.

But the Reeperbahm which, moments before, had seethed with color, heat, and dazzle now seemed reduced to monochrome, the murky grey of partially remembered nightmares. The night seemed drained of its allure, as though the Would-Be Savior, (who, Val thought, would probably have given up a frontrow seat watching sinners swim through seas of shit just to fuck one of the "whores" he so disparaged) had leeched some of her spirit. The street, until a moment before so vampish in its neon glitz, now looked cheap and tawdry.

Or rather, it looked now the way Val remembered New York's tenderloin, years ago and a lifetime away, when that same gaze of revulsion mingled with desire had been on her mother's face, the mission not one ostensibly to save souls but to spy upon the fallen.

And she could hear her mother's voice, raised up an octave with excitement, horror. "Look there, look there at that one. She's a whore, a hooker. She sells herself to sick men like your father."

Not exactly a standard education, thought Val.

She continued walking and traveled several blocks, ignoring those who would approach her, until she realized she was still carrying the knife concealed within her palm, that her fingers hurt from gripping it.

She slid the weapon back into her purse, almost wishing the young man had given her an excuse to use it, to open up his soft, smug face the way he had opened her to some of her least welcome memories.

Sadness crept across her heart.

Loneliness and bitter need.

Those most shameful, most unacceptable of emotions.

And to quell it, more than ever she needed the distraction she felt confident the City would provide.

She thought of Majeed, posing and preening on the bed like a spent Tom licking its genitals. Damn the little whore. She'd get to the City on her own. She didn't need his help.

But it was a lie, and the need to try to convince herself of its validity depressed her further.

She caught a cab and went back to the posh Vier Jahreszeiten Hotel where she had a room. Here the neighborhood was discreetly swank, the lighting sufficient for its purpose but lacking the mesmerizing rabbit-caught-in-the-headlights glare of the Reeperbahn. Couples strolled and tossed bread to the ducks and geese on Alster Lake, in whose black-purple waters the moon appeared to have drowned and lay submerged and glowing like a gold doubloon. In this more sedate environment, her thigh-revealing skirt and low-cut blouse were out of place. She didn't care. If some security guard had the temerity to question her presence there, she'd simply show him her room key—at the equivalent of two hundred dollars a night, she could damn well wear what she pleased.

She checked at the front desk for messages, thinking that Majeed might have called, contrite after their spat, or even that her little Iranian (though hardly *little,* she thought, remembering his heroically-sized dick) might have checked up on her to see if she was really staying at the Vier Jahreszeiten.

No messages.

The hotel lobby offered a bar with a nautical motif reflecting Hamburg's history as a port—gloomy oils of nineteenth century merchant ships struggling in typhoon-tossed seas, a wooden figurehead of a bosomy, dark-tressed wench that might have graced a pirate vessel. Val seated herself at the bar, allowing her skirt to ride up a couple of extra inches, and ordered wine. She sipped her drink, basked in the glow of male gazes, and felt her confidence reviving.

Within half an hour, a portly man in his mid-thirties gingerly approached and then arranged his ass with great consideration on the barstool next to her. He ordered beer and, when it came, leaned around the mug with a kind of protective wariness. Occasionally he peeked at Val in a way that made her think of a high school student stealing answers off someone else's test.

She knew he was going to speak to her half a minute before he finally turned and fumblingly asked, "Do you speak English?"

Val looked him over, deciding whether or not she could converse in any language in which he had even rudimentary fluency, be it English, German, or carnal.

"Yes. I'm American."

"American!" He said it like her nationality alone called for a celebration. Then he began to tell her about that subject which, clearly, he found most fascinating—himself.

He was a Chicagoan named Lou, a hefty man with the look of a former football player gone to seed, a bass player with a local band who taught classical piano on the side. He wore his greying hair in a ponytail, a tiny silver cross through one pierced ear.

His beer gut was starting to be prominent but still looked firm.

When he found out Val was new to Hamburg, he offered her a tour but Val, impatient to make the nature of the transaction clear, said she was available for that night only and then told him her fee.

To her relief, he looked neither shocked nor scornful, but openly delighted.

"I thought I'd have to wine and dine you for a week and take my chances," he said, putting his arm around her in a friendly, not proprietary way. "This is great. We can dispense with the preliminaries."

He didn't ask if Val had a room, but made it clear he wanted the encounter to take place on his own turf.

"It's only a few blocks away," he said, "and when we get there I can show you my collection. I call it my 'treasure.'"

"Let me guess, you're into porn."

"Oh, no, much better, but you'll have to wait to find out what it is until we get there."

Her curiosity aroused, Val agreed to go with him, but when they'd gone only a short distance along Alsterufer Weg, she stopped, reached down, unthreaded the straps encircling her ankles and slipped off her shoes.

He said with unexpected sharpness, "Please don't remove your shoes."

"My feet hurt," she lied. Her feet weren't what was bothering her. She'd had a feeling as they left the hotel, a very *bad* feeling, and if something terrible was going to happen, she needed to be capable of running, not hobbled by her heels.

"If you have to take them off, may I at least carry them?"

Val shrugged. "Sure." She handed him the shoes, slipped a hand through his proffered arm.

"Is your apartment much farther?" she asked, feeling gooseflesh ant-crawling along her shoulders and upper arms.

"Only another block."

"Good," she said and looked behind her, but saw nothing to alarm her, only a gaggle of teenaged couples, an older couple reading a menu posted in the window of a restaurant, a man hailing a cab.

"Something wrong?" he asked.

"It's nothing," she said. "Come on."

Now what?

Breen had finished the Schnapps he'd been nursing, stubbed out his cigarette, and slapped down several Deutsche Marks on top of the dimly lit corner table where he was sitting as soon as he saw Val and the fat hippie whom she'd picked up depart the bar. He'd checked into the Vier Jahreszeiten that afternoon, had phoned her room to satisfy himself she wasn't in, then parked himself in an inconspicuous corner of the lobby with a good view of the door to wait and see what would develop.

He'd considered picking the lock on her hotel room and waiting for her inside, but decided that was inadvisable. Too much security in the hotel, too great a chance as well that Val would have been a busy girl and wouldn't be returning to the room alone.

Then, just about the time he'd been ready to hang it up for the night and retire to his room (perhaps ring up an outcall service, have them send over something for *his* amusement, by God), there she'd come strutting in, the whore of whores, Queen of Cunts, hips undulating like she'd been fucked too much to walk straight, and it had taken her less than an hour to pull in a mark, effect some kind of sleazy interaction.

Of course, she'd never charged *him* for sex.

She wouldn't have dared.

About a block away from the hotel, Breen had to pause and pretend to be hailing a cab while Val took off those ridiculous shoes and minced in her stockings along the chilly Hamburg street. Her tubby swain seemed suitable solicitous and took Val's arm as they continued on their way.

Breen followed at a discreet distance, confident that there were still enough people on the street to make his presence half a block behind them unremarkable.

At the entrance to a narrow apartment building just off Alte Rabenstrausse, Val and her pudgy trick paused briefly. The man tilted her head back, kissed her while one hand roved underneath her jacket to the glittery fabric of the blouse. Val laughed at something. Then, with her preceding him, they went into the building.

Breen stood across the street and watched until he saw a light come on, identifying the location of the apartment Val and the Fat Hippie had just entered.

Bile and queasiness roiled in his gut. The old ulcer, the one that had developed when he was a teenager and which still chewed at him occasionally like a rabid ferret trapped inside his duodenum, had commenced paining him again.

He didn't like fat men.

He didn't fuck fat men.

He might make an exception, though.

Oh, yes, he surely might.

And this one—with his taste for low-class trollops in spiky heels—was going to be a treat.

Chapter Five

He was, Val decided, a man too much alone with his own thoughts and memories.

First he put a Chopin sonata on the stereo and showed her some pictures of his late wife, which were arranged atop the grand piano that took up the greater part of his tiny living room. He spoke rapidly, without benefit of periods or commas, in long sentences strung together like lanterns outside a Chinese restaurant, and he told Val much she didn't want to know.

Finally, when the verbal diarrhea ceased, he seemed to realize they were there for reasons other than social ones, and, in the quick, anonymous fashion of someone passing toilet paper to a person in an adjoining stall, he pushed a thick wad of Deutsche marks at her. She counted out the money, not out of any real interest in the amount but because this seemed professional, and tucked it into her money belt next to her Barclay Card and passport.

Then he showed her his "treasure."

It was on display in the second bedroom, a tiny room hardly larger than a walk-in closet. When they first entered it, the room was deeply layered in shadows, rimmed on three sides by what resembled miniature bleachers. He put a hand on her waist, preventing her from going in farther.

"Stand here while I turn the light on."

His voice rose with the thinly-contained eagerness of a young boy showing off a science project to a teacher he had a crush on. As he moved out of range of her peripheral vision, Val felt herself tense. Was Lou himself the source of the bad feeling she'd had earlier? She braced herself for whatever he was about to reveal—a dungeon stocked with store-bought sex toys or maybe a harem of rubber fuckdolls dressed up like his Mom.

"Well, what do you think? Aren't they beautiful?"

He had turned on a halogen light in the corner, and it cast a soft amber radiance, the golden sheen of an alien sunrise, on a room devoted to the worship of womens' footwear. They were displayed on a series of tiers, grouped according to color, with black and red or some combination of the two clearly predominating. None had heels lower than three inches; a few—obviously more fetish object than footwear—demanded the wearer totter on six inches of pencil-thin heel. Ankle-straps and buckles and sequins, coyly placed bows to accentuate an instep, laces that went half way up the calf, glossy dominatrix boots with silver studs and stirrups—Val had been in the shoe departments of major stores that, while perhaps catering to a more conservative taste, surely were no better stocked.

She noticed, too, that each pair of shoes was replicated three of four times, in different sizes.

"Try anything you like," Lou said, his voice grown husky with excitement. "I'd say you wear a seven and a half. Am I correct?"

"An eight."

"Good. I thought as much."

"You've obviously had a lot of experience at this."

"Since I was a boy. My wife—she had exquisite feet—she understood. She didn't have a problem with it. A lot of these shoes are ones I bought for her or that she picked out herself."

"You didn't say what happened to her? Did you divorce?"

"She died three years ago. Ovarian cancer. Since then, I haven't been able to find anyone…as accommodating as my wife. So I've hired prostitutes. It's better that way, really. No embarrassment, no awkward explanations."

"They're very nice." She felt like she was complimenting him on his children or his golf trophies.

"I have more, of course, too many to keep them all on display. But this gives you an idea. And some very special ones, very rare. Look, let me show you…"

He rummaged in the top shelf of the room's one small closet and pulled down a teakwood box which he opened to reveal a pair of what, to Val, looked like a small child's very old and tattered ballet slippers. Her stomach tightened at the unbidden mental image of Lou watching, covertly masturbating, while a little girl of four or five modeled her satin slippers.

"What are these?"

He all but clapped his hands in delight. "You can't guess, can you? No one ever does. They're over a hundred years old, very rare. The slippers of a Chinese woman after she'd had her feet bound. Lotus feet, they called them. Can you imagine any adult's foot that small? Amazing, isn't it?"

Val thought of the painful binding used to permanently deform the feet of little girls. She handed the shoes back to him, said nothing.

Lou selected another shoe, a red leather one with five inch heels. "I'd like for you to stick this up your pussy. Would you do that for me?"

"Maybe. What will you do for me?"

He looked outraged. "I paid you, didn't I?" but then he seemed to realize she was merely asking in a backhanded way what other activities he might enjoy. His voice changed then, took on a whiny tremulous quality more like a husky-voiced woman's than a man's.

"I'll do whatever you want, whatever you tell me to. I'll let you piss on me or whip me. I'll be a very good boy, a perfect boy. I promise."

"A perfect boy," said Val, warming to this unexpected role. "A perfect boy just like I'll bet you were for your mommy."

He nodded, wet-eyed. "Yes."

"Undress," Val commanded.

He eyed the red shoe in her hand.

"Now we'll see if you can watch me stick this up my pussy without coming all over yourself."

He disrobed quickly, awkwardly, staying on the side of the bedroom that the lamplight failed to illuminate. Shame—for his body, his desires, his being—clung to him like the scent of something unclean. His penis, Val noted, was hidden away, like some sort of tiny, vestigial snout, beneath the folds of fat that sloped down from underneath his pudgy tits to just above his pubic hair.

Nothing very appetizing here. Not this pale, thumb-sized appendage.

But she wasn't here to evaluate his manly attributes, Val reminded herself. She was here to act out a fantasy of her own.

She lay back in a chair, legs apart and skirt rucked up around her waist. She fondled the shoe. She tongued its length. Finally, she inserted a fraction of the heel inside her.

While this was going on, amazing things were happening to Lou's dick, which had transformed from puny slug to thick, majestic rod. She slid the shoe up another quarter inch.

Lou grabbed his cock.

"Did I say you could touch yourself yet?"

"No."

"Then why do it if I haven't given my permission?"

"I'm sorry."

Lou's cock, she noted, swelled even bigger, stiffer than before, when he apologized.

"Please," he murmured. "I want to come. Play with the shoe again."

"How about something else?"

She tossed the shoe aside and moved to position herself over his cock. No sooner had she commenced to lower herself on top of it, however, than Lou wiggled away.

"I can't do that. I want to watch you fuck yourself with the shoe while I jerk off."

"But not fuck me?"

He sneered. "I don't want to fuck you. I don't want to touch you. Just the shoes. That's all that I find sexy…just the shoes."

He sagged back upon the pillows, a portly odalisque with deflated pectorals and mounded gut. His penis, deprived of its fetish object, retreated snail-like under the protective folds of belly.

She looked at his diminished organ with distaste. "So I'm not good enough for you? The shoes are more enticing than my pussy?"

He hesitated, evidently trying to decide if this was still part of the game, then said sourly, "What the hell do you care? You're here to do what I want. I gave you money, didn't I, and plenty of it?"

Val crossed the room, yanked the money Lou had given her out of her purse and threw it at him. The large notes, twice the size of dollar bills, made a bright confetti across the bed.

"I don't need your fucking money. I'm not a whore."

"Then…why…?"

"Because I was bored," said Val. "Because I wanted to get laid. Because…I don't know why…maybe for the same reason you buy shoes…because I can't stop myself."

She'd said more than she meant to. Furious, with him and with herself, she got dressed, dialed for a cab, and waited for it downstairs at the door. She couldn't stand to be in Lou's apartment another minute. She couldn't tolerate having fed any obsession other than her own.

The cab was prompt. Val had no desire now to go back to her hotel. She gave the driver another address instead.

Majeed's.

From the shadowed alcove of a building across the street, Breen watched Val get into the cab.

Fine, let her go, he told himself. He knew where she was staying, and could intercept her there tomorrow. Renew old acquaintances. It was not all that improbable, after all, that they'd run into each other. Like her, he traveled constantly. Like her, he favored grand old hotels as homebase for venturing out to partake of the pleasures of less genteel establishments. They were still friends, after all. She'd probably be glad to see him. As he would her.

In the meantime, Breen had something else he wanted to accomplish.

Not because he thought Val would care or even ever know about it, but because he was in the mood to kill, and he wasn't ready to dispatch Val yet. No, Val's death was too long awaited, too much anticipated to squander in a few rushed minutes of slice and dice and filleting. With Val, he wanted time. Murder victims, after all, were much like lovers. There were those with whom a one night stand nicely sufficed, others with whom even a prolonged honeymoon was not sufficient to sate the desire.

Val, he felt, deserved a honeymoon.

Breen looked up at the fourth floor window, where a faint light remained on. The Fat Hippie changing the bedsheets maybe or soaping off the sex-scent from his groin.

Breen crossed the street and entered the apartment building. He felt elated, almost light-hearted in his mission. Val was his and, along the way, he'd pick off her little playmate, too.

A certain fat man was going to undergo the Arthur Breen Rapid Weight Loss Method tonight. Lose ugly flab and cellulite and maybe even bone as well. Become a shadow of his former self and a most unappealing corpse.

Chapter Six

There was no moon when Val crossed the courtyard leading to Majeed's squalid abode. She walked rapidly, her high heels tapping out a jittery staccato on the paving stones, her heart adrenalized and shivery against her ribs.

At the foot of the stairway, she stopped, considering what she was about to do.

What was she doing here? She knew she couldn't trust Majeed, an obvious drug addict and skilled manipulator whose grasp of reality was likely to be as dubious as his gender. To give him the satisfaction of coming back…

And yet what choice did she have?

I could go back to Paris, Val thought. *I could go to Asia or back to the States. I could check into a room next to Mother's and quietly rot. I could go anywhere.*

But there was no place that she wanted to go. The places were all the same, distinguished only by climate or architecture or geography. The people, once you got past the particulars of language and custom and coloring, all turned out to be, inevitably, the same person, the same body that she'd already fucked, grown weary of and left behind.

There was just the one place, really, that she still wanted to see.

If, in fact, it existed.

If Majeed could help her get there.

Finally, impatient with her own skittishness, she climbed the last flight of stairs and rapped on Majeed's door.

Inside was silence.

Val slammed a palm against the door. "Majeed? It's Val."

She heard the creak of bedsprings, followed by the scrape of feet that sounded like the resident of a retirement home shuffling painfully across the floor.

The door opened and Majeed blinked out. He was wearing a pale grey silk shirt that clung to him like fog, outlining breasts and nipples. His face was sheened with sweat. His full lips looked gnawed on, rouged.

"I thought you'd be back in Paris by now."

"We need to talk."

"About what?"

"I think you know."

Majeed seemed to consider this. "It's late. Come back tomorrow."

"No." In the silent hallway, the word sounded sharp as a slap. "Please," Val said, making her voice softer, "let me come in for just a little while. Unless, of course, you're entertaining someone."

"Only myself," Majeed said with a wry smile. "Until you interrupted." But he stepped back to let her in.

The air inside Majeed's small room was the color of a dowager's hair, all swirls of blue-grey tendrils and snaking wisps. Val's eyes immediately began to sting. She coughed and cleared her throat.

"How do you breath in here?"

Majeed shrugged. "I'm used to it. Pure air gives me asthma."

"Your lungs must look like pieces of burnt toast." She went to the window and began to move some of the incense burners aside in order to raise it.

Majeed stopped her. "Don't touch those, please. And come away from the window. If you're afraid of getting a contact high, you'll just have to leave."

"It's not the contact high I'm worried about. I just hate small, stuffy places."

"Ah," Majeed said, "a claustrophobe? Does that mean you're going to start to sweat and tremble and finally tear off all your clothes if I don't have a window open?"

"Don't get your hopes up."

Majeed took up his pipe again and drew on it. He slouched over to the bed, where sheets and blankets were heaped in an orgy of disarray, and collapsed onto a mound of tassled pillows.

"So you came back. And let me guess, you've decided you can't find your way alone to the City. You've decided you'd like to be my traveling companion after all."

"Only until we get there," said Val. "Then we'll go our separate ways."

"Assuming that the offer's still open."

She tried to mask her irritation. "I can make it worth your while."

"I'll bet you can."

"I mean I'd pay."

"I don't need money."

"Your habit must be quite expensive." Val arranged herself beside him on the bed in what she hoped was a provocative display. The smoke unfurling from Majeed's lips looked like the silhouettes of shadow women, all undulating heat and haze.

"Not as costly as yours."

"I'm not a drug addict," said Val, at once regretting the tone of derision that insinuated itself into her voice.

Majeed breathed out smoke and gave a guttural, cracking sound meant to be a laugh.

"Maybe not a drug addict, but an addict none-the-less. Otherwise you wouldn't be so hellbent on getting to a place you don't really know the first thing about." He croaked that smokey laugh again and lifted up the rumpled shirt, exposing cock and pussy. "Your habit's right between your legs…and here between *my* legs. And other legs. All legs. The legs of whoever you were with tonight. You'd like to fuck everyone in the world, but you can't, so you're feeling desperate."

"Or so you'd like to believe."

"What makes you even think the offer's still open? I quite enjoy traveling alone. And you don't look as though you need a chaperone."

Val sat up. "I don't know why I bothered coming here."

"Because I can give you something you want very much. As you know very well."

"I don't need anything that badly."

"What you need, for a start, is some humility. To admit you can't do everything yourself. To admit you might just need me."

"I did that by coming here."

"With resentment in your eyes and an attitude as big as my dick."

"How you flatter yourself."

"Better for you if you did more flattering and less demanding."

"I don't need this shit. Forget it."

"Now hold on. Wait. Do you always act in so much haste?" Majeed put the pipe aside. "I didn't say I *wouldn't* take you to the City. I only said you might as well admit your need. You're not just going there to sightsee. You're going there because you *have* to. You must. It's all that's left for you. Come on, sit down again."

He took Val's hand, their fingers intertwining in a loosely held latticework. "There's no harm in being addicted to pleasures of the flesh—and the pain. It's all one and the same. Most people are afraid of too much pleasure. They wouldn't want to see the City, even if they knew that such a place existed. They value their pleasant tedium, their safe little lives filled up with precautionary measures. And sometimes, it backfires, and they go crazy anyway."

"And sometimes they take prisoners with them into their craziness."

"Loved ones, of course," offered Majeed. "It sounds as if you've known a few like that."

"Unfortunately so."

"And run away from them, I'll bet."

"Something like that." She relented and relaxed against Majeed's breasts, breathed in the rich perfume of semen, musk, and flowers that permeated the room. "When I was a kid, I saw this horrible picture once of a fox that had gnawed off its own leg to get out of a trap—it was some sort of anti-trapping campaign. I never forgot that. I kept thinking what that must be like, to be forced chew off a part of yourself to get out of a trap." She shuddered. "Anyway, I vowed that if I survived my childhood, I'd make it up to myself. I'd live my life entirely to my own satisfaction."

Majeed sighed. "Spoken like a true Lost Child. One who never had a childhood."

"You could say that."

"You'll have to tell me about it."

"I don't think so."

"But we're going to be together, aren't we? That is, unless you've changed your mind *again*."

Val felt her pulse and heartbeat quicken. Her mind spun an erotic web—of decadence past imagining, depravities beyond the capacity of the mind to comprehend, and those few elect, the connoisseurs of flesh who would endure anything in order to experience everything.

Majeed took Val's hand and guided it underneath the covers, passing over his erection to the moist and avid opening beneath it.

"There's a selection of dildos in the dresser drawer. Pick one you like and fuck me, please. Afterwards, if I'm still awake, you can tell me how you came to lose your childhood."

When Breen knocked on the door of the Fat Hippie's apartment, the last thing he expected was that it would be opened immediately, without so much as an inquiry of "Who is it?" or an eye put to the peephole. But a voice started speaking English as, from inside, a chain was taken off the door.

"I thought you might be back when you realized that you left your…"

And then, of course, the door was completely opened and he saw Breen.

The two men stared at each other, the one impeccably and expensively attired, the other clad in a bedraggled terrycloth robe.

"Oh. Oh, my. Who…?"

Breen had rehearsed a line of patter in his head and now, though slightly flustered, he felt obligated to recite it all in German. "I'm afraid I've had a run-in with some thugs, and I need help. If you would be so kind as to let me come in and call the police…"

The man looked at Breen with narrowed, bloodshot eyes, as if trying to muster sufficient energy to send him on his way.

"Sorry, I don't understand you."

Breen repeated the plea in English. "Please hurry. They're still out there. Skinheads, I'm afraid."

The man hesitated, any Samaritan tendencies clearly warring with those of self-interest and self-preservation. Not for the first time, Breen counted on the fact that he always dressed impeccably, always looked and sounded like a gentleman. He appeared to be the kind of man you'd trust to come into your home or escort your wife to the opera, the type of prosperous businessman far more likely to be a victim of a crime than to perpetrate one. How many psychopaths, after all, wore hundred-dollar-a-bottle cologne and designer neckties?

Yet, even with Breen's sophisticated demeanor, the man whose post-coital sleep he had disturbed looked dubious.

"Wait here. I'll make the call for you."

"But you don't speak German?"

"Very little."

"Then the cops will get it muddled up and never get here. Please.

I'm really afraid for my life out here. Let me come in and use the phone."

Another beat of hesitation—Breen's nerves jittered for blood. Then the Fat Hippie stepped back and gestured him in.

And Breen was inside the apartment.

The living room in which he found himself looked just big enough to stable a large pony, and fully half of that meager space was taken up by a polished grand piano topped with photographs of a square-jawed, dark-eyed woman who was sultry in a peasant sort of way. From the bedroom came the kind of complex piano melody that put Breen in mind of black-clad harpists and high tea at the Plaza. Had Val and this guy actually fucked to that, thought Breen, and slid one manicured, ringed hand inside his jacket, feeling for the polished surface of the Glock 10mm that he always carried when abroad in the late night streets. One couldn't be too careful, after all. There were bad people out there.

"The phone's in here." said the Fat Hippie. He led the way toward the bedroom.

"Actually I don't want to use the phone at all," Breen said. "Although at some point I might like to take a look inside your refrigerator."

The Hippie made some muffled sound of exclamation. He was turning around when Breen brought the butt of the gun around in an arc against his skull, a gesture reminiscent of one christening a ship, the difference this time being that it was the object struck and not the weapon used that crumbled.

Their eyes.

Breen liked to watch the eyes of his prey when they awoke. Liked to see the gradual oozing back of darkness until consciousness was regained, the fluttering of lids, the registering of the pain unconsciousness had blocked while the glazed sheen on their pupils cleared and their sight refocused.

Sometimes, even at this point, they were still dazed and lay quietly a few more seconds, staring up at the ceiling as though expecting some celestial divinity, a *deus ex machina* angel complete with chariot and thunderbolts, to swoop down to effect a heaven-sent rescue.

That respite between nothingness and full, horrifying consciousness seldom lasted long, however, and if it did, Breen knew ways to jar the semi-conscious brutally alert.

But sooner or later, with or without any help from him, there came a gradual clearing of the head, the reconnecting of the massively insulted synapses, and the receipt of that all-important message: Something is wrong. Something is horribly wrong here.

That was just about the time they tried to scream and found that the sensation of pressure on their lips wasn't from some type of adhesive bandage covering a wound but a strip of duct tape that not all the torture in the world could force a scream past.

Then all else came rapidly: the frantic struggles to move bound arms and legs, the jerking, spastic flopping of bodies that often seemed to be attempting to dislocate their own limbs in their frantic struggles to free themselves from their restraints, the wildly darting eyes that looked like marbles zinged between the bumpers of a pinball machine.

The eyes, Breen knew, were always the last to admit defeat. The arms and legs, at some point, grew exhausted, but the eyes, right up until the end, sought some escape, searching the perimeters of their sockets again and again like prisoners looking desperately for some chink in the walls enclosing them.

The eyes were the last to give up, and when the light went out in them, even if the body stubbornly refused to die, Breen knew it was all over.

He liked that moment, awaited it, in fact, with some anticipation, because it was when the real death took place. Not the physical death, which could occur hours later, but the death of the victim's spirit.

Breen had been busy during the Hippie's little sleep. As was his habit in such situations, he'd first made sure the door was locked, then lugged the heavy body over and hoisted it up atop the bed where, after removing the robe, he'd used ties he found in the dresser drawer to turn the man on his side and hogtie his wrists and ankles.

He'd taken a break then, removed his own clothes and put them in a neat pile on top of the piano, a distance from which he felt sure—no matter how enthusiastic his coming indulgences—no blood would spatter far enough to soil them.

Next he went into the kitchen, perused the contents of the fridge, which was small and underprovisioned. He found only a half-empty bottle of mediocre Moselle and a tin of Leberkase, hot liver pate, to interest him.

More distracting by far was what he found in the narrow room off the bedroom. A shrine, no less. A place for worship of religious icons. Unless, of course, the Fat Hippie were a cobbler specializing in the footwear of hookers and exotic dancers, a possibility Breen thought unlikely. A pair of red leather pumps with ridiculous towering heels lay on the floor. Breen picked them up. Fashionable stilts, a woman wearing them would be as hobbled as a horse, a teetering and tottering absurdity. Had Val worn them? Had she stripped off her clothes and spread her legs, opening her petaled mouth to the Fat Hippie, while he salivated at the combined odors of pussy and shoe leather?

The teakwood box on a small display case—what Breen's mentor Miss Lee would have called a what-not shelf—caught his attention. He opened it, was disappointed to find the shoes inside so plain, so frayed compared to all the other, marvelously sleazy stuff displayed here.

And yet he'd flipped through enough art and history books in his time (for Miss Lee encouraged education, especially in the arts) to realize after a few beats what these shoes must be and why the Fat Hippie had provided them a special case. He'd seen a picture once, an old nineteenth century daguerreotype in a museum, of a tiny Chinese woman being carried in a chair by a pair of husky coolies. Her feet had been maimed in childhood so she couldn't walk. The museum caption had phrased it more delicately, but that was the gist of it.

Breen held the little shoes. He turned them in his hand. He sniffed them. He tried to imagine the broken, mutilated little feet they had adorned, the wailing, cringing of the dark, exotic child when her feet were bound. For several minutes, he stood in reverie, spellbound by the tapestries woven by his own imagination.

What heated fantasies some people conjured around something so pedestrian as footwear. What fantasies might Breen himself invent if he put his mind to it.

Returning to the bedroom, he used duct tape from the roll he carried with him to bind the Fat Hippie's mouth. Then he filled a glass with wine from the bottle of Moselle and upended it over his victim's head.

"I now baptize you in the name of Breen."

The man coughed and sputtered, groaning behind the gag as he returned to consciousness.

His eyes opened. He looked at Breen, who smiled down at him like an avuncular physician about to administer an anesthetic before the operation was to begin.

"Hello. I was beginning to wonder how long you'd keep me waiting."

The Fat Hippie began to strain and struggle. A vein in his temple stood out in brilliant cobalt against the skin.

"The woman who was in your apartment earlier tonight," Breen said, "She's an old friend of mine. A lover. I hope you aren't overly attached to her. Because I'm going to take my good slow time with you tonight and every ounce of pain and bead of blood I wring from you, I promise when the time comes, I'll do threefold to her."

The man blinked and shook his head, either to clear it or to indicate acute displeasure with Breen's plan.

"You fucked a woman who, in her own sordid way, means a lot to me," Breen went on conversationally. "You fucked a woman to whom I once proposed marriage, but she walked out on me. She left me and for that I'm going to kill her, slowly, taking back from her death all the pleasure that she owes me. But for tonight, my friend, I'm afraid you'll have to take her place."

So saying, Breen went to collect the objects that appealed to both his sense of sadism and of whimsy: a pair of pliers and five pairs of womens' shoes.

Chapter Seven

Val opened her eyes to a cluster of grotesque and gaping faces a few inches from her head. Cauliflower faces, swollen and pustular, faces pockmarked and jaundiced the color of corn, oily, dark faces with howling, eggplant-shaped mouths.

They appeared boneless, these vegetable faces, losing shape and squashing into each other until each face became a single feature of a much larger visage.

The looming face flattened and spread like a huge amoeba viewed from beneath a glass slide. The eyes, composed of many tiny, leering faces, focused its hungry gaze on her. The bulbous nose, sprouting green, broccoli-like growths, exhaled gusts of acrid steam.

Val tried to move, but a belt low across her hips and a strap over her chest held her in place in the passenger seat of a car. The tuberous mass oozed across the windshield, searching for a way to get in.

To get at her.

She struggled and flailed out. The multi-eyed, multi-mouthed creature had found a crack in a window and was pouring itself into the car. Taffy-like strings of gummy material ran down the inside of the glass and stretched toward her across the seat. The clammy muck reached her hand and braceleted itself around her wrist. She felt it start to ooze between her legs.

She screamed and kicked. Her foot hit something solid.

"Wake up!"

She opened her eyes and saw the nightmare face inches from her own. Huge eyes, charcoaled lids, a mouth deep and wide enough to swallow the world.

She screamed again.

Majeed shook her.

"Jesus, Val, it's me. You're having a nightmare."

"Oh, God."

"You kicked the shit out of me."

"I'm sorry."

She was shaking, her body drenched in a film of chilly sweat. "I haven't had that dream since I was a kid. I thought I'd outgrown it."

"What was it about?"

"Just…I don't know…hard to explain."

Majeed pulled her against him. "Come on, go back to sleep."

"No, I'm afraid I'll have the dream again. I want to stay awake."

"Make love?"

She shook her head. "Not even that. Just talk to me."

Majeed filled a pipe with hash and lit it. "I think you're the one who needs to talk. Tell me about the dream."

Val watched the smoke curl above Majeed's head. "I was in my mother's car. And there were faces outside, people trying to get in."

"That doesn't sound so bad."

"It was when I was eight."

"That's when the dreams started?"

"No, that's when my mother—Lettie—that's when Lettie started taking me on midnight rides. Her own peculiar brand of sex education."

Majeed frowned. "What was the idea?"

"I'm not sure." Some ashes drifted onto Majeed's breasts. Val brushed them away. "To teach me the wickedness of sex, I suppose."

"Somehow I don't think she succeeded."

"Quite the reverse." Val smiled for the first time since she'd awakened.

"Tell me about it then, your early introduction to the allure of the perverse."

"Only some of it," Val said. "The worst parts I never talk about."

She lay a hand across Majeed's cock and began telling him about her childhood growing up in a renovated twelve-room home on two acres of land outside Tarrant, New York. Her father, a Wall Street executive made the 90-minute commute to Manhattan twice a day. He had bought the showpiece home as an investment and as a haven from the tumult of city life, a safe harbor to enclose his wife and daughter while he went forth to do financial battle.

Unfortunately his final battle, which took place when Val was five, occurred not on the Floor, but in a seedy walk-up tenement where he'd gone to do some coke with a Latina hooker. The hooker rolled him while her pimp concussed his head in several places with a tire iron. The coroner's report indicated he spent a full day dying.

Val's mother, when she learned the circumstances of the tragedy, said too bad it didn't take longer.

Apparently Anthony Petrillo had been as clever at investing and amassing money as he was unwise in the choice of his companions. He left a vast amount of money—much of which Val inherited in due time—but little else. No memories to speak of (except the bitter ones left to his wife) and, for Val, just the blurry image of a man who left the house before she awoke and returned long after nightfall, harried, jittery, with the look of someone deprived of sleep for so long that exhaustion comes to seem the norm and recreation aberrant.

As an adult, Val still found it difficult to reconcile the image of that polite, precise, hard-working father with the shadow father who was murdered in the act of buying drugs and sex.

Perhaps, she thought, what he'd been really buying was a tiny window out of the tedium and humdrum of his life, much as the painting of sea-battered Orkney Island might have offered the illusion of a small window in the wall above his desk, into a remote world of mystery and possibility.

All she knew was that after her father's death, the painting, his books, all his possessions were removed from the house.

It was as if he were more than simply dead. It was as if he had never existed.

After her husband's death, Val's mother became afraid to leave the house. She claimed men followed her when she ventured out. The idle glances and chitchat of passersby became the furtive gaze of psychopaths, the soft babbling of lunatics who stalked her. Terrorized by the demons that nested in her head, she left Val and the house to maids and cultivated a sleazy romance with agoraphobia, preening for hours before the mirror but dressing in housedresses so shabby that the maid, discovering them in a pile next to the dryer, once mistakenly used them for rags with which to polish tabletops. She spent most of her time in her sewing room, sleeping or gazing out the one window or, occasionally, stitching together a dress or blouse for Val, usually in some wildly inappropriate material:

crushed velvet, lace and satin, jumpers cut from bolts of sequinned silk. And all the while she muttered in no language known to any but the denizens of her own internal world, reverting to normal speech only when necessity demanded that she order groceries from the local market or fuss with local school administrators who, after a year or so, began calling repeatedly to learn why her daughter wasn't registered for school.

Almost two years after her husband's death, Lettie's weirdness took a sudden shift, one which at first appeared to be for the better. She seemed to remember Val's presence in the house and spent time with her again. Hours were spent brushing out the child's hair, caressing her, teaching her to read and write from a book of fairy tales that featured stories about seductive hags who fricasseed their children, and coiled serpents that lurked under mattresses and crawled into the snoring mouths of sleepers.

And, as if her father's murder hadn't already taught Val enough about the cruelties and caprices of the world, Lettie decided, with that obsessive single-mindedness peculiar to the insane, that more instruction for her daughter was in order.

If Lettie had been a near recluse, afraid to leave the house, now she found a black new zeal, a morbid sort of daring.

She commenced to venturing out for night-time drives into Manhattan, trolling for dissoluteness and danger like a carrion-eating bird seeking dead flesh, a madwoman and her passenger, a wide-eyed little girl.

Val remembered riding in her mother's Mercedes through the rain-soaked, late-night streets of Manhattan's seediest enclaves. Lettie always drove a new car, usually one resembling a black barge, its leather smell still as fresh as when it had left the showroom. Val would sit close against her mother, staring out at the weird night-circus of the city, hoping that what she saw outside could not get in.

She remembered the sheen of stoplights reflected in oily puddles, the barred storefronts with their glut of tawdry merchandise, and the flashing neon, often with a letter or two burned out, so that the names of bars and liquor stores resembled gap-toothed grins. Often when she'd shut her eyes against the overbright display, she could still see the neon dazzle, as if one look had tattooed its garish message permanently on the inside of her eyes.

In some neighborhoods, Val remembered being most afraid when her mother stopped for lights, and the milling, seething faces passed within a few feet of the car.

Blacks and whites and Orientals, all combinations in between, and, though their skins were a multitude of hues, their expressions generally were less diverse: they looked bored and angry, angry and bored, and often they looked afraid.

Sometimes Val would imagine leaping from the car and running from her mother, disappearing into the crowd's dark and perilous ranks, and throwing herself upon the mercy of their world, but fear locked her legs. She was too afraid—not only of what was inside the car with her, but of what lay outside as well.

"Lock your door," Lettie would order, but she never believed Val's assurance that it was already locked. She always had to reach over and press the button herself, and sometimes—by mistake—in her haste, she actually unlocked it. And all the while, her eyes would gleam, her fear and enthrallment with that other world casting a sheen of rapt bewitchment across her face.

"Look! Look at those two women there," Lettie would cry, pointing out two cafe au lait madonnas in leather skirts the size of postage stamps and wildly bouffant hair.

"No, don't look yet! You don't want them to see you stare. Now! Turn around now. Look!"

It was a ritual that, by the age of eight, Val already knew too well. Her mother had a name for it—going for a ride." Presumably it was a form of education, in the wiles and sins and venalities of life, a graphic way of teaching a young child of life's rife and lurking dangers, and for a few months, Val had accepted it as such.

Only later, after she had grown too old to be trusted to remain locked inside the car on such excursions, did Val recognize the strange nocturnal forays were her mother's longing made tangible, titillation masked as moral guidance.

"See that man across the street, the one in the built-up shoes! That's a pimp, the lowest form of life. He lives off women, sells them for sex. And look there, there's his woman! That's the kind of woman that killed your father."

The hours spent cruising the tenderloin along 8th Avenue, then over to the docks where the chickenhawks prowled like lean barracuda, and finally up into Harlem, provided a seedy circus of vicariously-experienced trauma. There'd been the time a wild-eyed man, a tattooed troll with shocks of matted, grayish hair protruding at all angles from his skull, lurched up beside the car and tried to force the door open. He screamed that he was being pursued, that someone meant to kill him.

Val's mother ran the light, sped off. They were half-way up the block when Val heard shots fired and saw the troll, who'd run across the street and was badgering another driver, flop face-down in a mound of dirty snow, which promptly started turning red.

At other times, men with dark faces and Halloween smiles approached the car, thinking Lettie was a well-to-do suburban matron out to score some coke. (Or better business arrangement yet, to peddle her child's ass.) They cursed her when she sped away. One time a green convertible followed them through Harlem all the way to the Triboro Bridge, its occupants an Oriental with gold stars in his teeth and a woman whose head kept disappearing and reappearing next to him like some kind of dashboard toy.

"It's so you'll see the world for what it is," Val's mother would tell her as they returned from their nocturnal jaunts. "So you'll understand how dangerous and vile men are, how careful you have to be just to survive in this world."

Just to survive.

Sometimes Val wasn't sure she really cared if she survived at all.

"Later on," she told Majeed, "Lettie stopped taking me for rides. Things got much worse."

"Worse?" For a second, she thought Majeed was going to laugh and she regretted having told him anything. But he didn't laugh. He held her close. "What happened then?"

"I don't remember everything."

"That's hard to believe."

"Let's go to sleep."

Majeed said, "If you really don't remember, then I envy you. I remember everything about growing up—the loneliness, the taunts when people found out what I was. I thought I'd be better off dead. I still think that sometimes. Who knows what death is like—maybe it's the high that exceeds all others. Or, if nothing else, at least it's a cessation of all craving."

"But how can you talk like that? You're beautiful. I'd love to be the way you are, to be both sexes. Maybe then I'd feel complete."

"Or maybe you'd find out that what I am isn't male *and* female but something less than either one."

He reached for his pipe and filled his lungs, his cheeks sinking in and then expanding as he held in the smoke. He offered Val the pipe. She shook her head.

"You'd feel better."

"No."

"What can I do to make it better then?"

Keep holding me, don't let me go, was what Val might have said.

But she needed to escape her memories, put miles and lovers between her and the past and so she said, "Just fuck me hard. Then tell me about the City."

She had fallen asleep with Majeed still inside her, her head cradled between his breasts. She dreamed of soaring flight, then of suddenly being reclaimed by gravity and falling, a headlong spiraling plunge into a sure death. *Wake up,* she told herself, *it's just a dream,* and she reached out to cling to Majeed's soothing flesh—he wasn't in the bed, but crouched beside it, hunkered down with a look of terror on his face.

"Shh, don't make a sound."

From the courtyard below, footsteps sounded. They drew nearer, ascending the inner stairs, and approached along the corridor.

Majeed looked frantically around the room, as though trying to will some avenue of escape to open up in the solid wall or ceiling.

"What *is* it?" Val whispered.

"Shhh." He put a finger to his lips, glared at her with an urgency that brooked no dispute.

The footsteps stopped outside the door. Val held her breath.

"Majeed?" The voice was teasingly seductive and well modulated, a foreign sounding voice that twisted with difficulty around the German sounds. "Majeed, my love, I know you're in there."

The doorknob turned, but the door was both deadbolted and chained.

The voice dropped to a near whisper and said with renewed cajolery, "You shouldn't have run away from me. You shouldn't have stolen my pretty trinket. Now open the door, you little cunt. I want you to come home."

There was something about the voice that made Val's heart lurch into her gorge. It was too soft, too honeyed, the voice of a corrupt priest saying prayers while masturbating an acolyte in the confessional. And its persuasiveness reached entrail deep, for even as a part of her was terrified, there was another part longing to unlock the door.

"Come on, you pretty little turd. Unlock the door and show me what you've brought home to desecrate tonight. You know how much

I like to watch you whore around. So let me in, and maybe I'll forgive all your betrayals."

Val looked at Majeed, who'd gone bone white and appeared almost spellbound with terror. For some reason, she had the feeling that the talk outside the door was some kind of game, that had the owner of the voice desired to, he could have broken the door open without a moment's pause.

"You piece of cum-encrusted shit, you worthless bitch! You know this will only make me hurt you worse when I next see you. And I *will* see you again. You can't run from me. You *need* me. You'll come to me, and you'll come begging. You can't survive without me."

Those last words scared Val most of all, for something in Majeed's entranced stare argued for their veracity.

Nor did she expect the sweet-voiced brute beyond the door to leave peacefully. She was sure that in another instant the door would be kicked in.

But no blow came. There was silence for a few minutes, the would-be intruder evidently remaining where he was, listening no doubt, for signs of someone inside the room. To Val this ticking quiet was far more ominous than taunts and threats. The idea of someone lurking just outside the door, pretending not to be there but waiting for a chance to pounce or plotting his next move, aroused long-buried terrors. Her fear of being trapped slid into consciousness like a stiletto blade parting fat and muscle. She lay motionless, feeling the old fears swirling inside her, rising up to fill her chest, her throat, her mind, like flood waters over a drowned village.

"You little trick, I know you're there. Go ahead and have your fun tonight, but if you keep on running from me, there'll be no more chances. No forgiveness for the prodigal. You'll be forever exiled!"

The footfalls, a soft and shuffling tread, receded along the corridor.

Val breathed again. She slid out of bed and crouched down beneath the window sill, ignoring Majeed's protests. Presently, a figure emerged into the courtyard, a man in late middle age, tall and stooped, almost emaciated, but with a lush mane of jet hair threaded through with white that fell around his shoulders.

"Get down!" Majeed hissed.

The man crossing the courtyard paused and turned, directing his gaze toward the window through which Val peered. The room was dark, the courtyard lit with moon. She was sure he couldn't see her, and yet, she felt a frisson of both dread and longing, repugnance mixed with lust, as his eyes turned in her direction.

For an instant, just before he turned away again, she experienced the tang of want and craven need: it chilled her utterly.

"Goddamn it, don't let him see you!"

"It's all right. His back is turned. He's leaving."

Majeed cleared his throat, as though reaching for an offhand way to phrase his question, and said, "What does he look like?"

"What do you mean 'what does he look like'? Don't you know?"

"Sometimes he wears…disguises."

"Well, tonight he looks like one of those carved saints from the Day of the Dead in Mexico. Like he doesn't eat enough and never loves."

"Yes," sighed Majeed, as though that description were all too familiar to him.

"Who is he?"

"Just someone I've had some business dealings with."

"What's his name?"

"Why do you care?"

"I want to know."

"Dominick Filakis."

"Your pimp?"

Majeed did not reply, but got out of bed and put a fresh stick of sandlewood in one of the incense burners on the sill.

In the grey, rain-washed light of coming dawn, Val could see the ridges of his spine bisecting broad shoulders and tapered waist, the incongruous silhouette of full breasts as he turned again to face her.

"You're a prostitute," said Val.

"You say that like it surprises you."

"Very little surprises me."

"Then you haven't looked hard enough."

The room filled with scents of sandalwood and strawberries that mingled with the smell of sex to form a heady musk. Majeed slid back into the bed, pressed his persimmon lips to Val's.

"We need to leave. Right now."

"Leave? This minute?"

"Isn't that what you wanted? Isn't that what you came back here for? Don't tell me now you've decided you need more beauty sleep. Come on, get your stuff together. I don't want to stay here any longer."

"You're really afraid of him, aren't you?"

"I'm merely being…prudent."

"What will he do to you?"

"Christ, you ask too many questions."

"I'll need to go back to my hotel first. To get my things."

"Will it take long?"

"An hour."

"All right, look. Get your things, but hurry. You know where the train station is?"

"Yes."

"There's a coffeeshop in the main lobby. I'll be there. Don't make me wait."

"Filakis, will he come back?"

"Not today," Majeed said. "He has others to police. I'm small fry in his game plan. By the time he loses patience and kicks the door in, we'll be half-way to Africa."

"Africa?"

"I didn't tell you? That's where the City is. At least, that's where the entrance is."

"All right, I'll meet you then."

"You've got your passport with you?"

"Yes."

Val was pulling on her clothes. She picked up her money belt and saw, to her horror, that one compartment was unzipped. Her passport and traveler's checks were in place, but her Barclay Card and most of her German currency were gone. She had a sudden, sickening image of herself hurling wads of Deutsche Marks at a stricken-looking Lou, paying no attention to what she was pulling from the belt except that it was money he had given her and that, at that moment, she'd despised it and him with equal fury.

Shit.

"What's wrong *now*" said Majeed.

"Nothing."

"You looked…for a second you had a funny look on your face."

"I'm just thinking…I may not be able to get a taxi right away. I'll need more than an hour."

"Two hours then," Majeed said irritably, "but not a minute more. And if you're late, that's your problem. I'll take the first train going south. I'm not going to wait for you."

Pastel smudges, like the stains put on the wool of sheep to distinguish those intended for the slaughter, colored the underbellies of the clouds as the taxi Val had commandeered rushed her back to Lou's apartment. She was furious with herself. It had been stupid enough to lose her temper with that obsessed and foolish man, to give back the money she had rightfully earned in a fit of misspent pride. To have somehow left a credit card—with her *real* name on it—in his apartment was the height of lunacy.

But I can't just leave it there, she thought. *I need it and besides*—she shuddered, unable to imagine anything of hers, anything that bore her signature, becoming one of his collectibles, some sort of souvenir.

She asked the driver to wait and rushed up the stairs, her mind racing with unhappy possibilities. What if Lou was one of those who got up early to eat or exercise and wasn't home? What if he refused to let her in? What if he'd found the card but denied having it for whatever perverse reason? What if the card wasn't really there, but lost or stolen somewhere else along the way?

And now with Majeed waiting…so little time…

She rapped on the door.

Waited, knocked again.

Where was he?

"Lou?"

Dammit, he *had* to be home.

Then, despite the fact that his door being unlocked would defy all logic, she tried the knob. It turned and the door swung inward.

"Lou?"

The living room was as dark as when she had left it hours earlier and much more silent. But then he'd hardly leave the lights and stereo on if he were going out. Of course, he'd hardly leave the door unlocked for that matter, either.

"Hello? *Hello?*" The quiet twitched across her skin like an infestation of fleas. She took a few more steps and then her nostrils flared, assailed by a faint, but memorably unpleasant smell—an odor she associated with backed-up drains and the excremental ghettos of Third World cities.

Just find the damn card and get out of here.

The money, as she'd figured, had been gathered up. Her card, undoubtedly, along with it. To be put—where?—in his wallet, a desk drawer, trash basket? She didn't like being forced into the position of intruder in another's domain. He could shoot her for a burglar and be within his rights.

She called out again. Nothing. Even if he was in the bathroom with the water running, he'd have heard her that time.

It isn't worth it. Get out of here.

But then she saw the Barclay Card. Not stashed away, but lying atop a neatly folded newspaper on the arm of a chair. She crossed the room to snatch it up and, in doing so, was forced to walk past the Treasure Room, the door to which was opened wide. One of the red pumps that she had worn the night before had been tossed into the hall. Its towering heel had been torn off. Further on, closer to the bedroom, the shoe's mate lay mutilated in identical fashion.

And that smell—part hospital, part outhouse.

Although every instinct warned her not to, Val opened the bedroom door.

And almost laughed from shock, because—in the dim light—she didn't know what she was seeing. It looked like some bizarre expressionistic work of art or some practical joker's idea of a gag—in the same vein as those jolly wags who balanced spoons on the tip of their nose or inserted chopsticks up their nostrils in a restaurant.

A human head used as a shoe rack.

This isn't possible, thought Val, moving ever closer, feeling tugged as though by invisible wires intent that she view the horror from a better angle. Still at every moment, she expected Lou to shake his face free of its bizarre adornments and shriek with sadistic laughter.

Oh, Jesus God.

His arms were tied behind his back and lashed to his bound ankles. Whole sections of his torso glistened red. Flayed meat. Flaps of flesh, sliced from ribs and belly, hung loosely across his legs.

That was the least of it.

A white pump hung from each of his eyes, the heels brilliant red from the blood that had pumped out of his skewered eyeballs. Two more shoes hung from his ears, the spikes driven in deep enough to surely puncture the eardrums. Two more heels—these from the mutilated pumps Val had found earlier—had been driven up into his nostrils and held there with duct tape. One had penetrated with such force that the tip had smashed through the bridge of the nose and protruded next to an eye socket.

Added to these atrocities were the four shoes protruded from Lou's slack and gaping mouth, arranged there as a comic afterthought, Val suspected, after the man was already dead. A pool of thick, congealing blood had formed beneath Lou's buttocks and between his legs, hinting at other impalements she didn't want to know about.

The desecrated face stared up at her like some ghastly mask. Val backed away, although the distance from the bedside to the door felt like a day's march and the floor seemed to shift and tip like a ship's deck in uncertain seas.

In the living room she grabbed the Barclay Card, then tried to think of anything she might have touched when she was here the night before.

Nothing. Anything. Everything!

She'd touched the shoes she'd worn, of course, but the killer's fingerprints must be on them now unless he'd had the foresight to wear gloves. The Deutsche marks she'd thrown at Lou, those would bear her prints, but then surely hers would be only one set among the countless fingers the money had passed through. But the glass she'd drunk from, that was another matter. In the kitchen sink were several glasses. She rinsed and dried them carefully, then took the cloth and went into the Treasure Room where she wiped down any shoes that she remembered Lou had given her to examine.

There was something else…

The Chinese slippers! She'd turned them over in her hands, admiring them. They must be covered with her fingerprints.

But when she used the cloth to open the teakwood box, the shoes were gone. To search for them would have meant going back into the bedroom. Val didn't think she could stand the grotesquerie of that again.

A car horn bleated.

Suddenly she remembered asking the taxi driver to wait. She ran to the window and looked down just in time to see him driving off. Would he remember her? Would he read about Lou's murder in the paper and realize he had brought a woman to this building on the very day that the murder must have taken place? And who might have seen her here last night? Or, for that matter, this morning?

Panic tightened around her throat. She could go to jail. She could be held for questioning as the last person to have seen Lou alive except his killer. Unless they never found a killer. In which case, she would have been the last person…and now he was dead…horribly…and…

Val locked the door from the inside and closed it behind her.

She hurried outside to flag another taxi, wondering how long it would be before someone came to look for Lou. How long it would be before someone noticed the odor and investigated.

She knew she had to hurry.

Majeed was waiting for her.

Chapter Eight

The bitch!

Where the hell was she?

In the lobby of the Vier Jahreszeiten Hotel, Breen lit a cigarette and watched a buxom tour guide wearing a tailored blue and grey uniform dash about collecting her elderly charges, several of whom were apparently quite tardy. The logo of a British tour company bounced fetchingly on her chest, but pique and irritation were beginning to add unbecoming lines to her otherwise angelic face. Breen empathized. He'd been warming this chair seat much of the morning now, knowing at some point Val had to make an appearance. He assumed that when he saw her leave the shoe fancier's apartment the night before that she'd return here. Unless, of course, she'd gone somewhere else, picked up yet another companion. He considered the possibility that Val might appear in the lobby with an escort. That would be awkward, but not impossible. Under such a circumstance, he would trust Val's fickleness to work in his favor.

After all, he didn't want to kill her right away.

First he had to win her back.

The area of the lobby where Breen was seated was designed along the lines of a spacious living room. Two brocaded sofas and a quartet of commodious chairs flanked a marble coffeetable with inlaid tiles reproducing what Breen recognized to be a Pompeian mosaic. His only companion here was a softly pear-shaped woman who held on her lap a small dog that looked like a cross between a marmot and a feather-duster.

The dog yapped hysterically. The woman smiled indulgently, in the manner of a parent whose spoiled toddler has shouted naughty words.

"I'm sorry. She gets excited when too many people are around."

Breen replied in German, "It's all right. I like animals." He reached to pet the dog.

The woman lowered her eyelids slightly as though inviting Breen to pet her as well. He noted that she wore expensive jewelry—a clutch of gold bangles on her fleshy wrist, a topaz the size of a dime on her index finger. Her clothes were understated chic. In another situation, Breen might have been inclined to practice his seduction skills. He hadn't fucked a woman for some weeks now, and this was cause for a small, niggling unease. He liked to believe himself completely bisexual, utterly impartial as to whether it was a man or woman that he fucked. The gender of Breen's recent partners was currently weighted in favor of the males. Breen felt the need of a woman soon to maintain the gender balance.

Beneath Breen's touch, the dog ceased its barking and began to wag its tail.

"Nice dog," said Breen.

In fact, Breen loathed small, yappy dogs. They reminded him of his old love Miss Lee and her fondness for such creatures, a pair of which she often carried, Gabor-like, in her travels. She always worried about her height and girth and thought the presence of a tiny dog held in her arm made her appear more diminutive. Of course it had had the opposite effect. If she'd really wanted to minimize her size, Breen thought, she'd have gone about with a pair of Irish wolfhounds straining at their chains.

But for all her vanity and self-delusion, Miss Lee had been his savior. Breen never forgot that. She had educated him in the arts and languages and etiquette at a time when his idea of gracious living was a bag of pork rinds and a grimy t-shirt to wipe his fingers on. She'd taught him the importance of a clean and well-groomed body, of fresh flowers in a Lalique vase, of using the correct past participle and selecting a fine Bordeaux, of at least a dozen different techniques for giving head.

Eventually, she'd made him rich as well.

Before Miss Lee, Breen had spent his boyhood in a succession of motels and trailer parks throughout the southwest while his mother, JosieMay, eked out a living as skimpy as the outfits she wore dancing in strip joints in Laredo and Dallas and Tucson. Breen was JosieMay's only child, which was one too many, in JosieMay's point of view. She was fond of reminding the young Arthur how she had searched in vain for a reprieve from motherhood back in the days before salvation in the form of Roe vs. Wade. She'd ended up in a backalley clinic in Laredo, which got raided by the Texas Rangers just before it was JosieMay's turn to put her knees in the stirrups. They not only foiled her chance for an abortion, but one of the cops demanded a blowjob, too.

"So I didn't have no choice," JosieMay would say. "I had to go ahead and squirt you out, bald and screaming, just like a little pink pig."

Pig. Yeah, that was the word all right, except it was JosieMay and not young Arthur whose appearance verged on porcine. Addicted to junk food, JosieMay's size made it impossible for her to get a job working in one of the upscale places, like the Playboy Club in Dallas, where she might have made good money. She was a small woman to begin with, and she carried most of her hundred or so excess pounds in her gut and buttocks. The extra weight gave her torso proportions similar to those of an eggplant with breasts.

JosieMay's life was one long struggle with the weakness of her considerable flesh. Early on, when she was dieting rigidly, she'd put a padlock on the refrigerator and pantry doors and stash the key away, unlocking it only to prepare the leanest of repasts for Arthur and herself. Arthur, a skinny boy who'd inherited the runner's build and ruggedly romantic features of the cowboy/barfly who'd fathered him, rarely had enough to eat.

Hunger, and the rage that it inspired, became a constant in his life.

But there were other, less tangible ways, in which Arthur had starved. Early on, he'd realized that he felt little or no kinship with his own kind, that what others described as feelings of love and affection were off the scale of his emotional range.

To him, all others merged into one vast, unknowable and impenetrable Other—his mother, teachers, the kids at school, as bizarre and alien as microbes under a microscope, objects to be coldly scrutinized, made use of.

When he was ten he started breaking into trailers in the park, stealing whatever he could find and raiding refrigerators. Apart from the food and the booty, he had found an almost mystical attraction to the insides of other people's homes. With careful prowling, you could learn much. In his adventures, Arthur discovered a myriad of treasures:

love letters and dirty magazines, summonses and wills and diaries with all manner of confessions, threatening letters from jealous rivals and pleading ones from spurned lovers, and even once a suicide note composed again and again as the writer tried to explain an act that, so far as Arthur could tell, had not yet taken place.

With each discovery, Arthur found a clue to the Others. With each discovery, he wanted to learn more.

There came a time when rifling through other peoples' possessions no longer satisfied. Arthur had often fantasized how it would feel to kill. Now, in the oddly detached way of a practiced vivisectionist, he decided it was time to explore the contents of more than just the objects that other people owned.

He started with himself, by opening up his flesh. He found that, once past the initial pain, self-mutilation could induce a peculiar kind of trance. The pain became immaterial, like neural Musak he could easily ignore. And physical pain, in some strange way, anaesthetized all other kinds of hurt. To carve grooves into his upper thighs and watch the scarlet trickle made him feel invulnerable, powerful, and potent.

But to make others bleed, he later learned, was even better.

When he was thirteen, Breen had killed for the first time, smashing a cinderblock down on the head of a transient passed out with his bottle on an empty lot.

And again at fourteen—when he drowned a toddler in a wading pool and everyone thought the child's death was a tragic accident.

With both murders, Breen experienced something close to ecstasy, pleasure akin to orgasm but far beyond it. It was a feeling he would never forget and eternally attempt to recapture.

He left home the week before his fifteenth birthday. JosieMay had caught him smoking again and demanded that he eat an entire pack of Marlboros, which she fed to him, one after the other, with a smirk on her face and a pan on the kitchen table to catch the result of his stomach's inevitable revolt against this insult.

It had taken Arthur years to overcome the queasiness he felt at the mere thought of a cigarette, but he had done it. Just to spite JosieMay. Just to prove she hadn't really won.

A month after the Marlboro dinner, Arthur had left home, hitching rides until he got to New Orleans, where he quickly learned that a life of hustling and home invasion might feed him but would never give him the wealth and luxury he dreamed about.

In the meantime, though, he settled for burglarizing the better homes, which was how he came to break into a peach-colored Victorian mansion on an azalea-lined street in the Garden District. The owner had been thoughtful enough to plant concealing box bushes in front of several first floor windows. Arthur broke a pane, unlatched the window, and went inside.

After pocketing a few knickknacks, Arthur had gone straight to the refrigerator and begun to wolf down whatever he could find. He had been squatting there, like a savage entranced by the wedge of light put out by the refrigerator, cramming food into his mouth with both hands, when he'd heard the dog.

Not a big dog, the kind Arthur already knew enough about to fear, but a high-voiced, yappy dog with a bark that sounded like a knifeblade being drawn rapidly across a piece of slate. The pomeranian came skidding across the linoleum at him, barking furiously. It was no bigger than a cat and, in the darkness, looked to Arthur like a red muff with legs.

The desire to kill the little beast warred with his desire to flee and his natural fear of small and noisy creatures. But before he could take steps in either direction, the kitchen light had been switched on. Arthur, still crouched in front of the refrigerator, found himself looking up at a heavy-set but elegant woman, full-lipped and heavy lidded, draped in a turquoise and gold caftan with pompomed sandals on her feet.

The woman stared down at him disapprovingly. "What are you doing there? Can't you see you're upsetting my little Cayoudel?"

Arthur clutched the knife more tightly. She was a big woman. Should he try to kill her? Try to escape?

"Are you a burglar, dawlin'? Surely you must be a burglar, 'cause if you're a rapist, I'm afraid you're much too small. You'll never do."

And she began to giggle.

This was too much. Arthur lunged with the knife. The next thing he knew the woman had stepped quickly to the side, caught the wrist welding the knife with one hand and twisted his arm behind his back while her forearm went around his throat and pulled him against her.

"Not a very good idea, hon."

She laughed a throaty, theatrical laugh. Arthur had felt the hard-on underneath her caftan. It felt large enough to do justice to the winner of a Triple Crown.

"Now we have a couple of options here, dawlin'" the transvestite said, while Arthur continued to struggle in a useless effort to get free. "I can call the police, which is surely what you deserve. I can even use the knife that you were going to use on me and cut your silly little throat. I can claim it was self-defense. You'd deserve that, too. Or you can get back in my good graces by sliding down your pants and bending over. After that, I may be in a better mood to hear your side of the story."

But, of course, as Breen was to learn in years to come, when you were dealing with Miss Lee, there was only her side of the story.

His name was Lee Tuttle but "she" was "Miss Lee" to her friends, a coterie of queens who flitted about the French Quarter like vivid butterflies in the last days of their life cycle, a breed nearing extinction but brightening as much territory as possible in the meantime.

She was in her early fifties then, made wealthy from the ownership of two upscale bars, one that catered to the genuinely gay and TV crowd, the other aimed at tourists who wanted the experience of gawking at drag queens camping it up for the straights, and she took to Breen, who was skinny and unkept and sufficiently corrupt to remind Miss Lee of her own lost and tarnished boyhood.

They were together for as many years as it had taken Breen to get Miss Lee sufficiently attached to him to legally adopt him as her son. Then three more years after that, for the sake of appearances, while Breen waited for the opportunity he wanted. Breen was in his mid-twenties by then. He and Miss Lee traveled widely, sometimes masquerading as elegant matron mother and handsome son, other times cavorting openly as gentleman of substance and young lover.

There were always women, too, on the periphery of Breen's life, but he took care that Miss Lee never knew his compendium of perversions included tendencies toward heterosexuality.

Or toward homicide, for that matter.

In addition to her more exotic interests, Miss Lee had taken up diving while on a cruise with Breen to the West Indies. The initial attraction, as Breen well knew, had been a mocha-skinned diving instructor, but Miss Lee, whose athletic abilities generally extended no farther than the bedroom, actually enjoyed the experience and became an avid diver, a hobby she'd compelled Breen to share with her. It didn't matter that he was frightened of the underwater world, that in his mind, every shadow became a cruising shark and every coral crevice a hiding place for moray eels.

But the water had ultimately given Breen the greatest gift—his freedom.

The opportunity had come when they were diving in fifty feet of water on a reef in the Abacos. Their rented boat was anchored up above. Breen had another five minutes of air left in his tank when Miss Lee, who was heavier and tended to use up her air faster, tapped him on the shoulder and drew her fingers across her throat to tell Breen that she was out of air.

In this type of emergency situation, the procedure was to buddy breath on the way to the surface, passing the regulator back and forth between them. When Breen failed to offer his regulator, Miss Lee tried to take it. Breen blocked her and snatched away her mask, flooding her face with water.

Miss Lee had tried to do the only thing she could then—ditch her weight belt and ascend as rapidly as possible on whatever air her lungs already held—but Breen had grabbed her around the neck and forced her mouth open while her body filled with water like a douche bag held beneath the faucet.

Breen had collected his inheritance and lived well ever since, indulging his predatory nature on several continents. No one he'd really had a yen to fuck and kill had ever gotten away.

Until Val.

The bitch, the whore, the cunt.

The dog gave a sudden yelp. Breen realized he'd pinched its ear unknowingly. He'd forgotten the dog was even there. He'd been thinking only of Val's throat.

The woman gave him an indignant look, snatched up her pet, and stormed away.

Breen checked his watch. It was almost noon. His fragile supply of patience was exhausted. He decided to call Val's room. If she answered, he'd simply say he was in Hamburg on business, that he'd seen her going into the hotel the night before and wanted to renew old acquaintance before he left the city.

The desk clerk, a pimply youth with a neat beard and a persistent sniffle, shook his head while blowing his nose into a handkerchief. "She's checked out."

"What do you mean?"

"She called a few hours ago. Said she was leaving Hamburg and didn't have time to come back to the hotel for her things. She said we should bill her credit card for the room."

"Well, this is awkward," said Breen, struggling to remain composed. "I'm her attorney and I have some papers for her to sign. Did she say when she'd be coming back?"

"She said she wouldn't be returning, sir. That we could store her belongings or throw them out. She said it was of no importance to her."

"But that's...did she say by any chance where she was going?"

The clerk shrugged and sniffed. "She didn't say. Do you want to leave your name and where you can be reached? In case she calls, I can let her know you were here."

Breen shrugged and forced his face into a facsimile of a smile. "No, that isn't necessary."

"If I may ask, sir, is it some kind of emergency?"

"An impending death," said Breen. "The lady just found out she has a fatal illness. She hasn't long to live."

Chapter Nine

The trip overland to North Africa, which could have been accomplished by a few hours in the air, took Majeed and Val over a week. Majeed was terrified of flying and told Val that being confined to the cramped interior of an airplane made him feel like he was inside a coffin. Thus burdened with Majeed's unexpected fear, they traveled by train: Munich to Geneva, then south to Marseilles and into the tiny republic of Andorra, and across Spain, through Grenada and Seville.

In Gibraltar, they took a hydrofoil across the Channel, arriving in Morocco at Tangier, then took the train south to Fez, an ancient city at the foot of the Atlas Mountains. It was Val's first visit to North Africa, and she would have preferred to stay in one of the European luxury hotels in the French-built Ville Nouvelle section of the city, where the train station was located. Majeed, however, who claimed to know the city well, insisted that they stay in Fez El B'ali, the medieval heart of the city founded in the late eighth and early ninth centuries.

"Ten thousand heads," Majeed said as the taxi swerved and dodged around squealing children, cars, mopeds, and donkey carts, and men and women draped head to toe in *djellabas*, the long, loose outer garment favored by many in Morocco.

"What?" Val thought she hadn't heard him right.

"I was just remembering something I read. In the seventeenth century a new ruler, Moulay Ismail, came to power by defeating a rival faction. To celebrate his victory he sent ten thousand heads, including those of women and children, to adorn the walls of Fez. He wove the bodies of prisoners of war with rushes and made a bridge that his victorious army might cross."

"Nice guy," said Val. "Any others like him still around?"

"I doubt it," said Majeed, but he sighed as if he was disappointed.

The streets grew so narrow and congested that the taxi had to stop for minutes at a time before it was able to make headway. They were in the oldest part of the city now. Huge multistory buildings—Majeed said they were called *fondouks* and had been built around huge courtyards centuries earlier to accommodate traders and their animals—added to the oppressive feeling of seething, hive-like squalor.

Val was amazed that Majeed, who couldn't tolerate the enclosed space of an airplane, seemed unfazed by the blocks of tightly crowded buildings and the ceaseless flow of shoulder-to-shoulder humanity.

The taxi took them down streets so narrow two vehicles could barely squeeze past each other without the passengers on either side bumping elbows, and stopped outside an ornate gate near the Bab Boujeloud. They passed through a broad door decorated with intricate, hand-painted Islamic tiles, and were besieged by boys offering to be guides before ducking inside the Hotel Kaskade.

"It's better than it looks," Majeed said. "In the eighteenth century it was built as a pleasure palace for the local vizier."

"And hasn't been cleaned since," said Val, eyeing a cockroach the size of a half dollar that scurried across the wood floor of the lobby as a scruffy porter showed them to their room.

While Val bathed, Majeed went about setting up his beloved incense burners in both windowsills. By the time she came out of the shower, towels wrapped around her waist and hair, the air in the small room was cloyingly thick with the mingled aromas of a dozen fragrances. Majeed was lying on his back across the bed, sucking from his pipe.

"They sell dope here, don't they?" said Val.

Majeed looked as though she'd just said something of consummate stupidity. "It's Morocco, dear. Of course they do."

"I mean *here*. In this neighborhood. It's why you wanted this hotel instead of one of the newer ones."

"I like the atmosphere," said Majeed. "And please, try not to be such a snob. If you want to spend your money, there're some French boutiques across the street and a five-star restaurant next door."

"And what about the entrance to the City? Is that here, too?"

Majeed closed his eyes. "Must you be so impatient?"

Val grabbed her clothes, the same ones she'd been wearing for the duration of the journey since they'd made their hasty departure from Hamburg, and started getting dressed.

"I'm going to investigate those boutiques you mentioned. I've got to get something to wear besides these clothes. They're beginning to stink."

When she slammed the door, a few minutes later, the pipe had slipped from Majeed's hand and he was snoring. Val opened the door again and slammed it twice more, making as much noise as she could.

Majeed didn't stir.

The French boutique was as pricey as Majeed had indicated, staffed by a poppy-lipped Parisian women with sapphire-lined lids and gold bangles sufficient to make her arms ache. Val shopped quickly, buying several pairs of slacks, long skirts, and blouses. She left the clothes that she'd worn inside the fitting room and walked out wearing some of her new purchases, silk pants and a long-sleeved tunic top similar to some she'd seen the more liberated local women wearing.

When she went back to the room, Majeed was sitting up, sleepily refilling his pipe. Fragrant smoke eddied up from the incense burners. Val shook the contents of the pipe out onto the floor. Majeed glared at her so fiercely Val thought that he might strike her.

"Come on," she said, "you haven't eaten anything all day. I can't have you going anorexic on me."

And she tugged him almost bodily outside, where the air, though far from fresh, was at least less trance-inducing than the sickening sweet confection of aromas in their room.

She forced Majeed to walk around the Bab Boujeloud a few times, then led him to the restaurant next to the hotel that he had claimed to be five-star. Nor had Majeed exaggerated the merits of the establishment. They sat at a low table, eating with the fingers of their right hands only, sampling salads of oranges and carrots, thick, jammy mixtures of tomatoes and roasted peppers and lush tagines of meat braised with quinces, prunes, and the curious musty tang of preserved lemons.

Then, with one appetite sated, they went their separate ways, Majeed to satisfy his own proclivities, Val to explore the myriad maze-like streets of the Old City, intrigued by the exotic squalor of the Quarter's sights and sounds and odors. What Majeed did with his evenings was not discussed, but Val assumed he considered a night in which a few carnal transactions weren't carried out to be an evening wasted.

Few women braved the night-time streets of the Moroccan City and a passing foreigner, male or female, attracted hordes of young boys, offering their services as guides to the various attractions of the Quarter, both those listed in the tourist guides and those more dubious.

Val wondered if any of these children knew anything about the City. It had occurred to her that, if Majeed persisted in stalling their arrival there, she still might be forced to find a way in on her own.

Near midnight, rounding a corner near the Dar Batha Museum at the Place de l'Istiqlal, Val was startled to see Majeed not ten feet away. She started to approach him and then stopped.

Majeed was not alone. In front of him, half hidden by the darkness and Majeed's body, was a diminutive figure, a young Berber girl of eight or nine. Her black hair was braided intricately and covered with a patterned scarf fringed with small gold coins. Majeed and the little girl appeared to be deep in conversation. The child did most of the talking. Majeed looked uncharacteristically bereft. At one point his lips appeared to quiver and he put a hand to his mouth.

Although she couldn't know for sure the nature of the transaction, Val's immediate assumption was less than charitable. She hadn't known Majeed cared for children. The idea that he did repulsed her. On the other hand, perhaps the little girl was a connection for his opium. That thought did little to cast the situation in a better light.

A hustler, a drug addict, and now-perhaps-a pedophile, thought Val. *Even if he actually knows where the City is, how can I ever trust him to actually take me there?*

She ducked behind a passing donkey cart and left the square by a different route to make sure he didn't see her.

Chapter Ten

Breen unfolded the small rectangle of yellow paper that he'd been carrying in his pocket for almost a week now. At the bottom was a row of neatly printed numerals. He'd copied the numbers from Val's credit card before leaving the Fat Hippie's apartment.

This was a long shot, and he knew it. If Val had discovered the card missing, she'd in all likelihood have had it canceled and a new one issued. Unless of course she'd gone back to get it.

In which case, she'd have seen what Breen had left there.

He had to smile. That possibility was just too delightful.

Breen cleared his throat and dialed a toll-free number.

A woman's slightly accented voice answered in English.

"How may I help you?"

"My name is Lee Petrillo, and I'm afraid I have a problem with my credit card," said Breen, and he read off the numbers. "My wife and I have joint cards, and my wife is missing hers. She's not sure if she's just misplaced it, or if the card was stolen out of one of our hotel rooms." Breen's voice reeked of cultivation and sincerity. "I was wondering if you could check the most recent charges for me. There would have been one for the Vier Jahreszeiten Hotel in Hamburg about a week ago, and then perhaps one or two more that I'm not completely sure of."

"Just a moment. Let me check."

The clerk put Breen on hold. He fidgeted, tapping his finger impatiently against the desk of the telephone cubicle he was occupying at Hamburg's Fuhlsbuttel Airport. His thumbnail found a nick in the skin next to one cuticle. Absently, he began to pick at it until a drop of blood oozed.

"Mr. Petrillo?"

"Yes, still waiting."

"Your wife's name is...?"

"Val Petrillo."

"Yes, according to our records, Ms. Petrillo charged several items of clothing to a boutique in Fez—that's Morocco—called the Blue Parrot. That was on the fifteenth."

Breen almost shouted with joy. Val was still making charges on the card. That meant she'd been back to get it. Which meant she'd seen...

"Anything else?"

"The same day there's a charge for a room at the Hotel Kaskade in Fez, Morocco. And after that...nothing."

Breen scribbled down the name of the hotel and city.

"Excellent. My wife's traveling in Morocco right now, so obviously the card's just been misplaced. If it were stolen, the thief undoubtedly would have used it by now."

"Call us if you can't find the card, and we'll issue a..."

Breen hung up. Within a few minutes he was booked on a flight to Fez via Marseilles that afternoon.

Val had come into Breen's life almost two years ago, and—although Val would never have suspected it—she had saved it.

He was in Hong Kong, having flown there from Bali, where an ancient, bare-breasted soothsayer had read his fortune and told him he would die on foreign soil. Breen had believed her. He had a self-admitted weakness for superstition, and a manic-depressive attitude toward world travel. In the manic phase he traveled constantly and without anxiety, enjoying his adventures on exotic soil, killing coolly and without remorse when the appetite arose in him. In the depressive phase, some light died in him—a kind of dampening of the inner fire—and he craved only solitude and shelter. The mere sound of another human voice could make him wince as though flogged across the shoulders with a coathanger. At such times, he'd take a cheap hotel room and not go outside for days.

And so he alternated back and forth between convivial killer and misanthropic recluse.

In Hong Kong he'd entered the latter phase of the cycle with suicidal vengeance.

He'd intended to go back to the States, perhaps move back into the house in New Orleans that Miss Lee had left him. Some sort of snafu in his airline ticketing, however, had made it impossible (or so the representative for Garuda Airlines claimed) for him to fly directly from Bali to the States. The trip could be made most expeditiously by flying over a thousand miles north to HongKong, then picking up another carrier to L.A.

But on the flight to Hong Kong, Breen had been taken ill. Some sort of stomach upset. He'd spent the better part of the five hour flight locked up in the lavatory, both ends of his body competing to see which could spew forth more toxin in the shortest period of time. Breen arrived in HongKong and let the connecting flight go on without him. He checked himself into the New Kowloon, a Western-style highrise just off of bustling Nathan Road and spent several days there being violently ill.

When the illness left him, the malaise of the soul did not.

Adrift in the frenzied termite hill that was HongKong, whether meandering through the jade market or sitting next to the stage in a Wanchai bar while a beautiful Eurasian prostitute accepted a proffered bill in her magenta pussy, Breen felt not lust or even the familiar, adrenalizing urge to kill, but a profound, stomach-turning anxiety. His pulse would race, his pores would leak sweat as though he'd just stepped from a sauna. He'd feel dizzy and wonder if he was going to pass out here in this alien land and what would become of him if he did so, where would he be when he woke up, and with whom?

Breen had thought about the Balinese soothsayer's prediction and decided she'd been right. He was indeed destined to die on foreign soil. And it would be in Hong Kong.

The anxiety was worsening. It had taken all Breen's courage to leave his hotel room and walk the short distance up Nathan Road to the Star Ferry. The boat ride from Kowloon to HongKong Island took five minutes. From there he caught a cab to Victoria Peak. It was a clammy, chilling day. Fog draped the Peak in what looked like a wraith's tattered rags.

Breen had walked the Peak before, years earlier, in the company of Miss Lee. He remembered only that the day had been hot and blindingly sunny and that Miss Lee had wanted to find somewhere secluded where she could push Breen down onto his knees and have him suck her cock. In search of such a spot, they had walked all the way around the Peak, an hour's jaunt that offered breathtaking views of Kowloon and HongKong Harbor but nowhere a young man could conveniently fall on his knees to perform fellatio on his elderly cross-dressing companion.

Miss Lee had hated the place. But Breen remembered the cliffs.

And on this cold and foggy day, he'd found the spot he had in mind, an isolated overlook far from the main tourist area where only a low guardrail protected strollers on the path from the drop onto the rocks and underbrush hundreds of feet below.

Death would be painless and instantaneous.

The very opposite, Breen noted, from the kind of demises he'd inflicted on others over the years.

He had stood there, contemplating the angle at which he would hit the rocks, feeling no remorse and very little fear but only a consuming longing to be done with it all, to be free finally of the tiny, unsafe prison that was his skull when he had heard throaty laughter close to him and a woman's voice said, "I love heights, but they make me nervous. I always want to jump."

He'd whirled around, flustered with a confusing mixture of outrage and guilt and relief, to see who'd dared to read his mind, and *she* was standing there, haloed in fog. She wore khaki pants and a rather primly high-necked sweater under an open coat. There was fog in her eyelashes, fog clinging like a silk scarf to her throat. Breen had thought for a moment that she was created from the mist.

"I'm sorry? I don't know what you mean," he'd said, terrified down to the marrow of his bones that she somehow *knew*, that she was privy to the core of him.

"Heights," she said almost jauntily. "I'm always tempted to just say to hell with it and leap. Off ledges, cliffs, over the rails of ships or bridges that span a gorge. I don't, of course. It would be a stupid thing to do. But I always think of it."

He must have looked at her aghast, for she continued, "I can't imagine I'm the only person who thinks such things. Otherwise why would there be all these guardrails. I mean, no one's really going to *fall* over the side. An effort must be made. The guardrails just provide that extra second to think, 'Wait. What the hell am I doing?' and step back on solid ground."

He'd stared at her. For a moment, a vivid fantasy almost seduced him into action: he'd grab her arm and hurl her into the waiting void she craved, then follow her. The police would think it was some lover's suicide pact or a rejected suitor's wrath turned murderous. It would all be quite romantic, death with a lovely stranger.

Then she laughed again, low and melodious, and said, "I suppose I need more excitement than the average person. Are you that way, too?"

Breen had decided at that moment that her death could be postponed until he had time to fuck her. When they left the Peak together, they had a date for dinner. Breen's anxiety had lifted. His thoughts of death now seemed like the plan of some other man, some weak and foolish man-child that he didn't recognize, some feeble remnant from his past.

The two things he loved at once about Val were the same things he'd loved about Miss Lee before she grew old and sour: Val's appetite for sex was as exorbitant, as indiscriminant, as feverish as his own, and Val was wealthy.

It didn't take Breen long to realize she could provide for him all that Miss Lee had done and more. Great sex for as long as he desired it, then a replenishment of his resources when he killed her.

To accomplish the latter, of course, he and Val would have to marry, but Breen saw this as no great obstacle. When he was feeling confident and buoyant, his ego knew no bounds. He felt himself irresistible to virtually any partner, but particularly to women, many of whom coveted that rarest of combinations in a male: gentility, education, and a libido verging on insatiable.

Within moments after their meeting, Breen had mentally mapped it out and lived it in his head: the courtship, the marriage, then Val's unfortunate death. He'd even speculated on the possibility of letting Val give birth before he killed her—a baby, in Breen's mind, would be a toy of flesh and blood to mold in his own likeness. The deathwish, submerged in this fresh excess of plotting and ambition, had been vanquished. Breen felt powerful again. He had a Higher Purpose.

At first it was as romantic, as idyllic as Breen could have imagined. They spent whole days in bed together, indulged a spectrum of erotic tastes that spanned the Kama Sutra, and when they feared they'd tire of each other, hired callgirls and hustlers to come to the hotel room and expand on their erotic menu. For a time, Breen even flirted with the fantasy that Val—like him—might have a secret life, that she might be sizing him up as he was eyeing her—a victim for future butchery. He fantasized that they were truly brother and sister under the skin, that Val was the person he would have been had he been born a woman.

But, ultimately, Val announced that Hong Kong bored her and she was leaving for the beaches of Sri Lanka. Breen went with her. This time she was ready to move on in less than a week.

Australia next, she said and reeled off names that held no charm or romance for him: Coober Pedy and and Mt. Olga and Alice Springs. Breen didn't care to go.

Val made it clear that this was fine, but she was leaving anyway.

A game, thought Breen. A female ploy to force his hand to make more of a commitment. He wasn't terribly well-schooled in such things. His knowledge of feminine wiles came mostly from Miss Lee's dubious tutelage. In some ways, though he'd never have admitted it, Breen was as naive and callow as any schoolboy out on a first date. He knew a thousand different ways to make love and a hundred ways to kill, but was unversed in the specifics of real courtship.

He knew only that this seemed to be a moment that demanded action, when the balance of power must switch decisively from Val to him.

He had asked Val to marry him.

She told him no.

His ego would not allow him to show disappointment. He'd merely smiled and given a slight shrug, said 'so be it' or words to that effect. And made love with her much of that last night, the fires of passion stoked with the knowledge that he would kill her in the morning.

Breen had slept long and late. He awoke to find the bedsheets by his side unwarmed, the indentation of Val's head upon the pillow already fading. She'd left a note largely consisting of Hallmark-style platitudes—the 'I'm sorry's' and 'wish you all the best' of all generic Dear John letters.

She was gone.

She had left him.

Him. Arthur Quentin Breen.

Had robbed him not just of the potential wealth she represented but of the pleasure of her death as well.

Breen's rage was of sufficient violence that he had no choice but to wreck violence, if not on someone else then on himself, opening and peeling back his own skin the way he'd soothed himself as a boy.

He was an adult now, however, and not about to punish himself for very long if someone else could take the role of victim.

That night Breen had lured a prostitute out onto the beach with him, slit her throat, and sliced off sweet nibblets of her, which he'd greedily gobbled down. He'd felt better—but only for a little while. Thoughts of Val kept intruding on him, convoluted plans for revenge soared and dipped through his imagination like cancerous birds. In preternatural detail, he visualized their "accidental" meeting somewhere in the future: the feigned awkwardness on his part, the invitation, full of bittersweet innuendo, to have a drink together for old time's sake, and how, as she preceded him into the bar, he'd slide a hand up behind her neck, let his fingers close into a fist just for a moment in the sleek waves of her hair, knowing that she loved anything that smacked of honeyed threat, of domination, of a moment's pleasurable compromise of her precious freedom.

And on that future night, she'd follow him to bed, Breen knew she would, and what a night they'd have. Sex before her death and during it and after it as well.

Breen licked his lips discreetly and sent a mental command to his penis to stay put.

After his conversation with the Barclay's representative, he felt elated, infused with purpose. Connected.

As long as Val kept charging items to her card, he had a way to track her.

And soon, if things went as planned, he would be able to put his hand inside Val's chest and connect his fingers to her still-beating heart.

Chapter Eleven

Usually Majeed was late coming back to whatever hotel or hostel they were lodged in, but tonight his return preceded Val's. When she entered the cramped hotel room, scarcely bigger than a walk-in closet, with its damask curtains and faded turquoise spread, Majeed was reclining on the bed, incense and candles burning, the room redolent of spices and hashish. His eye were red and puffy, but Val was distracted from speculating on the cause of this by a scuffling sound, the source of which she couldn't locate, that ceased almost as soon as it began.

"Majeed? Are you all right?"

A halo of smoke drifted up from the pipe between his lips. In the dim light, his pale hair framed paler features, cascades of snow on snow. Through his swollen, slitted eyes he stared at her as though she were some acquaintance whose name he couldn't quite recall.

"You're back early," he said finally.

"I didn't know I had a timetable."

"Don't bitch at me. I've had a shitty night. Some faggot Frenchman paid me to let him give me a blowjob in the men's room of the Hotel Palais Jamai. Then he insisted on groping me and when he found my pussy, he thought I had an extra asshole, that some disease had rotted out a hole in me." He sighed theatrically and dragged on the pipe. "He didn't get his money back, though. Fucking faggot womanhater."

"That's quite a tale."

"Could I interest you in another one?," Majeed said, slapping his sleek rump. "We could start by taking a hot bath together. You go in first and let the water run."

Val plopped down on the bed. "I think I'd rather hear your stories about the City. I've been patient long enough."

"But we just got to Fez. We have more traveling to do."

"I thought you said Morocco *was* the gateway to the City," Val reminded him. "How do I even know there is such a place if you won't give me some details?"

"I'll do that. But first, why don't you run downstairs and bring us back a pot of that spiced tea with honey."

Val frowned. "Why don't you pick up the phone and call downstairs? They can send someone up with tea."

"Don't use that tone of voice with me."

"Then don't try to send me off on errands. First you want me drawing bath water, then you'd have me fetching tea. Next thing I know, you'll be trying to put me in a French maid's costume."

She heard the scuffling sound again. It came from underneath the bed.

"Are you hiding someone?"

Before Majeed could stop her, she slid off the bed, pulled back the spread and peered beneath it. Dark eyes gleamed back at her. Then whoever was beneath the bed rolled out from the other side and scurried toward the door.

Val got only a glimpse of plaited hair and dust-streaked clothes, but she recognized the Berber child she'd seen Majeed with a few days earlier.

"Wait," she cried, but the girl dashed past her, clutching tattered sandals in her hands, flung the door open and ran out into the hall.

"Now see what you've done," Majeed hissed. "You've frightened her."

"What was she doing under the bed in the first place?"

"She's extremely timid. She came in to read my fortune and when she heard you coming in, she ducked down there. Why are you looking at me like that? What's wrong?"

"I should ask you the same thing. I saw you with that little girl the first night we got here, but I didn't want to think the worst. Now I find her hiding underneath your bed and you naked. I haven't known you very long, Majeed, but I do know that you only live for sex and drugs, so what am I supposed to think when I find you with a child?"

"You think I'm a child molester?"

"And why would that surprise me? You're not exactly a person of high moral character."

"Coming from a whore like you, that cuts me deeply."

"Whatever else I might be guilty of, I don't abuse children."

"And I do? What do you think, Val, that I bought that little girl in a white slave market, a North African piranha bowl of pederasts?"

"Did you?"

"No."

"How can I believe that?"

"You trusted me this far," Majeed said. "Why not a little farther?"

"Because I'm tired of your games."

"Then allow me to show you a new game—one you may not have played before."

He offered Val the pipe.

"I don't want any."

"Please, go ahead. You're so upset your hands are shaking. Besides, it makes sex better. Just try a toke or two."

"You promise me you didn't molest that little girl?"

"I promise."

She took the pipe, pulling the sweet, narcotic smoke into her lungs and holding it until she felt the irritation seeping out of her, replaced by a warm and scented glow that bathed her cells in languor. She took another hit. This time the smoke didn't just fill her lungs, but traveled through her bloodstream, illuminating her muscles with what seemed to be a pale, internal glow.

She heard chimes in her voice. "What is this stuff?"

"High quality opium."

"It's nice."

"I think so. The only thing that's better is to have sex while you're doing it."

Val took another toke. Her head turned and she started to lie back, but the bed anticipated her direction and lifted up to meet her. Pillows, sheets, and mattress, all folded round her in a soft and pliant nest. It was hard now to remember the child underneath the bed, impossible to think why she'd been angry.

She was wriggling into this new womb, when Majeed crawled over to her, began unbuttoning her clothes.

The opium gifted Majeed's body with a beauty so intense that it was almost frightening. His cock, uncharacteristically flaccid, was sheened like polished ivory. Behind it, his labia unfurled like blossoms from some mutant flower, petals distended, redolent of musk.

He leaned forward to help Val remove her blouse. She reached up idly, ran a fingertip along his cleavage. Her gaze lingered on his face. There was something askew there, although Val was at a loss to know exactly what. The eyes, something about the eyes. That charmed-snake look. For an instant, she felt like a little girl again, a little girl who'd feared the woods around the house were filled with trolls and witches, only to find that worse that these were in the room with her, gazing down at her with an expression of hate mingled with lust.

It's just the opium, she thought, not even wanting to guess what her own eyes must look like now. She probably had test pattern written on the pupils.

"There's plenty more where this came from," Majeed said, offering her the pipe again.

She took it, sucking first from the pipe, then on Majeed's nipple, which dangled appetizingly in her face as he leaned across her.

Something cool touched Val's left wrist. She heard, as if far distant, the swish of silk.

"Now your other arm," Majeed said as he lifted away the pipe.

"What are you…?"

"I'm sure this isn't something unfamiliar to you," said Majeed, securing Val's other wrist to the bedpost with a scarf.

"But I remembered what you said about fearing confinement. Fear and arousal are so closely linked. I guessed this must be a major turn-on for you."

"It could be except…"

She was suddenly remembering the carved and crimson thing in the bed of the apartment back in Hamburg. How long had Lou stayed alive while the atrocities were being done to him? How hard must he have fought to free himself? And what was it she found so frightening in Majeed's strange gaze?

"…except you weren't expecting it," Majeed said. "That's even better. And this time will be especially memorable for you, believe me. Before we go on, would you like another hit?"

"No."

"Please. Go ahead." He put the pipe between her lips. Val drew in the fragrant smoke. "I want you to be high. There may be parts of this that are difficult for both of us."

Majeed leaned across the bed and put his mouth to Val's. When she breathed out, he caught the smoke in his own mouth and held it.

"You don't really need to see the City," Majeed said. "I can show you many of its delights right here. Tonight."

He was rummaging around inside his suitcase. Val watched, the narcotic effect of the opium blunting her perceptions in a way she found increasingly distressing. But being bound was always a pleasure of contradictory excitements: arousal and submission and panic like actors vying for center stage, each taking a turn before relinquishing the spotlight to the next. The trick, she knew from much experience, was similar to life: relax into the game, submit, and the ferocity of pleasure that resulted could be so kin to pain the two were almost indistinguishable.

"I'm afraid I received a disturbing message the other day," Majeed was saying. "I can't take you with me on our journey as I'd hoped to."

"What do you…?"

He turned around, the effect of the narcotic in Val's system making his eyes appear more feline than ever, gold-green slits that would have bewitched her gaze entirely had she not been suddenly distracted by the sight of what was in his hands—an eight-inch knife that curved up into a sweeping, saber-like blade.

"Don't worry," said Majeed. "I'm not going to use this now. I'm only going to let you admire it for a while."

He ran a finger up the blade. In the pale light, it gleamed like something living, like the horn of some exotic beast lacquered with the moonlight spilling in through the shades. Like Majeed's, its beauty was hypnotic. Val couldn't take her eyes off it.

"I bought it in the Bazaar tonight. It's lovely, isn't it? Sleek, elegant, well-crafted—like you."

He pressed the blade against Val's throat, nickingly close, then laid it flat atop her belly, tip pointed toward her eyes. In the warmth of the room, the steel was shockingly cold. She could feel the knobs and ridges of the heavy carved handle making tiny indentations in her flesh.

"Majeed, please…"

"Don't be afraid," he said, almost a whisper. "Remember it's just a game. Before we can continue, though," he added, "I need to buy more opium." He took a pair of underpants from Val's suitcase and plugged her mouth, then secured the gag with tape. She made a sound meant to be argumentative—it came out a powerless groan reminiscent of Santos' inhuman sounds.

"I doubt that you'd cry out, but one can't take the chance. Even if it is—" and now Val knew beyond a doubt that he was lying "—only a game."

He bent down and closed Val's eyelids, kissed them both, then unlocked the door, admitting for an instant a few words of an argument shouted out in Arabic up the hall, the aroma of couscous and lamb simmering from a nearby kitchen. Then he was gone.

Chapter Twelve

She lay there, staring at the knife blade lit up with moon. Her skin tingled at its proximity. Her fingers ached to touch its metal blade.

All right, she must believe him, that it *was* a game, a brutal one meant to seduce with terror. She reassured herself of this so many times it started to sound true, until Majeed's fundamental harmlessness seemed inexorable as the law of gravity. Yet something in her knew that, not only was Majeed lying, but, worse, that she was lying to herself.

She tried to work the scarves up over the bedposts, but found them snagged beneath some baroque convexity of the post's design, impossible to slide up any further.

Sleep seemed unthinkable, and yet she dozed, dabbling first at the edges of unconsciousness like one wading in the shallows of deep water before plunging, unexpectedly and with mounting fright, into dreams that rushed at her in fragments, like jagged glass. Nightmares flashing past in jigsaw form, held to no particular pattern except the terror they inspired.

"I've decided that the knife was a mistake. You don't deserve that. You deserve a more seductive death…the kind I'd want if I were in your place."

She thought at first it was another nightmare, this one masking its counterfeit nature behind a facsimile of Majeed's voice. Then the realization that this was no dream hit her, and she came awake with a muffled gasp.

Majeed stood beside the bed. His pupils were dilated hugely. In his hands, he held three feet of cord, the kind that Val had occasionally seen used to belt a tunic. This one was gold and woven through with gleaming metallic threads.

She tried to speak. The gag reduced her words to the gurgling of an imbecile or choking victim.

Majeed removed his clothing, then climbed atop her. Leaning down, he wrapped the cord around her throat.

She made a helpless, rasping sound. Her eyes followed his every twitch, beseeching leniency.

If this was a game, the point of pleasure was long past. Her wrists ached. Her heart stuttered with terror, its every beat pumping more blood into the bursting veins at her temples.

Her vision flashed with black striping at the edges. Centered in the ebony frame, she saw Majeed's pallid face, insectile in its out-of-focusness, bisected by the glimmering slash of gold cord in either fist.

She thrashed upon the bed, eyes darting from Majeed's hands to his eyes and back again and back…

She couldn't get Majeed to meet her eyes. That, more than anything he'd yet done, terrified her.

He teased her with the cord awhile, choking her almost into unconsciousness, then loosening his grip. At some point, she realized that he had penetrated her, that his thrusts were being matched with the tightening and releasing of his hands upon the cord. It was almost impossible to keep her eyes open, but when Majeed at last met her dulled gaze, her last hopes faltered: there was neither ice nor heat in them, only distance, as though he looked at her from some schizoid universe where pain and love were meaningless in equal measure.

The rope bit in, reducing light down to a pinprick point. The pressure behind her eyes increased, and her head filled with distant buzzing. Suddenly Majeed cursed passionately and slid out of her, releasing her throat. She realized that he hadn't come. He'd simply lost his hard-on.

"I thought this could be interesting for both of us," he fumed, "but you're spoiling it…you're ruining everything. Now I have to make myself feel better again."

Majeed seemed close to tears. Rapidly, he began assembling objects from the dresser. Hypodermic syringe and powder: the talisman of addiction. Soon he was busy with the paraphernalia of his habit. He tipped a bit of heroin from bag to spoon, then cooked it with a cigarette lighter held underneath.

All this Val watched with stricken eyes, imploring him to end the game but failing to find the least compassion in his vacant gaze.

When it came time to tie his arm off and shoot up, Majeed turned his attention back to Val. The pressure of the cord around her throat had caused her to swallow some of the silk panties Majeed had used to gag her with. Now even though she was no longer being strangled, she was in danger of choking to death.

Majeed reached down and slapped her. "Dammit, I can't stand to see you flopping around like a caught fish. If you're going to die, die quietly."

So saying, he ripped the tape away, snatched out the panties, and freed Val's mouth.

She coughed and tried to speak. Her throat felt like she'd eaten ashes.

"Majeed, if this is a game…?"

"It's what I have to do. I'm sorry. I really am. But I have no choice."

"What do you mean, 'no choice'?"

"It means I owe somebody."

"Filakis?"

"Yes."

"That little girl..?"

"She brought me his final offer, so to speak. A life, taken in a bloody fashion. That was the agreement. He's going to be furious if he finds out I didn't use the knife."

"Why me?"

"Your curiosity has a self-destructive bent. It led you to search for the City. It also led you to me."

"Why *my* life, Majeed?"

"Because the Turk enjoys inflicting pain and he knows I…" He grimaced, searching for the vein. "Look, just shut up or I'll find something else to gag you with."

"Don't do this. Please. I can't die yet."

He tilted a derisive eyebrow and concentrated on drawing the heroin up into the syringe.

"It's not as though most people expect to choose the moment. Besides, you told me you preferred dangerous…people. This was bound to happen sooner or later. Your lifestyle almost demands an untimely end, wouldn't you agree?"

"But not like this…not you. I felt so close to you. I thought in some way we were…alike."

"We're nothing alike. You're a normal woman. I'm something people used to pay two pounds just to gawk at. A she-male, the darling of the freak show and porno circuit."

"Stop it."

"But I'm also as competent a killer as the next."

"You said you'd take me to the City. Do that at least and then…"

"You don't know what you're asking for. There's no such place. It's a lie, a myth, dreamed up by people bored by everything else life has to offer, bored out of their minds, quite literally."

"Don't make me die like this. Not shackled like the way…."

"…the way someone once did to you? Who was it, Val? The friendly old physician, the priest? A funny uncle, or your crazy mother? What did she *do* to you?"

"What do you…?"

"No, never mind. It's too late now. Besides I'm tired of listening to you. When I'm not using you for sex, you're really very tiresome."

The syringe was full. Majeed squirted out a tiny bit to clear air bubbles. He struck at the vein and missed. His hands trembled so violently the needle appeared to dance.

"Majeed, what did you mean before? About why Filakis wants me to be the one you kill?"

"Shut up. It doesn't matter. I promised him I would or he won't let me back in…"

"The City? Is that it? So that's who Filakis really is—the Turk."

"What difference does it make?"

"Is the place that wonderful? That you'd kill me if Filakis said it was the only way you'd get back in? If that's the case, why did you ever leave? Why didn't you just stay there?"

Majeed's inability to hit a vein was making him increasingly distraught. Sweat beaded on his forehead, ran down his face.

"Is it like the opium?" Val pressed. "You want to stop, you want to leave, but you can't? It always pulls you back, and you pay any price for readmittance?"

"Shut up!" shouted Majeed and threw the syringe aside.

Val held her breath. The effect of the opium had diminished beneath the more potent effect of terror, and if she was still high, she couldn't tell it. She felt petrified, frozen in her fear like an insect trapped in amber, her muscles tense as wires, her heart unbeating stone.

If I'm going to die, she thought, *let it be something memorable*.

Majeed picked up the knife where he had left it and came over to the bed. He ran the knife between Val's parted legs, then lifted the blade to her neck. It popped the skin an inch above the hollow at her throat. Blood pooled there and then streamed down her ribs. The pain was distant, unremarkable; her senses focused entirely on Majeed.

"Why am I the one you have to kill?" she whispered. "Why not someone else."

"Goddamn you."

"Why me?"

Majeed raised the knife. His voice was barely audible, the low whistle of insectile wings.

"Because he knows I love you."

He raised the knife and brought it down—twice in quick succession. The blade slashed flesh, but only superficially. The main direction of the thrust was through the scarves that bound Val's arms.

Majeed waved a dismissive hand. "Go on and live your wretched life. You'll end up murdered anyway. It just won't be by me."

Val breathed again. She rolled off the bed, struggling into items of her clothing with arms that had gone numb as logs, no longer under her command but senseless stobs of flesh. She beat the circulation back into them, had managed to put on a pair of jeans when Majeed suddenly leaped across the bed and stood before her, the knife in hand.

His eyes were wild, his skin an unnatural, sickly cast, malarial.

"Wait!"

She thought he'd changed his mind about sparing her life.

"Please, Majeed, let's..."

His knife hand began to tremble.

Val lunged past him for the door. Majeed grabbed her arm and flung her backward onto the bed.

"I said you can't..."

But Val heard it now, the footsteps approaching up the hall. She had no reason to think they heralded disaster except by Majeed's reaction, which left little doubt as to his terror. He was darting about the room in a frantic dance of wasted motion, a trapped gerbil, running from window to window in a hopeless effort to find some avenue of escape.

"No," said Val, when it became clear Majeed meant to jump. "It's too high. You'll kill yourself."

Their room was three floors up. Both windows overlooked a narrow, stone-paved alleyway crowded not only with passersby but with a hodgepodge of vendors, their wares spread out on mats upon the stones. A fall from this height, though possibly not fatal, would shatter bones and rupture organs.

Still, Majeed was forcing one of the windows up and would clearly have taken his chances with the fall had not the door, which Majeed had locked upon his return to the room, suddenly burst inward.

The Turk, in all his corrupt nobility, strode across to the window and locked an arm that was all vein and sinew around Majeed's throat.

"You betrayed me, bitch," he crooned in Majeed's ear. "You promised me her life tonight. You swore."

Majeed responded by twisting with reptilian grace, the knife still in his hand. Filakis wrenched it from Majeed's grip and hurled it across the floor. Val heard fingerbones and joints crunch sickeningly. Majeed wailed.

"Don't," said Filakis, guessing Val's intention toward the knife.

He twisted Majeed around, so he could face Val. Behind him the open door tempted with the possibility of escape, but Filakis barred the way. He stared at Val—an odd and terrifying sizing up of her—that seemed rife with abhorrence.

Meanwhile, Majeed struggled in his captor's arms, choking and sputtering as Filakis applied more pressure to his neck. There was something odd about Filakis' palms, Val noted. At first, she'd had the impression that they were smeared with blood. Then, she realized the man's flesh was hennaed with jinn-spells and incantations, a practice designed to ward off evil spirits that she'd observed among the Berber women.

But Val had little time to reflect upon the oddity of the Turk's indulgence in this superstition. The knife he'd wrested from Majeed lay within easy reach, a temptation that, in the present circumstances, was irresistible. Val grabbed it, thinking to plant the blade in Filakis' neck and would have done so, had she not been halted by a crackling sound and the unfolding of a spectacle before her that rendered her immobile.

Tongues of pale green fire were licking at Filakis and Majeed. Mere tatters, at first, the flames soon grew, tonguing and plucking at Majeed's face and breasts, at his captor's opulence of hair. Majeed writhed and screamed in Filakis' grasp, but the Turk uttered not one cry as the fire climbed his torso, igniting flesh and clothing in its luminous embrace.

Majeed stretched out a hand to Val.

She reached to take it, but fire blossomed from her lover's fingertips like thorns. There was a moment's indecision, when she might have grabbed Majeed's hand anyway, but the flames were devouring him with ferocious speed. In the instant that she hesitated, Majeed tossed something at her. The object missed her and rolled across the floor. Then Majeed's hand was burned away, the fingers curling back upon themselves like withered foetuses.

Electric, crackling tendrils spread across Majeed's and Filakis' faces. Skin cracked and peeled. What lay below, shimmering suet and tendon and bone, was soon unveiled and melted down. All cries stopped and, presently, all motion.

The flame bulged out at its height and formed a funnel, which whirled like some inhuman dervish about the floor, consuming what remained. For several seconds, it danced and capered on the carpet with terrible exuberance, then lost volume and momentum and sputtered out into a tiny heap of ash and rubble on the floor.

Left behind, for an instant only, there glowed an afterimage: steepled towers and squat, dun-colored houses shimmering like bleak mirages behind medieval walls. The walls, when Val peered closer, appeared to be composed of writhing human bodies, living, faceless and crudely formed, all locked in carnal congress.

Val blinked—the scene did not disperse, but took on form, dimension. There was a moment when, remembering it later, she was sure she could have simply walked inside the rent in space that appeared open to her. But by the time she gathered wits and courage, the image turned translucent, its third dimension sloughing off like worn-out skin, the remaining threads of form and color liquefying into a few drops of dew-like mist that hovered in the air, then dispersed to nothing.

But even as the shock of seeing Majeed's fate rooted her in place, a small burst of celebration fired her heart. The place she'd glimpsed could be nowhere except the City.

That, or Hell, and she meant to find out, one way or another.

Majeed and his mysterious abductor had left behind a small pile of remnants on the floor. She went over to inspect it.

Swatches of cloth and leather, scorched and frayed as though they'd been through an incinerator, Majeed's opium pipe, or what was left of it, reduced to a lump of ivory and melted gold, dollops of glass, coin-sized, that must have once been a hypodermic syringe.

And, a few feet away, something else: the object that Majeed had thrown her, a pale green piece of stone, slightly smaller than a hen's egg, rounded at the top but with a flat base. Val picked it up and turned it over in her hand. The object was similar to a number of the incense burners Majeed had set out on the windowsill—in the case of the latter, the top could be unscrewed and removed to reveal the candle contained inside.

Unlike the incense burners, however, this jar offered no seam to indicate where the top could be twisted off. It seemed to be a solid piece of stone, onyx or malachite perhaps. If so, its function was entirely ornamental, yet so closely did it resemble its twins that Val couldn't help but think a seam existed somewhere in its intricately carved sides, but was simply far more subtly crafted and inconspicuously designed.

She turned the small jar in her hands a dozen times, yet found nothing to indicate it opened into halves. Its varnished surface was carved with some kind of complex floral pattern. Leafy spirals and overlapping whorls interlocked in patterns that at first appeared both random and simple, but, upon closer inspection, proved to be teasingly complex, provocative in its design. Stamen-like shafts writhed and twisted into budded knots upon the top while along the sides, carved blossoms formed fantastic arabesques that defeated each attempt Val made to trace them to their source in the design.

At length she put the object down, but not before it had revealed at least one secret. Upon the warming in the hands, it began to emit the faintest of odors, a musk so subtle in its fragrance that Val could sense it only with her nose pressed to the stone.

In any case, there was no time for further inspection. In the courtyard down below, a crowd had formed among the vending stalls, people gazing up at the room where someone must have seen the flickering of flames. Val heard shouted Arabic and French, the pounding of feet in the hall.

She had no wish to be caught and questioned. She grabbed her totebag with passport and wallet and headed through the shattered door toward an exit stairwell. The carved piece of stone she slipped inside her pocket with a promise to herself that it would yield its secrets to her yet.

For a few more days, Val remained in Fez in the hope that Majeed might somehow still be alive and make his way back to her, but restlessness soon overcame her. She took the train southwest to the beach resort of Agadir. From there, she traveled to the town of Taroudannt, a market center tucked in a valley between the High Atlas and Anti-Atlas Mountains. Always she kept the incense burner in her pocket, to be brought out and handled at odd moments, its complexities explored.

In Taroudannt, whose marketplace offered natural toiletries made from the musk of gazelle glands and desiccated lizards sold as potions to ensure good health, she spent hours studying the carved convolutions. It seemed to her that, over time, a pattern could be discerned and that occasionally, upon repeating a particular sequence of touch, the scent emanating from the jar became more powerful. At times, the scent was so alluring that she focused only on the jar, blind to the sights and sounds around her as she gave in to her obsession.

It was toward the end of her fifth day in Taroudannt, while taking refuge from the high heat of early afternoon in a cafe across the street from her hotel that Val first felt the minuscule beginning of a dismantling of the jar's design. A portion of its pattern seemed suddenly to be less than solidly attached.

She shut her eyes and traced the complex arabesques like Braille. There was a subtle sliding, followed by a snap, and an odor almost indecent in its seductiveness wafted to her nostrils. She looked down in her palm and saw a tiny aperture had opened up in the center of one carved whorl. A half inch wick, the kind found on any ordinary candle, protruded up.

Val stared at it. Was this the way? Majeed had disappeared into an emerald blaze. If she lit this, would the fire come for her as well?

She was turning the incense burner in her hand, working up her courage to return to her hotel room and strike a match, when she heard someone call her name.

Thinking that Majeed must have somehow returned, she looked up.

For a second she could only stare in disbelief. Then, in a stunned and whispery voice, she said, "Arthur?"

Breen bent down and kissed her cheek. "Val," he said, "I knew it. I knew someday I'd find you."

Chapter Thirteen

Val lay with her head on Breen's chest, her blood slowly seeping into the sheets.

"Do you love me?" Breen teased, stroking her cheek.

Val sighed. She felt drugged with sex. "I don't know. Fuck me one more time and ask again."

Her period had started the night before, while Breen and she were making love. He'd pulled out of her and squatted over her to fuck her mouth when Val had seen his cock covered in gore, blood running down the shaft.

For a moment she was fascinated. What he was about to fuck her with looked more like a bloody weapon than part of a human body. She licked the crown, explored the sharp metallic taste.

"You'd better wash," she'd said.

He'd shaken his head. "I like your blood. I like the taste of it."

And he went down between her legs, lapping her until his face was bearded and mustached in blood.

Later, in the night, he'd dipped a finger between her legs and written "I love you" in menstrual blood on her belly. She'd let the letters dry there and only this morning, with strange reluctance, washed them off.

Now she dozed, aware that Arthur continued to caress her face, her breasts, to stroke the thick mat of her pubic hair as though it were a living pelt. *Does he ever sleep,* she wondered. But no, the Arthur

Breen that Val remembered seldom did. Not when he could be having sex instead.

Val's body was pleasantly sated, but her mind kept questioning this most improbable of reunions. It seemed incredible that she and Arthur would have run into each other here in a small, out-of-the-way Moroccan city. Less incredible, perhaps, was the fact that as far as their mutual attraction for one another, nothing seemed to have changed at all.

Almost two years had passed since they'd last seen each other. Yet they still remembered every touch and texture of the other's skin, every favorite position and caress. They might have been making love with each other all along, if only in their minds.

How wonderful this is, thought Val, and it occurred to her that, since she'd looked up to see Arthur staring at her, she hadn't thought of Majeed, of the City until now. It was as if both had ceased to exist for her now that she was back in the arms of this man who'd been her lover, this man whom she'd walked out when he asked her to marry him.

"I still can't believe you're here," Val said. "The last time we were together you said you wanted to go back to your house in New Orleans, that there was nothing worth traveling around the world for that couldn't be found in the French Quarter or in Baton Rouge."

"I got bored," said Breen. "I went back to Hong Kong and lived there for a while. Then I started reading Camus and Gide and decided to see for myself if North Africa was as decadent as they described it."

"And is it?"

"I suppose—for those who take their decadence flavored with the tang of camel piss and unwashed groins."

She laughed. "Do you still have what you once described as an 'eclectic palette'?"

"Meaning do I still enjoy the company of attractive young men?" He leaned across Val's chest, tongued her nipples into puckered erection. "Not at the moment. At the moment young men are the last thing on my mind."

"Oh? You prefer my cunt to a boyish asshole and virgin dick? That's quite a compliment."

"One you don't deserve," said Breen. "Not after the way you treated me."

"You were too possessive. I didn't see any other way except to leave."

Breen reached across the bed for the pack of French cigarettes and lighter he'd placed there earlier. He lit one, then, as if in afterthought, asked Val if she objected.

"As long as you don't make a habit of it. When did you start smoking?"

"I never stopped."

"You never did before…when we were together."

"I hid it from you. One of those small vices I preferred you didn't know about."

"And now it doesn't matter?"

"Now I think I'd rather we be more honest with each other."

Val turned away. This was the part she'd dreaded—the Sincere Talk.

"I was always honest with you, Arthur."

"Even when you…" He stopped, regained control of his voice, said evenly, "Even when you couldn't tell me to my face that you were leaving. Even when you had to leave a note. That doesn't seem like honesty. It seems like consummate cowardice."

"I didn't know how to leave you any other way."

Breen turned his head, exhaled a plume of blue smoke toward the ceiling. "That's what I never understood—why it was necessary to leave at all."

"Because if I hadn't left you then, I was afraid I never would. I didn't want to be trapped, and at the same time, I could feel myself approaching a point where I wouldn't want to leave you ever. Especially when you brought up marriage. That was too scary for me. I had to run away."

Breen's left hand found its way into her hair, tightened sharply and then relaxed. "You hurt me. Waking up and finding you gone like that. How do you suppose I felt?"

"I'm sorry."

Breen sighed. "You sound like a little girl apologizing for eating too many cookies. Do you think 'I'm sorry' really makes up for what you did to me?"

Val disengaged herself from Breen's embrace, flopped over on her stomach. "Arthur, your finding me here in Taroudannt—was this really a coincidence?"

"What else?"

"You tell me."

Breen laughed. "Aren't you the egotist, my love. You're saying you suspect me of following you half-way around the world, of tracking you down after a two year absence? That I'm a stalker on an international scale? If I did that, it would mean I'm truly deranged or dangerously obsessed, now wouldn't it?"

Val ran her fingers down Breen's chest, traced a circle around his navel with her nail. "I was never sure about you, Arthur, whether you were dangerously obsessed or not. I suppose that was always part of the attraction."

"We could start over again. We could pretend those two years apart were just a misspent weekend."

"It wouldn't work. I haven't changed, you know. Besides, there's more traveling that I have to do."

"Here in Morocco?"

"I don't know."

"Well, if you don't trust me enough to let me know your plans…"

"It isn't that."

She was beginning to wish Arthur would leave if he couldn't stop asking questions. But how could she ask him to go when it was she who'd told him he could share her room for the few days that she remained in Taroudannt? He'd brought his things over that morning, only a suitcase and a leather kit for toiletries. She'd never known Arthur to travel so light or to visit a place as remote and non-luxurious as Taroudant. But maybe he'd changed. Maybe their meeting had really been coincidence.

What hadn't changed, of course, and what had been the deciding factor on Val's decision to let him share her room, was Breen's sexual appetite. Unlike many men whom Val had known, who fucked to achieve an orgasm, Breen seemed enraptured by the act of sex itself, of penetrating and of being penetrated. His body took its pleasure, but his mind—like hers—was never really satisfied.

Now, as she reached between his legs and felt him hard again, Val wondered how she had ever managed to leave him—the best lover she had ever known—without so much as a backward glance.

Fear, she supposed.

Fear that she would love him.

Fear that if she did, that love would bind her to him and never let her leave again.

"Tell me the truth, Val." Still lying on his side, Breen slid himself inside her, draped his legs between and over hers. "Isn't this what you want? Do you really think you're going to find something better somewhere else?"

"Now who's the egotist?"

"But it's more becoming in a male."

"Sexist."

"Granted. But you didn't answer my question."

"Maybe I won't find anyone better than you, Arthur, but what I will find is variety. I think you can appreciate the appeal of that."

At the moment, though, there was less conviction behind her words than Val would have cared to admit. She'd thought she'd never see Arthur again, yet here he was—the same muscular and sculptured body, the full and slightly crooked lips, those eyes, the most remarkable deep cobalt, like that point underwater just before the light no longer penetrates and that intense shade of blue is finally replaced with black.

Breen levered himself above her and repositioned her legs so that they were now atop his shoulders. He caught her wrists in one hand and pinned them above her head, deepening his thrusts.

"You shouldn't have walked out on me."

"If I stayed, we'd have become tired of each other a long time ago."

After that, she closed her eyes, refused to respond to whatever else Breen said. She'd always thought he talked too much during sex, sometimes obscenities and teasing threats, other times a low, almost inaudible murmur, as though he were not with her at all but off somewhere alone inside his head, talking himself through yet another masturbatory session.

It was a strange habit, and during their time together Val had trained herself not to listen, in part so that she wouldn't be distracted, in part in fear of what direction his solipsistic dialogues might lean. She focused only on the physical experience of Breen, the violent hunger in him which matched her own, the tang of rape implicit in the force with which he took her.

He rammed her cunt as though it were the enemy and cried out when he came, shuddering atop her for a few minutes while the sweat cooled on their bodies and they both regained their breath.

Breen smoothed the hair he'd so mercilessly tangled. He traced Val's lips. She sucked the proffered finger and tasted her own juices, musk and brine and copper.

"I loved you once," he said.

"I know," she said. "Last night. You wrote it in blood on my belly."

"I mean real love," said Breen. "The kind that doesn't wash off the next day."

"So you don't love me anymore?"

"I don't know. If you want me to fall in love with you again, you'll have to prove yourself worthy of it."

Val turned her head away so Arthur wouldn't see her smiling.

Worthy of love? That was the trouble with "love", she thought. It usually came with an exorbitant price tag. Even Majeed, who'd claimed to love her, had almost killed her first. As for Arthur Breen, Val doubted he was capable of loving anybody for longer than the duration of his orgasm. He wanted only to manipulate her, to make her feel she'd squandered something precious when she left him. Then she might beg him to take her back and he could have the pleasure of rejecting her.

Breen stubbed out his cigarette, reached for another. Sometime in the last few days, he'd given up his "only one a day" rule, and now the pack was empty.

"I need to buy some more of these."

"I wish you wouldn't. The room stinks as it is."

"Of sex."

"Sex and carcinogens."

"My love," said Breen. He kissed her forehead, eyelids, the tip of her nose, "the way you fuck, the last thing you need to worry about is carcinogens. At the rate you're going, you'll never live to see the age of forty."

He slid out of bed, put his clothes on. Val watched him dress, admiring the planes and contours of his body, the muscles that rippled across his naked back when he stooped to put on his shoes.

"There's a kiosk that sells cigarettes two blocks away. I'll just be a few minutes."

From the fourth floor window, she watched Breen thread his way through the crowded street, his blond hair and six foot height keeping him in her line of sight until he turned the corner.

God, she thought, *I've got it bad. Two years and I've still got him in my system.*

Visions of traveling with Arthur again, perhaps returning to Europe or living in that spectacular, turn-of-the-century home he supposedly owned in New Orleans, warred with her conflicting ambitions. In her mind, she toted up the pluses, minuses of such a union. Arthur was the most highly sexed man she'd ever loved, the one man whose appetite had always seemed to equal or exceed her own. That wasn't something she found every day. On the other hand, he could be possessive, cold, and taciturn. And secretive. She'd rarely known a man as miserly with the details of his past.

But still…how enticing to imagine that maybe he could really love her, that she might, indeed, love him.

A few more days, thought Val. Then she'd break away from this before the addictive quality of great sex wore down all her resolve. She'd light the incense burner's wick and see if it could take her to the City, to Majeed.

Idly, she fingered some of Majeed's incense burners and candles, which she'd lined up on the sill, but left unlit. The one he'd tossed her, the one she felt sure must hold the secret to entering the City, was hidden away in a pocket of her duffel.

Val took it out now, cradled it in the palm of her hand, admiring its whorls and intricacies. A part of her was angry at herself that she hadn't lit the wick when her manipulations finally opened up the incense burner to reveal it. Another part, less daring, advised further postponement.

As soon as Arthur and I part company, she thought. *Soon.*

She tucked the beguiling object back in its hiding place inside her duffel.

Secrets. She'd accused Arthur of being secretive, she thought, but look at her. They'd barely found each other, and here she was planning to run out on him again.

But he came looking for me. I'm sure of it.

His story that he'd lived in Hong Kong for a few months didn't ring true. Arthur had hated Hong Kong. Neither did his supposed interest in North Africa, young boys notwithstanding, seem plausible. She wished that she could see his passport, could find out where he'd really spent the last two years.

Breen's suitcase, an expensive Italian one, was pushed up against the wall inside the closet. Val toed it idly. Then she bent down and tried to open it. Locked.

Besides, he probably keeps his passport with him.

Even as she thought it, though, she was checking the one other possibility, the zippered shaving kit Arthur had left in the bathroom. She opened it, perused the usual array of men's colognes, deodorant, and aftershave.

And something else. A box of matches. It didn't shake like a box of matches, though. Val opened it and found a tiny key.

In seconds she had Arthur's suitcase open and was going through its contents. His clothes, of course, were hung up in the closet, and it soon became apparent that the suitcase contained little of interest. Certainly not his passport. Some extra pairs of socks and jock straps, a few boxes of condoms—some foreign brand Val didn't recognize—a Gucci belt, a bathing suit, a couple of pornographic magazines—transvestites and rubber fetishists and buxom Amazons wielding whips over the bare buttocks of trussed males.

Val glanced at these, then tucked them back where she had found them. Nothing.

And Arthur would be coming back soon. She had to...

Something else was balled up in one corner with some extra pairs of socks. Something that had been covered by the magazines. The material looked silky, shiny, but also worn and frayed. For some reason it also looked like something she had seen before.

She carefully lifted the object up and it immediately separated into two parts, which had been rolled up, but now came open to reveal a pair of tiny embroidered Chinese slippers.

Chinese slippers. And Lou hogtied and savaged, the dried blood that had run from his eyes and ears and mouth staining the many shoes on which his face was skewered. Punctured eyes and missing teeth. The pool of congealed blood that he was sitting in.

Arthur had done that. The man who'd spent the last half hour inside her body. The man who'd had his hands around her neck.

Arthur.

Chapter Fourteen

Val dropped the slippers, then forced herself to pick them up again and replace them just as they had been. She closed the suitcase, locked it with hands shaking so badly it took her several tries just to insert the key.

She grabbed a pair of jeans and a t-shirt and put them on, stuffed her passport and money into the pockets. That was enough. Arthur would be back any minute. She had to go.

She was in the hallway when she remembered that the incense burner was still in her duffel bag and she went back to get it.

That was how Breen found her, on her knees before the duffel bag, stuffing the small object into her pocket.

"What are you doing?"

She stood up so fast a momentary vertigo unbalanced her. She had to put a hand against the wall and take a breath.

"The smoke in here…it's giving me a headache. I thought I'd go out and get some air."

"Don't bother. It'll only make your headache worse. It must be over a hundred degrees out there."

She started to move past him. "Then I'll just sit downstairs for a while."

"I don't want you to go. I just got back. I thought I'd find you still in bed and here you are, dressed and leaving." His stare was narrow-eyed, invasive. "This isn't deja vu, I hope, me thinking all is well, you headed out the door."

"Arthur, don't be paranoid."

She turned to leave, but he stopped her with a hand around her upper arm.

"Let me see you."

She turned around, trying to appear merely annoyed at his suspicions.

"You can't go out like that. You've put your t-shirt on wrongside-out. People will think you got dressed in a terrible rush."

Val smiled weakly. "Guess I wasn't paying attention."

"Did you?" said Breen. "Did you dress in a terrible hurry?"

"Don't be silly," said Val. Unwilling to be even partially disrobed in front of him, she went into the bathroom, came out a moment later with her t-shirt righted.

He had used the time that she was in the bathroom to pull his suitcase out of the closet. He was on his knees inspecting it.

"Naughty girl," he said. "I see that you've been going through my things. I suppose I might have guessed you'd try to open it, but I never thought you'd be so diligent as to hunt up the key." He held it out to her. "Which you left in the lock of the suitcase after you opened it, my dear."

"And imagine my surprise at what I found!" She stood up, forcing herself to smile, and slid her arms around Breen's neck. "I'm really angry at you, Arthur."

"Angry? I find you snooping through my things, but it's you who claims the right to be angry. That's clever, Val, but it won't work."

"I understand now why you had to lock your suitcase. You were keeping something from me that you were ashamed I'd find. Your dirty magazines. All that lovely lace and rubber? How could you keep that from me?"

She tried to touch him. He backed away another step. Incredibly, it was he who seemed to be in retreat.

"It doesn't matter. You had no right to spy."

He took out a pack of cheap Moroccan cigarettes, tore off the top and shook one free, lit it with his Dunhill lighter. His hands were trembling, something Val had never seen in him.

"Come on," said Val, hoping to diffuse the tension. "Let's get in bed and look at the magazines. Maybe we'll find something to inspire us. I promise I'll make it up to you for being a bad girl. I promise I'll make you feel good."

She wondered how she'd be able to live up to that promise, knowing now that Arthur was a man capable of peeling flesh and plunging five inch spike heels into a human eyesocket. She wondered how she could touch him now without screaming.

"Well, Arthur?"

This time he let her touch his face and put her lips against his own. Nor did he change expression when she pulled away and promised him, like a mother offering extra sweets to a petulent child, "I'll even let you punish me."

"Oh, my dear." He took a deep drag on the cigarette while with the other hand he stroked her hair. "You'd let me spank you?"

She watched his eyes. They looked as remote, as lightless, as stars in a galaxy gone cold and dead.

"Yes."

"And bite your nipples?"

Was her voice giving her away? Could he tell how dry the terror had leached her tongue?

"Of course."

"And other things?"

She nodded. His lips were as close to hers as they could be without actually touching. She could no longer see his eyes, just his mouth as it moved above hers, smiling slightly and rimmed with even white teeth.

"Oh, my love, I'm only teasing. Do you really think that anything you did could make me really want to hurt you?"

He kissed her. Then he raised her right hand and kissed that, too, before, in one swift movement, he brought the hand that held the cigarette around and ground it out in the fleshy part of her palm.

She howled with pain. Breen backhanded her with the other hand, a blow that would have sent her sprawling, except that at the same time, he gripped and twisted her wrist more tightly, wrenching her to her knees.

"What did you find in my suitcase? What did you find?"

"Nothing. Arthur, stop it! I don't know what you're talking about."

"You fucking lying cunt!"

He seized her flailing arms and forced them to her sides, immobilized them there with his knees. She screamed for help.

He slugged her twice, blows that exploded in her skull like cannonfire. She tasted blood and saw him through a strobing haze of psychedelic neon.

"It could have been so different, so much nicer for both of us," he was saying. "But you had to go and ruin it, you snooping bitch, you had to fuck up all my plans just like you did before. I should have killed you when I first set eyes on you. I never should have waited."

She spat out blood. "You followed me here from Hamburg."

"Of course I did."

"The man that I was with…Lou…you killed him."

"And most appropriately, I think. He died with the smell of shoe leather in his brain, literally. He should have been in ecstasy."

"Who else?"

"Your studly little Persian, for one."

"Reza?"

"Well hung, I'll give him that. But just another one of the girls after I got through with him."

"Jesus, Arthur. You're a monster."

"You didn't think that when I was fucking you."

He reached inside his back pocket, brought out the Dunhill lighter.

"So I'm a monster, am I? Tell me, Val, what does a monster look like? Maybe it's someone with their eyes burned out, carrying their charred nose in their hand."

He flicked the lighter. The flame shot forth. He held it in Val's face, close enough that she could feel the heat against her cheek.

"Don't do this, Arthur."

She tossed her head from side to side in a useless attempt to evade the flame. He touched the fire to her earlobe. She screamed as she felt her flesh sizzle.

"Shut up!"

Breen grabbed the bottom of her t-shirt and yanked it up above her breasts. He clamped one hand across her mouth, fingers digging into her gums. With the other hand, he held the lighter to her nipple.

The pain was pyrotechnic red. She arched and caught his finger between her teeth, bit down until her teeth ground bone.

Now it was Breen's turn to scream. He flailed backward, flinging the lighter across the room and freeing Val's arms. She spun around—collecting a number of splinters in her back in the process—and kicked Breen in the face. He fell back into the bed, but was on his feet again in time to intercept Val as she got to her feet and tried to reach the door.

His left hand shot out and clamped in her hair, twisting and squeezing, as he pummeled her with his fist. The blows fell on her face and neck and shoulders. She tried to shield her face, and he punched her in the stomach. In one paralyzing rush of pain, the breath went out of her. Blackness webbed the edges of her vision.

And all the while that he was beating her, he went on talking. Not shouting now, but speaking evenly, methodically, like a teacher whose patience has been exhausted by dullard pupils.

"…stupid cunt…you fucked it up…could have loved you, but you wouldn't let me…could have killed you…loved you, killed you, loved you, killed you…" the words bounced back and forth, a kind of rhythmic metronome accompanying the blows.

When he let her hair go, she fell to the floor, blood running from her nostrils and her mouth. She would have screamed for help, but there was no breath with which to do it. The muscles that facilitated breathing had jammed, contorted. She could barely get enough air in to stay conscious.

Breen stood against the door, observing her with cold detachment.

"What a pitiful thing you are. I can't believe I wasted so much time on you. I can't believe I traveled so far, went to such great efforts. Just so I could have you where you are now, bleeding at my feet. Just so I could watch you die."

He took a slow step toward her. Val dug her elbows into the floor, pulled herself back away from him. Something dug into her hip—the incense burner in her pocket.

Breen grinned down at her. "Take those off. Right now—take your clothes off before I rip them off you. I want to see the bruises and the burn marks. I want to fuck you while I'm beating you to death. And then I'm going to fuck you after, too." He shrugged. "I want to see if it's true the meat is sweeter after it's tenderized."

She panted, "Give me a minute."

"Bitch, I've already given you two years of my life."

"I can't…breathe."

"Oh that's too bad. You're hurting, aren't you? Here, let me give you something to take your mind off it."

He kicked her in the ribs. She moaned and curled up on the floor, clutching at her sides. She could see light sparkling off the Dunhill lighter where it lay on the floor a few feet away. Breen kicked her again, sending sharp jolts of pain up her spine.

She let the blow turn her over. Her fingers closed around the lighter. Her other hand, buried in the pocket of her jeans, pulled out the incense burner.

She flicked the flame.

Breen laughed.

"Do you think you can hurt me with that little lighter? Do you think that frightens me?"

She bent forward, as if doubled over with pain, and touched the fire to the wick. It burned for an instant and went out.

Breen stood over her. "Get up onto the bed and take your clothes off. Now! Get up or I swear I'll kick you in the stomach until you shit your guts out."

"All right, give me…a minute."

She got one knee up as if to stand, touched the fire to the wick yet again.

Please, please.

It caught this time, burned almost instantaneously to the root. Wisps of green fire erupted around Val's hand. It caught her clothes, her hair, her flesh. It danced inside her mouth, licked at the wetness of her eyes, the hollows of her ears. Its touch caused her flesh to tingle with desire that was fierce and free and limitless, obliterating pain.

From behind the flames, she could see Breen cringing back against the wall, eyes almost bulging from his head as he tried to make sense of what he was seeing.

One time he reached out as if to test the reality of the vision, but pulled his hand back in fear before he could make contact.

Val looked down and saw her legs and lower body eaten away by the flame. Her flesh was going runny, like ice melting to the point of translucency.

A fierce wind keened. Through the mad gyrations of the flames, she glimpsed high walls and the slabbed roofs of cube-shaped, dun-colored buildings.

The fire seized and fed on what remained of her. There was no pain, but a cold and blinding dazzle that reduced her senses one by one until all that remained was the sensation of desire.

Desire suffused every pore and everywhere it brought oblivion.

Chapter Fifteen

Several minutes passed before Breen was able to bring himself to move and examine the spot where the weird green fire had appeared to incinerate Val before his eyes.

When he did so, he began to doubt his sanity. The wood floor, which should have gone up like a tinderbox, was barely smudged. All that remained behind were a few strands of burnt hair and charred bits of fabric.

Only the presence of Val's possessions in the room kept Breen from thinking he must have imagined having been with her. Her clothes were in the closet, her toiletries in the bathroom, the scent of her still lingered on the bed.

The Dunhill lighter, which she'd somehow used to effect her transformation into fire, lay on the floor where she'd dropped it.

Breen stood there in a stupor of confusion. He was not a man prepared to deal with mysteries. His mind was geared to the predictable, the mundane world of flesh that bled and bone that broke, things he could control, manipulate. To be so cruelly thwarted, duped, left him weak with fury.

"Damn her! Damn her! Damn her!"

A bellow of rage broke from his lips. With one sweeping blow, he cleared the dressertop—a mirror smashed into quicksilver shards, lipstick and earrings clattered to the floor, a bottle of Breen's hundred dollar an ounce cologne went rocketing into the wall and shattered into musky streams. He tore Val's clothing off the hangers and ripped them into rags. What was left, he slashed to pieces. When those remnants were sufficiently destroyed, he stabbed the pillow where she'd laid her wretched head and hacked the curtains into little more than silky fringe.

In the midst of his tantrum, he saw the incense burners and scented candles she'd lined up along the windowsill, and a portion of his mind cleared sufficiently for a single coherent thought to arrange itself within the turmoil of his consciousness: she'd used an object similar to those to make her escape. Who was to say he couldn't do the same?

Breen snatched the lighter off the floor. He commenced with the candle nearest him and worked his way up the line, lighting every stick of sandalwood, every wick.

For his efforts, he got fragrant scents and small, ordinary flames.

"God damn her!"

He hurled the lighter across the room and swept the sill clear with a mighty blow of his other hand, then looked about for something else he might destroy.

The only object in the room his fury hadn't touched was a bottle of cheap wine they'd opened and half-drunk the night before. Breen tossed aside the cork and guzzled. He carried the bottle into the bathroom along with the knife he'd used to wreck his vengeance on the room. There he removed his clothes and sat down on the floor. That done, he comforted himself in the way he had done as a boy—opening his flesh in long slow cuts, watching the blood seep out of him. As the blood flowed out, so ebbed his rage, and presently sleep claimed him.

Breen dreamed that a mob pursued him through a maze of narrow aisles and stairways. They carried bladed weapons and their cries rose up as if from one throat, a sound like that made by a hiveful of bees, milling and swarming.

They came closer. Hot sweat trickled along Breen's brow. He woke up to the sound of a woman's preternaturally loud screaming.

A siren.

Breen got up and opened the bathroom door.

And slammed it instantly.

Outside a wall of flame—real flames this time, not the emerald flames Val had mysteriously engendered—capered among the savaged curtains. Where Breen had torn and tossed them on the floor, they blazed before the door. The head of the bed, and parts of the floor were blazing. Smoke rose from the flames in a choking cloud.

Cursing himself for not having made sure the candles and the incense were extinguished, Breen slammed the door. His mind raced. He remembered having read something once about what to do in a situation like this—run water into the tub, soak towels and stuff them under the crack in the door, and wait for rescue.

But the room was an inferno, and the only way out was blocked by flames. No one was going to put the fire out in time to save him. No one even knew that he was in the room.

Outside he heard more sirens, running feet, and the excited shouts of the mob that had undoubtedly gathered outside to watch the spectacle.

For the first time in this life, Breen confronted a terrible truth: he was going to die and die most horribly, not in some distant future so far away he could convince himself it would never come at all, but here, in this miserable hotel room, alone in an alien land.

Not like this!

He couldn't stay and hope for rescue. He had to get out now.

He soaked all the towels he could find, wrapped one around his head and tied another at his waist. A third he held across his face.

Then, taking a deep breath of air, he flung open the bathroom door and hurled himself into a wall of flame.

Part 2

Chapter Sixteen

It was the wind that woke her. It was full of sand and stinging hot and yet, each particle of sand that blew against her skin was like a tiny, tingling penetration. Indecent and invigorating.

Her first thought was for the incense burner. It was clutched inside her fist, gripped so tightly that the swirls and loops of its indentations were imprinted in her palm. Quickly, she hid the treasured object inside a pocket of her jeans.

Then she tried to determine the extent of her injuries.

She hurt all over. There was the physical pain from Arthur's beating and then the other kind—perhaps worse—the despair of realizing what kind of man it was she'd slept with these past nights, what kind of man she'd been in love with.

A maniac. A monster.

Gingerly she explored her face with her fingers, trying to determine how badly she'd been hurt. The physical damage, at least, she could do something about. The rest—that would take longer.

To her relief, she found her nose and teeth intact, but there was a tender swollen area that extended from below her left eye to the middle of her cheek and a damp place near the back of her head where a clump of hair had been torn out. Nothing worse, however, and for that she was grateful.

She got to her feet, brushing off her torn clothing. She felt eyes on her. A bearded bedouin was staring at her from behind a donkey's dappled flanks. Man and beast made not a sound, but a slow and almost imperceptible thrusting on the man's part, a look of stoic boredom on the donkey's countenance, told her the nature of the mute transaction.

Such acts weren't to Val's taste, and yet she had to force herself to look away. The sand was nipping at her flesh like lovers' kisses, the wind hotly seductive as it dervished through her hair.

At first glance at her surroundings, it appeared to Val that she was still inside the city of Taroudannt, looking up at its earthen, crenelated walls, its decaying medieval ramparts behind which were stacked box-like dwellings, one upon the next, like something a child might erect with building blocks. But for the bearded sodomite with his equine mate, the streets seemed strangely empty. Only the evidence of commerce—huge burlap bags of grain, their contents in big golden piles upon the ground, bright yellow *babouche* or slippers, tapestries, and vegetables, and the pervasive scents of butter, couscous and spices—argued for some semblance of normal city life.

From somewhere in the winding, shadowed streets, a chime echoed. Its silvery tones shivered through Val's body. Its vibrations pleasured heart and lungs and entrails. The sound came again, melodic, light. Val leaned against a wall, flustered by her body's unequivocal response to the sound.

A parrot flew by above—a gaudy slash of green and scarlet against searing blue sky—and the sight brought delight that was almost unbearable in its intensity. Nor were simple, every-day sensations less capable of inspiring ecstasy. The odor of bread baking, of overripe persimmons and citrus smells and almonds, of musky human sweat that wafted from the cloistered doorways as she passed—each was author to an exquisite sensitivity of mind and loins, making of each pore a tiny vulva, ravenous for more.

She wandered the maze-like streets and tunneled corridors, aware of others who observed her with avid, hungry gazes, always remaining just out of sight.

Occasionally, in the rapid turning of a corner, the sudden glance behind her back, Val was positive she glimpsed some of the City's inhabitants. It was difficult, if not impossible, however, to keep her concentration focused—when the slap of her sandaled feet on paving stones, the metallic ting of chimes, the gold threads in an ornately woven rug glimpsed in an open courtyard wrung such sensual delight that she felt exhausted, frazzled, giddy with the unnatural opulence of her surroundings.

As her wanderings led her deeper into the labyrinthine streets, Val caught sight, here and there, of other people: an old woman lying splay-legged in an alleyway, her grizzled, thinly furred sex exposed. She held a musical instrument, a long flute-like thing with a curved end, which she simultaneously used to play and penetrate herself, moaning out the notes as she played herself to orgasm.

Beyond her, Val saw a queue of people bringing their own dough to be baked in a central oven, a practice she'd observed in Fez as well. Only after watching for a moment did she realize that, as they waited in the line to bake their bread, each also kissed and fondled the one in front and some of the women had lifted up their skirts, the better to accomodate the men behind them.

At another intersection, the narrowness of the convergence forced Val to step around a copulating trio, two men and a young woman locked in silent rut, one penetrating the woman's cunt, the other buggering her in an almost somnambulistic torpor. They barely moved as Val passed by, but the sex-scent wafting off them was enough to make her reel, her internal muscles clenching and releasing with contractions.

Still farther on, an archway opened up into a courtyard where two naked women embraced within the rippling shallows of a fountain, one sucking on the other's breasts while the first leaned back and spread her legs, the better to allow the cascade of water access to her clitoris. And there was the goateed man she passed who grunted and sighed out ecstacies as he made love to an ornately painted gourd, an aperture carved out of its pulpy meat to allow for such conveniences. He took no note of Val's presence, but bucked and thrust arrhythmically, the gourd's surface already slicked with evidence of previous man-vegetable love.

A dozen or so yards on, Val came upon a square devoted to magicians, storytellers, and oddities of every sort: here a tattooed boy made fire caper up and down his arms, then stroked his erect penis with the flames. A nude woman whose only covering was the strawberries and lemons sewn into her skin did a slow, lewd dance. A dark-skinned man picked dates and olives off the ground with a prehensile penis. Another bent his ten-inch cock backward and belabored his own anus.

At length, she forced herself along, although weariness was leaching at her enthusiasm for further exploration. Indeed, many of the people she encountered seemed depleted, slacked. Even some of those who copulated with each other did so not with the natural frenziedness of lust, but in a kind of stupor, like lewd sleepwalkers who, upon colliding with each other in a darkened hall, engage in mating more from habit than desire and without ever being aroused sufficiently to waken fully.

As the afternoon wore on toward dusk, she became aware of moving shadows, denizens of the City creeping out to find each other, meeting and merging with scarcely so much as a cry before interlocking lips and loins. Yet even then there was less a sense of passion than of a famished mutual feeding upon each other. Sometimes the wraith-lovers interrupted their mating to follow Val a pace or two, but they were slow and clumsy, their unsavory caresses easy to elude. More than once, she gingerly intruded on an embrace to ask about Majeed, but the inhabitants of the City seemed to understand no language but the one of touch and offered her no answers but their own slicked cocks and cum-encrusted thighs and parted, pungent vulvas.

The streets grew steeper, narrower. Hoping for an overview of the dizzying maze in which she wandered, Val climbed several flights of stone stairs up to a high, flat rooftop. From here she could see that the entire area was veined with *derbs*, narrow cul-de-sacs and pathways between windowless walls leading off from the main thoroughfare.

The breeze shifted and brought with it an abominable odor. Looking down upon the roof below, she saw a tannery where animal skins were soaked in stinking vats full of greenish liquid before being transferred to a row of dark, dank rooms. Here silent figures pulled the fur with ghoulish zeal, then stretched and beat the skin while others took the opportunity to yank their own hard meat, so that the smell of cum co-mingled with that of the tanning juices. The very repugnance of the place was sickeningly seductive.

Val didn't linger long. She crossed over to another roof and descended via a set of ladders to a convergence of streets through which she had not yet passed. Here she came upon a marketplace little different in outer appearance from those she had encountered in Moroccan cities of more conventional a nature.

Only many of the wares displayed, in addition to the normal items such as embroidery, silks and brocades, cedarwood and spices and gem-encrusted swords, were a departure from the usual—on one blanket, a treasury of dildos in every size and shape, on the next, a sadist's spree of whips and handcuffs and collars.

The area was the most densely populated Val had yet found.

Men and women, some wrapped head to toe in flowing white

djellabas, others in various stages of undress, browsed among vendors offering sizzling, stuffed aubergines, nipple clamps, perfumes and strings of fragrant sausages. Street musicians played double-reed pipes and rattled drums, obeying a scale all their own.

Across the way, a young man with a dark stubbly beard and hair long and blond as Disney's Cinderella provided a more unique distraction. He sprawled supine, his mouth plugged with a gigantic dildo which he offered up, beckoning to passersby to sit upon his face and take their pleasure there. He didn't lack for business; a line had formed and both sexes took their turn lowering themselves upon his phallus-mouth.

Val paused to watch the spectacle. A woman whose arms and legs resembled sausages of dimpled fat had hoisted up her skirt and lowered herself upon the proffered penis. She bounced jauntily, an expression of delighted greed upon her pan-flat face.

Then it seemed to Val the woman lost her balance and plopped down hard with her full weight. Nor did she attempt to rise again but sat as though resting on a stool, her enormous buttocks spread out in twin mounds over her suddenly unwilling partner's face.

The man beneath her began to struggle. His tanned and hirsute legs thrashed out. His fists beat on the fat woman's flanks, then scooped up handfuls of dirt which he flung in the general direction of her face. It won him nothing but her laughter.

Surely, Val thought, this couldn't be what it appeared. The man below the fat woman was in danger of suffocating—or even strangling if her weight forced the dildo out of her vagina and down his throat.

The man being squashed continued to buck and flail without the success. Meanwhile, the woman rested with the expression of a pleasured Buddha, arms folded Sumo wrestler-style across her ample chest. Those waiting in line to take their turn with the man were rapidly dispersing, evidently unperturbed by what was taking place.

Val could contain herself no longer. She rushed forward and grabbed one of the woman's porcine wrists. "You're suffocating him, can't you see that? Stand up!"

The woman glowered at Val and stood with unexpected swiftness, skirt swirling in a rush of fabric to her feet as she stepped aside. The man whom she had pinned spat out the dildo, worked his jaw. Blood trickled from the corners of his mouth. Val saw the reason he could so well accomodate the dildo—he had no teeth, and, judging from his youth, she guessed that they had probably been extracted.

"Are you all right?" she said, bending down to him.

Suddenly, women clad in dark, baggy garments came running to surround the still-dazed man. Their eyes were wild, their faces hellish with black and scarlet face-paint. In their hands they brandished knives and clubs. Their howls rose up in a frenzied ecstacy as they descended on the unfortunate man, who had barely risen to his feet before they were upon him.

One painted woman swung her club against the side of the toothless man's head. He toppled sideways and was seized and carried off by a half-dozen others.

A man watching the melee from the sidelines picked up a stone and threw it at one of the women. Another found a clay water jug and hurled that.

Someone grabbed Val's arm. She whirled and saw a cinnamon-skinned woman with kohl-smudged eyes and garish facial tattoos. Her nose was pierced through the septum with a gold ring the size of a dime. A similar ring pierced her eyebrow.

"Run!" she ordered in French, revealing the glint of metal posts that penetrated her tongue.

"Why?" said Val. "*Qu'est-ce qui ce passe?* What's going on?"

But by now more by-standers had gathered and were throwing stones and other objects at the fleeing mirauders.

The kohl-eyed woman hissed, "Come on. They'll try to kill you, too, if they see his blood on you."

There wasn't time for Val to explain the bloodstains on her face and clothing were her own, suffered at the hands of a psychopathic lover. Nor did she imagine that this explanation would carry much credibility with the rapidly assembling mob.

The woman tugged at her. "Run!"

A stone struck Val in the side. She needed no further motivation, but went with her would-be rescuer. They darted into an alleyway so dim with shadow that Val could barely see, then executed a twisting path, turning into other alleys, some so narrow that they allowed for little more than the width of a pair of shoulders.

The cinnamon-skinned woman moved with such unerring speed that Val had trouble keeping up. At one point, when she decided that no one was in pursuit, she decided to let the group go on without her. The woman came back and grabbed her hand.

"Hurry!"

Val pulled back. With the immediate danger past, she was

becoming aware once again of the pervasive sense of arousal that infiltrated every pore, was stimulated by every sight and syllable. In fact, with her adrenalin racing, it seemed to her the degree of sensory excitement had been turned up a notch. Even the beating of her heart seemed to pulse with the tremor of orgasm.

"No," she said and pushed the woman away. "I don't know who you are or where you're taking that man or why. I want no part of this."

With no change of expression on her tattooed face, the woman pulled out a knife and held it across Val's throat.

"We took him," she said, "for the same reason that I'm taking you. To make you one of us."

Chapter Seventeen

In the dream, he sank beneath deep water into lung-piercing cold. Miss Lee was leaning over him, in full and gaudy drag. She pressed her vermillion lips to his, breathed bubbles down his throat. Tiny spotted fish swished after one another, in and out of her eyesockets. Her chin was festooned with barnacles, her fingers encrusted with corals. She grinned and where her tongue had been, a lobster flailed its crimson claws.

Her fetid bubbles filled his lungs, caused his chest to rise and fall in painful spasms.

He tried to hold his breath, let go and die.

Impossible.

He wanted death, but death apparently did not want him.

Nor did the phantom figure of Miss Lee wish him to have it.

Yet.

All he had now was agony.

Breen opened his eyes to try to find the exact location of the pain, but the suffering extended over his entire body, everywhere the flames had kissed and lapped him. And they had touched him everywhere, like the caresses of an avid lover bent on licking every inch of skin, every wet internal membrane.

"Help me."

The sounds that came out were not recognizable as words, merely a whispery croaking.

His vocal cords—were they burned, too? He remembered dashing through the fire, while it seethed around him like something living, rabid. He remembered the towel on his head coming off, his hair catching fire and, looking down, seeing all the hair burned off his chest and the flesh black and smoking.

Like an ambulatory shish kebab, he'd run through the hallway toward the stairs, screaming and stumbling, but the stairs already seethed with flame. Smoke seared his lungs. He'd gotten down on hands and knees, crawling across a floor so hot that pieces of his burned flesh adhered to it. Finally he'd found an open door near the end of the corridor.

Smoke filled the room, but at least nothing inside was burning.

He'd crawled inside, slammed the door, and made it to the window, where he'd tried desperately to attract attention from the milling crowd below. His voice was gone by then, however, and smoke must have obscured him from their sight. No one had looked his way.

He'd gone to lift a chair, thinking to throw it from the window and, if that failed to get attention, to hurl himself after it, but the smoke he'd inhaled was smudging out his senses one by one by now, and his strength had burned away along with much of his skin. The last thing Breen remembered was lying on the floor, gazing up at a pitcher on a table by the bed, wondering if it contained water.

He had reached toward the pitcher, and it exploded into silver pinwheels, which in their turn, faded into nothingness, leaving him to grasp at only blackness.

"Help me."

He tried to move. His raw skin screamed. He was shivering uncontrollably.

It seemed odd to him at first that a man as badly burned as he must be should feel cold, but then he realized he was also a man missing his skin. He shut his eyes and moaned.

They'll come soon. Someone will come.

He'd heard the sirens off and on as he lapsed in and out of consciousness. Surely some sort of firefighting equipment was on the scene. Even now firemen must be entering the building, searching for the trapped and missing. Only a matter of time before they got through the fire on the stairs.

Only a matter of time...unless the fire got there first.

"Help me!"

A period of time passed that, from Breen's desperate perspective, might have been a minute or eternity. Then he heard footsteps coming up the stairs, slow and soft and scuffling.

"In here!"

Whomever was approaching came alone. At the top of the stairs, the footsteps ceased. Breen screamed again—or tried to—terrified that his potential rescuer might have encountered flames and been turned back.

But no, after a brief pause, the steps resumed, scraping the floor, furtive like a great snake sliding.

A door further up the hall was opened, the room apparently examined, the door shut again.

So help was on the way, thought Breen. Someone going room to room to search for victims.

But he couldn't bring himself to call out for help again. He lay very still now, listening.

The footsteps resumed. They didn't sound like firemens' boots at all, but something softer. Breen wondered if the person searching was another fire victim, someone in better shape than he was, who'd been trapped by the flames and now was venturing out to search for others.

But when every ounce of reason told him he should be crying out for help, he found himself holding his breath, staying silent.

"You're here, aren't you?"

The voice was male and sweet and lyrical, a voice that—had Breen been more conversant with the term—he might have described as compassionate.

"You're still in here. I know you are."

Breen's naked nerve endings pulsed as though immersed in ice. Great tremors racked his spine. It took all his effort to keep his feet and elbows still, to keep the massive shivering from causing his extremities to thump against the floor.

He had no idea what produced this terror, only that what was approaching up the hall—however honey-voiced and reassuring it might sound—was nothing that he wanted to contend with.

As the gently scuffling footsteps approached, Breen lifted himself up on his elbows and tried to drag himself under the bed. Patches of burned flesh on his legs and buttocks scraped loose on the floor. Breen clamped his lips together and choked back his screams.

"In here, aren't you?"

The door was eased inward.

Breen's shudders grew so great it was impossible to keep his body still. His legs and torso flip-flopped like a netted fish.

"Ahh, yes. I thought so. Here."

The man who entered the room where Breen had taken refuge was clearly no firefighter, but neither was he a victim of the blaze, unless he came from some floor higher up, somewhere the fire hadn't touched. He wore loose-fitting trousers and a shirt of fine, pale linen. His hair, black as a crow's but streaked with white billowed down to just below his angular, broad shoulders. His skin was pale and flawless, a powdered corpse.

Only his soot-blackened sandals showed evidence that he'd come through the burning hotel.

Silent and unsmiling, he stared down at Breen.

"So you're still alive. I rather thought you'd be. Those of your kind don't die easily."

Breen's voice came out a rasping croak. "I'm hurt. I need an ambulance."

"Indeed you do. Or, more probably, a hearse."

But he made no move to summon either.

Instead, he bent down and ran a fingernail across Breen's cheek. Breen shrieked. The pain was scalding. Something hung limply from the man's fingertip, like a strip of cellophane or very thin adhesive. Skin, Breen realized.

"It's amazing that you're still alive."

Breen grit his teeth, too preoccupied with withstanding the assault of pain to consider answering.

"I watched you after the woman entered the City. A rift was temporarily opened up when I could see you and rummage through the contents of your little mind. You have a vicious temper. There's half a dozen dead and many injured because of your unnecessary volitility."

Breen took a deep breath. "The fire—where?"

"Oh, don't worry. The fire's been contained. That's why I have to hurry. There'll be men up here before long, but first they're trying to determine if the floor's in danger of collapse. So we have a little time."

Breen grit his teeth. "Get. Me. Help."

"But I *am* here to help you. That's why I came. First, though, there's something that I think you really ought to see."

He crossed the room, removed an oval mirror from the wall, and wiped it clean of soot and grime with a corner of a bedsheet.

Bending down, he held it in front of Breen.

There came a moment when the physical pain was nothing compared to the gut-deep horror and revulsion at the thing that Arthur

Breen saw looking back at him. His burns were deep and covered almost his entire body. The towel he'd used to shield his groin was burned off in places; in other parts it fused to his flesh, a kind of clotted fester of blackened cloth and flesh. The hair was burned off his head, his groin. His ears were gone. As for the rest...

He shut his lashless eyes.

The older man sighed in a facsimile of sympathy. "Can't bear to look, can you? Well, I understand. You were quite a handsome man. Both men and women wanted you. I myself might have wanted you if I hadn't taken my oath of...chastity some time ago. And you were admirably evil. Inventively so."

Breen forced himself to stare into the obsidian eyes framed with shadowed pockets of fatigue. A horrible idea was dawning on him, an idea taken in part from his own fantasies, in part from his mother's oft-repeated prediction about where he was headed if he didn't mend his ways.

"I'm dead, aren't I? I'm dead, and you're...Satan."

For a moment, it appeared the gaunt man was going to laugh, but he contained it, the way a magnanimous host might choose to overlook a guest's blatant gaucherie. He bent down toward Breen.

His pale and haggard face seemed freighted with immense wisdom and great sadness and yet, below it all, ran an undercurrent of bemusement that frightened Breen most of all.

"Nonsense, my friend. You've read too many religious tracts. I'm not the Devil and you're not dead. In fact, you're very much alive. For now. Unfortunately, you haven't much longer to remain that way. Your burns are quite severe, and I doubt that Taroudannt has much in the way of burn. However—" and here the hint of mirth beneath the grim features burst into a resplendent, terrifying smile— "there is a way out of your predicament, if you're willing to consider it."

He bent down close, so Breen could hear.

"My name is Dominick Filakis, and I'm here to make you an offer."

Chapter Eighteen

"Run!" yelled the cinnamon-skinned woman, whose mane of disheveled hair hung past her waist. The hair was deeply waved, dark brown in places, in others, white as lime. Her eyes were dark ceramic beads recessed within her skull. She brandished her knife against Val's neck. "The crowd will kill you if you stay here!"

They fled through a maze of circuitous alleyways, beneath arches inundated with gloom. As she ran, Val considered her options. If she broke away, she could probably outrun her would-be captor and escape into the tumble of cubist-like dwellings. But what if the crowd from the marketplace was, indeed, still in pursuit? And how did she know whatever hiding place she chose might not prove just as dangerous?

They continued their flight through the warren of dark, narrow passageways until they reached a cul-de-sac from which there appeared to be no exit. Someone reached down and unlatched a door concealed behind a stairway to reveal an opening just large enough for one person to shimmy through.

"Get in." Val waited her turn and then slid down several feet onto a dirt floor. She blinked in the gloomy half-light, tasting dirt.

Getting to her feet, she took in her surroundings. The room was circular, no more than eight feet high, stuffy and windowless. Most of the scant light came from torches set in alcoves along the wall and from a brazier of coals that glowed over in one corner. Pallets of some satiny material were pushed up against the walls.

In the center of the room, the massive woman who had captured the Toothless Man was now chaining him to a metal peg, aided by several others who held the struggling captive.

Looking around the room, as if to make sure the others watched, she reached down and pinched the man's scrotum between her thumb and forefinger, eliciting a wail.

In response, the women uttered triumphant yips and fell upon each other in a frenzy so abandoned they might have been dislocating each other's limbs as much as making love. Determined hands removed what was left of Val's clothing. The woman with eyes like ceramic tiles grabbed her behind the neck and forced a kiss. The rows of metal studs that pierced her tongue clicked against Val's teeth. She smelled sweat and olive oil and the salty musk of menstrual blood.

"My name's Simone," the cinnamon-skinned woman said, her words colored with a heavy French accent.

Val said her own name. Then, nodding to the man in chains, "What will you do with him?"

"What do you care?" Simone said, her mouth stretching in a grin that made the bronze skin across her cheekbones tighten like drumheads. "For now, we're celebrating."

Her tongue explored the inside of Val's mouth, the rows of studs providing cold contrast to the softness of the surrounding flesh. Along Simone's bare thighs, tattoos of undulating serpents ended in tight, henna-colored coils atop each jutting hipbone. Her waist-long hair fell over Val's face and breasts. Wavy tendrils entered her mouth. It was like being smothered in wheat.

Two other women joined them, one partnering Simone. Val shut her eyes. She lost track of whom she made love with. Around the room, groups of lovers disengaged, reformed and recombined to make a squirming tapestry of flesh. Val found herself with a grey-haired crone with sagging dugs and wildly corkscrewed hair, her flesh crepey and papyrus thin. Her cracked and talonous nails plucked at Val's breasts.

"I worked at Miss Edwina's in London for eighteen years," she cackled, as though this information was of great significance. "I worked at Miss Edwina's. I fucked the Duke of Edinburgh, the Prince of Wales."

The tang of bile and rotting teeth spilled across Val's face. A carrion-sweet, diseased smell seeped from the old woman's pores. Blood clots floated in the yellow-tinged whites of her eyes.

"I worked at Miss Edwina's. Didn't you work there? Was one there once, a grey-eyed one, who looked like you, who..."

Val pulled away. The crone pursued on hands and knees. Her fingers, mottled like gnarled, twisted roots, groped at Val's feet.

"Let me lick your pretty feet. I'll suck your toes. Come on, I've done it for crown princes. You'll feel it all the way up to your clit."

Val drew her feet back, shook her head. The hag's pinched mouth contorted, and her jaw worked as though she were trying to chew something tough and sticky. "Are you rejecting me? You can't do that, you know. Not here. It's not allowed. Don't you know who I am? I worked at Miss Edwina's..." Her thin voice rose in trembly rage. "Jealous, jealous, that's what you are. Still jealous over that millionaire from Lebanon. I know you! I remember!"

"Hush." Someone rolled the woman over, lapped her withered genitals until she crooned.

"Crazy bitch," Val muttered.

"Have some respect. She used to be the highest paid whore in London," someone said. "Besides she won't live much longer."

Enormous breasts flattened out against Val's back. She turned around and was pulled into the pillowy embrace of the Junoesque Amazon.

"I'm Myra," the woman said. "Welcome." She leaned down and kissed Val between the legs.

Sheened with sweat, Myra's abundant flesh felt warm and slick, like greasy dough. Her small mouth, like a ruby valentine, rained moist kisses. Her touch was delicate, almost restrained, compared to the other women's, but her blue eyes were lusterless and full of greed, squinty and cold as a myopic shark. Val had never sexed with a person of this woman's size. She felt a moment's panic of being submerged, absorbed in her sheer volume.

Even so, their love-making was not without its own strange allure. With no other lover had Val experienced such a plenitude of bodily nooks and crannies and fleshy rolls, pungent folds for tonguing, deep crevices for sucking, a vast and wanton geography of softly sloping, overlapping hillocks, like a snowy mountainside melting toward an avalanche.

She was fascinated by Myra's freakishly abundant flesh, in her balloon breasts with their huge, cherry-tipped nipples, the folds of fat that hung from her thighs like kneepads in some high risk sport, the fatty wattles that joined torso and head. This lack of definition aroused in her a desire to probe and penetrate, to dig for bone and sinew like an archeologist excavating a buried city.

Determined to know Myra somewhere her true shape wasn't disguised with fat, Val eased apart the bulging thighs and pushed her head between them, but here, too, she found that Myra's body conformed to no normal physiognomy. Her tongue explored an alien and maimed terrain—thick ridges of scar tissue in place of labia, a healed-over excavation where the clitoris would have been. The rest was sewn tightly shut, but for a tiny slit hardly large enough through which to slide a dime.

The space left open was probably adequate for Myra to urinate and menstruate, but nothing else.

The sight made Val shiver uncontrollably. She tried to pull away.

Myra reached down and grabbed her hair. "What's wrong? You don't want to put your mouth there?"

Val answered honestly, "It's ugly. It's...disgusting...that someone would do that to you."

"I was eight years old," said Myra, "growing up in Cairo. My two aunts and my mother held me down. They thought cutting off my sex organs would make me pure."

"Can't you at least be...widened?"

"It doesn't matter. I'd still feel no pleasure there. This is what gives me pleasure."

She pushed Val away and shouted something in a tongue Val didn't understand. With sighs and groans, the fondling women uncurled and moved apart.

From a recessed nook in the earthen wall, Myra withdrew an enormous dildo fastened to a harness-like contraption designed to fit around a woman's waist and between her legs. She strapped it on while several of the women wrestled the captive onto his hands and knees and parted him.

With a sound like someone pulling off a muddy boot, Myra rammed the dildo home. The Toothless Man stayed silent, but long shudders traveled up and down his body so that his arms wobbled, and the muscles in his thighs convulsed. His eyes squeezed shut as tightly as if thorns had been thrust into them.

Myra's buggery was prolonged and ardent. When she withdrew, the man collapsed face-first into the dirt. The reek of blood permeated the room.

Other women took their turn, no less enthused than Myra, but with considerably less bulk to put behind their thrusts. The captive submitted to this awful stretching silently at first, but then began to scream and beg for mercy.

"Now you," a dark-skinned woman said to Val. Her eyes were the shape and color of pecans, her lips full and shiny as black leather roses. So numerous were the piercings on her face that her words were accompanied by a metallic tinkling as the many ornaments in her cheeks and lips clacked together.

She pushed the befouled dildo and the harness toward Val.

"Go on," said Simone.

Val shook her head. "No."

"Don't you want to?"

"Of course not."

But what a lie that was. Desire owned her. Her fingers tingled with anticipation, her heart pumped out adrenalin at the prospect of gratuitously inflicting pain.

"Don't worry. He's enjoying it," the pecan-eyed woman said.

Val doubted that. The pleas and sobs that issued from the captive now could only have been fathered by agony and fear.

"If he were enjoying it," said Val, "none of us would bother doing it."

The pecan-eyed girl reacted with a peal of bell-like laughter made more melodious by the way it caused her facial ornaments to ping and click.

Val took the phallus, pulled the belt taut around her waist and adjusted the center strap between her legs. The inside of the crotch strap was lined with tiny spurs, which came into instant contact with her clitoris. The slightest motion caused a gentle mashing and massaging of her genitals.

Some others got the captive on his knees again. Val aimed her hips and entered him. She clutched the man's sweat-sodden hair, thrust and ground her hips with vigor she could neither conceal nor countenance in a sex act that was one part lust to two parts cruelty.

Her own remembered pain flooded back, but with it came a rush of rage that empowered her to greater violence. She longed to stop and make amends. And couldn't.

The captive screamed. Val climaxed.

And crawled back to Simone, who kissed her mouth and wiped a strand of damp hair from her eyes. "You see now what it feels like? That the thrill of rape is not exclusive to one gender."

Val turned her face away from the center of the circle where the captive was undergoing yet more zestful sodomy. She drew her knees up to her chin and tried to scrunch her body closed, to use her arms to bind her legs and torso into a small and tidy box.

Her empty stomach roiled. Her throat was clogged with smoke and unshed tears.

The captive let out a stream of wailed entreaties. Several of the women fell upon him and turned him on his back. They held his legs apart while Myra gathered up his genitals and bound them with thick cord.

The prisoner struggled wildly. Myra looked over at Simone, who relinquished her knife.

Val looked away. When she turned back, Myra was crouched in front of her, an executioner's smile upon her face, excitement gleaming in the cold corruption of her tiny eyes.

"For you," she said and handed Val the knife.

Chapter Nineteen

The strange new world in which Breen found himself was not entirely different from the landscape of his dreams, his darkest and most private fantasies.

Nothing was concealed here, nothing camouflaged. Lust infested every breath and movement. Desire resonated in the pitch and timbre of every bird note, every swish of fabric and whispered word.

Nothing was hidden.

Therein, he realized, lay both the allure and the terror of the place. Breen had lived his life in hiding. He had crafted an identity of urbane good taste and wit and well-bred sophistication to deflect attention from the sociopathic personality underneath. He had learned to counterfeit love, so no one would suspect he was incapable of feeling it, had taught himself to feign tenderness when he had little sense of what it was or why anyone required it. He had donned personalities with the ease of a reveler at Mardi Gras trying on masks. He had lived among his fellow men and passed, not just for sane, but of possessing a certain masculine elegance and beauty.

Now that was over.

Now the frail pretense of sanity was no longer necessary, the charade of what passed for normal human emotion no longer required. As for his appearance, not the rags that he was wearing nor any form of face paint could conceal the ravages that the inferno had wrought upon him. The pitiable state in which he found himself was revealed for all to see. He had come through hell and been made hideous, but he was also strangely free.

And so, clearly, were his fellow citizens in this vast and on-going debauchery.

In the bazaar, not far from the foul-smelling tanneries, an old man approached him, naked except for the fishhooks skewering his chest and groin and connected by a webwork of chains. Breen flicked a finger across the hooks, causing a ripple effect that made the entire decoration tremble, the pierced skin rising into tiny peaks. The old man directed at Breen a gap-toothed, salivating leer, then was brought up short when he took in the full disfigurement of the creature that grinned back at him. He turned and loped away, chains jingling like some kind of living decoration at an S/M Christmas party.

Breen debated as to whether he wanted to pursue, decided that such prickly and emaciated quarry wasn't worth the effort.

Nor did he feel much beyond curiosity for the red-haired dwarf who'd split his penis into halves and pierced each of the two misshapen heads with rings and metal rods and was busily engaged in performing yet another piercing with the aid of a small mirror held up beneath his scrotum. The trollish oddity eyed Breen with slit-eyed suspicion, each of his twin penises sporting erections from which dangled a jangling display of metal paraphernalia.

But, like the old man, he scuttled off, cackling to himself in some babble of his own devising before Breen could initiate an intimate transaction.

In his haste, the dwarf had dropped his mirror, which Breen pounded into tiny glassine slivers with a stone before continuing on his way.

Not soon enough, of course.

In spite of his efforts not to look, Breen had peeked at his own image, which was not yet obliterated when he brought the rock down, but replicated in each fragment, erased only when he pounded the remnants into powder and threw his head back in a wail of grief and rage and self-pity.

He was beyond maimed. He was unspeakable.

The worst part, he was discovering, wasn't his scorched and hairless dome, resembling a rotting eggplant, his peeling deep-fried forearms, or even the condition of his penis, whose crispy folds now yielded rank-smelling pus instead of semen and from which passing even a few drops of urine caused a breath-stopping, heart-palpitating anguish.

The worst part was the mirrors.

This place possessed an abundance of them, he was discovering, for the inhabitants of the City took great pleasure in observing their own antics. Likewise, the taste of the voyeur had been amply catered to.

And so, often when he least expected it, rounding a curve in an alleyway or perusing the bazaar to see what new obscenities were on display, he'd find himself confronting a visage of such horror that he would have to touch his face to convince himself the creature in the mirror was really he, that all charm and debonair good looks, all masculine allure had been burned away and that what remained was this charred and raw red nightmare.

The monster in the mirror was really he.

Worse, though, even than this was the reactions of other people, a squeamishness made still more galling in this place with no shortage of the maimed and weird and freakish.

People gawked and stared and murmured as he passed. In a place where promiscuity was God, no one sought out his attentions or seemed eager to reciprocate an overture.

He tried consoling himself with the knowledge that, he was at least, alive. That surely Filakis had been right. He'd been a doomed man, guaranteed an awful death if he'd remained in the smoldering hotel in Taroudannt.

But maybe I'd have been better off...

He shook that notion off. He feared death, would keep it at bay at any cost. Even if the price was coming through the terrifying green flame to be the underling—Filakis hadn't used that word, but that was what it came to—of an anorexic despot whose sexual proclivities remained outside the ken of even he.

An arrangement of mutual benefit and convenience, that was how the skull-faced Turk had summed it up.

Breen would stay alive—thanks to what kind of sorcery Breen couldn't know—in his new and radically altered form and in return would be available to serve Filakis' needs.

"My whims," the Turk had told him, his eyes slit-thin and sad, heavy-lidded in a facsimile of bereavement, "are minimal. They also coincide with some of your own tastes. For the most part, you may do as you will—as long as what you will to do amuses me."

What did that mean, Breen wondered. Was the Turk able to spy upon him, even now, as he moved through the shadow world of tunnel-like streets and featureless mud brick dwellings through whose narrow windows bewildered or beseeching faces sometimes peered out at him from behind carved wooden grills? Did Filakis smile as Breen paused to thrust the stubs of three burned fingers into the vagina of a woman who spread her legs and lips to be fucked or fondled by all passersby? (She was among the few who didn't flinch away from Breen's caress, bound as she was by chains set into metal posts). And was Filakis titillated when Breen observed a bit of flesh peeling off his rib cage and plucked it loose, popped the raw morsel into his mouth and experienced a small frisson of horror and, worse, an appalling titillation?

It mattered not. Breen had accepted the offer of the City's high priest, its fallen Pope. Agreeing, after all, was no great feat. He'd spent a decade agreeing with Miss Lee. When necessary he could fall back into that mode, appear dotty and docile as an old man on Thorazine.

When necessary...

Rounding a corner in the maze, he came upon a couple locked together, lips fastened in a frantic kiss as though all the breathable air in the world were contained within the other's mouth. Long necks, white and supple, an elegance of form and limb that, in another lifetime, Breen might have found quite ravishing. Their cocks, both handsomely erect, rubbed heads like two rams preparing to do battle.

Breen gaped and licked his rare-beef lips.

The young men, aware of an observer, looked up at the same time. Identical blue eyes shining from identically shaped alabaster faces. Seeing Breen, identical expressions of appalled disgust that were doubly mirrored in each of the twins' angelic faces.

Breen experienced a moment of such scalding shame that it was unendurable and transformed itself immediately into rage. He made a menacing gesture, which put an end to the siblings' love-making and sent them scurrying like albino ferrets through the nearest doorway.

Amuse me.

Was Filakis skulking somewhere close, observing even now?

Breen steeled himself and looked down at his naked torso. But for a scrap of fabric around his waist, he was nude. In his first days here, he'd attempted to procure some clothes—money, evidently, wasn't necessary, as most things seemed free for either the taking or the plundering—but even the lightest whisper of silk rent pain from every pore.

So he'd experimented and found, miraculously enough, that he was able to touch flesh, immerse himself in other people's skin, without suffering the agonies that other contact gave him. Perhaps the delights of the erotic canceled out the pain. He didn't know.

He knew only that one thought alone had dominated his thoughts since his horrendous transformation.

Val.

This was her fault. It was she whose actions had rendered him unfit for human eyes, revolting even in this place where the most obscene debaucheries were commonplace and public.

It was she who'd robbed him of his seductive body and aristocratic face, the very qualities that it made it easy to attract prey, easier still to dispatch them. His victims had rarely ever suspected anything. Because he'd been a handsome man who spoke with a cultivated voice that bore no trace of his humble origins. Because he could discuss Nietzsche and quote Baudelaire and looked like what most men wanted to see in their mirrors and most women and quite a few men wanted to find in their beds.

Had looked like.

And she was here. Somewhere. Locked in some carnal congress, impaled on a dildo ridged with studs, fucked senseless by a mob—somewhere she was here and he would find her.

He ached to put his hands on someone, something.

He paused next to a cart piled high with persimmons, plucked one of the purple, plum-like fruits and sank his teeth into it. The fruit was unripe, astringent, but he ate three more, desirous less of the bitter taste than the sensuality of biting, chewing, swallowing. He had not been hungry, really hungry, since he'd come here. He was too preoccupied with adjusting to his new appearance, too consumed with the potential for satisfying appetites other than hunger to give much heed to the rumbling of his stomach.

But now he ate, in haste and anger, cramming the fruit between his blistered lips until the juice dripped off his chin and dribbled down his scorched chest and bits of red pulp and seeds flew from his mouth like gory spittle.

One hunger briefly satisfied, he then went in search of someone to fill a greater need.

He found her sprawled out on the ground, her long hair fanned across her face, arched beneath a leggy wolfhound in the center of a shadowed courtyard. She'd placed two velvet pillows underneath her rump, the better to accommodate the dog. The glistening ruby stalk of the beast's pencil-slender penis slid in and out between her thighs. She reached up, clutching the matted fur. The animal snarled and snapped at her face.

With Breen approaching, the cur disengaged and fled. The woman remained on her back, eyes close, legs parted in expectation of another phallus, human or otherwise, to take its place.

Breen knelt down and roughly flipped her over onto her hands and knees.

"You want a dog. Then you must like it doggie-style."

She tried to scuttle away. He yanked her back by her long hair and straddled her, clutched the root of his erection with one charred hand and tried to plunge it into her.

"All right, don't be so rough," she said through gritted teeth. "I'm into beasts, not pain."

"Well, I'm a beast who loves inflicting it," said Breen, but his damaged voice came out a guttural croak, making it unlikely that the woman even understood what he had said.

Apparently convinced of his determination, though, she ceased resisting, reached back with one hand and tried to guide him in.

Breen's cockhead disappeared inside her. Pain only minimally muted by desire rocketed through him, stole his breath and, in its nearly unbearable intensity, made his erection pulse still harder. He stopped pushing. The dog-fucker turned to frown at him.

"Go on," she panted. "Do it."

An inch of hard-on throbbed inside her pussy. Breen ached to ram it home. But at what price?

He pulled back gingerly, watching, horrified, as even that minute amount of friction caused skin to flake and slough away. Folds of skin hung from the foreskin like a condom only partially peeled off. Hatred hotter than the fire that had maimed him rose to a crescendo of white noise inside his head.

Her fault.

The woman, aroused now by his partial entry, tried to back herself onto him. Enraged, he jerked her head back harder and was appalled as pieces of his palm were left glistening in her hair like red-black beetles.

She squirmed and yanked her head free. She took Breen's wrists and placed his hand atop one breast. Three of the fingers of that hand were stubs that ended in black cauterized wounds below the second joint. The thumb was gone entirely. What cupped the woman's breast resembled less a living hand than something excavated from a Phaeronic tomb.

When she saw what she was touching, Breen's would-be partner made a hissing sound of fear and disgust. She pulled away too quickly and won a souvenir—a flap of skin from the head of his charred penis went with her. Pain etched indelibly with a hideous pleasure seared through Breen. His penis stiffened even as it peeled. Never had he felt such need. He longed to fuck the woman until his dick penetrated her body and burst through her teeth.

The woman scuttled away from him, got to her feet. Breen kicked her in the knee and sent her sprawling. Standing over her, he grabbed her by the hair again and clubbed her with his fist until she sagged, while skin spattered from his knuckles, freckling her breasts bright red.

By the time she regained consciousness, he'd broken out a window in one of the courtyard walls and selected a shard of glass, one end of which he'd wrapped in rags to protect his hand from further mutilation. He didn't let her see the weapon, though, but laid it aside. When she woke up, he had her legs spread and was holding up the fist that had her blood on it.

Passersby took in what was going on, but kept going.

The woman implored someone to help her.

No one offered aid, but a few stopped to watch and masturbate.

"What's your name?"

Breen spoke slowly and with great effort, determined that she understand him, but even then it took him several repetitions, either because his voice was barely human-sounding or she was still dazed enough to make comprehension difficult.

"Your...name?"

"Desiree."

"Ah, how apt. Tell me, Desiree, have you ever had a fist so far up inside you it filled up your womb like a baby waiting to be born?"

She peered up at him in silence, not knowing perhaps what answer might win her further injury.

"No?"

Breen furrowed his brow in a mock frown. "Oh, I doubt that now. I really do. Any woman who'll spread her legs for a hound is probably no stranger to less esoteric sex."

The words came out a garbled croak. Tiny gobbets of flesh spewed from Breen's cracked lips. The woman named Desiree, though she clearly hadn't understood a word, nodded with forced enthusiasm.

"And you'd like it, wouldn't you? Having a hand stretched all the way up inside you, all the way to the elbow?"

She murmured an ascent.

"Good, good. Then you'll enjoy this."

The woman spread her legs accommodatingly.

Only when she realized what it was Breen planned to do to her did her eyes go wide with terror and her screams begin.

Chapter Twenty

Val looked at the blade in her hand and at the Toothless Man, who lay spread-eagled and bound at her feet, his genitals swollen and jutting above the rope that bound them. It was how animals were sometimes gelded, she thought. The pain had to be excruciating.

Yet, a dark part of her, cancerous and seductive, whispered in favor of the knife. She could even justify the action—what might the women do to her if she refused? And what might the experience be like for her, that moment when metal parted flesh and the severing began?

That, in itself, was the final horror—that she could anticipate, even relish, the deed.

Which meant she was no better than the worst of history's butchers.

"If you're going to cut him, do it yourself. I won't." She threw down the knife.

Myra fixed her with a venomous stare. "I told you to..."

"And I told *you*..."

Simone reached past Val and snatched up the weapon. Crouching over the captive, she swung her arm in the motion of one scything grain. There was one terrible scream—then silence, except for the sound of blood spurting. Simone waved her gory prize. Warm droplets struck Val's face.

Simone threw the grisly trophy like a bride tossing the bouquet.

The women flung themselves upon it, fighting like unruly children competing for a handful of tossed sweets.

Myra's tiny eyes were hard as glass shards imbedded in her face. Going to the brazier, she lifted a hot poker from the coals and plunged it onto the wound of the newly-created eunuch. The man made not a sound. The stench of burning flesh filled the low-ceilinged lair.

Val's vision blurred. She realized she'd been holding her breath.

"How could you do that?" she whispered to Simone.

"If I hadn't, Myra would have. Or you."

"No, never."

"Don't be so sure. I said that once myself."

"Is he dead?"

"I doubt it, but he may die soon. When it's done like this, not many live."

Val felt her stomach heaving. She put a hand across her mouth and crawled in the direction of the passageway that led up toward fresh air. But no sooner had she begun to climb up out of the hidden room than hands were reaching for her, pulling her back. Her breasts were pinched and fondled, her body penetrated with hands and polished dildos. Her mind was numb to this excess of touching, focused only on the mutilation she'd just witnessed, but her body had no such compunctions and responded eagerly.

During this forced pleasuring, Myra took Val's toes into her mouth and sucked them one by one. The tickly feeling was delightful, unfamiliar. Val closed her eyes. She heard a metallic click and realized too late that Myra had snapped a cuff around her ankle and connected it to the same chain that had been used to restrain the torture victim.

"What are you doing? Let me go!"

"Don't," whispered Simone. "It's only for a little while—until you get used to things."

"Let me guess: until I realize what I really want is what you want as well."

"It might surprise you, but that's true."

"The man you mutilated might not agree."

Simone tapped her tongue against her teeth. It made a tinny clicking. "If you'd been willing to do the cutting, Myra wouldn't have to chain you."

"I'm not a sadist."

"It didn't look that way when you were fucking him."

"The fucking wouldn't have killed him—being gelded probably will. You said so yourself."

"He came to the City like the rest of us—to have experiences outside the normal realm, to experience arousal that eclipses everything else, every pain and distraction and sorrow. And sometimes what the City offers is painful, too, maybe worse than whatever you were running away from, but it doesn't matter. You're here now. You don't get to choose what happens to you, and neither does he."

"But I don't belong here."

"You came with us, didn't you?"

"But I prefer men."

"And you just had one."

"You know that isn't what I mean."

"Don't worry," said Simone, "you'll have men you may allow to fuck you. But you stay with us."

The Toothless Man died during the night. Several of the women carried his body up to the street. Perhaps they traded it to someone who had a use for mutilated corpses, because they brought back food and wine.

Simone took her share and offered Val a flat hunk of bread and a glass filled with a dark, ruby-colored liquid. Val made a face and waved it away.

"It isn't blood, if that's what you're thinking, for Heaven's sake. We're extreme, but we aren't insane—not like the ones who actually eat flesh. It's only wine."

Val took a bite of bread and sipped the bitter liquid, felt its glow thrill warmly through her body.

"That's better," Simone said. "You need to eat to stay strong. People forget to eat and sleep here. There's no replenishment. That's why there's so much sickness—skeletons trying to copulate, dying men with one last hard-on begging someone to come and sit on their dick, women too exhausted to spread their legs or part their lips still crying out to be fucked. Starvation in the midst of plenty is the rule here."

Val glanced at Myra's porcine bulk as she nibbled butter-slathered bread from between another woman's lips. "She doesn't look in any danger of malnutrition."

"Myra has her own ways of experiencing sex. She doesn't have a clit, but she does have a tongue, and that's her sex organ."

Val chewed the bread and sipped the wine. She thought of flesh and semen. Of Santos and Reza and Majeed.

"I didn't think it would be like this," she said.

"No one does. I didn't."

"Then let me go. Take off the chain."

"They all say that," Simone said. "It's too late now. We need you. And you, believe it or not, need us."

"You can't keep me chained up forever."

"Only until you decide you want to stay with us. That will take less time than you imagine."

Val slapped her hard enough to nick her hand on Simone's eyebrow ring. Simone looked more shocked than injured. Blood beaded in her eyebrow, wended its way to her lips. She tongued it off as though the taste were sweet.

"You'd better learn the rules before you get into real trouble. The City isn't a forgiving place. That's why you ought to be grateful for a chance to join our family."

"That doesn't exactly warm my heart."

"You came here because you wanted to, didn't you?"

"I wanted to come to the City, but not to wind up chained by a bunch of psychotic sexists."

"So you'd rather fuck men than mutilate them? Do you know there're people here who would consider that a perversion?"

She bent down and drew her studded tongue slowly between Val's thighs. Val allowed it, but did not respond. When Simone looked up, dark pubic hairs were caught between her teeth.

"It may not seem like it right now, but we are a family. The only one that most of us have ever had. Just trust me for a while. You'll see that this is much better than being on your own in a place where women get fucked to death every day."

Val shook her head and clenched her thighs together, refusing all Simone's attempts to resume her artful licking. Finally, Simone said, "Get some sleep then. Tomorrow we go back to the desert."

"The desert?" said Val. "What do you mean?"

But Simone had moved away to fondle someone else. The other women were either sleeping now or making subdued love.

Val tried for a while to squeeze her foot through the manacle, but it was hopeless and she soon lay still. No one touched her. No kisses or caresses fed the naked expanse of her skin. She felt alone and small and needy, and her fear of being held against her will was surmounted by a greater one, the fear that she would somehow be shunned, that she would never again be touched or kissed or penetrated. And if that happened, that she would cease to *be*.

That her skin would starve and her heart shrivel.

The primitive depth of the fear shamed her. She curled up on the pallet, trying to ignore the near-by sounds of flesh exploring flesh, and sipped the tears as they slid into her mouth.

As if in a murky dream, she thought, *I wanted to find this place, so I could be free, and I'm less free than ever. What have I done?*

After that, she touched herself until despair gave way to distraction, and she took temporary refuge in sleep.

Chapter Twenty-One

Breen was learning, not just to tolerate the mirrors, but to enjoy them.

He held a mirror between his knees, opened his mouth wide and, using a nailfile filched off a corpse, re-shaped one of his front teeth into a fang.

He could look in the mirror now without turning away in sick despair. No more wasted lamentation for his ravaged appearance. It didn't matter. If lovers didn't flock around him willingly, he'd just take them anyway, replace the courtship faze with force and torture.

Not a bad trade, after all.

And in the meantime, there were things he could do to improve his looks—home dentistry, for one.

While Desiree was still alive, but no longer capable of fleeing, he'd amused himself (worked up an appetite, so to speak) by filing his front teeth and incisors. There'd been some discomfort—not like anyone was there to offer Novocain, after all—but by now pain, to Breen, seemed so much part and parcel of existence that it was like a kind of neural Muzak, a repetitious ditty largely overpowered by the lusher symphony of pleasures he experienced.

He blew enamel dust between his teeth and angled the mirror closer to best admire his impromptu orthodontistry. Slightly simian, but over all, not bad. In his old life, Breen remembered, he'd been a dentist's dream, a stickler for oral hygiene, brushing and flossing and staving off periodontal disease with anal-retentive zeal. Now all he had to worry about was keep the points filed sharp.

He walked over to Desiree and knelt beside her head. Much of her face was already gone, but he tested the biting and tearing quality of his new fangs on what remained and found it excellent, like carrying a scalpel in his mouth.

Her taste, however,—slightly gamier than most human flesh he'd sampled—was beginning to sit badly. Perhaps fucking dogs, he thought, had given her a canine tang.

A tree hung heavy with oranges over the courtyard wall. Breen plucked one, bit through the rind without bothering to peel it, and sucked the fruit dry with several slurps. He tossed the puckered hull away. It landed over one of Desiree's empty eyes, fitting over the socket like a jaunty pirate's patch.

With his cock now in its unfortunate condition, he'd have to rely on his teeth to do the necessary penetrations. They were the only part of him the fire had left untouched, although the tip of his tongue had been badly roasted. A portion of it had fallen off while he was eating Desiree.

The oranges, of course, were merely dessert. Something to clear the palate after the main course. And Desiree had been alive to share much of that meal with him, even though, sadly, she'd declined to participate. Her body—which had finally breathed its last while Breen was nibbling at her ear—lay sprawled in the courtyard where he had found her, sniffed at with no sign of grief by her former, four-legged lover.

Her arm, which he'd severed just above the elbow, was now buried deep in her vagina. The bloody stump protruded from between her legs, making it appear that she was giving birth to a child whose skull had been lopped off.

He continued eating, flinging the empty orange skins away, gobbling down the fruit until his bloated stomach protruded between his rib cage like a shiny pinata ready to be popped by a strongly swung stick.

The sun rose high, drawing black swarms of flies to Desiree, making Breen's burnt flesh throb. He crawled into the shade and lay down across the cool cobblestones. Soon he was spiraling down into a sleep inhabited by thousands of sharp-toothed, spotted fish, and as they bit him, every fish turned into one of Miss Lee's drowned and bulging eyes.

It was dark when Breen awoke from the dream. His throat felt like he'd been screaming. His stomach lurched, and gas passed from his rectum in staccato bursts.

And he was hungry. No, not belly hungry. It was his new teeth, his teeth were hungry. Sharpened now, they ached to bite and tear. The blood throbbing in his gums sang for flesh.

The wind, flecked with sand, scourged his face. The night pulsed with a thousand couplings, a host of depravities. Clumps of bodies, like a single, many-tentacled beast, roiled and grunted in the shadows. Breen made his way among them, ignoring the occasional entreaties that came his way by virtue of the darkness. At night his horribly burned skin and naked scalp were no deterrent to his participation in the on-going orgies. His penis, though, was still swollen purple-black and scorched skin still peeled off at the slightest touch.

Breen noticed the blonde woman lingering beneath an archway because she was one of the unpartnered few. She wore a garment made of scarves wrapped judiciously about her body so that her breasts and genitals were revealed while her shoulders, waist, and thighs were concealed beneath the flowing fabric.

As Breen watched, two men approached her, and he almost withdrew, assuming their intention was to fuck her. He didn't mind a buttered bun, but hated having to stand in line for it.

The men got within a few feet of the woman and stopped as though encountering an impenetrable wall. Words were bantered back and forth. The woman laughed and lifted a breast, aiming it at the taller of the men. A jet of milk arced from her nipple and splattered on his face. It streamed down his forehead and glistened in his heavy brows. He licked it from his lips and chin.

The second man had taken out his cock and was vigorously pumping. The woman bent and bathed it in a stream of milk that mixed with the spurting semen. At that, the first man fell to his knees and commenced to suck the other's streaming organ. The other bent to lick the beads of milk that shimmered on his face.

The woman turned around. Her eyes met Breen's. She beckoned with a slender hand whose moon-illuminated flesh resembled mother-of-pearl. The breeze made her hair dance wildly, a Medusa's crown of writhing, moon-streaked ringlets.

Breen followed her around the courtyard wall, where they lay down beneath the orange tree. She offered him her milk-swollen tits. He put his head between them, breathed in the scent of flowers and fruit, of strawberries drenched in cream.

He rolled her tender nipples between his fingers. His teeth ached to bite and chew.

"Thirsty?" she asked. With both hands she squeezed a breast and shot forth a stream of pale, fierce-smelling liquid.

Breen caught the musky outpouring full in the face. He grimaced and recoiled. Viscous and muscusy, the semen dripped from his hair, drenched his face.

"A good trick," he said, recovering from the shock. "What did you do, bitch, eat so much cock your tits squirt cum?"

He grabbed one of the woman's scarves and laid it across her face. The material was translucent. He could see her darting eyes, the outline of her slightly parted lips beneath the fabric. He pressed it tight, cutting off her air.

Beneath the silk, her mouth curved with amusement. Breen crouched above her, held the fabric tighter until her face was mashed beneath it, the features flattened and distorted like a smeary watercolor.

As he commenced to choke her, she got her hands free and squeezed her breast again. A clear, acidic liquid struck Breen's raw chest and burned along his belly. The tinny background noise of pain that he was learning to ignore swamped his synapses with agony. Red and black flames pinwheeled behind his eyes.

"Bitch!" he screamed when he could find the breath to do it.

He pinned her down, intending now to kill her as painfully as possible, to peel her like an orange with his newly acquired fangs and leave her skinned alive.

But before he could rip her face raw, the woman's body moved and shifted shockingly beneath his hands. Her bones seemed to rearrange themselves, her body to dissolve and flow into some new configuration. Breen had the strange sensation that the wind was blowing her apart beneath his fingers, that she was being reduced to swirling sand and, in that moment when he thought he'd lost her, he felt a surge of grief and panic as though she were a lover being swept away from him forever.

He screamed with rage and drove his fist into the blurry maelstrom that undulated underneath him.

His hand sank wrist-deep into the flux and flow of her fleshy current. For a second, he could see the writhing zebra-patterns of her ribcage embossed upon his knuckles, the outline of her strumming heart like a fluid tattoo upon his wrist, and he yanked his arm free of her transforming body with a shriek.

The creature's hands, spade-shaped now and tufted with bristly hair, swung forward and boxed his head with an explosive force that threatened to drive his eardrums into his cranium and tore out the little hair still clinging to his temples in bloody clumps. A second blow spilled black neon behind his eyes and sent him sprawling in the dirt.

Beneath the scent of blood welling in his mouth, he smelled the spicy tang of cloves and saffron and a pungent hint of garlic.

When he finally dared to open his eyes, the Turk was standing over him, his somber countenance freighted with a mournful weariness that suggested less a sadistic bent than a man fulfilling an unpleasant obligation.

His face contorted suddenly and, without a word he stepped forward and kicked Breen in the throat.

Then his expression became composed and dour again. Without a trace of rancor, he said, "I could kick you until you puke up your own intestines. I could make you wish I'd left you to die in that hotel room in Taroudannt or to suffer in some Moroccan hospital while the doctors try to make you a new face from skin grafted from your ass."

Breen choked for breath and tried to speak.

"How did you...? What happened to the girl?"

"The tart you were in the process of strangling? She was never here. I only made you see me as I wanted to be seen."

Breen forced himself to take deep breaths and tried to recover some of his bravura. No easy task, crumpled naked and bloody in the dirt, his ears still playing some off-key version of the Hallelujah Chorus.

"What is it? Hypnotism? Mirrors? You just say some fucking hocus pocus and turn into a piece of pussy anytime you want?"

"No," said Filakis, "anytime *you* want. You're only capable of seeing what you're already predisposed to see."

"Bullshit. I didn't *want* to see that girl. She was just there squirting milk out of her tits and looked like someone I'd like to kill. Is that what you're pissed off about?"

"You arrogant simpleton," said Filakis. He made a shooing gesture with his hand. The remaining oranges on the tree erupted into fire. Tiny ocher and vermillion tongues danced from the fruit's burning centers. The sick-sweet smell of burnt citrus filled the air. Then, as Breen watched, the oranges burst, sending forth a swarm of yellow wasps whose stingers blazed with flame.

Breen screamed, got to his feet, and tried to run. The wasps settled on his chest, his face. He pinwheeled his arms, swatting madly. Filakis made another gesture. The gaudy insects shimmered and shrank down to yellow pinpricks before turning into the kind of common gnats that swarmed throughout the City.

"I can make that happen to the oranges in your belly, the ones being digested even now," Filakis said evenly.

Breen tried to still the trembling in his voice.

"Why are you doing this? What the fuck did I do?"

"Destroyed something that I valued."

"You mean...the woman I killed?"

"The dogfucker? No, I was tiring of her antics anyway...I think the dog was, too. No, I meant the oranges. That was my favorite tree. I can see it from one of my balconies. The sunrise lights up its fruit like the balls of a golden bull. It's beautiful...a work of art, the ripe fruit against the lush green of the tree, the scent of citrus I wake up to every morning, something I look forward to. You wouldn't understand an appreciation of the aesthetic. You plucked a whole branch bare and gulped it down the way you used to work your way through the contents of other people's refrigerators."

"Jesus," murmured Breen. "How do you...?"

"Too late for Jesus. Why not try a brief but heartfelt apology?"

Breen reminded himself who he was and balked. He wasn't meant to grovel. He was Arthur Quentin Breen, he'd killed and traveled on five continents, he was a man of quality and of taste. He was...

The Turk's face suddenly turned fluid, a permeable mask of flesh tones and browns backlit with the lush magenta of blood seething through a complexity of arteries and veins. His outline blurred and redefined itself. Breen smelled mint leaves and bourbon and the unmistakable odor of Chanel #5.

Then Miss Lee was towering over him, her emerald eyelids rimmed with spidery false lashes, mouth stretched wide in a smirky smile, bright coral lipstick smeared on her front teeth.

"You stupid boy, get down on your knees. This instant. Now! You stupid, stupid boy. I ought to make you suck my dick till you require kneepads."

Breen quailed.

Miss Lee began to change. The skin of her skull unraveled with a sound like wet cardboard tearing. Her flesh took on a moldy cheese cast and hung from her body in tatters, so that the emerging bones seemed draped in worm-grey fringe.

The toothless, lipless mouth puckered like a dark and gaping sphincter. Something silvery and wet-looking, what Breen took to be saliva, gathered in the hole. Miss Lee grimaced and spat. A horde of tiny fish and crabs flew from her mouth, spattered Breen's face and nested in his hair.

He screamed, and the image vanished.

In its place, the Turk returned in all his morbid grandeur.

"I'm sorry," muttered Breen.

Filakis shifted his weight so that one foot came forward as if to administer a kick. Breen flinched and raised a hand to shield his face. Filakis shook his head disparagingly, like a schoolmaster appraising a particularly doltish child.

Breen covered his face and sputtered out the words.

"I'm sorry, I'm sorry, I'msorrysorrysorry..."

"Better," said Filakis. "With work, you may even come to be suitably obsequious. In the meantime, though, I expect you to serve me with twice the boot-licking, ass-eating eagerness you attended your flamboyant faggot friend. The only reason you're still alive, in fact, is so you can serve my needs. Instead you act like the City is your personal playground—your private killing ground. I don't object to that, because you're more interesting to watch than many here. What I do object to is when the only way that I can get your attention is to make myself into your next slaughter victim."

"What do you want?" said Breen.

"Obedience."

"How?"

In the distance, beyond the City's walls, a dust storm howled like something disemboweled.

"Do you think you could last a few days in the desert?" Filakis said. "Not that you really have a choice in the matter, mind you."

Breen nodded grimly. His heart and lungs felt like they were in a tug of war, depriving him of sufficient blood and air. His teeth clacked hungrily against one another. Without thinking, he reached down, peeled a sardine-sized strip of flesh from his belly and popped it in his mouth.

His body's reaction was electric. Pleasure shot from his teeth and spread into his gums, filling the space behind his eyes with light and chimes.

Filakis, watching, made a sour face.

"You have a friend who's hiding in the desert," he said contemplatively. "I believe her name is Val."

Breen stopped chewing.

"It seems she's stolen the affections of an old love of mine," the Turk went on. "This concerns me very much. I believe it's time I had her killed."

Breen nodded so vigorously his neck hurt. "How do I find her?"

Filakis told him.

"Oh, one thing more," Filakis said. "I want her to die, but not to suffer. No fucking and no torture. Dispatch her quickly and painlessly, as you would a beloved pet. Are you capable of doing that?"

Breen saw the amusement behind Filakis' glowering visage, knew he was being toyed with.

"Quickly and painlessly," Filakis said. "Repeat it, if you will."

"Quickly."

"Painlessly."

The words might have been runes from some forgotten tongue.

Breen said them, but he didn't know their meaning.

Venturing outside the walls of the City was as frightening than anything Breen had ever done.

Like leaving his hotel room when he was in the throes of one of his depressive phases.

Like running through the fire in his hotel room in Taroudannt.

Like stepping outside his skin, or what was left of it.

A small and hellish death.

Painless and quick, Filakis had said.

Well, so far nothing about this experience had been either quick or painless for *him*. Despite the protective garments in which he'd wrapped himself, grains of sand strayed in and scoured the flayed expanses of his flesh. At night the desert tormented him with cold, by day it parched and blistered him. He moved only at night, like a tarantula, and holed up in the daylight in whatever shade he could find.

When he got bored, he ate his own scorched flesh, then retched it up and ate some more.

The last remnants of his sanity dispersed like sand and, without a struggle, he slid willingly into madness.

In some oddly detached way, however, he was aware of the subtle, psychic dislocation of his mental process and aware, too, that the madness felt more comfortable, more *right* than anything he'd known before.

He followed the tracks of wild camels and smeared himself with the shit of Barbery apes and, to amuse and cheer himself, added up the killings he'd accomplished over a lifetime by piling pebbles: five stones per pile, seven piles and four left over—an even five when he got through with Val.

Except that "quick and painless" business. That enraged and confounded him. He was a man unused to self-denial. The thought of forfeiting a prolonged and brutal death for Val because of some strange whim of Filakis' was as unthinkable as chucking diamonds for a cache of cubic zirconia.

So he traveled at night and he brooded and bled, and when at last he found the camp Filakis had described and spied upon the tribe of pierced and phallic women, the urge to kill and mutilate was powerfully upon him.

The need to love—and to love brutally—was on him, too.

There was great risk, but he knew then what he had to do.

He intended for Val to have the most torturous death he could invent. A honeymoon of slow dismemberment and ardent peelings, a prolonged and exquisite romance with pain.

But the desert was not the place for this long-awaited idyll.

Her death must be a private matter, as intimate as the lushest lovemaking, a sacred moment between Breen and the woman he loved. Until that moment came, however, there were still ways he could amuse himself.

To hell with Filakis' absurd order.

And to hell—one of his own devising, in his own time—with Val.

Chapter Twenty-Two

In the City and the desert that surrounded it, hours passed at an eccentric pace. At times, it seemed to Val the seconds hobbled, drawing out what should have been a brief incident into a small eternity. At other times, so intense was the quality of experience, that it seemed whole lifetimes passed within a day or hour.

Val would try to calculate how long she'd been with Simone and Myra and the others, but would be unable to determine if it was several days or many weeks. Her existence unfolded in a kind of slumberous rapture, an ebb and flow of erotic tides that could comprise an orgy among all the women or an activity as simple but as sensuous as nibbling dates and slices of ripe melon.

The women captured other males, but these were never castrated and were usually set free as soon as the women had made use of them. A few wanted to stay, be castrated, and live as women, but these were driven away with hoots of mirth and barrages of rocks. Val noticed there were often a few camp followers to the group—usually young boys who hung around hoping to be made the center of an orgy.

Often they got what they were hoping for and more than they ever wanted.

In their camp outside the City, the women raised sheep and lived in primitive tents which they set up against the rocky hillsides for protection from the wind. Here the south wind blew all the time, and the sand stung like small serrated teeth, each grain producing a prick of pain that quickly transmutated into a profound and greedy hunger for more stimulus.

Val had always imagined the desert to be a barren moonscape, with miles of wind-driven sand leading to an unbroken horizon. Indeed, some parts of her current environment did fit that description. More often, though, the women camped near ponds or *gueltas* surrounded by ancient cypresses, fig and olive trees, tamarisk trees and date palms. Maned sheep, the aoudad, antelope, and wild camels often visited the ponds. Fennec, the tiny desert foxes with fur yellow as marigolds, chittered outside their burrows.

The women slept two or three to a tent, simple shelters made from canvas slung over wooden frames and carried with them when they moved from place to place.

At night Val usually went to Simone's tent or Myra came to hers. If it was Myra whom she coupled with, then she had to resign herself to accepting the woman's touches without attempting to reciprocate and of feeding and being fed as a central part of their love-making. Most of the time, it seemed that Myra literally ate her way to orgasm. Buttered bread in place of breasts. Plums instead of pussy. The tongue and teeth as sex organs.

Sometimes Val felt pity for her, but then there'd be some new act of cruelty, a young man whose libido and bravado led him to go off alone with Myra into the desert and who was never seen again. From these assignations, Myra always returned alone, the befouled and bloodied dildo swinging at her side like a policeman's truncheon. And whatever appetite and affection Val might have commenced to feel toward her would vanish.

For the time being, however, Val had postponed her thoughts of trying to leave the camp and found it easier to settle into the dubious comfort of this strange sisterhood.

The night before, a trio of young boys had been lured, not unwillingly, into the camp and passed around, one a black boy with lips as plump as figs, the two others sleek and muscular as acrobats, their erections as big around as their wrists.

Val had taken a turn, marveling at how young the boys looked, how hard they tried to seem unafraid, then not to scream, when penetrated by dildos of increasing girth. The black one Myra had taken off by herself. Val hadn't seen her since.

Of the remaining two, one boy had died, another had crawled away, delirious, blood streaming from his rectum.

In the early evening, a harsh, hot wind had commenced blowing from the south, flinging sheets of sand, making the date palms rattle and the cypresses moan. The temperature dropped abruptly, and the women took refuge in their tents.

Val and Simone cuddled in each other's arms. "I hate the wind," Val said.

"I know. It sounds like a woman keening at the funeral of her children." Her hand roved to an unexpected place on Val's body. "There, do you like the way that feels?"

"Very much. Do you like this?"

"Oh, yes."

"That boy that Myra took out into the desert the other day," said Val, "do you think she killed him?"

Simone sighed. "I don't want to know. She may have."

"But why?"

"Who knows? There've been male serial killers preying on women and children since the dawn of time. Maybe Myra thinks she's helping to rectify the balance. Or maybe she's just *folle*—or as you say, fucking crazy."

The touching seemed less pleasurable now. Val rolled onto her back, staring up at a moon no thicker than the gold rings that pierced Simone's dark nipples.

Simone leaned over, lush wheat hair tumbling around her face. "*Qu'a-tu?* What's wrong?"

"I was just...remembering. One of those young men, the one who died, reminded me of someone."

"In your other life?"

"Yes...and no. I met him earlier, but now he's here. At least I think he is. His name's Majeed."

And she described Majeed, how they'd met, and how she'd last seen him snatched away by Filakis.

In the darkness Val could see the luminous white of Simone's eyes. "You know him then? The one they call the Turk?"

"I saw him twice, once at a distance when he was crossing a courtyard, then again when he came to take Majeed."

"If your friend is with the Turk, he won't come back. Or if he does, he'll be so changed you won't want him anyway."

"I've got to find him."

"Don't be stupid. If he's really here, whether he's with the Turk or not, he's probably forgotten you. Haven't you noticed that? How difficult it becomes to remember a specific person—how sooner or later, it's impossible to distinguish one body from another. They all blend together like a single sex partner, a single sex organ."

Val had observed this and found it frightening.

"It doesn't matter. I need to go and look for him. I have to try, at least."

"Now you're the crazy one," sighed Simone. "It sounds like you're in love with him."

"I'm not sure. For a long time I thought I loved a man named Arthur, and he turned out to be a psychopath, a murderer. The worst part is I believed Arthur loved me. Sometimes I still think he does. But he tried to kill me. That's what I know about love."

"That it kills?"

Val nodded.

Simone said, "You don't have to worry about that here with me. You're safe here."

Safe, yes, thought Val and she remembered the excitement that she'd always felt, meandering alone in foreign cities, the sweet safety of her anonymity, her isolation, wandering those unknown streets and byways. Like being the only person in the world, like no one could ever hurt her, see her, become aware of her existence, her fears and needs.

And the awful loneliness that came with that feeling and, at the same time, the serene sense of invulnerability.

The safety that Simone talked about was something very different.

"How did you come to be here? What was your life like before?" Val asked.

"That was a long time ago."

"Tell me anyway."

Simone gnawed delicately at her lower lip. "I had two children, a boy and a girl. Their names were Marc and Ariel."

"Where are they now?"

"Teheran, as far as I know. With their father. We were married in France and lived in Nice for eleven years. The children were two and five then. Mustaffa wanted to take them home to Iraq for a month to meet his family. I knew it was a mistake to let him take them, but I wanted to be rid of him and of the children, too, to tell the truth, for a little while. I had a lover."

"A woman?"

"No, a man who worked at the same school where I taught

English. I thought with Mustaffa and the children away we'd have a whole month together, a honeymoon. But Mustaffa took the kids and all the money from our joint accounts and disappeared. He called me, demanding a divorce, saying he'd found out about the affair, that I was an unfit mother, he should have slit my throat, cut my tits off, on and on, the usual macho garbage."

"There was nothing you could do?"

"Not with him and the children in Iraq. I was his wife, so I had no rights. If I'd gone to Iraq to try to get the children back, he could have held me there. I might have been murdered or, at the very least, never managed to escape."

Tears, like clear beads, unraveled from the corners of her eyes. Val watched, entranced. The wetness emerging from Simone's eyes looked like polished quartz. It was the first time since she'd entered the City that she'd seen anybody cry.

"How long ago did you lose the children?"

Simone shrugged and licked the sand off her lips. Sand had collected in her hair, webbed it into clumps like grainy peanuts.

"A year, a month? You must have realized time spins round and round here, like fish being flushed down a toilet. All I know is, after I realized Mustaffa would never bring my children back, I dropped the man I'd thought I was in love with. I began to drink too much. I slept with many men. I started sleeping with women, too, then women and men together. Nothing was ever enough."

"And then you heard about this place."

"From a woman I'd met in Marseille who was a dominatrix. She talked about it while she whipped me."

The harsh wind bullied the sand into whirling cones. Beneath the skeins of moonlight, the desert seemed to be alive with spinning dervishes in pale brown robes.

Val said, "Have you ever wanted to leave here? *Could* you leave?"

Simone wiped her tears and gave a little grimace. "And do what? Go back to France? Use my new talents and make pornographic films? What point would there be to leaving here? I hardly ever think about Marc and Ariel anymore. Only sometimes..."

"What?"

"Sometimes it bothers me because I can hardly remember them either. The face of my little girl and boy—I've forgotten what they looked like. I've forgotten the sound of their voices and what toys they played with, what t.v. shows they liked. It's like they were some other woman's children that I only heard her talk about, and now it doesn't feel like they were ever mine."

"Why don't you at least try to get out of here and find them? It's possible, you know. There are people in your situation who've gotten help and had their children returned from foreign countries, either through legal means or by force. You can't give up."

"I gave up when I came here."

"If you love them, how can you *not* try to go back and find them?"

"How could I face them? The things I've done here, the things that I've enjoyed doing...I'm not the same person I was then. Even if I could find them, my children wouldn't recognize me as I am now."

"So you'll just forget about them?"

"If I can."

"I don't believe that."

"Oh no? You're a fine one to talk. I don't see you in any hurry to find your dear Majeed. Apparently having your cunt lapped day and night has caused his memory to fade."

Val squirmed and turned away.

"Maybe you're right. Maybe searching for Majeed is easier to talk about than do. But your children...children are supposed to be different from lovers, aren't they? They're always your children, no matter what. You love them, but you're not *in* love with them. Isn't that the way it is?"

"A little of both, I suppose," Simone said. "When they're babies, it feels like you're in love with them. A husband, lover, means nothing for a time. But then they get bigger and become more independent. You realize they aren't part of you, and you fall out of love.

"Marc and Ariel aren't real to me anymore. It's better like that. It's less painful." She stroked Val's hair. "You told me once you can't have children, but I can. I've thought about letting one of these little boys who hang around the camp give me a child. We could raise it together, you and I. What would you think?"

"I thought you came here because you wanted excitement, variety. Now you sound like you want a family."

"Is that so bad?"

"You *had* a family once, and look what happened."

"I know. I made a terrible mistake, and I'd give anything if I could take it back. But I can't. All I can do now is make the best life that I can. And I'd like to have a child again, a family. You wouldn't want that, too?"

"Sometimes," said Val, "I think I'd like to *be* a child again, if I could be with someone kind and loving, someone who wouldn't hurt me. But it's too late for that."

"No, it isn't. Not if we provide the love we didn't get when we were younger to each other and to our child."

"How domestic," said Val. "And I suppose we'd rape and castrate only as a hobby?"

Simone's shoulders trembled. She began to sob quietly. "Those things don't please me as they once did. I have bad dreams now. I feel ashamed."

Val held her, feeling wonder at the tears flowing down Simone's face onto her shoulder, at Simone's capacity for remorse. "Since I've come here, you're the only one I've met who cries. It frightens me."

"Because you can't?"

"I think so."

"If you go back into the City," said Simone, "you know the pleasures won't be the same as when you first got there. Everything changes with time. The price for pleasure gets higher and higher. What starts out as heaven gets closer to hell."

And even if you find your Majeed, one day I'll bet he will betray you."

Val smoothed the damp hair off Simone's face and kissed her. "Then I'll have to take that chance."

Outside a woman's voice screamed along with the wind.

There was the sound of footsteps running and voices shouting.

"What is it?" said Val.

"I don't know. Come on."

Hurriedly, they draped themselves in hooded, multi-layered djebballas to protect them from the wind. Simone lit a torch. They rushed outside and, following the sound of voices, climbed a rocky promontory to find a group of women gathered around what appeared, at first, to be a mound of sand. Then Val realized it the body of a woman, almost concealed by the blowing sand.

The others were on their hands and knees, digging her out.

Simone held her torch closer, then gasped and looked away.

Val saw, but couldn't believe what she was seeing. She stepped closer.

The folds of Myra's djellaba had been rucked up, exposing her mutilated genitals. Between the massive thighs, Myra's head had been positioned so she could eat out of her own vagina. In her arms, like a dark, round melon, she cradled the head of the boy she'd taken off to rape. His eyes, Val realized, had been bitten out.

In the stunned silence following the macabre discovery, Val found herself thinking about Majeed. She realized, too, that no one, not even Simone, was paying any attention to her.

She made a small choking sound, murmured something about being sick, and moved off into the darkness with a hand over her mouth.

She'd gone about a hundred yards when the moon rolled out from behind a bank of clouds like a gold coin sliding out of a magician's fingers. A bright, quicksilvery light illuminated the dark trunks of the cypress trees. An irascible camel bellowed. She saw its humped silhouette moving among the date palms, followed by two other, smaller beasts. The three camels trudged with funereal slowness, backs to the wind, elongated heads bobbing like huge cobras.

Simone shouted her name.

Val looked for somewhere to hide, but Simone had already seen her and was running to catch up.

"What are you doing?"

Val could think of no lie that would be believable. "Please go back. Pretend you never saw me."

Simone's hair flapped around her like a bedraggled cape. "I could call the others. I could have them force you to come back."

"But you won't, because you love me. I know you do."

Simone hesitated, then reached under her djellaba and unstrapped a knife from where it was secured to her waist with a cloth belt.

Val took a step backward and looked for a weapon of her own.

Simone handed both belt and knife to Val.

"Take this then. You'll need it."

Val turned the weapon over in her hand. "I thought you were going to...I was afraid...thank you."

From the camp echoed the high, ululating cries of a woman mourning Myra. "You'd better get back before they miss you," said Val.

She fixed the knife to her waist, turned to go.

Simone called to her. "Val? About this Majeed you want so much to find...you might want to talk to the Deadenders."

"The what?"

"The ones who live up in the mountains near the burial ground...the Deadend, it's called. If Majeed's dead, they'd have seen his body."

"How do I find them?"

Simone laughed. "How do you think? You follow the vultures."

Chapter Twenty-Three

A sadist's Disney World, that's what Filakis' dungeon was!

After his journey to the desert, Breen was drawn to its cool, ill-lit corridors and entranced by the excesses of pain endured in its underground cells. He was never sure if the captives here suffered as a form of punishment or willingly, in some perverse pursuit of pleasure that, over time in the City, they'd lost all capacity to feel.

All he knew was that, according to Filakis, *everyone*—if they remained alive in the City long enough—sooner or later made the journey to this low-ceilinged, subterranean lair, where the baked earth walls exuded a dank and noxious moisture and an unsettling, sweet putrescence tainted the air.

Richer with unholy marvels than even the rest of the City, its terrible delights were of the most exquisite kind, its subtleties and excesses spanning a broader spectrum on the palate of pain than Breen had ever hoped existed.

In the corridors and tunnels beneath Filakis' private domain, Breen imposed upon himself a form of limited captivity. Here in these dark vaults, he spent most of the daylight hours, sleeping in an unlocked cage whose small dimensions were snug and comforting, lullabied to sleep with cries of pain. There was a sense of safety in this Spartan cloister; the wider world was becoming one whose stimulations he could tolerate for only a short time.

For distraction, he would wander among the sufferers on display in their narrow cells, observing those who might have died or—more interestingly—who'd crossed the line into masochistic madness and reveled now in the very pain that, but hours and days before, had fathered only screams and pleas for a swift death.

He might spend hours squatting before the cages of the unfortunates whose nether regions were being opened up with dildos of formidable girth and length. Each day the dildos had to be replaced with larger ones, the suffers impaled upon them and chained tightly so that the only movement possible was the kind of hopeless writhing that only served to make the phalluses penetrate more deeply.

Sometimes a victim of such torture would split internally before Breen's eyes. One poor catamite began to scream unceasingly while a splitting sound, like fabric being rent, accompanied by a copious gush of blood.

Then there was the woman who was tied in place, her genitals smeared with the estrus of beasts, and left to be mauled and mounted by wild animals. And others, gagged and trussed so cleverly, that they were kept constantly aroused with no hope of any respite from the agonizing intensity of unfulfilled desire.

Breen watches these torments as, in an earlier time, he would have viewed a pornographic movie, his initial arousal diminishing to mild amusement, then fading to disinterest and ennui. Eventually, he lived in anticipation only of those days when the Turk devised some small atrocity for him to perform.

He was not permitted to rape and kill at will, however, but only those whom Filakis singled out, inhabitants of the City who, for one reason or another, had annoyed the Turk or devised some minor treachery against him.

And always when Breen squinted into the bleak confines of a cell or peered into the black maw of a pit, he was fantasizing about *her*, the bitch whose perfidy had led him to this place.

He delighted in having spared her life that he might later take it and marveled at how delicately the fabric of hate could be interwoven with the occasional strand of love.

But then, upon reflection, it had been that way with others in Breen's life, Miss Lee and, of course, his mother.

Breen missed them both and hated them and, sometimes, in the anonymity of some late night atrocity, his lust was suddenly overwhelmed with something worse, more sinister and scalding, and he wept like a little boy.

Lately, since becoming an inhabitant of the City, Breen had begun to feel more and more like a child. He got sudden, nerve-prickling flashbacks to the trailer camps in Texas. Sometimes he could smell the pungent odor of his mother's unwashed hair and cheap Wal-Mart perfume. Other times he woke up with his sinuses so full of fishy reek and the chemical strawberry concoction that she douched with that he could swear he'd stuck his face into her pussy.

In his childishness, he came to feel all-powerful, to veer toward a solipsistic grandiosity tempered only by his terror of Filakis. He imagined the City to be an invention of his own creation, where the Turk's dominion was surely an illusion, and God only a code-word employed by those too feeble-minded and faint-hearted to use the pronoun "I".

In the meantime, he had begun treating the burns on his face and body so he wouldn't repulse his fellow fornicators unduly, as was now usually the case. He'd begun this process by plucking off and gobbling the dead and peeling skin. Even when his complexion was more even, though, there were still numerous craters and discolorations, what looked like huge port wine stains spilling asymmetrically across his face and chest and backsides.

Breen took to smearing himself with mud in an attempt to cover the disfigurement. On his face he blended the mud with blood to achieve what he imagined to be a ruddy glow. On his charred scalp, he mixed mud with ashes and sculpted the few remaining strands of hair into something resembling a cockscomb. His skinned penis he covered in an even thicker layer of mud, deadening it to the point where pain and pleasure were equally diminished and erections within the gourd-like sheath were almost impossible.

Then he crouched outside one of the cells in Filakis' dungeon underground, as he watched a woman being tortured with an infestation of beetles lured into her vulva, he pined for Val and for a time when he could love her to death, love her with knives and cock and teeth, and know she loved him back.

His reverie was interrupted by Filakis' sibilant and sarcastic endearments murmured behind his back. Breen leapt to his feet with cur-like obedience.

Filakis stooped to get through the low doorway into the passage of cells where Breen was kibitzing on the torture. He wore a rustling, tawny robe of some rough material that looked like a dried-out hide. He looked aloof and somber, like a priest come to pronounce a few words at the bedside of the deceased.

Breen found himself shivering, causing bits of the carefully applied mud coating to flake off his arms and shoulders. He kept his eyes downcast, away from the face of the brooding Turk, and awaited his next instructions.

He hoped it was to kill another woman.

Better yet, a child.

So caught up was Breen in the weaving of his psychotic day-dreams that he paid scant attention to Filakis until the Turk's hennaed hands signed out a spell and brought forth a bloom of flame.

The mere sight of fire was enough to wring a scream from Breen. His seared flesh quailed at the remembered horror.

Filakis gestured with the flame. The hand-held blaze elongated. It dripped down in tear-shapes from Filakis' fingers like a molten neck-lace, thin tendrils reaching avidly toward Breen.

"Do you know," said Filakis conversationally, "someone once said that a baby, given sufficient power, would destroy the world?"

Breen was beyond answering.

Filakis went on.

"You, my friend, are one step more dangerous. You have a certain amount of power, but not the intelligence or self-control to use it to your advantage. Your self-will blots out your senses. Furthermore, with each drop of blood you shed, your I.Q. seems to drop. Do you know what I'm talking about, Arthur? Can you guess why I'm displeased with you? It couldn't be that you'd have lied to me, now would it?"

In truth, Filakis might as well have been speaking Hindi for all Breen took in of that speech. The flame held him mesmerized with terror.

"Did you kill a woman in the desert as I asked you to? Did you, Arthur?"

Breen nodded with a head-jerking gesture so fierce that beads of sweat flew off from forehead. Filakis took a step back to avoid the unsavory secretions. The fire, however, did not, but rippled redly toward Breen's feet.

"Which woman was it that you killed, Arthur? Was it Val? Answer me!"

"Stop it!" Breen screamed. "Just stop it. Take the fire away!"

"You didn't kill Val, did you?" Filakis sighed almost seductively. "You killed some other woman and a boy, both of them entirely inno-cent of any wrong-doing, either because the fire from which I saved you fried your brains or because you found yourself incapable of meting out a merciful death to anyone, least of all the one I wanted you to kill. You hate her too much, don't you? You love her too much, too. You undoubtedly thought me a weakling as soon as the word 'painless' passed my lips. How you underestimate me, Arthur. How you fail to realize when I'm testing you."

Breen covered his face and quailed.

"You disobeyed me, Arthur. I tested your obedience, and I found it just as limited as your wits. How gravely you disappoint me."

Filakis lifted his arms. The flame roared up like a monstrous phoenix and seared Breen's face. The mud that he'd so carefully applied was baked upon his skin. In the fierce heat, it cracked and fell to the floor like broken pottery hards. Breen threw himself at the Turk's feet, weeping.

Filakis stepped over his prone body. "And since you can't seem to accomplish killing your friend Val in the manner that I'd asked, that means I'll have to take care of it myself." He paused and favored Breen with a dreadful smile. "Eliminating that nonsense about a quick and painless death, of course. About that, I was only joking."

Chapter Twenty-Four

The corpse of the young woman with the blonde braid was listing to one side of the saddle.

Val twisted around on her own mount and tugged on the mare's lead rope. The animal nickered in protest, before plodding alongside Val and her horse.

She leaned over and shoved the straw mat in which the body was wrapped toward the center of the mare's back. Leather creaked as the ropes tying the body frictioned against the saddle. The horse shook its head, dispersing a troop of worrying flies that buzzed briefly away and then resettled, seeking out the mare's lugubrious cargo and the moisture available at her mouth and eyes.

Val unscrewed the top of her canteen, tilted it back and gulped water. Even in the short time that she'd been traveling, the seasons seemed to have altered, going from the baking summer of the craggy low country to the wet chill of the northern slopes of the Atlas range. In the distance, she occasionally saw stone houses with rain-shedding overhangs protecting the packed earth walls. Passing near a village, a bearded man with his head turbaned in white muslin offered her two pigeons for her supper. She refused, wondering if he guessed from its shape the nature of her cargo.

Now, toward mid-afternoon, the sky was thick with fat, dirigible-shaped clouds. Amber slants of sun revealed the higher peaks ahead, strung out like the silhouette of a gigantic rollercoaster.

As she drew closer, Val could see green slopes leading up to cliff-sides topped with dark rocks, like a line of blunt brown molars. She urged the reluctant horses on, wondering if those she'd talked to in the City were right: that a pilgrimage into the mountains to join the lovers of the dead, if her tastes did not incline in that direction, was folly enough to render her either an object of pity or of mirth.

The young woman was an offering. She'd been told it would be unwise to make the journey to the mountains without some token, preferably a pretty one not too far gone into decay and rot. The lovelier the better, of course, but few in the City died with their looks intact. Most expired from exhaustion, worn thin and ancient-looking as a tribe of preying mantises, skins scabby with infection, minds unmoored from any but their own untrustworthy versions of reality.

Val watched the wooded hills unfold above her and wondered at the strange obsession that had brought her to the City, the other obsession—with Majeed—that now prevented her from attempting to get out. Her hand reached for the incense burner where she had sewn it into a pouch inside her clothing and rubbed the heavy, walnut-like shape for reassurance.

Its flame had brought her here. She hoped its flame might also return her to Taroudannt.

As soon as she found Majeed, that is. And after he agreed to leave with her.

After Myra's murder, she had made her way back to the City to inquire about Majeed and to restore herself with food and rest after the deprivations of life in the desert. As before, she'd found that merely to wander among the City's winding streets stirred her skin to fresh arousal, made desire rove her body like avid hands. Even normal commerce, the vendors hawking brilliantly colored spices, heaps of dried grass used by the Berber women for cleaning teeth, and the strong-smelling aged butter called *smen*, was still infused with an almost mesmerizing sensuality. Minutes could be lost as easily in the contemplation of a pot of apples and black olives in honey-sweetened sauce or in the trill of a tinglingly sweet bird call as in the adoration of a lover's eyes.

There was an ebb and flow to the City's life, she discovered. While much activity still took place during the day, in the plazas and the courtyards, where all could stare and see, it was at night that the most frantic coupling occurred, when those neither beautiful nor well-endowed slunk out to seek each other, often piling in great writhing nests of limbs and genitals, so it was impossible, without deliberate inspection, to determine exactly who did what to whom, to tell who partnered willingly and whom against their will.

Val had lingered only long enough to determine that no one she spoke to knew anything about Majeed. That reenforced her worst fear—that Majeed wasn't in the City at all. That he was dead and his body had been taken to the mountain ranges beyond the City where the rapt attention of the vultures was the least of the indignities inflicted on the dead.

"Don't bother going to the mountains empty-handed," a bare-breasted woman wearing a print sarong wrapped around her waist had told Val. She had a baby sucking at one swollen tit, a grown man with his teeth clamped around the other one. Both man and babe made pleasured, cooing sound. Milk gurgled in their mouths and streamed down the mother's pregnant belly.

"The Deadenders won't waste their time on you if you don't have nothin' to give 'em. Find a body and take it to 'em quick, 'fore it starts goin' bad." She'd paused to kiss the silky crown of her baby's head, then the dark locks of the man. "Somebody young and pretty is the best. Those they prize so much they'll fight over 'em."

"How do you know this?" Val had asked.

The woman laughed, showing chipped, stained teeth. "My husband—them that's deceased is his thing. Used to spend all his paycheck hiring fancy girls to lay down in fake coffins, pretend that they was stone cold dead. Spooky sort he was.

"'Course, he's up in the mountains with his own kind these days, but I hardly miss him. Got me more'n enough to keep me busy as it is." She prized the baby off her tit, lifted him toward Val.

"You want a go, luv? I know you ain't got milk, but here a women can get off just from bein' sucked on. Even men get off that way sometimes, takin' a babe to titty."

Val had found the woman's proposition an unappealing one and was abashed to find her pulse was quickening none-the-less. How disobedient her body was, she thought. How vulnerable she was to the temptations of self-will and excess.

Acquiring a corpse proved easier than Val would have imagined. In the City, after all, there were no cemeteries, no crypts, no crematoria. People died primarily from exhaustion, from murder at the hands of a sadist lover or an autoerotic "accident", and from suicide. The latter, in fact, was common. As the need for sex grew more insatiable, even the City's pleasures ceased to delight. Those residents who'd been there longest grew jaded, restless, hungry for something more.

But there was no *more.*

Only death and a cessation of all hungers.

And so they shot and stabbed and starved themselves in droves, often helped on their way by some lover whose own erotic tastes inclined toward cruelty.

When death occurred the bodies were hauled on donkey carts to the northern end of the City, where they were taken outside the walls and left a mile or so away, to await collection by those who inhabited the mountains. The Deadenders came daily, drawn by the promise of new diversions for their own macabre tastes.

To find the kind of corpse she wanted had required only a few days wait, time that Val used to trade her sapphire ring for two horses from a trader in one of the souks, preferring to use the ring rather than the other kind of currency available to her—the owner of the horses was a pockmarked man with oily hair and eyes like two small balls of pan-fried grease, not one to arouse in her much zest for coupling. She then roamed the periphery of the City in the early morning hours, when the newly dead were most likely to be found.

The corpse that she was now transporting had been propped against a well, a slender, darkly pretty woman whose nose apparently had once been broken and crookedly reset. Otherwise she was unmarked but for the small, swollen puncture wounds visible underneath her neck when Val had tried to lift her.

In so doing, she had disturbed the creature that had been nesting in the moist shadow beneath the dead woman's skirt, a foot-long cobra that rippled like a mottled penis, rucking up the gauzy fabric of the skirt as it exited its lair so that Val could see the copper coils slithering wetly from inside the vagina it had occupied.

When she recovered from this sight, Val had wrapped the woman's body in a sleeping mat, hefted her over the back of one of the horses, and secured the burden to the saddle.

Now, after the exhausting journey from shimmering heat to fog-misted chill, Val could see the aerial choreography of the vultures above a nearby ridge—what must be the City's burial ground.

The trail grew steeper, tapestried on either side by holly, cork oaks, and olive trees. High above, where the cliffs soared to unscalable sheerness, Barbary apes and monkeys perched on the rocks, tails curved into furry question marks, showering down walnuts.

The horses, already bedeviled by the barrage of walnuts, smelled the burial ground before Val did. Spooky with the nearness of the death smell, they began to whinny and tried to turn around on the rock-strewn path.

Val urged her mount on while keeping a firm grip on the other horse's lead rope. As they progressed, she, too, could smell the odor. It permeated the warm breeze like poison-based perfume, sweet and sickly, rich with the coppery tang of blood and the charnel house smell of putrid meat.

She tried to look away when they passed the area of open rocks where the bodies had been left, but found herself turning to take in the macabre scene despite herself. The more recently dumped bodies, those the vultures concentrated on, still had flesh, albeit in tatters, and some kind of human form. Others had been reduced to only lard-encrusted skeletons and carelessly strewn bones.

A half dozen or so large vultures, flinty-eyed and bald-necked, fixed surly stares on her and the horses. Their taloned feet dug into decomposing flesh. The feathers on their chests were stained red like bloody bibs. They screeched and flapped from one portion of the feast to another, gore-flecked beaks dipping down to pluck out the softer morsels.

Val urged the horses on.

She was approaching a bend in the trail flanked by several boulders when her horse shied away and tried to turn back. The mare, too, was acting skittish, her ears pinned back, nostrils flaring. The focus of both horse's fear appeared to be the boulders to the right side of the trail.

A snake, a dead thing, or something worse, thought Val. Some kind of ambush maybe? She had still not recovered from the shock of Myra's death. Violence inside the City and beyond was swift and senseless. Did the Deadenders always wait passively for corpses to be brought to them or did they perhaps speed up the process and hunt down the living, too?

Val walked the horses back down the trail and tied them among a stand of olive trees. Then she circled around and approached the pile of boulders from the opposite direction.

Two sounds caught her attention. The first, the soft and hissing cascade of water over rock, promised a needed opportunity for the horses to drink and for Val to refill her canteens.

The second, less easily identifiable, was an irregular splatting, occasionally interrupted by a harsher, clinking sound as though light tools were being struck against each other. The combination of the sounds made Val think of someone doing dishes, scrubbing plates clean with a sponge, then stacking them in a pile so that the polished surfaces clattered gently.

She listened for some minutes, unsure of what to do, while the muscles in her thighs cramped and her back ached from the prolonged squatting position.

Finally, she inched her way forward on hands and knees and squinted through an opening among the rocks hardly larger than the lens of a camera.

What met her eye was nothing Val could at first identify. The lopsided, asymmetrical structure she was seeing looked like some sort of primitive creation, a shrine or *marabout*, as they were called, or perhaps only the crude sculpting of a demented artist. She had only just realized that the angular assemblage was made of bones when a small figure moved into view and she saw a dark-skinned child wearing a chiffon head scarf. The girl was also veiled from the nose down, a practice Val had seen occasionally when she and Majeed first came to Fez, but never in the City or its environs.

Perhaps, though, the veil was less modesty than practicality, she thought. A way to deflect some of the smell when the wind shifted the wrong way.

The child crept deftly on her hands and knees, foraging through the grisly refuse pile. Her black hair hung in spiky snarls, the wispy tendrils at the tip reaching midway down her back. She wore baggy brown trousers tied with a rope belt, scuffed moccasins, and an oversized blue shirt embroidered with some white stitching up the sleeves. Deeply absorbed, her tanned forehead knitted with concentration, she selected and then rejected several possibilities, before settling on a slender bone Val thought to be a tibia. Having made her choice, she moved so quickly that Val ducked down, thinking that she must have been seen, although why discovery by the child should so alarm her she was at a loss to fathom.

But the little girl was only going over to the stream, at the edge of which she'd diverted enough water into a shallow depression in the soil to create a glimmering pond of diarrhetic-looking mud. Into this brown lublolly, she dipped her hands, slapping out two mud pancakes into the desired consistency, and applying them in globs to both ends of the tibia.

This done, she added the bone to one end of her crude creation, one end resting on the knob of a femur, the other fitted inside the buck-toothed maw of a skull.

The girl's exactitude was worthy of an architect. Minutes passed while she adjusted the tibia to exactly the right angle to insure stability and compensate for the skull's slight overbite.

Then she returned again to the bone pile, perusing it for her next choice like a careful shopper mulling over produce.

While searching for her next selection, she began to sing. Her voice was soft and lilting, clear as the notes of a xylophone.

"Tibia, scapula, and femur will do, coccyx and ulna and clavicle, too."

She repeated the ditty over and over, sometimes varying the rhyme with the names for other bones.

"Tarsal and sternum and jawbone will do..."

Val's thigh muscles were paining her severely. She decided to take the chance of revealing herself to the child, although in truth the meticulous construction of the bone house held a fascination of its own for her. In other circumstances, she might have watched for hours.

She stood up slowly, smoothing down her rumpled, sweat-stained shirt and cleared her throat in hopes of getting the girl's attention without frightening her.

The child spun around in alarm and hurled the bone that she was holding—a tibia with a deep fracture at the mid-point.

Val ducked as the arm bone whizzed past her and shattered on the rock behind her.

"It's all right. I won't hurt you." She held up her hands in a gesture of appeasement.

The girl's dark eyebrows bunched together. Beneath the translucent veil her mouth turned southward in a wary frown.

Val said, "That's quite a song. Where did you learn the names of all those bones?"

"My mother taught me. And the bones are mine, and I can do what the fuck I want with them. You leave them alone. Go find a corpse, you fucking Deadender."

"I'm not...you don't understand." Val took another step forward. "All I want is a drink of water. You don't mind if I get that, do you?"

The child considered this. Finally she pointed to a stony area on higher ground a few yards away and said, "Go that way then. But don't walk near the castle. Last time I let somebody come close, they knocked two whole rooms out with their big clumsy feet."

Val assured her she'd be careful. She drank from the stream, keeping the child in sight in her peripheral vision each time she bent her head, then splashed cool water on her face and neck. The little girl stayed at a distance, eyes fixed suspiciously on Val.

"I have horses, too. I'd like to let them drink."

The child agreed this time with less reluctance. "I like horses. I have a horse of my own." She pointed to an area where the a dozen or more ulnas were angled down to form what might, in a child's fantasy, have passed for a corral.

"In here."

"Can I take a look?"

"If you're careful you don't knock anything down."

Val swore she'd behave as though she were in a museum. And, in a way, of course, she was. For the child's creation was far larger and more ambitious than Val's limited view from behind the rocks had led her to believe. The castle comprised an area as large as two tent sites, a macabre marvel of rooms made from tibia and roofed with femurs, rib bones that curved together to make arches connecting different sections of the structure, jaw bones piled one atop the other to form toothy towers. Inside some of the rooms, the child had fashioned tiny chairs and tables by interlocking toe and finger bones.

"And here's the living room and the bedroom and the body pit..." she indicated a shallow pit in the corner of one "room", which she had filled with tiny bones, "and the torture rooms..."

"Why torture rooms?"

"To kill people, of course," the girl replied, clearly impatient with Val's dullness. She either didn't catch or simply chose to ignore the edge of horror in Val's voice and went on enumerating other features of her castle: the yard for holding camels, the bedroom big enough for orgies, the tower like the one in London.

"You mean the Tower of London?"

"Yeah."

"Have you been there?"

"A long time ago."

Val was surprised. She'd thought all the children in the City had been born there. "Who brought you here?"

"My mother."

The child resumed her work, using a handful of mud paste to affix an arch of yellowed vertebrae to the knobs of a pelvic bone. Sunlight glanced off the bones, casting weird and abstract shadows.

"What's your name?" said Val.

"Rema."

"I'm Val. And I think that's a wonderful castle. It must have taken you a long time to build such a beautiful thing."

"Weeks."

"And you've been living up here all this time?"

"Uh huh."

"With your...mother?" Val said, although she hated to think what sort of parent would allow a child to roam this austere, vulture-ridden land.

"No."

"You said she taught you the names of the bones."

A mournful look crept into the child's face. "That was a long time ago."

"You mean you're alone?"

Rema nodded. "She doesn't want me. She says I'm an embarrassment. I only see her now and then...when I have a message to bring or work to do."

"What kind of work?"

"It depends. Sometimes the Turk even sends me outside the City, but I always have to come back when he tells me to."

"Where's your mother now?"

Rema pointed out one of the castle's bleached and leaning rooms. "In there."

Val was at a loss to know if this answer was symbolic or simply meant that Rema had no mother other than the one that she imagined. Before she could inquire further, Rema indicated another room and said, "I live there."

"Oh, in your imagination," Val said and then regretted it.

The child's black eyebrows squashed into flat black bars. Her face took on an abstracted, distant look as though she peered at Val from the back window of a train, getting ever smaller and farther away.

"No, it's where I live," she said defiantly. "It's my secret place. I go there to be alone."

"I see." Although, of course, she didn't, and was at a loss to imagine what sort of aloneness might be more profound than that the child must experience in these death-plagued mountains.

"Aren't there others that live up here. Where are they?"

"There's Egg, but I'm afraid of him. He looks at me real weird. And some others, too, but they leave me alone. They don't want to fuck with live people."

Val shuddered at the matter-of-factness of Rema's comprehension of the situation. She'd been debating whether or not to ask her about Majeed, but the child seemed unfazed by the proximity of death or the perversions drawn to it, so she decided to proceed.

"Where do you get your bones?"

"The burial ground."

"So that means you see the bodies?"

"Sometimes. It's not like I hang around, you know. The vultures look at me the same way Egg does."

Briefly, with as much circumspection as possible, Val described Majeed. "I need to know if he's still alive or if...he was brought here."

"Why do you care?"

"He's my friend."

"You mean you fuck him."

The word, coming out of the child's mouth, made Val recoil.

"My *friend*," she repeated. "He put himself at risk for me. If he's dead, it may be because of me. Have you seen him?"

The child shook her head. "I don't know any man like that. Besides, I wouldn't want to. I'd run away from such a freak."

She was having trouble erecting her arch of vertebrae. The bones must have been very old, or perhaps belonging to someone suffering from osteoporosis. They bent stiffly, close to popping apart. Little bits of bone dust drifted down. Looking at the child's bent back, Val had the impression of a wizened, near-sighted paleontologist trying to reassemble some prehistoric creature.

With a popping sound like a gun firing, the arch of vertebrae snapped at the middle and collapsed. Rema gave a frustrated cry and threw the useless halves away. They ricocheted off a rock, then skittered into the dirt like two skeletal snakes.

"Are you sure you're okay here?" Val said. "What do you eat? Who takes care of you?"

To her surprise, the little girl began to sniffle, then to cry. Her slender body trembled. She ran to Val and pressed against her, snuffling into the crook of her arm and clutching at Val's clothing.

"There now, it's okay," Val said, stroking the girl's hair.

She knew little about children, having had none of her own and no sisters or brothers. She only knew that they intimidated her, with their savage candor and their awful neediness, which invariably left her feeling inadequate and helpless.

Now she did her best to comfort Rema, murmuring stock consolements, drawing on the scattered memories of the few times Lettie had attempted to sooth her and hoping they gave solace.

"I know it must be scary out here. I know you must be lonely."

More sniffling and half-swallowed sobs.

Val went on, "I know how it feels to be alone..."

With a shriek of glee, Rema jerked loose from Val's arms and spun away, capering and dancing on the periphery of the bone castle. Her eyes gleamed with trickster malice as she clutched the incense burner taken from Val's clothing and waved it in her hand.

"Give that back to me. Now!"

Val struggled to control her voice, but the sight of the child tossing the incense burner, which until now had been kept safely sewn into the lining of her trousers, made her heart clutch.

"Give it back."

The child scrunched her face up until nose, mouth, and eyes were compressed into a tiny portion of her head. "Give it back," she mimicked.

She angled back her arm like a pitcher getting ready to hurl a curve ball.

"No, don't," said Val. "That's mine."

"No, don't. That's mine."

"Please."

"Puh-leazzze."

"Stupid brat." Val lunged and grasped the child's wrist. She pried the incense burner loose from Rema's fist and held it up. The precious object was intact, although red dust had filled in the indentations of the intricately carved surface.

With a smile of tight-lipped disdain, Rema watched Val tuck the incense burner back inside her pocket. "*That's* how I take care of myself. By taking what I need from people who're too dumb to know I'm robbing them. I can steal the false teeth out of an old man's mouth while he's still chewing his food. I can swipe the jewelry off of dead people and trade it in the City."

She planted her small hands on her hips, shot Val a bitter dare. "I can take care of myself. I don't need my stupid mother and I don't need you. I don't need anybody."

Her eyes shone in tearful defiance. Yet she looked so small and so alone—standing there in her fantasy land of mud and human bones—that Val felt a moment's panic for her. There were few children in the City and its environs, and those that were tended to run in packs or cling to a parent or a "guardian," however dubious the term. This child had no one.

"That was wrong," said Val, "but I'm sorry I called you a stupid brat."

Thinking: *You're certainly not stupid.*

"Look, I have to go, but I don't want to leave you here alone. Why don't you—"

The high-pitched whinnying of frightened horses interrupted her.

"Oh, shit," said Val. She turned back to Rema. "Stay here. I want to talk to you some more. I'll be back as soon as I find out what's going on."

Chapter Twenty-Five

Val took off running toward the stand of olive trees where she'd left the horses. As she approached, the bay mare galloped past, its saddle empty. Val tried to head her off, but the panicked animal veered around her and kept going.

Reaching the grove of trees, she saw a powerfully built, bare-chested man with a yard-wide back and a pigtail of flaxen hair sprouting from an otherwise bald dome untying the remaining horse. On the ground, only a few yards away, the body Val had transported lay sprawled and partially unclothed. A second, considerably smaller man was in the process of zestfully violating her. Rhapsodic sighs and grunted endearments issued forth in abundance.

Val reached inside her waistband, grabbed the knife Simone had given her, and flicked it open. She seized the violator by his hair and inserted the knife between his teeth, so that the tip of the blade angled up to jab the roof of his mouth.

"Get off."

The outpouring of ecstatic murmurings faded into a gurgle of dismay as the knife pricked his flesh. A thin crimson stream stained his teeth.

"What is it? What did I do?"

"Lose the hard-on and pull out," Val said.

"Sully, He-ee-lp."

The wonder of testosterone who was in the process of making off with Val's other horse turned around to see what was happening to his partner. Glaring at Val, he flexed muscles so heroically proportioned they made him look deformed. With his oiled pecs and laddered abdomen, he resembled a small, plated dinosaur.

"Stay where you are," said Val, "or the knife goes through his brain."

The bald man blinked and scowled but seemed more interested in maintaining his grip on the horse's bridle than on coming to the aid of his comrade.

With a soft sputtering sound, the squirming Deadender disengaged. Val released her hold on his hair. He stood up, folding himself back into his trousers and spitting blood.

"Look what you did? Now I'm bleeding! Is she your lover or something?"

"I never saw her alive," Val said.

"What does that have to do with it?" The small man's eyes glinted feverishly. "I asked is she your lover?"

"Christ, no."

"Then what's the problem?"

"I didn't say that you could fuck her. Not to mention scaring off one of my horses." She turned the knife in the direction of the would-be horsethief. Noting the man's glossy pate with its one wispy sprig of hair, she said, "Don't tell me...is your name Egg?"

His face flexed in confusion. "I'm Sully."

The pervert with the glittery eyes stammered meekly, "I'm Egg. You want to see why?"

"I'd rather not."

But he'd unzipped himself anyway, revealing a minuscule appendage completely hidden in a cocoon of foreskin, thickest at the mid-point and tapered at both ends, smooth and white and egg-like.

Unimpressed, Val turned away. She walked over to Sully and snatched the horse's reins out of his ham-like hands. He grinned arrogantly, but made no move to stop her.

"And you, stay away from my horse."

"It's our horse now. That's how we do things here. We share."

"I'll bet."

"Not just the bodies. Everything—food, shelter."

"Good," said Val. "Then you can share some information."

She told them about Majeed.

When she was finished, Egg said, "If the Turk took him, he may not be dead, but he'd probably like to be."

Sully's forehead creased; from the back, his skull looked like a gigantic, worried embryo. "Rumor and hearsay, that's all that is. I don't think the Turk's anything to fear. I think he's one of us."

Val said, "That's not exactly a character endorsement."

"Come on," said Egg. His cloyingly unwholesome voice took on an edge of urgency. "Let me show you what we do with the bodies that are brought to us in good condition."

"Forget it. I don't want to know."

"It isn't what you think," said Sully. "Just have a look."

Keeping her knife at the ready, Val followed the ghoulish pair to a sheltered area thickly fringed with scrub willows and oaks. A small pool, apparently fed by the stream where Val had left Rema, gleamed with clear, icy water.

Next to the pond, rocks had been piled up to form a crude alter, upon which rested the body of a young man laid out on an ornately patterned rug.

A disagreeably sweet odor emanated from the corpse. Akin to the scent of decay, but something else, crushed orchids and the languid perfume of lilies rotting on a stagnant pond.

Val covered her mouth.

"My own concoction," Egg said. "It keeps the flies away while minimizing natural odor."

Val gingerly approached the body. She'd seen enough of death since coming to the City to extinguish any prurient curiosity. This corpse, however, was so bizarrely painted, decked out like a life-sized sex doll tarted up in drag, that she couldn't help but scrutinize Egg's dubious accomplishment.

The body was that of a muscular young man with what must have been a formidable cock. His red hair was tied back in a ponytail, and an elaborate necklace of turquoise and amber beads circled his thick neck. The natural contours of his abdominal muscles and pectorals had been enhanced with cosmetic shadow. A pearl as big as a pea occupied the cup of his navel. Grasses trailed between his legs, giving the impression that esparto grass and coiled grapevines grew from the crack in his ass.

His lips and cheeks were tinted the color of bruised peaches, the eyelids shimmery aqua with ivory underneath the brow. His eyes had been left open, the better to insert two scarab-backed beetles, the spindly legs of which overlapped and intertwined with the young man's own abundant lashes. The backs of the dead beetles were painted with bright turquoise orbs which, at a distance, gave him an expression of wide-eyed astonishment at his own deceased condition.

"Amazing," murmured Val. "Would it be in poor taste to say that he looks bug-eyed?"

"Less bad taste than cliche," said Egg. "You'd be surprised how much I hear that since I started using insects instead of flowers."

"Why not just close the eyes?"

"Too bland. I prefer something festive."

Val touched the beaded collar around the man's neck. Beneath it, the color of the skin was purplish-yellow, in places almost black.

"He hung himself."

"A certain amount of attrition's to be expected," Sully said. "We had another suicide here just the other day. A Swedish boy, young, a mouth to die for, climbed up onto the rocks and sat there for hours, so motionless the vultures did everything but land on his head. He wouldn't talk, wouldn't come down. Finally he just stood up and made like one of those rock divers in Rio. Except no forgiving sea to break his fall. There wasn't a lot left besides snack food for the birds."

Val gazed down at the body. She jiggled the beetle coverings over the eyes, rolled the pearl in its tiny cup and saw a fleck of lint appear on the other side. She let her index finger trace the line of reddish hair from pearl to pubic hair, then drew away.

"He must have been very unhappy here."

"All I know," said Egg, "is that he was stupid and impulsive and he deprived himself of a few thousand lovely orgasms."

Val looked at the body on the alter. "He couldn't leave here, could he?"

Egg scowled, the fatty area between his eyes dimpling deeply. "Don't talk about leaving. I don't know why this one hung himself. It might have been accidental. Maybe he only wanted to choke himself unconscious, get a rush. We see a lot like that up here, the accidental deaths. It's best to have a partner for that kind of thing." He stroked the dead man's waxen cheek. "If you don't like the Deadend, why did you go to so much trouble to come up here?"

"I can't leave until I'm sure Majeed's not here."

"He sounds remarkable," said Sully, and his voice took on the salacious breathiness of a phone sex customer. "One like that I'd have remembered."

"I as well," said Egg, "but of course we only deal with the best specimens. Now Danielle, there's someone who might know. She likes all kinds. Come on and bring along the pretty blonde girl with her unfortunate proboscis, and we'll go ask her."

"I have to go get someone first," said Val, remembering Rema. "A little girl, she's too young to be alone here."

"Young hooligans," said Egg. "It's best to keep away from them. They'll steal from you. They comb the burial ground and rob the corpses."

"Just the same," said Val, "I don't want to leave her here."

While Egg and Sully waited, she followed the rocky trail back up the slope to where she'd last seen Rema.

The child was gone.

Strewn across the muddy ground, the bone house lay in ruins, bones mashed into the soft earth and tossed about helterskelter. Imprinted in the moist river bank were muddy hoofprints. *The mare must have run through here when she bolted*, thought Val.

Bleakly, she surveyed the destruction.

Oh Rema, I'm so sorry.

She stayed in the area a long time, calling her name, but there was no more sign of the child.

Chapter Twenty-Six

In the land of the dead, Val soon learned, the living moved like ghosts, invisible, unreal. They dwelled in ramshackle, stone hovels with roofs supported by layers of poles and twigs and waterproofed with a thick coating of clay. At night, with the wind banshee-wailing, they huddled around a central fire, dipping bread into melted three-year-old butter washed down with the ubiquitous mint tea.

Sometimes the Deadenders spoke of loved ones left behind in the "other" world. They talked of spouses, children, careers, of cities Val had visited in her ramblings and obscure towns and villages through which she'd never passed. They complained of head colds and of rain and the resulting mudslides that sometimes took whole houses with them, they praised spring wildflowers and celebrated loudly when someone returning from the City brought wine or beer to break the monotony of tea.

They died, too, of malnutrition or accident or the same diseases that would have felled them, albeit less quickly, had they never traveled to the City and beyond it, but their own dead were never violated, but left unceremoniously for the carrion-gorging birds.

The one topic that was not discussed, the singular taboo, was the very thing that drew them there, proximity to that largest of all human tribes, the feared and holy dead. Except for those rare cohorts like Egg and Sully, what was done to the bodies took place in private rituals and was never spoken of. The inhabitants of the mountain were merely a tribe of hillspeople, raising sheep and goats and living off what meager food the land provided, not the notorious Deadenders whom those in the City so feared and abhorred.

Like the rhinoceros in the living room that no one notices, thought Val, remembering something a psychiatrist had told her once about denial in those days when she was still willing to lie down on a couch without opening her legs.

Nor were the dead ever acknowledged to have been otherwise except as they arrived in the mountains. They had never lived or possessed names, sired or given birth to children or fallen in love, dreamed or prayed or cried out for help in that last fearful moment when they realized they were dying.

They simply were the Dead, and had never been alive or harbored any relation to those who violated them.

The body that Val hauled into the mountains won her a guarded welcome, but nothing in the way of information. Few seemed able to say with any certainty whether they had seen someone like Majeed at all. It was as if the Deadenders suffered from a collective quelling of any awareness of a body's individuality and made love—over and over again—to some idealized wet dream.

"When a body comes to us in good condition, we decorate it and hold a ceremony in its honor, a Death Day feast," said Danielle, the teen-aged girl whom Egg and Sully had wanted Val to meet that first day in the mountains. She and Val were eating dates and drinking mint tea inside the stone house that Danielle shared with Egg and Sully.

Danielle claimed to have been a Druid in a previous life and had come to the City with her boyfriend, a bisexual poet and drug dealer who frequented the underground sex clubs of San Francisco.

Now she wore jeans so tattered and frayed that a plump rectangle of her backside was exposed and a madras halter top that showed off the top of one pink nipple and an inch of tattooed cleavage.

Danielle had discovered her taste for making love to beautiful dead men at the age of fifteen, when she looked into the open casket of an ex-boyfriend who had been gunned down on Castro Street.

"When I bent over to kiss him, I slid my other hand inside the coffin and I groped him," she told Val. "I ran my hand up his body and I could feel his dick and the outline of his nipples under the shirt. I started to crawl on top of him, and his Mom and the minister come runnin' over and drug me off, and after that they put me on tranks, all kinds of shit. But it didn't stop me thinkin' about doin' him, from wanting to be like him in some way without having to be dead myself."

Val told her about her fruitless search for Majeed.

"There's one more thing you could do, but you probably won't want to."

"What's that?"

"Go look around the burial ground. If your friend is dead, that's where he'll be. There might be something left you'd recognize."

Val felt the bread and dates she'd eaten earlier do slow backflips in her stomach.

She said with more conviction than she felt, "If Majeed had been brought here, someone would remember him."

"Because of him bein' a freak."

"Don't call him that."

Danielle laughed, the moist and throaty sound of a woman sated by a multiplicity of orgasms. "What if his body's been mutilated or it's already decomposed? The vultures might not have left anything to find. On the other hand, maybe he's still alive somewhere in the City."

"Then I'll have to go back there."

"You don't have to, do you? Not right away. Not ever if you don't want to."

Danielle smiled at her. Val skimmed a fingertip along the girl's finely chiseled neck and down between her breasts, where a tattoo of a thorn-filled rose garden blossomed across her breasts. Their mouths met and mashed together. Val buried her hands in Danielle's hair. She wanted to forget Majeed. She wanted to forget everything about her life before she'd come here.

"You're such a pretty girl, you know that? You have hips like a boy and tits like a woman nine months pregnant. And with all this death around, you make my pussy water like I haven't fucked for days."

"Would you like a man, too?"

"If he can fuck us both."

"I'll get Sully. He can get the biggest hard-on that I've ever seen on a man who wasn't dead."

Chapter Twenty-Seven

In her sleep, Val became dimly aware that someone had crawled beneath the blanket and nestled next to her.

Smooth, supple flesh, the faint odor of ash and unwashed hair.

She smiled in her sleep.

Sully, she thought, *or Danielle.*

Her new bedmate burrowed in beside her, slid an arm inside the folds of her djellaba and explored among the layers of her garment with the subtle stealth of a heat-seeking scorpion. Val moaned and turned over. The hand inside her clothing quickly retreated and came to rest on her waist.

"Go away," Val murmured, but she was speaking to the person in her dream now, to the sudden image of Lettie with a mask across her eyes, beckoning her closer.

"I'm sorry, but I have to do this."

Did she actually hear those words or was it some strange voice-over from the dream? She tried to reach that semi-lucid sleep state where one can actually control the way the dream unfolds or decide to come awake, but this dream-sleep had a seductive quality that sapped her will, lured her deeper. Up steep stairs, through darkened hallways, past a trio of sleek and baubled women hobbled like horses in their needle-slim heels.

In here.

Lettie opened a door for her, stepped back, and gave a mocking bow. The mask she was wearing turned runny and dripped down her cheeks in goopy strings. She dug at her empty eyesockets. Waspy, winged insects crawled out of the scar-tissued craters, hissing as they flew at Val's face.

She batted them away and peered into the room.

On the bed, a man lay gutted and bloody as something destined for the window of a butcher shop. Between his legs, a knife protruded.

"Go sit on him," cooed Lettie. "It's what you wanted, isn't it? Go sit."

Val commanded herself to come awake, but the effort had little effect on her dream-self, who stood above the phallus-knife and spread her legs.

"Sit," said Lettie.

"Ssssssit," hissed the insects emerging from her empty eyes.

Val reached beneath her garments, spread herself, and sank onto the blade. Internal membranes ruptured. The knife twisted and elongated inside her. Her lungs and heart were speared before the blade traversed her throat and pricked the jellied meat inside her skull. Twirling behind her eyes, it cored out a primitive lobotomy.

She tried to scream and found her voice was gone.

"I know where you can find your friend."

Gasping, she tried to emerge from sleep's terrifying murk.

For a few seconds, she was fully awake, but unable to move.

Then small, sharp teeth gnawed at her neck. Val yelped and her eyes flashed open.

In the darkness, the gold coins on the headscarf the child was wearing tinkled and flashed. She was unveiled, but in the darkness, Val could see few details of her face.

"What...? Rema?"

"I was cold. I came to sleep with you."

"I thought you were...someone else."

"I know." She wriggled closer.

"Be quiet if you're going to stay." Val nodded toward the sleeping forms of Sully and Danielle, who were spooned around each other in the corner. She put an arm around the child, unsure how to say what she needed to.

"Your bone house...I'm sorry it got trampled. The horse was scared and..."

"It doesn't matter," Rema said. "I built another one. A better one. Somewhere no one will find it. A safe place inside my head."

Val took the child's hand. It felt small and cold. "You shouldn't be here in the Deadend by yourself. It isn't a good place."

"As good as any."

She shrugged and the gold coins on her scarf pinged gaily. They reminded Val of something, but before she could say anything, Rema spoke. "I told you already, but you were sleeping...I know where he is."

"Majeed?"

"Yes."

"Where?"

"The burial pit."

Val felt as though her heart dropped to her stomach. The night breeze felt chill and noxious as a corpse's kiss. She lifted her hands to her face.

"Are you sure?"

"You said he was a man-woman, didn't you?"

Val nodded.

"Then it's him," said Rema, snuggling closer.

Val lay back and tried to sleep, but it was useless. She felt depleted, drained, half-sick from her earlier exertions with Sully and Danielle, sicker to have learned Majeed was dead. And yet, even as she became aware of how exhausted she was, her physical emptiness again demanded filling. An impossible craving, enough hunger to devour the world and still not be sated, throbbed in her body's cavities and crawl-spaces.

Majeed is dead, thought Val, *and I still want to fuck.*

Rema reached out and touched Val's head. "What is it in your hair?"

Val fingered the stiff strands where Sully's cum had run down her mouth, encrusted the hair. *Majeed is dead.* She tried to stop herself, but the desire was irresistible. She slid the cum-caked locks into her mouth and sucked the mildly pungent paste. The faint sex-taste made her throb inside.

When she finished the cat-like cleaning of her hair, Rema was smiling slyly.

She knows what it was, thought Val and burned with shame.

"If you don't hurry, the vultures will get him first," said Rema.

Sully moaned and twisted in his sleep. Danielle opened an eye, saw Val with the little girl. She smiled wickedly. "You didn't tell me you like kids."

Val ignored her. "Let's go," she said to Rema. "Take me to where you saw Majeed."

A pale tusk of a moon hovered just above the mountain peaks as Val and Rema made their way along the rock-strewn path. Daybreak was making its first encroachment on the night, shadows gathering and bunching, gossamer silhouettes of trees and hillsides taking shape where earlier had been but solid black. At the horizon a thin ribbing of pewter lined the undersides of the clouds.

"There," said Rema and pointed to where Val could make out the gloomy sweep and glide of the vultures. A few would hover and land, then several more take off.

Like an airport, thought Val, *or the take-out window of a fast food restaurant.*

As they approached the burial ground, Rema hung back, staying in the shadows.

"Aren't you going with me?" Val asked.

The child shook her head.

"Are you afraid?"

The little girl didn't reply, but looked away, scanning the eastern horizon. In the distance, too far away to see clearly, lay the City's towers and walls and minarets and within, its teeming, carnal heart.

Rema's small hands twisted the frayed hem of her blouse. She shook her head, eyes stricken. "I can't come with you."

"But I need you to show me..." Then she thought about what sights the child might have to witness and relented. "All right, never mind. I'll find him."

Rema nodded and gave Val directions to where she'd found the body she believed to be Majeed's, saying it was near the edge of the burial ground beneath some olive trees. She didn't look at Val, but gazed off toward the City. It occurred to Val that she had never really had a good look at Rema's unveiled face.

"Listen, I want you to wait for me. If it's Majeed, I'll bury him. After that, I'll come back here."

"That's not allowed."

"What do you mean?"

"You can't bury him. You can't bury anyone. It's forbidden."

"By who? Why?"

"It's forbidden," Rema repeated, as though this were something Val should be expected to know. "Bodies at the Deadend are to be used up to the very last. By the Deadenders first, then whatever's left goes to the vultures. No funerals, no graves. The Turk forbids them."

"But why?"

The child turned away. From the determined set of her shoulders, Val saw that she would get no further with her questions.

"All right, I understand," she said. "No burials. But I still want you to wait for me."

"For what?"

"Before I leave, I want to say good-bye."

The words, as soon as she'd uttered them, seemed woefully inadequate, making all too clear her intention not to take Rema with her when she left the Deadend.

Rema muttered something Val didn't understand.

"What did you say?"

The child kicked a small rockslide of pebbles down the trail. "I said it doesn't matter if we say good-bye or not. I don't care if I ever see you again."

She turned and trudged away.

"Wait! Rema?"

The child broke into a run. Val watched her go without attempting to follow. She felt an ache of helplessness, inadequacy. For a moment she wanted to run after Rema, but for what? What was there she could say to make things better? What was there she could do?

She turned away and went to search the burial ground.

Within minutes the dove-colored dawn had brightened to an amber dazzle that lit up half the sky. With the light, the vultures seemed to grow more sluggish. They perched on rocks above the burial area, a few squabbling over choicer morsels, but most resting immobile, their long bodies and plucked and scrawny necks creating silhouettes that resembled crude, crooked lamps whose shades had been removed. With malevolent and greedy eyes, they watched Val pass.

A large part of the burial ground was comprised almost entirely of bones. Val skirted this area until she saw the olive trees that Rema had told her grew out of a rocky slope overlooking the burial ground. She approached with skittish steps and heartsick trepidation, afraid to look and yet afraid not to. Worst of all were the bodies among which she now meandered. Many, having suffered the night-long attentions of the vultures, were too terrible to look at, their internal organs strewn about half-eaten, mute testimony to a surfeit of flesh and the vultures' profligate feasting.

Occasionally, too, she spied a body wounded in a way suggesting, not a vulture, but some other type of fiend. Holes that gaped too neatly and symmetrically, passageways plowed into flesh where no natural orifice offered itself for use, the size of the wound implying penetration by something larger than the beak of a carrion-seeking bird.

Others, with their mouths agape, were lacking any teeth.

There was little blood, for apparently the teeth had been removed postmortem, but the lips were invariably coated with the pasty evidence of those for whom the dead mouths had offered temporary diversion.

A fly crawled up Val's forearm. Another attached itself to the leg of her trousers. Two more found a bead of cold sweat in the hollow of her neck between her collar bones.

More flies gathered. They massed and formed one airborne entity, roiling together in a single seething cloud.

Val hurried on, then leaned weakly against the first thing that presented itself, an olive tree. When she felt steady enough to go on, she glanced down and at once gasped with recognition.

"Oh, God!"

The body was the most perfect she had seen, showing no sign of violation, eerily serene in death. Hair swept back, hands folded comfortably across bare breasts, lips parted just enough to show the teeth were still intact, the tongue pink and life-like, ridged with studs.

Simone looked exactly as Val had last seen her. Even her various piercings were still intact, unusual, since most bodies here had been meticulously stripped of their adornments.

"Simone, no." She put a hand to the still face. The skin felt cool and rubbery. She ran her fingers down the woman's neck and touched her breasts, her belly, appalled that grief and prurience should be so closely mated.

How had she died? Val could find no signs of wounding.

Illness? Exhaustion? And what of Majeed? Was Simone merely the first whose loss she had to grieve?

Thus far, Simone's corpse lay unmolested by the vultures. The tanned skin was smooth, unmarked. If anything, Val thought that she looked too composed, almost obscenely peaceful.

And how to bury her? For all its penetrability, the ground might as well have been bricked over, and she had no tools to dig with.

Finally she decided on the only feasible option. The hard ground offered a profusion of stones. If she couldn't dig a grave for Simone, she could at least build a burial cairn.

Scooping her arms under her dead lover's shoulders, she dragged the body to an open area, rearranged the corpse's hands as she had found them, and went to gather stones.

The work was grueling, the number of stones required to cover up a human body were more than she would have guessed. At times, the combination of stench and physical exertion rendered her almost delirious. Thin brown shadows flitted past the edges of her vision. The moment that she whirled to catch them, they retreated further, staying always just at the limit of her peripheral vision, tempting her to turn continually, making herself dizzy.

Once she thought she saw Rema peeking from behind a boulder. She dropped the stone that she was hauling and ran to catch her, eager to see another living human being.

But the only creature she encountered was a wild sheep that gazed down at her from a rocky ledge before climbing out of sight.

Burial is forbidden.

Val heard the words as clearly as if Rema had murmured them in her ear. She flinched and whirled around but no one—not even the sheep—was spying on her.

Only Simone's head was left exposed now. Val lifted up the piece of cloth she'd draped across the woman's face and looked at her former lover a final time.

"I'm sorry, Simone. I hope you remembered your children's faces before you died."

The buzzing of the flies was becoming an ever louder drone. They gathered in a fluid, winged mass, shifting, seething, changing form.

Val slapped them away. They exploded briefly into hundreds of individual flies, then regrouped at once, reformed their cluster.

The massing flies, the unnatural heat, the smell—it was unbearable.

"Good-bye, Simone," said Val and bent to kiss her before she put the final stones atop her face.

The cold lips moved. Simone returned the kiss.

Val gasped and pulled away. Simone's mouth curved into a wide and terrifying smile. The stones began to fly off her with such force that Val had to throw herself to the ground to keep from being struck.

Simone sat up, shaking off the stones like a large dog shedding water. She reached out and grasped Val in a rib-fracturing embrace.

Val struggled fruitlessly, her nails sinking into mush and mire. Simone's face was liquefying, the features collapsing in upon themselves, reforming.

Sand spun and swirled inside the creature's permeable skull, sand coated its diffused anatomy, clung to the ridges of its unhinging spine and dusted its disintegrating heart.

Val felt herself lifted and flung into this maelstrom, enveloped in the flux and flow of the Simone thing's restructuring anatomy.

She looked down at her hands. They had sunken into the changing other's transubstantial flesh. Her fingers clutched a nest of capillaries. Arteries still pulsing blood looped around her arms like dark red grapevines.

I'm going to die, she thought. And then: *No, worse, I'm going to be absorbed inside this thing.*

She strained to free herself, but she was fighting sand and wind and the fragments and gobbets of flesh flung off as the thing disintegrated.

"It's time I dealt with you."

She opened her eyes and glimpsed the drawn profile of a morose, world-weary saint, three quarters of whose skull was a roiling stew of vapor and liquified matter. Even in this bizarre, fragmented form, she recognized the dark and troubled eyes, the sparse and tight-knit lips.

The Turk, she thought.

After that, the sand turned black and filled up her head entirely.

Chapter Twenty-Eight

Val awoke in darkness so impenetrable that her first thought was that she'd gone blind. Her second thought was that she was close to having an orgasm. The pleasure came in glistening waves. She sensed that, should she choose, she could succumb to the sex trance, pleasure herself unceasingly and die with her emaciated body still demanding more.

There was a certain morbid seductiveness to the idea. She forced her hands to her sides and eased herself up into a sitting position. Even such a minor effort produced a pain that felt like scalding wires probing inside her skull. She lay back. The pain rewarded her by ebbing slightly, but in its place, she became aware of a dull, cottony feeling behind her eyes, a blurring of her thought process as though she were coming down from a hellish drug trip.

Presently she became aware that near-by, she could hear what sounded like the muted crackling of a fire.

The fire promised light. Spurred on by that incentive she struggle to a standing position. In the darkness, the sense of unreality and the resulting vertigo was daunting. She took a few deep breaths, then felt her way cautiously with outstretched hands until her fingers came in contact with a wall.

She felt her way along it, inching along its twists and inclines until she came through a tunnel so narrow she had to turn her body sideways to negotiate it. Entering a rock-lined chamber, she confronted the source of the sound.

At first glance, her eyes, accustomed as they were to darkness, mistook the brilliant cascade for some sort of waterfall, ferocious in its splendor, unnatural in its crackling energy.

Then, stepping closer, she realized she was looking at a living river of writhing, licking fire, the same green flames—albeit a grander version—that had transported both Majeed and herself to the City.

The fire, however fiercely it might blaze, emitted no heat and, in defiance of all reason, seemed to be flowing downward, more like a lava stream than normal flame. In its seething center, Val saw smaller tongues of flame, spermatozoan in their flux, milling like tiny eels. She didn't need the incense burner in her hand to guess that the configurations here must replicate those incised into the stone.

The seething motion was impossible to look at. She shielded her face.

On either side of the fire, Val's stinging eyes made out two naked figures, a female and a male. Both were so bizarrely maimed that it took her several seconds to deduce the true obscenity of what had been done to them.

The man's hands had been amputated and then tacked back onto his torso in the most lewd of postures. Like grizzled crabs, the dead hands clung to either side of his testicles. Shriveled thumbs from which the nails had either dropped off or been torn met at the head of his penis.

While Val was still reeling from the sight of him, she was confronted with the horror of the female. Her breasts had been sliced off, one sewn into her mouth so that she was permanently nursing on a lifeless nipple. The other breast drooped from her vulva, giving the impression that a single-teated udder swung between her legs. Her eyes, just visible above the horror fastened to her mouth were cloudy, glazed. She made soft suckling noises at the breast.

Val staggered against the wall. Her fingers dug into the stone behind her as the fire unfurled new designs. In its many tongues converged pencil-thin shafts of color that stained the earthen walls and reflected glossy rainbows off the monstrous couple's wounds.

In the trough of shadow next to the flame, there occurred a subtle rolling and remolding of the shadows.

A voice, soft and avuncular, almost melodious, said, "The first time I saw the fire, I couldn't look away. I thought that I'd been hypnotized or lost my mind. But in a prison for sexual deviants in Izmir, madness was as expected as an infestation of cockroaches in the stew."

"If we're going to talk," Val said, averting her eyes from the maimed ones, "at least come out where I can see you. Or whomever it is that you're impersonating at the moment."

"No illusions this time. Shapeshifting drains me severely. My limits are too quickly reached."

So saying, an area of shadow dislodged itself from the larger dark. Filakis strode forth. He looked depleted, haggard.

The streaks of silver in his beard and hair appeared more numerous, his long and elegant hands almost cadaveresque in their bony thinness. He wore a brown cloak that scraped and crackled audibly against his skin with every movement. Val imagined it must have felt like being swathed in sandpaper.

"The last time you saw me in my true form," Filakis said, "was back in the hotel in Fez. I'd come to discipline my little freak. You tried to grab him and pull him away from me. I almost took you with me then, but I thought Majeed would suffer more if I left you behind."

"Majeed—where is he?"

"Not anywhere you'll find him. He's being punished."

"Where?"

"It doesn't matter. You won't see him again."

"I was told he was dead."

"I know...that little bastard girl." Filakis steepled his spidery fingers against his beard. "Like most children, deceit is her native language and lies, her toys. You were a fool to believe anything she said."

"And Simone? Why did you trick me by impersonating her corpse? What was the point?"

"Need there be one" said Filakis, "beyond my own amusement? It was a test, if you must know—one which you failed. I like to test people, find out their capacity for cruelty, compassion. I rather expected you to fail this one, but I wanted to give you every benefit of the doubt."

"How did I fail?" said Val. "Because I bought into your illusion? Because I thought that it really was Simone?"

Filakis waved a hand dismissively. "No, no. You really don't understand, do you? In order to have passed the test, you'd have had to either remain unmoved by the body or make some use of it...for a moment there, when you let your hands wander into areas that the prudish avoid even when their partners are alive, I almost thought I might have been wrong about you, that you truly were beyond redemption." He smiled, revealing a brown incisor in need of extraction. "But then your nobler nature reasserted itself and you decided that the right thing to do was bury her."

"And burial is forbidden."

"As I instructed Rema to make clear to you."

"She's your child?"

Filakis grimaced. "God, no."

"But she lied to me about Majeed because you told her to?"

"She had no choice. I have something that she values."

"And you, do you value Majeed?"

"Very much."

"Then why won't you let me see him? Why is he being punished?"

"I asked that he prove his loyalty to me in the most insignificant of ways—by killing you—and he defied me."

"Because he loves me."

Filakis scoffed, "Majeed never loved you or anybody. He succumbed to a romantic fantasy, that's all. You happened to be a convenient focus. Majeed's incapable of living outside the City for any length of time. He's incapable of living without me, for that matter. He would have betrayed you."

"I don't believe you."

Filakis gestured toward the man and woman wearing amputated parts of their anatomy. "Neither did they."

"So you're God here, is that it?"

With groaning weariness, Filakis eased his lanky frame down onto a stone bench cut into the wall. "Not quite. But if you like, you may think of me as a minor deity."

Despite her efforts to avert her eyes, Val found herself gazing at the kaleidoscope-like fire. The multi-hued flame flowed counterclockwise now, narrowing down like water spilling through a drain. Then, just as suddenly, it reversed direction and spun outward like a Catherine wheel, a tiny molten universe being born again and again in a multiplicity of forms.

"Is that the same kind of fire that brought me to the City?"

"In essence, yes."

"And can it get me out of here?"

"Forgive me for destroying your illusions, but even if you had the incense burner in your hands, I'd never let you leave. This is your home, for the brief amount of time that you have left to live." Filakis smiled like a Halloween trickster doling out rat-poisoned sweets.

"I see the patterns in the fire fascinate you. Would you care to see the price I paid to have dominion over it?"

That the question was pure rhetoric, Val had no doubt. She'd been weighing what her options were when Filakis asked it. Should she try to run or attempt to keep him talking? Or should she try to light the incense burner and take the chance that she might escape from here before the Turk could stop her?

Without waiting for her response, Filakis untied the cord around his narrow waist, allowing his robe to fall open.

"At this point I believe the proper line would be, 'drop to your knees, bitch, and suck me off,' but, unfortunately, the first rule of oral rape is that it helps to have a penis."

"Lucky me," said Val.

"Indeed."

She came closer, remembering the man that Myra and her band had tortured, as she looked at the dense crosshatching of scar tissue where Filakis' genitalia should have been. But for the puckered wound marking where the root of his penis had once joined his body, nothing remained to indicate the Turk had ever possessed a normal male anatomy.

"Touch me if you like," Filakis said, as though conferring some great boon.

Val did. The marbled skin had the dense and fibrous texture of a rattan mat. Mid-way down, her exploring fingers found a tiny, puckered hole, little more than an inverted nipple, through which urine must pass.

"I think I understand," she said. "In order to have sex, you have to shapechange."

"Either that," Filakis said, "or watch. Or submit to buggery. But I frankly got my fill of that in the prison at Izmir. By the time the guards got through with me, I could have shat a watermelon as though it were a chickpea." He sighed. "Regrettable how the human body breaks down with overuse."

"The guards, they did this to you?"

"Made me a eunuch? My goodness, no. They were just horny cretins, lacking all imagination. They'd have been as happy sticking it in the backside of a chicken or a hole in a wheel of goat cheese."

"Then what...?"

"In my youth I suffered the burden of great appetite and even greater curiosity. Like many young men, I was obsessed with death and sex, and I wanted to devise a marriage of the two. I took a girl out in the woods and raped and tortured her with a winch handle from my father's shipyard. I should have been put to death, I suppose, but my father used his influence and I was sent to a prison in Izmir for the criminally insane.

"I shared a cell there with a man who belonged to an old and venerated Moroccan tribe. I doubt you've heard of it, unless you've spent time studying Moroccan history. It was called the Brotherhood of the Aissawa, and it was founded in the eighteenth century by a holy man named Sidi ben Aissa. Supposedly Ben Aissa conferred upon his followers magic powers. My cellmate claimed to be one of his descendants. He saw promise in me and offered me a chance to be his successor. Of course, I thought he was a madman—until he made the spells tattooed into his hands turn into fire and spin miracles before my eyes.

"He offered to pass his knowledge on to me, to burn the spells into my palms with Ben Aissa's fire."

"You must have shown great aptitude for perversion," Val said.

If Filakis noted the sarcasm in her voice, he chose to ignore it.

"Indeed. But his knowledge came with a very high price." He touched the area of his missing manhood with wistful fondness, then closed his robe. "The price was, of course, my sex. I had to do the cutting with a straight razor and use nothing to kill the pain.

"Of course, the guards thought that self-castration was just more proof of my insanity. I was near death. My mentor sneaked into the hospital ward that night and burned the spells into my palms."

He moved his long hands languidly. The tattoos on his palms seemed to separate from the flesh and orbit near his fingertips, changing designs. Val forced herself to look away.

"As I said, I was nearly dead—I'm told the doctor who examined me the next day pronounced me so. But in my temporarily altered state, before I was brought back to life, I was able to follow the spells on my hands to their source. I discovered there are rivers to existence. Currents and eddies and streams, where all consciousnesses intersect. One has only to be able to tap into them. In my near-death, I encountered that flow of consciousness where all humanity's darkest dreams converge in a malignant tide. Such collective repositories of human want are like giant vulvas. With sufficient will, they can be penetrated."

"And you did?"

"The spells he carved into my hands can summon up the fire, can conjure any desire I—or you—could dream of. You asked if I am God here. In a sense, I am. Your desires may have brought you here, but mine created the opening through which you passed."

"Does that mean that if you die, the City ceases to exist?"

"I told you," smiled Filakis, "if I'm a deity, I'm but a minor one. It was I who opened the door, but that state of mind from which the City was born, that has existed through eternity and always will."

"Then I'm in a world your mind created?"

Filakis pursed his full lips as though he'd tasted something sour. "You say that as if you find the thought unbearably repugnant. No, this is a world of humankind's collective creation, meaning your little mind has made its own puny contribution to the general stew. Does that please you?"

"What I need to know," said Val, "is why my mother suffers from terrifying visions in which she describes a place, a hellhole—her words, I'm sorry—presided over by a gaunt, mutilated despot. If it's the City she's describing, how could she know about it?"

"Desire finds a way," Filakis said. "Perhaps she taps into that collective repository of the perverse when her need, like yours, is strong enough. Ah, don't look so appalled, my dear, mothers find their way here, too. And I'm sure you do acknowledge the naturalness of inherited tastes."

"Having her genes doesn't mean I share her inclinations."

Filakis smiled gently. "If it pleases you to think so."

Val stared into the fluid musculature of the flame. Its unnatural brilliance was painful to look upon, but she took a few steps closer to it, squinting as her eyes overflowed and tears streamed down her cheeks.

"If you have such great wisdom and power, it shouldn't bother you to humor me with a minor request. Let me see Majeed."

"I think not."

"But you said that he's alive..."

"Only because I find him highly entertaining. But I'll wager at the moment, he wishes he were dead—as soon enough, you will be."

As he spoke, Val's hand slid between the folds of fabric in her djellaba. In its sheath next to her leg, she felt Simone's dagger. She let her fingers brush its reassuring heft. But the pouch which she'd stitched shut with the incense burner inside was open now—and empty.

"Looking for something?" Filakis grabbed her by the hair, spun her around.

"I don't know what you're talking about."

"The incense burner's not there, is it?"

"What do you...?"

"Stop playing games!" Then, lowering his voice again, Filakis said, "How ironic that you've already tired of the City. That you're already bored with a place you went to so much trouble to find?"

He nodded to the two maimed creatures. Before Val could move to stop them, they caught her arms and twisted them behind her back, the handless man exerting surprising force and dexterity in the use of his stumps.

"I've something special planned for you here," Filakis said. "It's time to take a look at it."

He nodded, and his two disciples dragged Val between them directly toward the flame. For a moment, she thought they meant to hurl her into it and wondered if Filakis could possibly mean to exile her, to send her from the City the same way she had come. Unable to stare into the fire's brilliance, she shut her eyes. When she was able to open them again, the green flames were above and on both sides of her, cascading down around her and her captors in a licking, leaping arch. Her head sang with the ferocious crackling.

Then they were beyond the flames, traversing a narrow tunnel supported by crude arches and slitted windows no wider than the thickness of a hand. At intervals light streamed in from holes cut in the ceiling, piercing the gloom with gauzy light aswirl with dust motes. Val's sense of claustrophobia was acute as they progressed more deeply into the maze. Occasionally, she saw narrow *derbs* branching off from the main route, but whether these led to some other part of the City or merely deeper into Filakis' lair, she had no way of knowing.

At one point, she could hear cries and moans, muffled pleas that sounded not quite human and emanated from beyond the faienced walls.

Val cringed.

Filakis gave her a chaste pat and said, "Think of their cries as music, the sounds produced when pleasure reaches its upper limits and turns into something even more intense."

"You mean torture."

"Torture is only pleasure toward which one lacks the proper attitude. You'd do well to contemplate that principal."

They passed beneath a low arch to where a low stone wall overlooked a pit a dozen feet below them. A collection of ragged carpets had been strewn across the dirt floor. Most were bunched into lumpy piles, as though some sort of wild activity had taken place upon them, either frantic copulation or a savage fight. Val thought their stains, which were difficult to distinguish from the overall design, were almost certainly blood.

Along the sides of the pit, at intervals of about six feet, metal grills sealed off what looked like lightless passageways. Too low for anyone but a child to walk through, Val assumed they must be intended for some kind of animal. She had visions of wild dogs rushing through the tunnels to tear apart their prey, for dogs were the only animals she'd seen in the City that were sufficiently large and fierce to kill a human being.

"You should be grateful to me," Filakis said. "I'm going to make it possible for you to literally die of pleasure. To die while taking part in the one activity which you prefer above all others."

Val tried to pull her arms free of the mutilated creatures' grasp, but their grip—especially the pressure exerted by the wrist stumps of the handless man—were amazingly strong.

"Listen to me, I have something for Majeed. A memento. You said you wouldn't kill him. At least, if you have to kill me, give him this for me..."

"It's too late for sentiment," Filakis said. "When I'm finished with Majeed he won't remember his own name, let alone some whore he's unwisely consorted with. But I'm curious what kind of foolish bauble you think might please him."

"Then make them let me go."

With a wan smile, Filakis assented.

Val brought her arms around, trying to massage the blood back into them.

"Let's see what she's got besides her tits and pussy inside those clothes," Filakis said. He nodded to the gruesome couple. "Undress her."

But in the fraction of a second before the maimed pair seized her, Val slid one hand inside the folds of the voluminous djellaba and pulled forth the knife.

Filakis was the one she wanted, but the other two were in the way. She slashed the man first, opening up one of his wrist stumps so that the raised, keloidal scar tissue split, pumping forth fresh crimson. He screamed and reared back, so that the next blow, which she was aiming at his jugular went off the mark and instead sliced off a portion of his nose. She saw one hairy nostril fly, spewing blood across the dirt floor like a grotesque and gravely wounded insect.

The woman wedded to her awful pacifier lunged at Val, forcing her to take a step backward toward the wall surrounding the pit. Val struck at her throat but managed to open only a bloodless wound in the dead flesh sewn to her face. She ducked a blow and turned to flee, but the woman locked both arms around her waist, lifting her up.

Val arched backward, trying to break the woman's grip as she brought the knife down alongside her adversary's spine. She felt the point of balance shift. She started to fall backward. At the last second, her antagonist realized what was happening and tried to let Val go. Val gripped the woman's hair. They seesawed for an instant, then fell together, landing on the dirt-caked carpets.

When Val opened her eyes, the woman who had fallen with her was sprawled nearby, moaning. Her leg was twisted under in a way that anatomy made impossible assuming her deformities did not include a second knee joint midway down the calf.

Filakis stood above them, peering down in avid expectation.

As Val got to her knees, he made a gesture with his hennaed hands. The grills blocking off the tunnels slid open.

"It's even better that there're two of you," Filakis said. "This way it will take longer. The record for this kind of death, by the way, is fourteen and a half hours, but with two of you, it may take a day or more. Internal ruptures, hemorrhaging, that takes place eventually. You'll understand what I mean when things get started." He peered down. His smile was gluttonous. "Don't worry. I'm not leaving you for long. I'll be back in time to watch you die."

From deep inside the tunnels, Val heard a mounting noise, feet scuffling over stone, harsh breathing that might have belonged to man or beast. Desperately she looked around for the knife and saw that the hilt protruded from beneath the woman's mastectomied chest.

As she reached for it, the approaching noise became a guttural roar and what Filakis had seen fit to set upon her burst out of the tunnels.

Chapter Twenty-Nine

When he heard the deafening commotion in the tunnels leading to the torture pit, Breen was crouched upon the flat roof of Filakis' palace enjoying a new game. He squatted on his haunches, nude except for a cotton loincloth and the most gossamer of shirts that protected his sensitive flesh from the sun. Around his waist, he'd strapped his own approximation of a workman's toolbelt, a pouched belt that held some of his favorite toys—an ice pick and a pair of pliers, a set of handcuffs and a handful of two-inch nails.

Painstakingly, he was peeling small strips of skin off his forearms and belly and tossing the fragile wafers down below.

Below him, several stories down, clustered a motley gang of such assorted trolls and fiends and madmen as Breen had ever seen. Such a frenzy did his meager offerings create among them that it was like showering down the Host upon a contingent of religious fanatics.

The would-be cannibals fought and clawed and snarled over the skimpiest of morsels, the slightest bit of Breen.

Breen had heard tell of this wretched tribe, as despised as the Deadenders and more greatly feared. The Deadenders at least confined their violations to the dead. The Skinners consumed both the living and the dead. They got their name from their predilection for skinning meat alive before the feast in the manner of a persnickety child cutting the crust off a slice of toast. A bit of tissue or cup of blood from a living body aroused them to a pitch of lust no mere sex act could equal. They were the City's sharks, cruising for the wounded, the aged, and the ill.

Because of the raw and oozing burns that mapped his body, the cannibal tribe gravitated toward Breen like hounds on the scent of venison. He'd seen them lurking in the shadows or peering out of slitted windows, inept ghouls whose tendency to compete with each other for prey led them to spend as much time spying on each other as on potential victims. Even with their numbers, they never dared attack. Breen's state of physical health, however repugnant to the eye, was not sufficiently in shambles to give the impression that he would be easily dispatched.

And the Skinners, like all addicts, could be toyed with.

Now Breen observed with fascination how they swarmed and struggled over the scabby bits he threw them. Once, in hopes of precipitating chaos in their midst, he used a razor to slice off the end of a toe and watched as a half dozen of the gaunt and savage creatures came to bloody blows for possession of the treat.

Breen leaned down over the wall and bared his wolfen teeth.

He spat upon his devotees. Then, no longer amused by their morbidly hungry gazes, he commenced to hurling stones.

The Skinners dispersed like a bevy of waterbugs.

That was when Breen heard the sound beneath his feet, emanating from deep within the building where the warren of tunnels housed Filakis' torture chambers. Not cries of pain, which he'd become sufficiently familiar with as to find almost uninspiring, but howls of lustful glee. Male voices raised to savage pitch.

Not one to miss out on either spectacle or opportunity, Breen decided this clamor was worthy of investigation.

Making his way back to one of the rope ladders that connected the third story of the structure with the roof, and keeping a watchful eye out for the Skinners, he started climbing down.

Filakis' prisoners, when they burst from the tunnels into the central pit, were in no frame of mind to be intimidated by Val's knife, which they soon wrenched away from her. They seemed, in fact, impervious to pain, their phalluses engorged and held tight with painful cockrings.

A half dozen of them had swarmed over the woman whose breasts had been removed, ripping away the awful tokens sewn to her mouth and genitals.

Val's body, of course, offered no such bizarre impediments to violation. Her djellaba was shoved up around her hips, the men striking out and quarreling with each other in their desperate haste to make use of her.

She was dry when she was penetrated. The thrust felt like her assailant's cock was wrapped in sandpaper.

Above her rapist's head, she could see the others crowding round.

For the first time in her adult life, all desire left her.

Even the City's hypnotic sensuality couldn't mute her terror. Her body was a pillaged prison now. All was pain and invasion and the suffocating sense that she no longer belonged to herself, that even her death would not be private, but only the loathsome conclusion to this hideous melee.

There's no escape from this, she thought, as the man on top of her was pulled away and another took his place.

She hoped Filakis was wrong about the time factor. She hoped she would die quickly.

Breen exited the tunnel with a feral grin upon his lips, the tang of blood and semen already palpable in the stagnant air. He had heard the sound of women's screams—sweet music that caused his blood to quicken and his cock to twitch—as he made his way through the dizzying tunnels.

Some new sort of torture taking place, he assumed, and hurried like a glutton in danger of arriving late to a sumptuous meal. When first he saw the two women being gang-fucked, he squatted in between to observe the action, making bets with himself as to which of the two men currently raping would climax first. When he realized that the cockrings the men were wearing made orgasm impossible, he giggled with sadistic mirth.

In the state of voyeuristic glee in which he found himself, it took Breen a moment to recognize the woman nearest him, the one who, at least to Breen's trained torturer's eye, appeared to be already dead.

Dead?

This couldn't be. Not Val. Not *yet*.

Not when she still belonged to him, not when he had suffered the Turk's wrath by sparing her life in the desert so that he might inflict on her a sufficiently brutal death later on.

The knife that Val had dropped was lying in the dirt near the edge of the pit. Beset with killing rage and lust, Breen seized it up and joined the fray.

She had been wrong. There was, indeed, an escape of sorts still open to her. How, in fact, had she forgotten how to get there? She'd known how to do this as a child, when the merely impossible became the unendurable. The skill had been forgotten, but not lost to her.

There was a place and it was deep within, so deep it verged on death. In this spot, she disconnected from her body, exited her flesh. In here, her attackers couldn't touch her, and though they raped her, she could be penetrated by neither pain nor fear.

She was hovering above the scene now, watching the men violate her body and that of the maimed woman. Her own body appeared to be lifeless. The rape, she noted with some critical detachment, would have progressed more quickly had not the various participants continually squabbled among themselves. No one seemed willing to vacate his place to the next one in line. Thus the violence kept escalating, with one man pulling another off her and that one being pummeled bloody by a third.

Then into this dismaying havoc leaped a monster, a scabrous creature who appeared to have been skinned alive. Patches of dried mud were plastered in the crevices of his body. His hair was gone, his scalp a raw and festering wound. A sickly rictus of a smile caused blood to seep from the cracked corners of his mouth.

Yet for all his appalling condition, the man seemed not to lack for strength. He snatched up the fallen knife and thrust it so hard between the shoulder blades of the man mounting her that she could all but feel the scrape of metal against spine. Her rapist stiffened and howled, then fell thrashing to the dirt.

The madman with the knife was shouting something, keening it through ruined vocal cords.

Two others ran at him while a fourth took advantage of the abruptly vacant pussy to fall to his knees and try to drive himself inside her.

The half-naked knife wielder kept screaming. His words were incoherent as he flailed at his assailants, but one word sounded like "Mine!"

The man assaulting her was having difficulty making entry through the unlubricated lips of her vagina. He turned to duck as the screeching madman drove his weapon through another assailant's femoral artery, bejeweling the air with scarlet.

Go back, Val's mind commanded, but she was loathe to leave her vantage point. Her position as a disembodied spectator was safe and comforting. She felt serene. Death held no terror.

I could stay here forever.

Go back, go back, go back.

Then the body that still belonged to her twitched feebly and her viewpoint on the carnage shifted suddenly. Now she was no longer gazing down from the ceiling, but looking up at it. Her body was dotted with spattered blood. Her insides felt like she'd been gutted with a poker.

The man who crouched between her legs provided a perfect target. She launched a kick with all the power of her thigh muscles behind it and felt his balls squash nicely beneath her foot. He shrieked and tumbled across the body of a fallen cohort.

She crawled away and, while the other's were still occupied with fending off the armed attacker, scuttled on her hands and knees into the closest tunnel.

The tunnel was just high enough for a person of medium height to run at a crouch. Val moved as quickly as she could, guided by light that filtered down through grillwork in the ceiling. In several places the tunnel forked, offering the possibility that anyone pursuing her might be misled.

Up ahead she could see a cone of light descending from an opening to the outside.

That the space in which she found herself was a type of dungeon was immediately clear. Also—distressingly—was the fact that there appeared no exit.

Along a central corridor, grilled windows offered a view behind a dozen or so heavy wooden doors. A few of these were open and unoccupied—Val assumed her attackers had been housed here and freed for the occasion of some recreational rape.

A few of the doors stood open. The prisoners inside, manacled or handcuffed in numerous inventive ways, were in no danger of escaping. But among the doors that might have offered access to the outside, she could find not a single one unlocked nor was she able to pry loose any of the grillwork covering the few windows that looked out over the rooftops of the dwellings lower down.

From further down the row, she heard low, ecstatic moans. Investigating, she discovered a naked woman reclining on a bed of straw. A leather riding crop protruded from her spread vagina and she was plumbing her own depths with dangerous fervor. No chains restrained her, but she seemed oblivious both of her surroundings and of the blood that welled between her legs.

"Is there a way out of here?" Val asked, although she had scant hope of receiving any sensible reply.

To her surprise, the woman interrupted her own gouging and fixed her with an intense and lucid gaze. "In there," she said, pointing through an archway leading from her cubicle into the one beyond. That an exit from Filakis' awful lair existed where anyone might gain access to it seemed to Val unlikely, yet she had to take the chance.

Ducking through the arch, she found herself in yet another cell-like space, confronting a latticed wooden door. She tugged on it with all her strength, but the door refused to budge.

She had paused to rest, debating in which direction to flee next, when the door, seemingly of its own accord began to move beneath her hands and open inward.

Val thought her efforts had freed a latch or unstuck a stubborn hinge. Suddenly the door burst open with such force that, had she not moved aside with sufficient speed, she would have been crushed between it and the wall.

Before her, its flesh raw and seeping, the half-skinned creature from the pit roared out an indecipherable noise. In one maimed hand it clutched the knife that Val had dropped, the two good fingers of that hand aided by the stubs of the others.

Its face split in a savage grin and she saw its teeth, filed to jagged, crocodile-like points. It fixed on her a glare of wild, unblinking lust.

If Val had harbored any hope that the madman's intervention in the pit was on her behalf, she saw now the folly of that notion. Whatever the monster had been attempting to accomplish, it was certainly not to rescue her from rape and death. She darted back toward the archway she'd passed under earlier. The creature followed, swishing the blood-soaked blade and clicking its gruesome orthodontal work like a chef sharpening knives prior to carving up a roast.

As it pursued, the maimed man kept up a steady yodeling howl, the same syllable, mantra-like sputtered out through liverish lips.

In some awful way, the sound wasn't entirely unfamiliar, but such was Val's state of terror, she had no time to try and put any sense to it. The monster was advancing. Soft shafts of light that filtered through the ceiling gave a luminous cast to the blade.

She took a step back and her stalker advanced three, lashing out with the knife. The blade made a sound like fabric tearing. Hot pain lanced through Val's shoulder. She saw blood seeping around the edges of a new gash in the rags of her djellaba.

She ducked the next blow so that the blade imbedded itself briefly between two unmortared stones. In the seconds that it took her assailant to scrape it free, she hefted a loose brick and swung it at his skull. He dodged and caught the blow on his muscular back, but a tongue-sized flap of skin sloughed off, and the ravaged vocal cords emitted a guttural howl.

Pain proved, however, no deterrent. The next sally sent the knife singing past Val's face, so close that tendrils of her hair were snipped off and drifted to the floor. She darted into the cubicle behind her. There, the woman pleasuring herself had given up her grievous coring to try to crawl out of harm's way, but to no avail. Val gained some time when her pursuer paused long enough to strike the woman a brutal blow across the neck. She toppled backward against the wall.

Val took a running step and felt her ankle seized. All balance left her. She plunged forward onto the hard-packed dirt, arms splayed in front of her. Blood from the knife wound in her shoulder spattered the earthen floor.

She freed herself by kicking at her pursuer's head, her efforts rewarded by his grunt of pain, but no sooner had she regained her feet than he had slammed her up against the very door that she was struggling to get open. The knife tip prodded underneath her breast. The man's fecal-smelling breath assailed her.

It was only then, with his face pressed so close to hers that she could see where his eyelashes had been seared off, that she understood that the word he was repeating was a familiar one and that the word was "Breen."

Chapter Thirty

"Arthur?"

The recognition stunned her so greatly that for a second all fear left her and she was filled instead with horror and pity for his awful injuries.

"How did you get here?"

"Following you."

"But how...what happened to you?"

He pricked the knife up into the crease below her breast. She felt blood seep beneath her garment.

"You mean you don't find my new appearance...appealing?"

How to answer? At first she'd thought he'd said "appalling." She had to strain to get his words. The syllables were garbled. His burned tongue seemed to singe and melt the consonants.

"Arthur, please don't do this."

"I saved your life back there."

"I know and..."

"So now I'm going to take it at my leisure."

She tried to move her hands. He jabbed her again with the knife. Beneath the loose-fitting garment he was wearing, she felt his penis stiffen.

"Don't you even want to fuck me before you kill me?"

"Oh yes. But first I want to carve you up." He brought the knife up level with her eyes. "A long time ago, you told me your mother once took out her own eyes. I've given a lot of thought to that. I want to see how you'll look with yours cut out."

He pressed against her. Val gave up all resistance and made herself go limp. The sudden ceasing of her struggling took Breen by surprise. She slithered down the wall, then flung herself sideways and scuttled on her hands and knees between Breen's legs, toppling him over backwards in the process.

She reached the woman Breen had felled just as he tackled her again.

Expecting to feel the knife sink between her shoulder blades at any moment, she hurled herself forward and grabbed the last few inches of the riding crop protruding from the woman's bloody labia.

The leather shaft slid out between the parted legs with a meaty pop followed by the burbling exit of trapped air escaping. The woman never moved, but toppled forward silently. Val saw the fatal knife wound at the base of her skull.

There was no time to try to turn or to take aim. Val brought the riding crop up and back over her head, striking Breen with sufficient force to wrench forth a scream.

He released his grip upon her legs. She rolled over and saw the leather lash had opened up his cheek. One eye was closed and seeping crimson tears.

Before he could recover from the blow, she slashed him again, back and forth, bits of skin and mud flying as though a filthy rug were being beaten. He reeled and stumbled backward. Darting past him, Val reached the door that had been left open when he came after her. She ran through and slammed it shut behind her, then pushed the bolt across and leaned against it, sobbing with relief.

A few seconds later, she heard the slit-throated screech of Breen's ruined voice and felt the door rattle on its hinges under his assault.

She put her lips to the crack between the wood and stone and said, "I'd tell you to go burn in hell, Arthur, but it looks like you've already been there."

She barely moved her face in time before the knifeblade came through at the spot her mouth had been, probing for her futilely before it was withdrawn.

"Fuck you, Arthur," she said at a safe distance, but in reply there was only an icy, eerie silence in which Val thought she felt the hatred emanating toward her from behind the door.

The monster, at least for now, was locked in that section of the dungeon. How easily and quickly he could find another exit and come after her again, Val didn't know, but she wasn't waiting to find out.

Ahead of her stretched a dimly lit, rank smelling corridor—another section in the cluttered warren of Filakis' subterranean abode. Light from the overhead airshafts was even more scant. Thick, unpleasant odors clotted the still air like dung-covered magnolias, the air tainted with a sewer stench that made her stomach heave.

The section of the dungeon in which she now found herself was so eccentrically constructed as to defy all her attempts to create a mental map. Paths forked, stairs descended into darkness profound and rank, other staircases ascended along the walls, like handholds set in stone for a mountaineering party.

Occasionally, baffled and exhausted by the maze, Val paused to catch her breath and heard, emerging from a deeper portion of the maze, the most distressing sounds, plaintive wails and frenzied keening, the staccato yap of tongues convulsed by insanity or pain.

Afraid to proceed, yet more afraid to try to find her way back to where she'd last seen Breen, she continued in the direction of the cries.

A few paces farther on, the narrowing staircase petered out entirely at a hole in the wall where a stone had been removed. It was from the other side that the sounds of suffering intensified. She crouched down, saw a faint light on the other side, and slithered through the opening.

She found herself in another corridor, this one even grimmer than the one she'd just traversed. On either side were narrow cells, each one containing an isolated occupant, and each endured their own ordeal—some hooded, with clamps attached to swollen genitals and nipples, others suffering cockrings of heated metal and brutally snug corsets, bindings so unnaturally tight the flesh popped between the ropes like risen bread. One man, a contortionist, was positioned on his back with legs behind his head. His cock came within a millimeter of his mouth, but so cunningly was he secured that not even his most ardent struggling allowed his tongue to reach his other head.

Val wandered on, appalled and mesmerized by this symphony of frustrated arousal. The floor became increasingly wet. She heard a soft sloshing and, rounding a bend in the torturous hallway, saw an oblong pool just large enough to accommodate a body. In it, nude and bound, leeched utterly of color, floated face-down an emaciated angel, dead to all appearances but with a breathing tube resembling a flute extending from its mouth.

Given its pallor and stillness, Val was highly doubtful the thing was capable of breath at all.

She bent down to it and then gasped with recognition. No ethereal being this, but quite the opposite—Majeed. But in what condition! Foetus-like, he floated in his swollen sac of womb. Naked, touching nothing, ensconced in dark and silence.

Val reached into the pool and floated Majeed over toward her until she could untie his hands and flip him on his back. Dead, she thought. Pale and, to all appearances, devoid of life, his clammy flesh seemed formed from tallow and oiled with ashen mucus.

Yet she had already witnessed sufficient wonders in the place not to concede Majeed's lifelessness too soon.

She lifted his head out of the pool, removed the tube from his mouth and shook him hard. His head lolled back and forth, his eye whites gleamed.

He didn't seem to breath, but, with a hand between his breasts, Val felt the ticking of his heart, its pace so slow that her own heart beat a dozen times to Majeed's one.

"Majeed!"

She slapped his head from side to side, then bit him on the ear until the coppery taste of blood filled her mouth.

His eyes came slowly into focus, squinting into the painful glare of the flashlight. His skin and hair, always fair, were alabaster. He looked, Val thought, like an albino eel raised in some subterranean cavern, its translucent flesh never touched by sunlight.

"Majeed, it's Val. What has Filakis done to you?"

Majeed began to shake convulsively. With Val's help, he managed to drag himself up over the side of the pool where he collapsed shivering, his nerves capering in mad jigs beneath the skin, tics working at his face and muscle twitches making his limbs flail.

"Can you talk? What's happened to you?"

She tried to hold him in her arms, but his body now was seized with cruel spasms. He alternatively flailed and shook, like a child in the throes of night terrors.

She realized then the nature of his peculiar torture. In a world where even the rustling of leaves produced erotic shivers, Majeed had been deprived of even the most meager stimulation—even his precious opium had been denied him.

Val's hands were covered with the liquid from the pool. She became aware now of the coolness and viscosity of what at first she'd taken to be water. Not water, though, she realized now, but cold and clotted semen.

"Majeed? Come on, get up."

She hoisted Majeed to a sitting position and struck him in the back. He took a gasping breath of air, another.

Then his eyelids fluttered open and he gazed at her, as mindless as an idiot child before leaning over and vomiting into the pool.

"Are you all right? What happened?"

Majeed's eyes were glazed under semen-clotted lashes. "I was in the strangest place... children with eyes like chunks of quartz and archangels with huge penises..."

"Majeed, get up. We haven't got much time."

"...and a hermaphrodite who curled up in a ball and fucked himself."

Val slapped him hard. "You were hallucinating. It happens when people are deprived of all sensory experience. It's a form of torture."

Majeed rubbed his eyes. He seemed to be concentrating hard.

"How did you find me?"

"It doesn't matter. Right now, we've got to hurry and find a way to leave the City."

"Do you still have the incense burner?"

"No, it's gone. But there's a place Filakis showed me where the green fire cascades down like a waterfall—I've walked beneath it. If we can find it and jump into it, maybe it will take us out of here."

Pulling Majeed to his feet, she led him back along the corridor with its rows of cells of naked captives, through the opening in the wall where she had first gained access. A stairway at the other end descended into what appeared to be a still deeper level of Filakis' catacombs.

"Down here," said Val.

"No, wait." Majeed grabbed her hand. "I think I hear someone. "

Val heard nothing, but she was willing to concede that Majeed's long sensory deprivation might have made his senses preternaturally acute. A shadowy niche in the earthen wall offered a hiding place. They ducked inside it.

Long minutes passed, their bodies pressed together in the narrow space. "Come on, " said Val, "I think it's safe. "

Instead of answering, Majeed pressed her fingers to his groin. Something had been added to his anatomy since his captivity, a set of gold rings that penetrated labia and scrotum. The piercings made a bell-like tingling as he rubbed against her.

"Do you know what Filakis' said he'd do to me if I disobeyed again? He threatened to turn me into a neutered creature like himself. The whole time I was in the pool, that was what I thought about. "

"Then don't give him the chance. Help me find the fire, and maybe we'll get out of here."

"And if we don't...?"

"We'll die. "

"Then fuck me one last time." He thrust against her, making the rings clink and ping together in urgent song.

Val said, "Majeed...the noise... " just as the vulval bells were stilled too suddenly.

She tried to turn around, but her wrists were clasped behind her.

From the corner of her vision, she saw Majeed slump to the floor. Behind her, she smelled an unspeakable aroma, a perfumed breath, rich with death and strawberries.

She managed to twist around. Filakis stood before her, lean and dour as a medieval saint. His hennaed fingers roved her face as though its contours held the meaning of some mystery. His lips, drawn tight in monkish gloom, bestowed a cold kiss on her forehead.

"I only want to leave here with Majeed," Val said. "Let us go."

"Majeed is going nowhere," Filakis said. "He doesn't *want* to leave. And if you believe he loves you, then you're a fool. He isn't capable of love."

"You're hardly an expert on the subject."

"At least my expertise extends to knowing what's real and what's wishful thinking.

"In any case, your haste to leave verges on insulting. I thought you wanted pleasure. I can't let you go away disappointed."

He touched Val's throat while keeping a tight grip on her wrists. The long, emaciated fingers wrung forth a rain of gold and silver coins behind her eyes. The coins clattered against the inside of her skull, while, as if from the bottom of a deep and water-filled well, she heard Filakis say, "I want to find out if what you most deeply dread is also what you secretly desire."

Chapter Thirty-One

Looking up, Val saw her naked body reflected back to her in the ceiling's mirrored tiles. From neck to pubis, biceps to wrists, her body appeared to be the canvas on which a demented seamstress had created a masterpiece of color and design. A hundred needles pierced her flesh, and through the punctures had been woven the most colorful of threads, which crisscrossed in a splendid zigzag of geometry. The threads, in turn, were secured to hooks affixed to the bed's headboard and sides. The slightest movement agitated the needles and caused her nerves to scream.

Movement created pain so sharp and constant that after a time, it crossed a psychic border and became a kind of lunatic arousal—desire not linked to pleasure, but a perverse and masochistic lust that fed on misery and terror.

She realized this in her strange and all too familiar prison, a room she had only to glimpse to know its perimeters and furnishings, the contents of its bookshelves and its dresser drawers, to know, without going near the window, what view she would see: not crenelated walls of a Moroccan Casbah, but plowed fields and distant tree-clad hills, a decaying barn belonging to some unknown neighbors to the east and a silo above whose entranceway a hex sign had been drawn. To know that if she were free to turn the photo on the desktop to face her, she would see a picture of the child she used to be.

How this illusion of a return to the chamber of her childhood was possible was lost on her. She assumed, at first, a temporary dementia on her part, that Filakis might have slipped her some powerful hallucinagen. This belief was comforting since, at some point, the drug might either wear off or be overcome by sheer force of will. She resolved not to give in to panic but to accept her situation for the moment and await the next development the way one allows a nightmare to run its course.

When she heard a key in the lock, Val hoped to see Filakis, even as a part of her mind braced for something worse. It came—her mother Lettie or an identical imposter, perfect right down to the dimple in her cheek, the heart-shaped mouth, the missing eyes.

"Filakis!" hissed Val.

The Lettie creature turned her blind head, uncomprehending. "What did you say?"

"You don't fool me. You're another of Filakis' illusions."

"I don't know what you're talking about," her mother crooned. "You must have been having a bad dream." She minced her way gingerly across the room, until she could put her outstretched hand into Val's hair.

"Did you enjoy the drive last night? Did you like looking at the whores? How are we feeling this morning?"

"These needles...whatever they are...they *hurt*."

"Well...yes, I guess they do," said Lettie, no more moved by Val's predicament than she'd been twenty-five years earlier. "That's so you won't get up and leave. But I remember what the laces look like—they must be quite beautiful, I think." She strummed a lacquered fingernail idly across the weave. Like falling dominoes, Val's nerves responded to the wiggling needles. Fire shot beneath her skin.

"...this design in particular I find attractive. A cat's cradle is what it feels like, the thread's as soft as your skin. Much more becoming than clothing, I imagine."

The pain receded. Val tried to focus on the appalling vision at her side. Lettie was almost as she remembered her from long ago, plump and auburn-haired, artfully lipsticked and rouged. But for the shockingly empty eye sockets, she might have been a Vegas showgirl gone to seed, a soiled and faded starlet.

"Make her go away," Val said. "I know it's you, Filakis. Make it stop."

"What are you talking about?"

Lettie made a shushing sound and reached beneath her skirt.

When she looked up again, her mouth was crammed with threaded needles which protruded from her mouth like quills. Her fingers walked their way across Val's body. Pinching up a bit of flesh, she ran a needle underneath Val's jaw. Val gasped, but dared not struggle, for any movement caused the other needles to shift and dig.

"This must look so lovely."

"Please stop."

"I only wish that I could see it this time."

"Let me go."

Lettie frowned. "But then you might run away. The world is such a dangerous place, especially when you've got eyes to see the temptations in it. Fortunately, I don't. But you might go and hurt yourself."

The words were spoken with the correct tone, the perfect inflection that the real Lettie would have used. Val blinked and tried to dismiss the illusion from her mind. "You're not real. My real mother's in a hospital in Virginia."

"Hush now. All that was only a bad dream. It's over. Lift your head up and look out the window now, and tell me what you see."

"That's going to be a little difficult."

Lettie sighed. "Yes, I suppose it is. I'll have to help you."

As she touched her fingers to Val's eyelids, Val's mind filled with long-forgotten images. The winding, dun-colored streets of the City grew hazy in her memory, as if her head were filling with fog. Now it was spring in upstate New York, and the earth smelled fresh and thawed. Green buds were visible on the trees, and swallows, so far away they looked like asterisks against the sky, did airborne lifts and plummets. On the road beyond the untilled land, a man was riding a horse. He wore a cowboy hat and metal-tipped boots that reflected blinding shafts of light. He moved farther and farther out of sight, until his horse and he were no bigger than the swallows, his boot heel a tiny spangle of light. He was, thought Val, the most beautiful thing she'd ever seen and as unattainable as the most distant star.

Tears filled her eyes. She knew the scene was an illusion, produced perhaps by Filakis' trickery or her own weary, traumatized mind, but the needles in her flesh were real. With the slightest hint of movement, the arabesque of threads across her body tightened and a hundred tiny wounds were enlarged and deepened. Blood seeped from her like sweat.

"Do you like the view?" said Lettie.

"Of course."

"But your face is wet. Why must you always cry and ruin everything for me?"

Val tried to turn her face away from Lettie's fingers, but even this small effort was rewarded with a myriad needle stings, sweet silver bees that set upon her at the faintest shiver.

"It's painful to look out there and see the world and not be part of it."

"I know *I* wouldn't want to be out there," Lettie said.

"Why not?"

"The dangers..."

"But think," Val said, "of the possibilities for pleasure."

"No!" Lettie's face closed like a fist. She made a choking, half-mad sound, and stamped her feet so fiercely that the vibrations reached the needles and set each one to shivering. A thousand penetrated nerve endings sang with pain, Val's synapses ignited, burned. She struggled and her efforts meant more nerves were pierced until her body shivered in the cold fire of a hundred small impalements.

And still Lettie screamed. "You're lying! You're evil and you're lying. The world's an evil place. I'm glad that I can't see it. Only here is where it's safe. Just here. And you and I will never leave."

That said, she squatted beneath the bed and brought out what Val recognized to be her mother's sewing box. A heavy picnic hamper-type box, when opened, it revealed all that Val recalled and more—threads in a hundred colors, dull muted shades to glittering metallics, pastels diluted from the sea and sky, a dozen nuances of crimson comprising all the shades of blood—from freshly shed to tacky moist to the dull scarlet of dried gore.

To go with these—a shimmering hierarchy of needles, from the thinness of a human hair to those with the length and heft to penetrate a heart.

"This will surprise you," Lettie said, "but I'm not doing this to hurt you. I'm doing it because I want to keep you safe and innocent, as I wish someone had done for me."

She used her hands to feel her way and pierced a threaded needle through the skin of Val's groin. Quickly, with hands that moved so fast their speed was almost magical, a conjuror's hands, plucking miracles from the air like doves, Lettie pierced Val's labia half a dozen times in swift succession.

The pain produced was anything but magical—dazzling and sickening in equal parts. Val screamed and dug her teeth into her tongue.

"You'll come to understand this later," she said, touching her own mouth to Val's. "You think the needles keep you bound, but it isn't really so. It isn't even the pain, although that will come to seem like pleasure, too. It's the seduction of confinement that will keep you here." She laughed, a hollow, mirthless sound that teased dread from every pore. "The day will come when I could snip every thread, remove every needle, and open the door wide, and you'd beg me not to make you go, not to turn you out into the world. You'd weep bitter tears at just the thought of being asked to leave this room."

"Try me," said Val, tasting blood and honey from her mother's mouth.

"Believe me, dear," Lettie said. "Someday you'll come to love this..."

"You said that when you mutilated me the last time...when I was just a child."

"It's different now," said Lettie. "Since I can't see, I'm going to teach you how to sew. But first, I have a surprise. Two surprises really. I'm not sure what they look like, but one of them is very strange. I can't tell if it's a woman or a man, and it doesn't seem to know either."

So saying, Lettie gave a gleeful grin and beckoned to someone out beyond Val's line of vision. Majeed stepped forth, leading Rema on a leash. He wore make-up and a woman's silk pants and a cleavage-revealing blouse.

"Majeed, what's happening?"

He shrugged. His pupils were dilated, his face slack. He seemed not to recognize her.

Val turned to the little girl, whose unveiled features—now that she saw her with Majeed—were suddenly familiar.

"Rema, it was you—you were the girl I saw with Majeed in the bazaar in Fez and then, later, under his bed. You lied to me about Majeed being dead. You tricked me. Why?"

"Filakis told her to," Majeed said sullenly. "If she didn't, he said he'd never let her see me again. Just as she won't see me again if she doesn't cooperate now."

Val turned to Lettie. "Let them go."

"Don't worry" Lettie said. "I'm only going to let the strange one you call Majeed watch for now. It's the child I'm interested in."

Val shuddered with disgust. The needles in her nipples tingled like erotic acupuncture, sensations that traveled all the way into her vulva, her womb.

Rema clutched at Majeed's shirt, trying to hide her head.

Majeed turned away from the child. "Rema, get away," he said. "I've told you not to touch me."

"You see how lucky you really were," Lettie said to Val. "See how some mothers are. Won't even comfort their own offspring in distress."

"Mother?...My God, Majeed, are you...?"

But his inability to respond was sufficient answer.

"Your daughter...not the daughter that you fathered but that you..."

"No one was ever supposed to know," Majeed said. "She was a secret."

"But why?"

"Because I can't bear myself this way—not male, not female, but less than either one. I never thought I could have a child. I didn't believe it could be true until too late to...undo the damage. After that, I took steps to make sure it could never happen again."

Lettie bent forward, ran her hand down Majeed's back until she found his buttocks, and patted them approvingly.

"Since Majeed no longer wants this child, perhaps she can be yours, Val. And you can pass on what you've learned to her."

"The only thing I'll pass onto her is how much I despise you."

"Not after you learn to sew."

"You're wasting your time. I'd never do this to someone else."

"You'd be surprised," said Lettie, "what people believe that they're incapable of doing. Even the saints are capable of the worst atrocities—it's when they recognize that that they decide to become saints. You're capable of anything, especially that which you've already suffered. What has been done to you, *believe me*, you can do to others—especially to your child."

Lettie held a threaded needle up to her sightless eyes. "I could have used one of these in the hospital that night. It would have been better, so much better than the spoon."

She groped for Rema's hand and found it. "Now hold still, dear, be good or something terrible will happen to your mother, you hear? Or is she your father? Such a strange anatomy. Anyway, I'm sewing in the dark, as you can tell, so you've got to hold very still. I wouldn't want to put this through your eyeball by mistake."

And then, to Val: "You'll learn to do this to her, too."

"No! Don't!," Val and Rema cried almost simultaneously.

Needle penetrated flesh. A drop of blood flowered on Rema's skin. Rema cringed and Lettie looped the needle back again, cajoling Rema to stay still. The distressed child looked toward Val.

Val closed her eyes.

There was a moment of black titillation when Val felt she might, indeed, be capable of wielding the needles, of making this child suffer as she once had. To have the tables turned and play the role of victimizer instead of victim. To pretend that she had never been as Rema now was.

"All right," said Val, "let me sew her. You're only going to botch the job trying to do it blind."

"Good girl," said Lettie. "I have a feeling you'll excel at this. Just your arms, though. It's not time to free you yet."

She reached across the bed, plucking loose a few of the more deeply imbedded needles. Her fingers, in their clumsy haste, kept making contact with Val's skin, a touch Val found more unendurable than the steel piercing her flesh. It made pain seem, in fact, a blessing.

Trying to roll away, Val strained herself against the remaining lacings. There was a teetering moment of agony and inheld breath when the combined strength of the remaining sutures held her fast, pulling at her stretched and bleeding skin. Then she flung herself against the lacings in one final effort. Hooks and needles parted company. Blood-soaked threads broke snapped, while the greater part of Lettie's design, the shimmering cat's cradle, remained intact, covering Val's torso in a gory arabesque.

"Get away from me!" Val leaped to her feet, knocking Lettie to the floor. Her hands flew to Lettie's neck, as they had done in fantasy a thousand times.

The woman flailed and kicked beneath her, but there was scant conviction in her struggles. It was as if she was resigned to accept whatever fate Val deemed appropriate.

Val realized her tears were dripping onto Lettie's face along with blood. Images came to her—of midnight rides under skies so black they snuffed the stars, of haggard, frantic faces pressed against the window, of glossy women, swaying in their spike-heeled strut, savage women, electrical with desperation and crackling need. She saw her mother's face, entranced and lustful as she peered out at that other world, the vast Outside, the object of all her lust and terror.

You see what a terrible world it is. Just look at that. You see.

Her mother's face, as Val remembered it, was full of loss and longing.

"Oh, God," said Val, and she let go of Lettie's throat.

Lettie coughed and rubbed her neck. "I knew it." Her voice was tiny, dry, the sound of petals being plucked from long dead flowers and crushed to powdered scent. "I knew you'd try to kill me someday. I knew you hated me."

"I did," said Val. "I wanted to kill you when I was just a little girl. I used to plan it sitting by the window in my locked room. But then the police found out that you'd kept me prisoner and tortured me with needles, and they took you away before I got the chance. I hated you so much. It seemed unfair they took you away from me."

"I hated you, too," said Lettie.

That startled Val. She'd seen herself as Lettie's victim all these years; the newspapers and magazines, the neighbors, the teams of tutting psychiatrists and clucking therapists who'd worked with her after she'd been freed and put in a foster home, had viewed it the same. As one tabloid had put it, Lettie was *The Monster Mom Who Kept Her Child in Chains.*

"I hated you for being free," said Lettie. "For seeking out the dark places I was afraid to go."

"But you're the one who showed me those dark places."

"Just to scare you, so you'd never want to leave me."

"And I never have," said Val. "I've carried you around the world with me like a heavy chain. I've carried you in my dreams. I've hated you for being there in every place I ever went to, every bed I ever slept in. You've always been there, haunting me, spying on me, watching."

"Then forgive me," Lettie said, "and I'll go away."

"Unlock the door."

"I can't do that."

"Don't lie to me. That's what you used to say when I was a little girl."

Val raised her hand up in frustration, then brought it down without delivering the blow. The accumulation of her wounding made her weak, but Lettie's sadness weakened her still more. In the shadows, Lettie's face appeared to dance with minuscule pinpricks of light that mimicked the crosshatchings of the cat's cradle.

"Forgive me," Lettie said again. "I only hurt you because I was afraid you'd leave."

The thaw in Val, though incomplete, was tenfold more painful than the freeze, a blossoming of anguish. She was conscious of Majeed watching her in a trance of immobility, as silent as an inheld breath, waiting.

Rema ran to her and pressed against her.

"I forgive you," Val said, though each word felt like it cost her a lifetime's worth of pain. "I can't love you, but I forgive you...Mother."

Or Filakis, she thought. *Or whatever you are.*

But the transformation Val was expecting never came. Lettie's hands lifted beseechingly, but there were no tattooed palms, no reforming into the Turk's scourged flesh and ribby torso.

"I knew there was a place like this," said Lettie. "They said that I was crazy, but I knew...I knew you'd be here. If only I could see..."

She rubbed the gouges in her face. For an instant, Val thought she glimpsed the pea-green walls of her mother's hospital room, smelled piss and disinfectant, and felt the terrible caress of leather restraints. Then Lettie was gone, and the room in which she, Majeed, and Rema stood began to fold in on itself like the wings of an origami swan. The bed, the sewing basket, the window with its unreal view of New England fields dismantled into shreds, the shreds reduced to tatters, and these to gaudy flecks that spiraled through the air like sequined confetti.

In its place appeared the dank and winding corridors of Filakis' grim abode.

"He's letting us leave?" said Val, incredulous.

Majeed seemed to have shaken off the effects of whatever he had inhaled or injected. "Don't kid yourself," Majeed said, helping Val pluck the needles out of her body. "He thrives on building up false hope. But come on, let's go anyway."

"But how do we get out?"

"The child knows the way. She's spent much of her life down here."

Val was suddenly overcome with despondency. "But what difference does it make? We still can't leave the City."

"We'll worry about that later," said Majeed. He took off the flowing blouse, beneath which he was naked, and handed it to Val. "Come on before it's too late."

Where the locked door had been was now replaced by a twisting staircase of clay bricks. Val took Rema by the hand and they lost no time in climbing it.

Chapter Thirty-Two

Above ground, the City's winding alleyways were swathed in darkness. And if by day, the inhabitants of the City copulated in seclusion, nightfall had brought a lurid change to that.

Now bodies writhed and twisted on the cobblestones, locked in violent congress with each other and themselves, with objects, animals, and beings that, glimpsed in passing, Val could not identify as either alive or dead. If lethargy infused the sex act by day, at night savagery and madness ruled it.

Nor were those erotically engaged so concentrated in their efforts that they ignored Val, Majeed and Rema. Tongues flicked out to touch their skin as they passed by. Hands pinched and pressed. Fingers fluttered in mute cajolement.

They avoided the on-going orgy as much as possible and plunged into the blacker corridors where, by daylight, the marketplace had offered its obscenities. Now the streets were empty of all merchandise except the human trade. In the pale illumination of a paltry moon, Val saw the abominations that the light of day had shamed into concealment. Around a heaping, stinking mound the tribe of shiteaters squatted, dining with their hands. No sooner was their vile repast consumed than their bodies evacuated the meal again, and they recommenced their feast. Forced to pass within an arm's length by the narrowness of the passage, Val and Majeed were prey to dozens of soiled fingers dangling out at them, dripping enticements as they proffered their foul treats.

Rema scrunched her face up and said, "Yechh." Val tugged her on.

Beyond stretched the open stalls that, in daylight, comprised the butchers' market. Carcasses festooned with flies swayed softly, like huge melting lumps of tallow. The smell of putrefying meat hung in the fetid air. Majeed slipped and went down on one knee. Val and Rema stopped to help him. Liquid ran cold and clotty on Majeed's leg. Val's hand on his skin came away reeking of copper.

She'd barely had time to register the fact that they were skidding in a pool of blood when the moon skimmed out from under cloud cover again, revealing a huddled cluster of figures, the deformed and mutilated Skinners, the self-created amputees, eaters of their own and others' flesh. Val whispered something to Majeed, who'd faltered again, perhaps from shock at seeing the display in front of them.

"Cannibals?"

Majeed stood mute. Less shocked, thought Val, than riveted in abject fascination at the strange self-mortification the group was undergoing. With razors and small, thin-bladed knives like those used for peeling fruit, they sliced off tiny portions of themselves and popped these awful delicacies into their mouths, chewing with ecstatic sighs, while the men's erections hardened into steel-like batons, and lubricant oozed between the women's thighs. They paused in feasting only long enough to rut against each other's blood-streaked skins before returning to the next course in their grisly repast.

The appearance of three newcomers provided an unexpected distraction and the possibility for fresh and undiscovered flavors. As one, the Skinners stopped snipping at themselves and cast admiring glances.

"Come on!" Val shook Majeed. He seemed entranced, but came alert and followed Val and Rema in among the swaying rows of carcasses.

"Wait here until they leave," said Val. They crouched down behind the mottled meat, trying to ignore the flies that were drawn to their sweat.

Val looked up and bit back a scream. The carcass nearest her was that of neither sheep nor goat, but the flayed and headless torso of a man. She tried to prevent Rema from seeing, but the child had already followed the direction of her gaze and was looking up at the red abomination.

"It's all right," she said to Val. "I know the Skinners store their food in here. I've watched them do the skinning."

In the far corner of Val's peripheral vision, something shifted, turned.

A breeze-borne carcass rotating?

"Sometimes the men come when their penises are skinned," said Rema.

Then, a metallic clinking.

"They come screaming and then they go into shock and die."

A carcass near the back, striated, red, was emerging from amid the other dripping slabs of meat. The makeshift toolbelt of a sadistic handyman jangled at Breen's waist. In his maimed hand, he held a gleaming, tusk-shaped sword.

"Rema! Majeed! Run!"

Val pushed Rema out into the street as Breen's sword sliced the space between them. Air sang beneath its whistling descent.

The next stroke, aimed at Val, went wide, the blade burying itself deep in a goat's decaying carcass.

While Breen was struggling to dislodge his weapon, Val, Majeed, and Rema plunged back into the seething commerce of the streets.

They'd run only a short distance when Rema looked behind and screamed, "He's coming!"

Val whirled in time to see Breen using the sword to hack his way through the band of Skinners, whose orgy of self-mutilation blocked his passage. Screams and growls issued from the wounded.

Blood spewed blackly into the night. The injured ones at once were set upon by the others who, from what Val could see, were all too practiced at tearing their fallen comrades limb from limb.

They darted through an open doorway into a darkened foyer. The floor was a breathing carpet of pumping, thrusting flesh. Other doors led into connecting dwellings. A wooden ladder offered access to the roof.

Outside Val heard cries of dismay and alarm—Breen, no doubt, his advance temporarily slowed by the cannibalistic frenzy his bloodletting had engendered.

She put Rema's hand in Majeed's. "I'm the one he wants the most. Let's separate. If I can, I'll try to find you later."

Rema cried out, "No, wait! I have to tell you something," but Majeed pulled her with him through the doorway into the next series of dwellings. Val grabbed the ladder and began to climb.

She had just reached the top and was hauling herself onto the roof of the lower level when she felt a shaking of the ladder underneath her and saw Breen recommencing his pursuit.

"Come give me a kiss," he croaked. "You might as well. Don't you know I'll never rest until I shove this sword so far up your pussy, the tip comes out your mouth?"

Val dropped down, braced both feet against either side of the ladder and kicked. It teetered backward, but didn't fall. She kicked again and this time heard the satisfying thud as Breen and ladder hit the ground.

She moved so quickly that she was almost out of earshot by the time his curses started.

Chapter Thirty-Three

He was close enough behind her that she could hear his raspy breathing and the frantic ticking of his heart, like a bomb a few seconds from explosion.

Then she realized it was only her own breathing, her own heartbeat that pursued her as she crossed a half dozen of the clay rooftops and climbed another ladder to a third-story section.

Still, she imagined she could hear his sandpapery whisper, imagined with every footfall that she could hear the silken swish of air as the sword descended to cleave her skull. When she dared to look behind her, she expected to see him covering the distance between them in great sweeping strides, the weapon raised above his head, its deadly metal winking at her in the moonlight.

But there was no sign of his pursuit, even when she lay flat on her belly, head hanging down, and peered over the edge onto the roofs below.

The rooftops of the City's crowded warrens were banded in moonlight and shadow. In places rows of towers and turrets sprouted like stone goblins from the flat roofs, leaving only the narrowest of ledges to walk on as she eased her way around them.

She decided Breen had either lost her or chosen not to follow. The latter was a still more harrowing possibility, since it meant he'd probably gone in pursuit of Rema and Majeed. She found herself on an empty stretch of rooftop, edged with crenelated faience through which the moonlight played like a mad artist lobbing skeins of color at a wall. In other circumstances, the stillness and the moonlight would have made the setting almost unbearably lovely. Now she could only continue on as rapidly as possible, staying in the shadows, checking below each time she passed a ladder leading up or down to another section of the elaborate structure.

A rope ladder to a fourth level presented itself. She debated, then decided greater safety lay in continuing to climb.

Breen probably knew the layout of the building little better than did she and could easily become lost and confused searching for her on the lower floors.

She grabbed the sides of the ladder, which swung stiffly under her weight, and commenced pulling herself up. Nearing the top she reached both arms up to climb the last few feet.

The bright blade hissing downward almost shaved off an ear. Breen's skinned and seeping face leered down at her, its surface cratered with cracks and fissures, runneled with sour-smelling pus. He raised his arm to swing again. The curved blade of the sword flashed like a demented smile.

Val released the ladder and fell backward just as Breen slashed again. The blow severed one of the vertical ropes. The ladder sagged and twisted. Val grabbed for one of the footholds to break her fall, but missed and thumped down hard onto her back. There wasn't time to register the pain of impact. She rolled to her feet and ran, hoping the ladder was now sufficiently unusable that Breen would have to find some other means to follow her.

She jumped a short gap between two rooftops. On the other side, she risked looking back and then wished that she had not. Breen hadn't been deterred in the slightest and was even now shimmying down the single rope that remained intact, his profile that of some berserk primate descending a jungle vine.

Moving across the rooftops as fast as she dared to in the darkness, Val tried to think what to do when she reached a point at which she could proceed no farther. She knew that ladders and stone footholds provided access to all levels of Filakis' quarters except the ground, that, unless she jumped, she'd have to find a way back into the maze and seek an exit through one of the ground-floor passageways that led to the outside. At the moment it seemed insurmountable. Her wounded shoulder had commenced to bleed again. Exhaustion gave everything a slightly unreal edge. The gaps she was required to jump between rooftops were coming up at her too fast, the distances to the other side too difficult to gauge, as though some internal control panel were starting to misfire.

She no longer looked behind her. To see him gaining on her would be too much, to have her last conscious image that of his grotesque visage bearing down on her. She wondered if he'd be swift and efficient with a killing blow. Somehow, even if he possessed sufficient skill with the weapon, she doubted that would be the case.

A veil of blue-sheened clouds obscured the moon. She plunged ahead in semi-darkness.

The smell of what she was approaching suddenly hit her. The impact was swift and stunning. One minute she was sucking in lungfuls of air, the next she gagged on an odor so foul it was like inhaling feces.

Behind was Breen. Ahead the horrifying reek. She held a hand across her nose and mouth and forced herself ahead.

She'd smelled this stench before, although nowhere nearly as close at hand when she'd first come to the City.

Amazing, Val thought, that any odor could be worse than what she had endured while searching for Majeed's body in the burial grounds, but this was more sickeningly concentrated, more potent with the promise of impurity.

Her foot hit a patch of slime. She clutched at something flapping in the dark and found herself clinging to a dank skin hung up on a line to dry. All around her similar skins swayed in the light breeze, their silhouettes making that section of the rooftop appear strung with lines of stiff, dark flags that emitted an intense and fetid odor.

Moving too fast among the drying skins, she almost plunged over the roof's edge onto a terrace. The drop was only about six feet to the roof below, but had she fallen, it would have proved disastrous.

Below her, the entire rooftop was taken up with deep vats used for soaking skins. The strong smell of the animal skins, dye mixed with cow urine for preservation, and the lingering reek of human sweat was all-pervasive. The close proximity of the stone vats left only a few inches of slippery walkway to pass among them.

At intervals, small torches set into the walls on metal hooks threw a sulphurous glow onto the vats. Val could see the outlines of what looked like obscene shadow puppets copulating in the corners, oblivious to anything except their own sluggish fucking in the ghastly half-light.

Lowering herself over the side of the roof, she dropped onto the terrace. The stones here were slick with ghoulish muck. Moonlight made the viscous liquid in the vats resemble a repulsive gruel.

Above her, she heard Breen's lumbering approach, the garbled curses when he, too, apparently narrowly missed stumbling over the edge. She knew he'd caught himself in time, however, because a moment later, as she crouched below a row of hanging skins, as far as possible from the nearest of the torches, she heard him prowling along the edge of the rooftop, unconvinced perhaps that she would jump down and risk a drop into the stinking cauldrons.

If that was where he least expected her to be, thought Val, then that was where she should go.

As silently as possible, she lowered herself into the horrid muck inside one of the vats. Slimy animal skins swished eel-like around her legs, were trodden underfoot. The stench rising from the vat was overpowering.

So engrossed was she in conquering the urge to vomit that she barely heard the wet thump when Breen jumped down onto the terrace and began creeping stealthily among the vats. She held her breath and prayed the moon would not betray her.

Breen passed so near that, for a few seconds, she was eye level with his burned and filthy feet. The hitch of his breathing was audible, the metallic clink of the weaponry attached to his belt produced a weird, atonal song.

Then he moved on, passing behind more rows of hanging skins.

Minutes passed. There was no movement on the terrace. Val dragged herself out of the vat, consigning her sandals and the outer layers of her sodden djellaba to the muck, squeezing out the rest as best she could.

From behind the rows of drying skins a shape moved swiftly forward.

Val gasped and started to run, but she was seized from behind.

"Wait!"

"Majeed!" She clasped his hand. The slime squelched between their fingers.

Behind him, Rema darted sure-footedly between the vats.

"You stink," she said, appraising Val.

"How did you find me?"

Majeed said, "This one, she knows every passageway and tunnel inside the building."

"Can you lead us outside the City's walls?"

"She doesn't have to," said Majeed. "She's had the way out all along. The little thief..."

"What do you mean?"

"I *tried* to tell you." Rema plumbed the pocket of her garment, pulled out an object wrapped in dirty cloth.

"My God," said Val. "You stole it from me that night in the Deadend, didn't you? What were you thinking of? Didn't you know it could save us?"

"I didn't know what it was," the child said with a look of studied innocence. "I thought it was a pretty thing that I could sell."

"I don't believe you. You knew very well what you were taking. Give it to me."

Rema folded her fist tight around the incense burner. "No."

"Stop this. There isn't any time to waste with games."

"I took it so you wouldn't leave me, and I won't give it back until you promise me."

"Promise what?"

"That you'll take me with you, that you won't leave me again if we get out of here."

"If we leave here," Val said, "I can't promise you what happens after that."

Rema cocked her arm and bluffed a throwing gesture.

"No!" cried Val.

"That's why I didn't let you know I had it," Rema said. "I knew you'd make me give it back. You'd leave without me or maybe you'd even take me with you in the beginning, but then you'd dump me someplace after that. You're just like all the rest. I know you are."

"Rema, I can't make the kind of promise that you want. But if Majeed and I get out of here, you will, too. After that, I don't know."

"No. You have to promise I can stay with you."

"Why would you want to be with me? Why not Majeed? He's your...parent. You need to be with him." She looked helplessly at Majeed for confirmation.

Majeed shook his head. "I...can't."

"Can't what? Admit you're Rema's mother?"

Majeed shook his head. "I can't take Rema with me out of the City, because I've decided not to leave."

"What? But if you stay behind, Filakis will kill you. Or Breen will. Or..."

"The Turk won't hurt me if I choose to stay here willingly," said Majeed. "He finds me too amusing. I'm the only freak like myself in his menagerie. And as for your psycho admirer, I don't think he gives a rat's turd about me. It's you he's after."

"But why would you want to stay here? How can you even think of it? And what about..."— the words caught in her throat like chips of glass—"...me?"

"If I come with you now, I'll only wind up leaving you eventually to return here." He nodded at the child. "Her, too."

"But I thought..."

"That I loved you? Even if I do, it's not enough to keep me away from the City permanently. At least I know myself that well."

"Then Filakis was right. You're a lying little whore. You don't love me. You never did. All you can think about is your next fix, your next pipe or your next fuck. I can't believe I came back here looking for you."

Majeed's skin looked like pale saffron silk, translucent in the glow of the lamps. He tried to meet her eyes and failed. Unthinkingly, perhaps, one hand cupped his genitals, another idly spooned around a breast as though, for a baffled instant, he were trying to make a choice between the two. Then his hands came away and he took Val by the shoulders.

"I wish I could love you more. I wish I could love Rema. But the City keeps me distracted from what it is I am, from looking at myself. My need for those distractions is greater than my ability to love anyone."

He started to kiss her, then must have seen the rage and anguish in her eyes and pulled away. "I'm sorry."

"Sorry? That's all you're going to say? It's one thing if you don't care about me, but what about Rema—your child, Majeed, whether you like the idea or not."

"You don't understand...the City...it's more important than you and Rema. It takes away my pain, something you can't do."

"But it creates *more* pain. "

Majeed shrugged and looked away.

"I'm sorry I ever loved you. You aren't worth it."

"At least," Majeed said, "take comfort in the fact that however much you may think you hate me now, I hate myself much more."

"Then don't do this. Come with us. Set yourself free from this place."

Majeed smiled sadly. “It’s not so easy. If you succeed in getting out of here alive, you’ll understand how difficult it is to live outside the City once you’ve been here. In a little while, you’ll have forgotten all the bad things. All you’ll remember will be the excitement, the variety. You may come to regret you ever left. You may spend the rest of your life trying to get back.”

“Majeed, please. I’m sorry about the things I said. Please don’t...”

“I can’t. I find that it’s beyond my power to leave.”

He nodded toward a threesome mashed groin to buttock in a corner. “Would you believe that even at this moment I feel an urge to join them? ”

“Then fight it! You don’t have to give into it. You can be free of the City’s spell if you just try.”

Majeed shook his head. “If you believe that, Val, then you really *don’t* understand. ”

He moved away, his pale figure melting into the darkness.

Val ran after him. “Don’t do this! Come back! You don’t have to be a slave to this place. You can set yourself free. ”

Majeed pushed her gently away. “I can’t come with you. But maybe you’re right, after all. Maybe there is a way for me to be free. ”

He turned away again. Val started to follow, thinking for one mad instant that she’d give up her own chance for escape and go with him.

Then she heard Rema calling her.

In the flickering shadows of the lamps, the child held out the incense burner.

“Promise you won’t leave me.”

Val looked up for a last glimpse of Majeed’s departing back. There was no sign of him. She reached out to the little girl. “I promise.”

Rema relinquished the incense burner, and Val hurried to the nearest of the torches. On the first try, the perfumed wick sizzled briefly and went out. Val cursed and said a prayer and tried again.

She heard the clink of metal above her an instant too late. Breen dropped from the roof, slashing the air above her and Rema’s heads with the sword. The incense burner dropped from her hand and rolled into the darkness. Rema dove after it, crawling out onto one of the ledges between two of the tanning vats.

While Val’s eyes were on Rema, Breen turned the sword and drove the handle into her stomach. As she doubled over gasping, he yanked the pair of handcuffs from his belt and fastened her left wrist to the metal ring in which the torch was set. In doing so, he let the sword drop and then kicked it out of Val's reach before going in search of Rema.

Unwilling, perhaps, to trust his footing on the slippery ledges between the vats in order to pursue her, Breen turned his attention back to Val, who was struggling to force her hand through the opening of the cuff. It was a hopeless effort. Desperately, she looked around, thinking Majeed might have heard the scuffle and returned to help her.

Then, like an answer to her unspoken prayer, she saw him standing atop the high roof of an adjacent building. Surely he saw what was happening. Surely he would find a way to help her.

Breen saw him, too.

Val screamed for help.

She thought, for a fleeting instant, that Majeed looked toward her, but that was all the action that he took.

Then he stepped off the rooftop.

From somewhere on the far side of the terrace, Val heard Rema give a strangled cry that almost, but not quite, drowned out the meaty thump of Majeed's body breaking on the cobblestones below.

Even the copulators on the terrace interrupted their compulsive rutting to take in Majeed's leap. For a moment, they appeared to shake off the spell of sex that bound them, to surface from their lust-trance. Then the truth of their circumstances proved too unbearable. Mouths found mouths again and clamped to genitals. The soft wet sounds of flesh on flesh murmured in the night like a subdued humming of insects.

From below, however, there came a chorus of other sounds, feral yelps and smacks and growling.

Breen flashed a ghastly smile at Val. "Don't go away."

He walked over to the roof's edge and peered down. He stared at whatever was taking place below only a moment—or so it seemed to Val who had realized she had but one chance left and was trying to reach the sword that Breen had left just beyond her reach.

"Remarkable," said Breen. "The Skinners are tearing him apart like a tribe of uncouth dinner guests dismembering a turkey. There goes the liver...ah, the heart...as fine a job as I might do myself, if somewhat messier."

He giggled hoarsely and turned back to Val.

"You know why I didn't kill you right away? Not up to answering that, are you? Well, I understand. Fortunately for your friend Majeed, he was dead when he hit the ground. But you...I think I'll whittle you away piece by piece. An ear here, a bouquet of toesies there, a nipple or two, and feed them to the Skinners while you're still alive. If I do it right, you won't die for a long time and you can watch your own flesh being turned into lunch meat. Maybe you'll even want to sample it yourself."

He looked below again. "Do you know they use a rock to crack the skull and scoop out the brains?"

In the moment that Breen turned away again to look down at the carnage, Val reached the sword with her foot and dragged it toward her. Almost dislocating her trapped arm with the effort, she reached down and snatched it up.

Breen whirled around. He smiled broadly, exposing the jagged outline of his teeth.

"Do you think that frightens me? You're caught, you aren't going anywhere. All I have to do is walk around behind you and take the sword. You can't even turn around in that position. There's no way you can strike me."

He took a step forward.

"Stay back," said Val.

Breen cocked his head, as if trying to fathom this show of fruitless courage. "The only way that sword can help you is if you fall on top of it, and I don't think you've got the nerve."

Val took a deep breath, steeled herself.

The nerve, yes, she had to find the nerve to do this.

"You stupid bitch, you never understood the truth: I really loved you."

"You know what," Val said, "I really like your new appearance, Arthur. It suits you. Now your outside is as repulsive as your inside."

Breen made a tsk-tsk sound. "Oh, my, how very cruel you can be. But that's why I loved you, isn't it? Your innate capacity for evil always showed through. We're alike, you and I. Oh, that upsets you, doesn't it? You don't like thinking that we're spiritual siblings, carnivore kin."

He moved closer.

"You would have learned to kill someday, when you got bored enough with your tiresome promiscuity. It was only a matter of time and you'd have put a razor up your cunt and started keeping dicks in a display case like Purple Hearts."

"What about your dick, Arthur? Does it still work or did the fire melt it permanently?"

"You'll find out soon enough."

Now or never.

With all the strength in her free hand, she brought the sword down straight across her shackled wrist. It chinked and snagged briefly on the bone, then went on. The flesh parted like warm butter. The gushing, glove-like thing flopped to the ground. Blood from her maiming geysered into Breen's stunned face. He staggered back. She lunged and buried the sword in his belly.

Breen screamed and clawed at the protruding steel. Val thrust all her weight against it.

Breen stumbled backward into a glistening pool of slime. His feet flew out from under him. The sword came loose, and with a cry he tumbled backward into one of the tanning vats.

He surfaced once, pawing and tearing at the edge, trying to hoist himself up. Val ran the blade into his mouth. He splashed back into the muck again and did not resurface.

Only then did the magnitude of her injury hit her and she sank to her knees in an ever-expanding pool of blood, clutching her gushing wrist while the world pulsed black and red like a flow of lava and static sizzled in her ears.

"Don't die! Don't die," cried Rema.

She rushed past Val and thrust the incense burner's wick into the flame. It didn't catch. *I'm dead*, Val thought. Then green fire nibbled forth, first in snaky tendrils, then a gathering blaze until a whole wall of incandescent fire illuminated the night.

"Hurry," Rema said. "Let the fire close the wound. Otherwise, you'll bleed to death."

Val clutched the child's hand with her remaining one. She crawled forward a few paces before struggling to her feet.

With Rema preceding her, she took a deep breath and threw herself into the fire.

Epilogue

Val watched as the coffin was lowered into the ground.

Rema, standing beside her, tugged on the prosthesis attached to Val's left wrist. "Now both our mothers are dead."

Val nodded.

"They weren't very good mothers, were they?"

"No," said Val, "they weren't."

"But they can't hurt us anymore?"

"Not unless we let them."

The cancer had been nibbling away at Lettie all through the winter after Val's return from the City. Beginning in her lymph nodes, then spreading throughout her body, insidious, invasive, finally penetrating bone. At the end, she conversed with phantoms and babbled in her sleep about a place where the very air induced an orgasm, where a severe, wan priest presided over an ultimate debauchery.

With her blindness, she had died not ever knowing the mutilation Val had suffered.

Nor did Val ever wish that she should know.

The funeral ended. Val said good-bye to a few relatives and friends of her mother's. Then she and Rema drove from Tarrant back to New York City where they caught a British Air flight from LaGuardia to Glasgow. There they caught a domestic flight to the town of Scrabster, near Thurso, on the north coast of Scotland.

En route, Val found herself watching the people, sizing them up, weaving familiar fantasies. There was a dark-haired man with skin so golden it might have been basted in honey. An older woman with lush wet lips and a triple strand of pearls. A young man with a punk rock haircut and powerlifter arms.

She watched them and felt the old cravings, the tug of emptiness inside her, the inexpressible, all-encompassing desire for something more. An escape of some sort. Distraction, delusion.

More.

She shook it off. This was a new life. A new beginning.

From Scrabster, they got on the St. Ola ferry for the crossing to the port of Stromness, two hours north across the choppy North Sea. They leaned against the rail, eating meatpies they'd bought at the snackbar below deck and throwing bits of bread to the gulls.

Rema wiped the grease from the meatpie off her lips with the back of her hand. "Where will we go after Orkney?"

"Maybe nowhere. Maybe we'll like it and stay."

"In the same place?"

"We could try it."

"For how long?"

"I don't know," said Val.

She felt very young, like she was running away from home, like she'd never been out in the world before on her own. For a moment she felt very afraid. She remembered the man with the muscular arms, imagined the taste of him, the aroma. And the woman with her creamy choker of pearls, her vermillion lips—what might she have been like?

Then, in her mind, she was seeing them not as they'd been when they'd passed in the airport at Wick, but as colors and geometric designs, a medley of texture and shading. Plum-red for desire, cool cobalt for caution, restraint, grey for the hint of ungrieved loss in the woman's slate-colored eyes.

Rema tossed the last bite of meatpie to the gulls and turned back to Val. "What if you get bored here?"

"I thought I'd try painting again. It's always been a secret ambition of mine. Once I was quite good at it. A long time ago. Before you were even born."

The misty shore of Orkney Island was getting closer. They could see the grey silhouette of Brinkie's Brae, the hill overlooking the town of Stromness, and the outlines of waterfront gables, slipways, and jetties, just as Val had first seen them in the painting in her father's study, a lifetime ago.

"Come on, let's go get our things. We're almost there."

She took Rema's hand in her right one. With her left, she fingered the object in her coat pocket. She'd found that she preferred touching it with her prosthetic fingers. They couldn't feel its curves and whorls and so the contact seemed less intimate, less dangerous. Even so, as she caressed it, she imagined that it still emitted, very faintly, an odor of temptation and desire.

Since leaving the City, she had tried to dispose of the incense burner a number of times. If she held onto it, she feared the day might come when she'd no longer be able to resist its possibilities. She'd light the flame and step inside to be consumed.

Or she could pitch the object out into the dark depths of the sea this minute. Hurl it high and far and never suffer its obscene allure again. Now was the perfect opportunity, with the churning North Sea offering up its depths.

Perhaps in time she'd make that choice.

But not yet, she thought, stroking Rema's hair with her good right hand.

Not yet.

Lucy Taylor's work includes the collections *Close To the Bone, Unnatural Acts and Other Stories, The Flesh Artist,* and *Painted In Blood*, as well as numerous short stories. A novella, *Spree*, and *Dancing With Demons*, a novel of erotic horror, are two of her most recent works. *Eternal Hearts*, a vampire novel, and *Sub-Human*, a novella, will be out in 1999.

Taylor shares a home with her partner Don and their five cats in Mead, Colorado.

www.ingramcontent.com/pod-product-compliance
Lightning Source LLC
Chambersburg PA
CBHW021515240626
47154CB00002B/633

* 9 7 8 1 8 9 2 9 5 0 1 2 3 *